ISBN 978-1739375 2-1-8

Previously available as separate novels as follows:

Captain Random vs the Sandman ISBN 978-1-99 9865 9-2-4

Captain Random and the Eater of Souls ISBN 978-19998659-3-1

Captain Random and the Rainbow Chasers ISBN-9 7-19998659-978

Printed and bound by Lightning Source, Milton Keynes, UK

www.haydengribbleauthor.com

THE CAPTAIN RANDOM

ADVENTURES

VOLUME ONE

HAYDEN GRIBBLE

Also by the author

The CAPTAIN RANDOM Adventures

Captain Random and the Stratos Conundrum
Journey in the Randomverse
Captain Random and the Battle for Rodas

Other titles by the author

The Man In The Corner
Tales From Another Me
Child Out Of Time: Growing Up With Doctor Who In
The Wilderness Years
The Lurking

The CAPTAIN RANDOM Adventures Volume One

CAPTAIN RANDOM

VS THE

SANDMAN

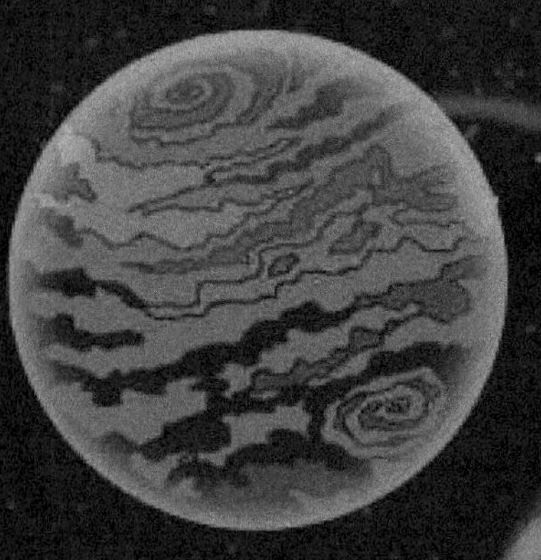

HAYDEN GRIBBLE

CAPTAIN RANDOM

VS

THE SANDMAN

HAYDEN GRIBBLE

For Sophie

PROLOGUE

A barren, desolated wilderness greeted the eyes of the travellers as their spaceship settled down on the sand dunes of the decimated world. The landing gear let out a whine - groaning under the stress and strain of hundreds of tons worth of titanium and seda metal that crunched the legs of the Venus II further into the ground, like a mallet hitting a tent peg into place.

Its battle worn colours and bleak, dense appearance blended in well with its surroundings on this occasion but given any other landscape and it would have attracted all the military and television crews of the galaxy to its whereabouts.

In fact, given the huge exterior, that's what the Venus II normally did. But on this occasion, there was no fanfare. As the dust snaked and roared around the bottom of the ship, it began to settle on the stabilising pads that the Venus II stood on.

The only sound that could be heard now was the faint vibration of the inner door mechanism whirring away. All of a sudden, there a mighty hiss from the hydraulics and the door began to slowly drop down from the belly of the beast.

Footsteps could also be heard clattering down the metal gangway. Well, if there was anybody around to hear it.

The shadows of three bodies illuminated the gangway – exposed by the bright, white lights from inside the spaceship. The first figure stood at the front of the pack and made his way heavily down the bottom of the ramp.

He bent down and touched the sand with his gloved fingers, feeling the coarse grains fall through the gaps between his digits. Sniffing, he shot a look back to his two companions. A young boy, who was no more than ten years old, stood on the ramp scratching his blonde hair, whilst observing the calm that surrounded them all.

The third member of the party, a girl of Earth-Indian descent, played nervously with her bag that swung irritatingly on her right shoulder. After several seconds of awkward silence, she decided to speak.

'So, we made it then?'

The first person looked away, knowing the answer but not wanting to dignify his friend with a response.

'Yes,' he croaked. 'Yes, we made it.'

'It's not what I expected,' cried the blonde-haired boy.

He looked up at the strange fluorescent moon.

Even though the moon was as bright as anything he had ever seen, the horizon still looked as dark as a harsh winter night back on Earth.

'I was expecting huge towers high in the sky and flying cars. What happened here?'

'The war to end all wars,' exclaimed the leader of the party as he straightened his legs and stood up. He could make out a faint outline of the once, great citadel in the far distance. 'Yet, it still rages. For centuries my home planet has been a battlefield. Millions upon millions have died and it was my responsibility to stop the fighting.'

The girl tore forward and put a reassuring hand on the shoulder of her companion.

'None of this is your fault, Random!' she insisted.

Random turned towards her and gave a glimmer of a smile from his dour expression. For all of the adventures both he and these two earth people had experienced, all the fun and laughs and the ever so slightly dangerous places they had visited in the quest to get back to this world, he knew he had made a terrible decision bringing them here.

'Anji, you will never know what suffering I have caused. It's time I made up for it.'

'How?' the boy asked.

'By making sure that this is the final day. I have to put it right, Jake. It is my destiny.'

Jake was worried. He had never seen Random so serious, so morose and so determined before.

Was this really the same boy that had whooped and cheered his way down a thousand-foot rainbow on the planet Spectronia? Or the same spiky haired, funny costumed wearing guy who had used a discarded feather to tickle his way out of the prison tombs of Catacombe 62? Gulping hard, he took Anji's hands and followed his friend towards the unfriendly outline of what looked like a city.

Together, these three had been through so much. It had been the Earth children's choice to leave their planet behind and join this funny looking boy who fell from the stars and since they didn't have a home to go back to anyway, it didn't matter to them if they ever made it back. But at the same time, both Jake and Anji didn't want to get hurt. So far, they had endured many bumps and bruises on the planet hop back to Random's home world, but this time, there was a full-scale war staring them in the face. And why had Random allowed himself to be talked into bringing them into the hornet's nest?

If I had a dad, he'd never have let me come, Jake thought to himself as he trawled along the sand, which had entered a hole in his favourite pair of trainers and was causing more than a little irritation to his left foot.

'Back when we first met, I had no intention of letting you come with me,' Random said as he walked, the chilling night air carrying his sentence back into the general direction of his two friends. 'I just wanted to forget about my responsibilities, run away and never come back here. But you two, you two showed me how to be a better person and for that I thank you, but after we assess the situation and analyse what our next move should be I am taking you back to the Venus and locking the door. Do you understand?'

Jake and Anji nodded as they clambered through the soft sand.

'And what if you don't come back?' Anji's lips were beginning to feel sore as the wind continued to blow the sand in her face.

'Then Skateboard will pilot the ship to wherever you want and you can live your lives out however and wherever you like.'

'But you are coming back, aren't you?' Jake craned his neck to see if he could make out Random's face in the gloom.

Random felt terrible. Although he had the physiognomy of a boy just a couple of years older than his counterparts, he was in fact a far more advanced being than they were.

He was not as susceptible to illness, disease and trepidation like humans were but right now he had a throbbing feeling in his chest that he had never felt before. The most human of emotions.

Fear.

The trio jumped as Random's wrist communicator crackled into life. Over the wind, he could just make out a metallic voice.

'Sir, I must warn you that my sensors have picked up hostile lifeforms in your vicinity. It would be wise to come back to the ship as soon as possible.'

Random strained to be heard as he continued to walk.

'How many of them?'

'Fifteen, Sir. They appear to be on land hawkers, roughly 80 clicks away.'

'Okay, no problem. We are getting close to the edge of the citadel now. I will report back to you when we get there.'

The electronic voice was fast becoming less static than usual. You could almost say, it sounded emotional.

'Sir, I really must protest. Going on may result in your capture, or worse, deaths!'

'We have got the picture, Skateboard.'

'They will want to pluck all of your hairs out one by one whilst dancing the tango on your broken toes.'

'We get it-'

'...And they will dip you into a pit of boiling acid after making you wear dresses made of cat food so that their hammerhead tigers can have a bite at your-'

'SKATEBOARD...THAT IS ENOUGH!' Random bellowed. Jake and Anji jumped in fright. They had listened to every word. Maybe they should have stayed on the ship after all.

'Await my instructions,' Random ordered before clicking a switch on his communicator and returning to the task in hand.

'Would they really do that?' Jake enquired.

'Do what?'

'Make us wear dresses?'

Random sighed for so long it was heard by future generations. 'Come on, we are nearly there.'

The trio got down on their hands and knees as they negotiated the slight curve on the ground that licked up into the sky. 'Stupid bag!' Anji grunted as she swiped it over her shoulder, almost knocking Jake out in the process.

After a few minutes crawling in the dirt, they heard something they had not heard before.

The wind had died down and all they could hear now was the sound of explosions, screams of pain and terror and the occasional whizz of hyper-jet fighters and laser fire.

Random's heart was thumping so loud that he thought he could hear it over the sound of destruction.

'Right, that's it. Back to the Venus now, both of you!'

'We are not going anywhere,' Anji protested. 'We are staying by your side and that is final.'

'What? Are you mad!' Jake shouted. 'Can you not hear that down there!? Let's go while we still have the chance!'

'I'm staying.'

'Oh yeah? Well, I'm going!'

The boys' protests were interrupted by an explosion so loud it made the ground tremor for almost a minute.

'...On second thoughts, I'd better protect you, Anji!' Jake declared, despite cowering and holding onto the legs of his friend. She shot him an unimpressed glance.

'Stay low now, we have to get to the edge,' Random implored.

The three youngsters crawled their way closer and closer, the pitch-black landscape was giving away to a blood red horizon, like a doomed sunrise. Slowly, they pulled themselves up to eye level and saw one of the most indescribable scenes of devastation it had ever been their misfortune to witness.

'Anji...Jake,' Random stuttered. 'This is the citadel of the planet of Rodas. My home...'

CHAPTER ONE

ORIGINS

Every story needs a hero, a person who influences the lives of those around them in a positive way and generally saves the day. Somebody who wanders into town and rights the wrongs they see in front of them. Where there is danger, they make people safe. When the time of adversity comes, they hold their hand up to the storm and say, 'hey, you...stop!' Someone who will sacrifice themselves when there is no other option but to lay their life down to save many. Well, this story doesn't start with a hero. In fact, the word hero will not be used to describe our main protagonist until near the end. This is the story of... an idiot.

It started during the Galactic War of Ursa-17. A quadrant in the Galiony system, roughly 13 million miles away from the outer edge of our universe. The war had been raging since the system had first begun to shatter, like a window pane after a football is kicked through it. The proverbial football in this instance was an argument between the heads of two rulers of the planet known as Rodas.

It was a beautiful planet, where one side of the hemisphere was a crimson wash of red and the sun was a glorious yellow, irradiating the people with a warm orangey glow that kept them happy and blissfully unaware that they were being taxed heavily, that the international crime figures were high and that Paxley Dreamywonder, everyone's favourite celebrity reality television star on that side of the planet had been dead after tragically losing his life after a magazine coupon incident.

On the other side of Rodas there was a stark contrast. That side of the planet was a calming shade of electric blue and the sun looked more like a pinkish grey that bamboozled the people of that side of the hemisphere and had a habit of making them tired and irritable, especially when the moon was a florescent yellow that pierced even the blackest of black out paint. On this side, the people were not happy and were all too aware of the problems their world had inherited.

Due to lack of sleep, the employed were forever falling asleep at work. There was next to no crime either, mostly because the criminals had a habit of only working at night and as the night

time was lighter than the day, they simply didn't bother and just
chatted to each other on webcams instead. Their Prime Minister
had very little to lie about or cover up as there was simply nothing
to keep secret. It should have been a happy place but it wasn't.

The frustrations of both factions soon came to a head when the
rulers of the two sides, Cardinal

Beutoch of the red side and Cardinal Flavalboombuzzer of the
blue, met for their annual senate meeting in The Grand Halfway
Mountain on the equator of Rodas. It was a magnificent sight to
behold. The mountain was a glorious amalgamation of all the
colours of the known galaxies. Yellow, sepia, burnt orange,
electric lime, screaming emerald, the colour formerly known as
Prince and the one that was named after a man from the Wilburn'l
system called Norman Astley.

There was however, one glaring omission from the canvas of
colour and that was the one shade of light that neither had ever
managed to create; that neither Parliaments had ever cracked or
discovered, no matter how much of the public's money went
unknowingly into its research. It seems silly now that this would
seem such a humongous sticking point between the friendships of
the good people of Rodas and the one thing that the people of the
red and blue planet continued to fight about. They had never
found a way of making the colour purple.

And so, for what seemed like the latest millennia of debates,
Beutoch and Flavalboombuzzer sat wearily in their chairs at
either end of the long, long delegation table. It was so long it
stretched across international time zones and both leaders and
their advisors had to speak through a combination of megaphones
and intercom systems just to be heard. During this particularly
tiresome session of deliberation, Flavalboombuzzer put down his
goblet of hot milky tea right on his assistant's hand which was
resting on the table and screamed his frustration down the
megaphone so hard that it took the hair off the head of the
scolded assistant.

'For god's sake, man!' he cried. 'Why will you not accept my
advice and give it a go?'

Flavalboombuzzer waited a full seven minutes for the reply.

'...What!?'

The elderly cardinal put his hand to his brow and wiped his golden fringe away to the side of his head.

'I said,' he sighed, 'why don't you just give it a go? Why won't sapphire and sodium work? It's the only combination we haven't tried!'

After a further seven minutes of waiting for his counterpart to respond, the intercom system fizzled into life.

'You mean YOU haven't tried! I've told you before how we have been conducting important experiments away from the public's view and not one of them worked.

When we did add sodium to the pure sapphire crystals in our possession, the explosion was so devastating that we had to cancel the month of August and blame it on a change in the ecosystem,' Beutoch retorted. 'Our only action is to conduct our experiments in space out of harm's way so that we will not endanger the lives of our subjects.' He paused for a moment to read a set of notes handed to him by his personal assistant.

'Now let me see, what about white marzipan and wild watermelon? That should do the trick.'

Flavelboombuzzer grunted in an impatient manner down the intercom. He exhaled deeply, emitting hot breath so loud that it reverberated around Beutoch's side of the table.

'Why do you think we sent that team of scientists up there?'

'To do that same experiment?' Beutoch enquired, his green skin perspiring in a way that made him look like a sunbathing lettuce.

'...To do that same experiment!' Flavalboombuzzer replied.

'And do you know what it did? Opened up a wormhole and dumped our scientists in a nude holiday resort on the other side of the galaxy!'

'Well...' Beutoch stalled. 'At least they were happy and safe on the other side.'

'They would have been if the nudist camp was not populated with deadly cyborgs who were giving their circuit boards an airing!'

Flavalboombuzzer screamed!

This debate went on for days. It rolled on for so long that Beutoch missed his 166th birthday party and Flavalboombuzzer missed his wedding anniversary, his divorce proceedings and finally his annulment.

Eventually, there could be no other way to settle this other than to declare full scale war on Rodas. It was news that plunged the whole planet into despair. The young men were recruited to join the armed forces. The children, who had been relatively happy in their well-funded and lovingly taught schools, were forced to attend work camps based on training them up to become the next generation of soldiers.

The elderly men and women were made to become nurses and medics where they were needed most.

The war raged long and hard and both Beutoch and Flavalboombuzzer both passed away during the early conflict.

Beutoch passed away from old age and his rival died after an unfortunate choking incident with an olive when his ship had to make a sudden emergency stop.

Soon, the other planets in the system also took the option of force to put an end to the bitter war. Some, like the Holy Planet of Xmir stayed unbiased and impartial to the events until someone pointed out that the very existence of religion in that part of the galaxy was based on war and conflict in the first place.

The fighting became so acrimonious that neighbouring planets struggled to keep out of the devastation. The Glogmeister Planet of Glop, where the inhabitants were sort of jelly like creatures who spoke out of the ear-shaped pods on the tops of their heads, were so afraid that they would also get caught up in the war that they moved planets to the outer system known only as 'for sale.'

Others so appalled at the reasons for the fighting, decided to hide the secret of the colour purple from the people of Rodas and also refused to take refugees in, saving them from the horror that ensued on their war-torn burning planet.

After two centuries of fighting, Rodas had become a bad word in an unforgiving galaxy, an outlawed fable, told to warn others off that part of space. The tales of Rodas were so bad that even the Hard as Nails Space bikers of Snotpoo 97 turned the other way when they were on the outer edge of Ursa-17.

If only someone had been smart enough to point out the obvious that red and blue make purple then many lives would have been saved.

But then again, our idiot would never have been brought into existence…

II

Blent stood with his arms crossed in the doorway, leaning against the cold marble. He stared unblinking into the main hall of the citadel of the blue side of Rodas.

It was night time, which of course meant it was the brightest time of the day for the occupants of that side of the planet and not the best time to have agreed to a secret meeting with a traitor. His pulse was racing like mad, scared that he would be caught and thrown into one of the many prison camps that had been built over what had seemed a lifetime ago. He had heard stories and they were not pretty ones.

His allies had created many unpleasant ways to torture those who had been captured. They were forced to take hour long baths with an animal called the Fargnot. The Fargnot looked like a mad scientist had managed to find a combination of a frog, a rabbit and a 17-tonne whale and it petrified the prisoners, especially as it would sing for six hours a day involuntarily and relentlessly.

The penalty for those who even attempted to escape was to ride the Fargnot around the camp with no clothes on whilst their fellow captors were made to fire hot lead at them from super soaker-like water pistols. Blent shuddered.

Who would want to suffer that kind of punishment?

He looked down at his watch. It was three in the morning. He had disappeared into the night and left his wife and child at home all alone. He had to get back soon, to protect them from the bombings and the attacks from the red side – who by now had called themselves the Crimson Empire. He lived just a few miles from the citadel, where the main bombardments happened. If all went to plan tonight, then the war would soon be over.

The old hall had so many memories for him; so many moments that would stay with him forever. This was where the people of the hemisphere had crowded upon the coronation of Queen Davinal around 900 years ago, long before the war had become a bleak, bloody mess that had no end in sight. As she took over her regional duties from her Father, there was an air of optimism and excitement that filled the sapphire side of Rodas. A promise was made that day; that the war would be over by the end of the year.

Sadly, after Her Majesty's mysterious disappearance, there was nothing but never-ending chaos and bloodshed.

It was the last time that Rodas had dared to dream of a new world as the current one plunged further into chaos.

Blent's train of thought was disturbed by the sound of distant footsteps. He jolted, his eyes darting like mad from side to side, looking in desperation for a place to hide. There were none. The citadel was nothing but smooth spherical shapes, cobbled together by a designer who thought that straight edges were just as dated as flared jeans are on planet Earth.

A sense of panic began to grip Blent, who pulled the collar of his long, dark trench coat up to his face and then tip-toed across to a half-mooned crevice that would fit his seven-foot-tall frame. It was at moments like this that he wished he hadn't inherited his uncle's ridiculously lanky frame. He thought to himself that he probably looked like a large worm cowering behind a small crisp.

The footsteps were getting louder and louder until all of a sudden, they stopped. Blent dared himself to sneak a peek from his not-so-hidden hidey hole.

He slowly reared his head up and over the crevice, which still would have given a lot away as his head was almost as long as his body. His forehead was so large that a family of hedgehogs could happily call it their holiday home. Nevertheless, he just had to see who it was who was making his...or her...way into the citadel.

For a few moments, there was nothing but silence. It was the most unnerving experience of Blent's life so far. He was just one sneeze, one cough away from a naked ride on a Fargnot.

Sweating profusely, he strained his vision to see the outline of a lone, dark shadow, sprawling out long onto the citadel floor.

'Hello? Is anybody there?'

Blent sighed so hard he nearly sucked his lungs up into his throat. He strode out like a different man from behind his hiding place, confident and assured. The sound of a woman's voice, soft and as beautiful as a nightingale in the moonlight beckoned him closer.

'Thank zark it is you. I thought I was a goner for a minute there!'
As Blent walked closer towards the shadow, he saw the figure of a
much smaller person come into view.

'I'm sorry I'm so late. It's a nightmare to get past the soldiers at
this time of night. Also, I may have got a little bit lost. I've never
been to this side of Rodas before.'

Blent looked upon the face of his ally. It fitted the voice
perfectly. Strong, assured, intelligent, determined, beautiful.
Whilst studying her face, he also noticed something he had never
seen before about her. Her face was a crimson red. Crimson
Empire Red.

'It's a good thing I recognised your voice,' he said. 'The only
people I have seen with that shade on their skin have either been
after my blood or imprisoned in the camps.'

His female companion shook her head. 'Is that what this planet
has come to? Torn apart by colour? Lesser planets have learned to
resolve their petty discriminations. It is a disgrace that ours never
has.'

'If all goes to plan tonight, Niva...it will.'

Blent held his arm out, beckoning Niva to walk with him.

'Come, there is little time.'

The pair walked down the long, white corridor of the citadel at a
pace that would make the average person gasp for air after a few
hundred feet.

There was no time for small pleasantries or catching up. They
were lucky to have got as far as they had.

It had all started when Blent, sitting alone in his laboratory,
intercepted a message on his mailing list.

He had long given up the desire to end the war by discovering
the colour purple and after a number of decades had decided to
cease his experiments, making him the latest in a long line of
Government-enlisted academics who had attempted to crack the
case and failed.

Instead, seeing how bad things had got and worrying for the
safety of his family, he decided to secretly research the
underground revolutionaries who had begun to fight for peace.
He had heard rumours that the revolution groups were a mix of
people from both sides of the planet.

At last, unity! And not just that, but these people were peaceful.
He was entranced at how they worked towards a better future. All
those meetings, all those sing–a–long's about ending the war. All
those bonfire evenings under the crust of Rodas, hidden away
from view like moles, and like moles, they were slowly digging
up to the surface.

As the revolutionaries grew in number and Blent became more
and more involved in the peace efforts, the revolution was taking
measures to infiltrate the main army bases on both sides and
sabotaging them from within.

There were many people like him who had also been employed
by the Government, so access was easy. They all went by
codenames to protect their identities and went about trying to
bring down the establishment from within.

But slowly, the armed forces had worked out what was
happening and had started to clamp down on the revolutionaries.

Blent had been lucky not to have been found out so far. He
knew this was his last chance.

He had been put in contact with a mysterious woman called
Niva through one of the remaining revolutionaries. The numbers
had dwindled as those who were discovered had been imprisoned
in camps and punished severely. So, to maintain secrecy, neither
of them had seen each other's face. They had only contacted
through instant mailing and scrambled telephone conversations.
This was their first proper meeting and if they failed, then they
both knew that they would never see their loved ones again.

Niva looked to her right and saw the pensive look on Blent's
face. Like he, she had been driven to desperate measures to ensure
that the Rodasians had any future at all. She was from a more
military background than her co-conspirator.

She had been enlisted as a young child to become a pilot in the
Sedlich Infantry and aged just 15 she was flying her way into
warzones, taking out the enemy and using her armed combat
skills to take prisoners who had dared infiltrate the red side of the
planet.

But after years of fighting, her resolve was destroyed when the
Crimson Empire decided to dye the armies' skin a permanent red

colour as a reminder of who they fought for and where they came from. Like so many others, Niva knew that this was wrong and that it would inspire more hate from their opponents. This war had gone too far. Her innocence and youth had been taken by the conflict, and now so had her identity.

Luckily, Niva was discharged from the army after she faked her own death on the day of the bloodiest battle the war had ever seen. The day of the emergence.

III

'Are you sure this is going to work? Niva said without looking at her partner in crime. 'This kind of thing has never been tried before.'

Blent stared at her, as if she had just told him that she thought he could not spell. Or count.

'Of course, it will work!' he snapped. 'I have been working on the formula for the last five years. It hasn't been tried and tested, granted, but I know this is the answer to all of Rodas' problems.'

Niva sighed. She had second thoughts. It was an ambitious project and she had more confidence in a man surviving a fall from a thousand feet into a cushioned yoghurt pot than what they were attempting. 'But how did you come up with it?'

Blent gave a moment's pause to draw breath. It was a long story.

'Back when I was project leader on the Nirmamas Outposting Scheme, I attended a conference about how the discovery of the only colour to be missing from the spectrum could be sliced from the memories of species from the outer reaches of our galaxy.

Since the peoples of the universe had turned their backs on Rodas long ago, the chair of the conference, Professor Travemant, had started experimenting on prisoners of war; extracting memories, skills and abilities from them to be implanted in soldiers who were lacking all of the above and turn them into a kind of super-warrior.'

'And that's what you're going to do here? Simply make another warrior? I don't suppose it may have escaped your attention but we have enough of them as it is! In fact, you could say that the

27

vast quantity of soldiers in this world has led to centuries of war!'
Niva spat. She was so angry that she had left the red hemisphere
to risk her life just to make another killer. 'There has been enough
bloodshed. One more soldier is just another drop in the polluted
ocean.'

Blent stopped in his tracks. He looked hurt, his eyes squinting to
see through Niva's perspective. He looked down at her, eclipsing
her like the moon shutting out the sun.

'I'm not going to add to all of the death and destruction,
Niva...I'm going to create a miracle. For you, for me, for Rodas, for
the rest of this stupid, idiotic galaxy. I'm going to create life.'

The lanky scientist continued down the long, white corridor,
leaving Niva to stand on the spot for a moment.

'Oh, my god,' she thought to herself. 'He's flipped!'

She looked ahead and saw that Blent had sprinted away from
her. Breathing in, she ran off after him. The clock was ticking...

*

Meanwhile, high above the citadel, a heli-fighter continued its
patrol of the burning capital. Inside the dark, cramped, hawk-
shaped machine were two soldiers, both dressed in black leather
combat suits, which kept their bodies thin and nimble but
compressed their flabby, middle-aged frames into that
reminiscent of a body builder.

The Pilot had set the steering console to automatic control, so
that he and his counterpart, a young, stick-thin boy fresh from the
academy, could watch the intergalactic football match between
Gloicchester United and the Steaming Vom Wiglacers of Nubulus
3.

As they squinted to see who had possession of the ball, which
was spherical but with metal spikes in it as to make for a harder
game, it was clear that the pair had neglected their duties.

Instead of being on watch for intruders inside the citadel and
warding off any unwanted spies from the Crimson Empire intent
on bombing what was left of the capital, they were arguing over
who was the better side, even though the Steaming Vom
Wiglacers of Nubulus 3 were currently edging the tie 45-3.

'I'm telling you son,' the Pilot garbled to his young ward through a homemade turkey sandwich. 'Gloicchester will never stand a chance if they insist on playing without a goalkeeper.'

The youngster squinted away, trying to make out the players on the pitch through a haze of bad reception that had turned them into static, explosions of colour on the relatively small television screen.

'True. But perhaps they would if your side didn't have thirty-nine players on the pitch! I thought intergalactic football was a five-a-side affair?'

The Pilot gulped the remnants of his lunch down. 'Ah, you'd have thought. But you know what that business is like. Offer the referee a bribe or two and the pitch is your oyster!'

He itched his torso with some discomfort. These suits were incredibly stuffy and suffocating. After a while, they became like a second skin.

The suits had been constructed to give a more dynamic and professional feel to the armies of the blue hemisphere.

What they disguised underneath – for the majority of the armed forces – was middle aged spread. The problem was that these suits were designed with a special compression containment field on the inner lining so it kept the illusion on the outside. They were impossible to take off. You had to spend all day in them. Eat in them, sleep in them, bathe in them. Going to the toilet was only possible with the installation of special zips at the front and bottom of the wearer and even that mostly proved tricky...and messy.

Now that the army was old and knackered and had no idea how unfit it was thanks to the ignorance installed by the miracle suits, some of them had started to breakdown. Little tears in the fabric had begun to emerge and the inner fibre had started to make the wearers itch and scratch. There were dark, grizzly stories being told about what happened to the men as their suits tore apart. It didn't make for easy bedtime reading. But the duo was ignorant of what was in store. As the Pilot continued to claw at the patch on his stomach, something he had been doing for some time, he ran his fingers over his taut six pack.

'I never thought I'd live to 57 and still have a body like this,' he said. 'Still, it must be all the fighting we have been doing. Keeps you fit, son, keeps you fit.'

'But you told me the other day that you haven't seen combat in twenty years,' the ward pondered. 'You told me that your regiment had been attacked and you lost the function of your legs.'

'Well,' the pilot rolled his bottom lip. 'I may have told a fib here and there.'

'Indeed. I knew you were lying because you've walked ever since I got posted here three months ago!'

'Too late to dob me in now, lad. Who would you go to? My superior officer is dead.'

'I know,' the ward replied. 'You killed him!'

'It was a mercy killing.'

'He was on holiday! You managed to fix a timed explosive to the alarm clock of his holiday villa. I'm sure you would have got away with it if you hadn't tweeted the whole thing was your doing.'

The Pilot grimaced. He was pleased that social media has since been banned on all planets within Ursa-17.

'It's amazing what comes out when you've had a few too many ginger ales.'

The Pilot leant forward to pick up his beverage of choice; a ginger ale. Not that he had spotted it, but a tear had begun to form in the area of his suit that he had been scratching.

'That's why I was given this post. Call it exile it you like. Whatever you call it I'm afraid you're stuck with me.' He took a look at his counterpart. The leather suit was so large it looked like he was a little boy wearing his dad's wedding jacket. Pathetic, he thought to himself. 'Why hasn't your suit started to fit your frame lad?'

The ward looked down. His long, dark hair dangled over his face, hiding his pale, white features from view as he glanced at his puny body.

'I don't know,' he replied. 'Maybe mine had a defect.'

'You won't last long in front of a hail of bullets if your suit isn't doing its job!' The Pilot took a swig of his ginger ale and leant back in his chair. As he did, the tear got a little larger in length.

The heli-fighter lurched in the sky as it continued its pre-planned sweep of the city. Little did it know what place it had in the creation of the potential saviour of Rodas.

The ward looked up and saw the pile of leftovers shoved into the corner of the small craft. It was hideous how much the Pilot was eating.

'Maybe if you shared the grub, I would fill it out!'

The Pilot grunted like a warthog struggling to fit into a summer dress.

Ignoring the fact that he did overeat, and had done for decades, he replied, 'What with the measly rations we are given? Huh? You stick to what you're given mate!'

The ward sat slumped in his chair and looked at the altitude dial. It was ever-so-slowly decreasing. He furrowed his brow, perplexed as to why this could be.

'Sir.'

'Not now, young lad. Gloicchester have just pulled a goal back. This could get tight, this match! It's 45-4 now!'

The Pilot heard a squelching noise emit from inside his suit. He thought little of it, but then he felt a constricting sensation in his left leg.

'Then again, it's not the only thing that is getting tighter...'

What happened next filled the young ward with terror. Right in front of his eyes, he witnessed the pilot change. At first, there was the sound of tearing fabric. The suit began to rip without mercy. The Pilot's face was awash with horror and fear. He started sweating, his face became hot with anxiety and his eyes grew evermore bloodshot.

'It's the compression containment field...it's breaking down!' he screamed as he got up off his chair.

His left leg began to feel swollen and painful like an army of hornets had stung it mercilessly.

Soon, the feeling spread up his body, into his torso, which began to bulge against even more tears in his suit. The Ward reached the intercom system.

'Zeta Major, this is Black Hawk we have a problem here.'

The intercom sparked instantly into life. A computerised voice replied through the metal grill of the speaker.

'Roger that Black Hawk, what is the situation?'

'The Pilot...' the ward broke off as he watched his superior continue to swell in random parts of his body. He was starting to develop thick rolls of fat under his chin and his limbs were now out of proportion with his body. His arms were so flabby he was having trouble lifting them as the suit continued to tear apart.

'...his suit has broken down. He is getting bigger and bigger, Sir, what do I do?' The panic in the ward's voice was reaching fever pitch.

The intercom went dead. The youngster struggled to make anything out over the screams of the Pilot, who was getting very large by now.

A balloon-like, pinkish belly was poking out of the hole in the torso of his suit. It looked like he was going to blow.

The ward looked at the heli-fighters instruments. They were still losing height. He was panicking so much now that his right hand that was resting on the console had started to shake. All of a sudden, the intercom came to life again.

'I have spoken to my superior and he has asked me to relay this message...FOR GOD SAKE, GET OUT OF THERE MAN!'

The loud volume of the latter half of the message made the ward jump. He was so frightened he had been frozen on the spot. He daren't look at the Pilot, who by now had grown so fat and big that he had crushed the TV against the pile of rubbish in the corner. He looked terrible. Like a man who had been blown up by a foot pump.

The heli-fighter began to spin uncontrollably. It scraped the main tower of the citadel with its propeller as the ward, who had been forced to snap himself out of the shock of what was happening, tried to wrestle some control back from the craft.

'It's no good, lad. Save yourself!'

The Pilot yelled. His voice sounded wheezy and strained, as though his vocal cords were now swimming in the fatty deposits exploding all over his swollen body.

The first tear in the Pilot's torso shredded across his jelly-like skin and he screamed as he continued to get bigger. He was now six times the size of a normal person. The compression containment field had gone haywire and was now stretching him to breaking point, pulling him apart.

'Shut the door lad! You won't want to see this!' he demanded.

The ward did just that, knowing there was nothing he could do to save the pilot. He flicked a switch on the console and the door slid shut. All he could hear was the screams and the failing engines. The heli-fighter was getting closer and closer to the ground. The ward realised that he had blocked himself off from the only exit he could have used to escape.

He knew that when the craft went down, it would probably mean the end of him too. For a few ghastly seconds, he let that horrific thought wash over him like a wave of death. Then suddenly, he heard a final terrible yelp from the pilot before it got much worse.

A massive explosion ripped through the craft, sending the ward crashing up against the console and then up against the viewing window.

The sound was deafening. Flames omitted from the outer shell of the heli-fighter as the explosion hit the fuel tanks and the ammunition that was stored directly below the section that the pilot had been in. The fire spread along the small craft but stayed out of the control room as the ward regained his seating position.

He grappled with his senses and ignored the pool of blood that was running down his face from a fresh gash in his forehead. He tried to pull the craft up but it was no use. The heli-fighter was about to crash into the citadel...right where Blent and Niva were about to formulate their plan...

IV

Blent and Niva were agonisingly close to the laboratory, blissfully unaware of the madness that was ensuing high above them. Niva was blowing hard, doing her best to keep up with her impressively tall counterpart.

Her cheeks were puffed out and she made an effort of conserving a gulp of breath for a few moments before exhaling loudly from her screaming lungs. She was having a rough time keeping up with Blent but then that was to be expected.

After all, watching him sprint further and further away made him look like a daddy longlegs trapped in a bathtub. She would have giggled if he wasn't so damn fast and their mission was so grave.

'Come on!'

The scientist had decided that they needed to run to get to the safety of his laboratory as he had grown anxious about the possibility of them being discovered and failing in their mission.

He clutched his inside pocket with his right hand.

Inside, Niva had given him the essential ingredients to his experiment and he would do anything to make sure that they were not damaged.

A thought crossed his mind as he was just a few metres away from the door. He held on his person the only thing that could save Rodas.

Blent finally made it to the smooth, silver coloured door that opened up onto what had been his working space for the last few years. He tried to turn the handle but it failed to budge.

'Oh, of course!' he muttered. 'Silly me. Don't worry Niva; thank zark I remembered the key.'

'Yeah, like you're going to leave a laboratory full of top-secret files and research open in a war zone,' Niva screamed at her companion. Her reply echoed down the corridor. Blent sighed. She was miles away. Still, it gave him a little time to dig the long, serrated key out of his pocket. He dug deep into the murky depths of the multitude of pockets on his coat. First, he checked his left-hand-pocket. Nothing but an old tissue and a green, disappointed looking chocolate sweet in the shape of a ques-bear he had taken from home a month ago but had forgotten to eat.

He quickly searched the other pocket. There was what felt like a card that had got stuck to the frayed inner stitching, which was clinging onto the card like its life depended on it.

He pulled and pulled until he heard a huge tearing sound that echoed through the dark, long corridor.

Wincing as though he had just dropped some expensive china on a glass floor, Blent looked inside the envelope and gazed at the front of the card. The words 'Happy Anniversary' were emblazoned in pink and red font on the front. Blent sighed. He had been so preoccupied he had forgotten to open the card. He grunted when he realised that his anniversary was a couple of days ago. *If we make it out of this alive,* he thought, *it will take more than a card and a peck on the cheek to keep her in my life.*

Shaking his domestic problems from his thoughts, Blent reached inside his inner pocket to put the card away. As he did, his long, snakelike fingers clumsily knocked Niva's secret leather pouch from its relative safety. Blent gasped and for a few seconds his life seemed to be running in slow motion. His eyes grew wild with horror as he bent down to the ground to catch the pouch but he expected he would not make it in time.

If the components in the pouch broke on impact on the cold, marble floor then that was it.

All of his hard work, all of the jeopardy and danger he had faced with the revolutionaries had led to this moment and now it was about to go up in smoke.

Out of the corner of his right eye, he saw a hand dive out towards him, reaching out low to the ground.

His eyes followed the pouch as it dropped softly into the palm of the outstretched hand.

Blent breathed a sigh of relief.

'What do you do for an encore?' she inquired. 'Stand in front of a nuclear blast!?'

'Sorry, Niva. I'm just nervous. I'm not normally this clumsy.'

As the word 'clumsy' left his lips, Blent's hand slipped on the floor as he tried to get up and he whacked his chin hard on the ground. Niva rolled her eyes before offering her other hand to her fallen comrade. She bent down and helped him up.

The red-faced girl took the key from Blent and jammed it hard in the lock. She manipulated it; turning it left and right until she heard the lock click open. She pushed the heavy door and spilled inside the laboratory, pulling the still-startled Blent inside. With a great effort, Niva pushed the door closed behind them, allowed herself a sigh of relief and looked at her comrade. What now?

'We'd best leave the lights off. There is a glass ceiling above us. Wouldn't want to light ourselves up like a star going supernova now, would we?'

Blent started to fumble around on the harsh stone floor. Niva looked at her surroundings. The laboratory was a pig sty.

Piles and piles of paper covered the work benches, glass beakers we left all over the floor and there seemed to be a chalkboard that had overturned and fallen flat on another desk that was now smothered by shattered glass. Niva took a peek at what had broken the fall of the dilapidated board. It looked like a cage of some sort - transparent and hard – at least it had been. Just as Niva bent down to take a closer look, a strong, repugnant and sickening smell surged down her nostrils and made a nest in the back of her throat. Suddenly she leaped back. Something had been alive in that cage when the chalkboard slipped off its buckled haunches and obliterated it. From the smell, it definitely wasn't alive now.

'Remind me never to ask you to pet sit for me!'

Blent ignored the remark and was already busy pulling a large piece of tarpaulin off a machine in the centre of the room. Niva gazed at the monstrosity that eclipsed her thoughts for the poor deceased lab pet.

The machine was roughly twenty feet in height, thin and silver and stood like a tower in the dark.

'How long did it take you to make this?' she asked.

'Oh, not long. As soon as I had run a few tests and realised that it was possible to fabricate new life from Professor Travement's original notes, I just knew that this would be our salvation.'

'How does it work?'

'Well, imagine that this is a food blender...'

Niva huffed. 'Right...not the best visual comparison Blent.'

'Just imagine that it can mix up all of the ingredients of a cake, or a smoothie, take your pick! Then it filters out the pips and leaves us with; a completely invincible, physically tough, devastatingly intelligent...'

'Smoothie?' Niva interrupted. 'Okay I get it, just press the start button already. I have a feeling that something bad is about to happen.'

'Will you relax?' Blent looked at her with calm, reassuring eyes. 'Nobody can get to us now. We are just one step away from completing our mission and then...Rodas will be saved.'

'Well, if you're sure...'

'Look, I'll let you stand guard at the door if needs be.'

Blent turned towards the machine and flicked a switch on the crude keypad which looked like it had been added to the cylinder as an afterthought.

He jabbed a few buttons and a compartment popped open.
Inside were several vacant file holders with what looked like the
lip of another cylinder on top.

This was where the liquid from within the tubes was going to be
sucked up into the machine and life would be created.

Niva crossed her arms, gazed up through the glass roof and
sighed. Her attention then went back to the cylinder, which was
beginning to hum into life. Blent furiously managed the controls
like a madman playing a reaction game and she braced herself for
the worst.

'There we go...now we wait. It shouldn't take long. Give it a few
minutes to sift through the information and then we shall have
our miracle!'

Blent's optimism would be crushed in a little over four minutes.
Unknown to the duo, their plans were about to unravel quicker
than a ball of wool tumbling down an endless flight of stairs.

Just moments before the process was complete and the
proclaimed saviour of Rodas was fully formed, ready to end the
bitterness that had engulfed the once-mighty planet, the glass
ceiling splintered into a thousand pieces, showering down like
razors on the unsuspecting freedom fighters.

A heli-fighter plummeted through, crashing to the laboratory
floor in a dust cloud of smoke and fire.

Blent and Niva reeled back as the force of the crash hurled them
against the wall; knocking the former unconscious and the sonic
boom of the blast permanently damaging Niva's hearing for the
rest of her life. After what seemed like an eternity, the perished
heli-fighter came to rest on the floor and the laboratory decimated
beyond all recognition.

Slowly, Niva stirred and picked herself up. The first thing she
noticed was that there was an insistent ringing in her ears that
hadn't been there before. It was overpowering and frightening
that nothing else was audible. She gazed around the room in
horror. She could imagine the sound of the flames licking
maniacally around what looked like a crashed Crimson Empire
heli-fighter. There was no point checking for survivors, she

thought to herself. No-one could have survived such a hideous accident. Her attention then turned immediately to Blent.

She recoiled in devastation as she saw that her ally, the man who had given hope to the people of Rodas, lay lifeless on the ground; his head slumped against the wall.

A trickle of blue blood had smeared down the wall from the point of impact. She looked at the lifeless form and noticed what looked like a card poking out of his lab coat.

Forlorn, Niva swooped for the card, knowing that it had some sentimental value to the scientist but not knowing the reason why. She knelt down to check for a pulse in vain hope but it was no use. Blent was dead.

Suddenly, the scientist's machine started to yawn with greater ferocity than before and the whole cubicle started to shimmer. In all the turmoil, Niva had forgotten about her mission objective. It was a miracle that the damned contraption hadn't been damaged in the accident! She staggered over the broken glass and twisted metal to the impossible contraption. Niva peered inside the class container and noticed a humanoid body suddenly whirring into form, as the fog cloud within slowly began to combobulate.

Niva started to feel dizzy; an effect from the smoke emitting from the crashed heli-fighter. She gasped as she realised that the craft ran on methane and bromide fuel and when unleashed with oxygen, the effects were toxic. Niva started to pant heavily, sweat forming on her brow as it dawned on her that she didn't have much time left...

She clasped her hands up against the glass as the humanoid's form became solid, the seconds ticking away before its 'birth.'

The machine shook more violently than before and as Niva began to slip slowly down the shaft, her life force leaving her body, the hum from the cubicle grew louder and louder and LOUDER! Until...

DING!

The sound of an egg timer signaled the end of the birth.. and the beginning of life. The chamber door creaked open and clouds of smoke spilled out like a milky tide of fog into the decimated laboratory. Niva blinked upwards from her vantage point on the ground, gasping for air. In her final moments she saw the large shadow of a man loom over her, engulfing her frame. Her lungs began to burn. Gulping and fearing that this was the end, she struggled with all her might to stay alive long enough to set her eyes on the man that she had helped create.

Sadly, her final breaths were accompanied with a feeling of failure and utter humiliation. As the figure in the chamber stepped forward, his shadow diminished in height to a little over five feet tall. She shook her head as her bloodshot eyes screamed out in agony.

'Bloody...scientists!' she hissed to herself as her head collapsed to the ground.

What Niva and Blent had struggled to create, all those man hours, dangerous meetings and life-threatening missions they had both taken part in, had led to nothing. For in the chamber door, stood – not the man who would put an end to the bitter war on Rodas – but the body of a young boy...

V

The boy staggered out of his cocoon and into a world of chaos. Opening his new-born eyes for the first time, he saw nothing but devastation, death, broken glass and twisted metal. He blinked through the smoke which brought tears to his eyes like a freshly cut onion. He cried out in shock as he noticed the dead form of Niva at his feet. Scrambling away from the corpse, he then noticed another dead body in the corner of the room and shivered. Although he was just moments old, he was already well aware of the finality of death. He was surrounded by it!

His mind and thoughts darted all over the room. The fireball in the middle of the laboratory, the two corpses, the turmoil; it was all too much for a new being like him and before he knew it, the boy was running.

He had no idea where, but his naked legs were carrying him as far away as he could, away from the horror that was now scarred into his memory.

As he pelted like a thunderbolt down the cold, dark corridors of
the citadel, he heard a voice in his head that was telling him his
purpose – what he was supposed to do.

It was too much to take in. Save a planet!? He wasn't even
wearing any clothes! And why should that responsibility rest on
his pre-pubescent shoulders? Why not that of a great general, a
battle-scarred hero? The questions continued to rain down upon
him. Who was the lanky, blue man in the incredibly white coat
and the red skinned girl who both lay dead by his feet? Were they
his parents?

He didn't even have time to look down and observe his own
form – he didn't care how he looked. He just wanted to escape
and get out of there.

*

'Sergeant, they came down in what looked like the medical
centre on the west wing of the citadel.'

The crash of the heli-fighter had not gone unnoticed by those
conflicting factions over the sky of the citadel – not to mention
those in the tactical war room back at the Crimson Empire's base.
The call taker sat feverishly typing the developments into his log
book.

Sergeant Everald stood gazing out of the observatory window,
taking in the view and pondering his next move.

The Tactical Ensign had informed him minutes earlier that the
pilot's suit had malfunctioned and the chaos that had ensued had
caused the accident. His crossed arms dropped to his side and he
marched over to the operator's station.

'Send a recovery team in to retrieve the black box. No-one
outside of this room will find out about what happened. We don't
want the enemy to know our suits are degrading. There's no way
that I am giving them the upper hand and I certainly don't want
members of the boardroom getting word of our weakness.'

The operator felt a sharp sensation swipe across his cheek...well
one of the four cheeks on his face he had at his disposal. He felt
his hot, aching face and looked in fear into the eyes of his
superior.

'I will not hear that word in my presence!' Everald spat. Regaining his composure, his voice returned to its cool calm tone.

'Can we hack into the citadel's security system? I want to know what happened as soon as possible.'

The operator gulped and turned back to his work.

His fingers flickered against the keys in quicksilver fashion and although he was doing his best, he could hear the tap-tap of the Sergeant's boot clanging impatiently on the metal gantry floor. Mercifully, he managed to infiltrate the security system after bypassing the firewall mainframe – which was practically a room with computers in that ran the security systems in the citadel and could not be reached as there was a wall in flames in the hacker's way.

'All done, Sir,' he declared.

Together, Everald and the operator saw it all; Blent and Niva, the genesis machine, the crash of the heli-fighter and eventually the unnatural creation of a brand new being in the glass chamber.

With intent, Everald lent closer into the viewer screen.

'Show it. Show it on the ultra-screen!' Everald barked.

The operator pressed a few buttons and transferred the images onto the giant fifty-foot awning that dominated the room. Every man and woman stopped precisely what they were doing. From the military to the pen pushers, every single person paused in their steps and gazed in shock and awe at the fantastic sight.

Even the secretary who was making the Sergeant his late-night coffee had her sight fixed on the images and found herself pouring the muddy liquid all over the floor instead of his mug.

'I don't believe it,' Everald gasped. 'Get a search party down there, now...NOW, gadzuke it!'

The operator turned back to his post and radioed in to the foot soldiers.

'All units...I repeat, all units. Engage the citadel. I repeat. Engage the citadel!'

Everald gazed up at the image. Something he had never seen before, so brilliant yet devastating he was struggling to work out what to do next. In front of him, projected for all to see, was a boy...with purple skin...

*

The newborn continued to race through the citadel, totally oblivious of the chaos his very existence was about to cause.

His legs carried him at such a vast speed that the broken glass and masonry that littered the floor pinged off his naked soles like bullets against a wall of steel.

He had no idea where he was running, but an overwhelming sense of fear and desperation led him to flee anywhere. His mind was still empty, except for two voices that kept crawling over his thoughts.

'You are the only person to save us all,' said one of the ghostly apparitions.

It was the voice of a woman, whilst the other was that of a man and it was encouraging him to, 'be the bridge between a world that is divided.'

He didn't even know what a bridge was!

Choking as the air was replaced by the poisonous concoction of poison and fire, the boy tore through a wooden door into the open hallway of the citadel. The place was amber with flame, with one half of the outer wall ripped open. Skidding to a halt, the boy caught his breath and surveyed his surroundings. A cold wind chilled through his cloth-less form and he shivered as he looked for an escape route. Before he could take in another breath, a crash of sound broke above him and a halogen light that burnt deep into his newly formed retinas pushed the boy to the floor. Shielding his vision with his arm, he tried in vain to protect his ears from the piercing scream of engines above him.

'Alright, now we don't know who you are or what you are, but you've got to come with us, kid.'

The boy looked away, confused and alone. The voice came from the whirring contraption above him and sounded like it was coming through some form of amplifying contraption.

'Stay where you are and we will come in and get you.'

The voice spoke with the utmost authority as it buzzed through the cold night air. The boy began to convulse, his body in shock at its first few moments. Tears began to form in the corners of his eyes and no matter how hard he tried to blink them away, they showed no signs of stopping. Resigned to his fate, he curled into a ball and wept.

'Iron Hand, Iron Hand, this is…erm…the Sacrificial Lamb here.' The young Private shook his head at the indignity of his call sign. He could not wait until he was no longer the new boy in the squadron so that he could relinquish the agonizing title. 'We have found the child, Sir. We will proceed with the pick-up and report back when the mission is accomplished.'

Everald stood incandescent with his arms fixed like tent poles over the intercom system. 'Don't just stand there, man!' he barked into the microphone. 'For flibs sake, get on with it!'

'Yes, Sir…'

The Private's reply was cut out by a savage blow to the speaker, delivered from the impatient hand of the raging Sergeant. The speaker hissed and a puff of smoke emitted from its mangled mesh as the whole room stopped in fear.

They had seen the Sergeant like this before – and when his anger reached fever pitch like this, it always meant that the next couple of hours were going to be the most crucial in the Crimson Empire's cause and that the control crew's desk was going to need to be fixed again for the fourth time that month!

Without a moment's hesitation, Everald wheeled on his heels and marched smartly into his office in the corner of the main operations bay. He pushed his palm against the print recognition screen and the door sliced into the wall allowing him entry. Stomping to his desk, he poured over the list of buttons that accompanied his own personal intercom.

Much like its wounded counterpart, it too was dented and mangled from many an encounter with the iron fist of the cantankerous Sergeant.

As if like a sentient being, it almost squirmed in its place as Everald punched the big red button at the top of the list.

He waited for the buzz to whimper into life before a light hologram in hellish red descended from a projector hidden in the roof of the office. The picture flickered before revealing a hooded figure.

'What do you want?'

'My Lord, I am sorry to disturb your slumber but we have received news that a boy has been found within the ruin of the citadel.'

The hooded man leaned forward; his voice so sharp it could shred paper from 100 paces.

'What concern is that of mine?'

Everald gulped, his brow moistening.

'This was no refugee, Sir. As you might recall, we intercepted plans not long ago that rival crimson and blue factions were formulating to end the war.'

'Yes, a foolish notion.'

'Well, it looks like they might have succeeded…'

The hooded figure twitched in surprise.

'You have my attention, Sergeant.'

'In days of yore there was a prophecy that a child would be born of the red and blue inhabitants of this world; a child that would bring peace to our cause.

I believe that the prophecy has come true. We have isolated a young boy who we believe to be the one to bring Rodas together. Of course, this would mean the end of our campaign, Sir.'

'Churlish nonsense, Everald. Not one being in the known cosmos can stop the tide of the Crimson Empire.' The figure waved a skinless hand in the air, dismissing the Sergeant's claims.

Everald bit hard on his bottom lip before continuing. What he said next would put him in the direct line of fire from his superior.

'I'm sorry, Sir, but I believe that you may be wrong.'

The figure rose before him, eclipsing his form like a shadow.

'You'd better have a very good reason for your insubordination, Sergeant.'

'I do, Sir.' Everald shifted in his place, fists clenched so hard by his sides that his knuckles were turning white.

'And what proof do you have of this miracle child's existence?'

Everald wet his lips, his mouth gasping.

'He is purple.'

Instantly, the hooded man shot into life.

'DESTROY HIM!'

*

'Please remain calm. We just want to help you.'

The voice continued to buzz through the megaphone in a clam yet authoritative manner.

The child of Rodas stayed close to the floor, cowering from the strangers in a dark, desolate land. And then, he started paying attention to the voices in his head.

The man and woman's soothing tones somehow gave him strength. He could feel his resolve growing, his confidence blooming, and his eyes opening. The boy unfurled his ball-like form and gazed deep into the search light. All of a sudden, a wash of composure engulfed his very being, flooding his veins with a godly power. He slowly straightened his posture and met the harsh gaze of the heli-fighter's halogen search light.

'Please do not move. I repeat, do not move. We just want to help you.' As the Sacrificial Lamb looked down upon the child, he sensed that all was not in his power.

The purple boy walked towards the heli-fighter.

'Stay where you are!' the voice through the megaphone grew tense and desperate. To everyone's surprise aboard the vessel, the boy spoke.

'Why?'

'Why what?'

'Why should I stay where I am? You're not my Mum! At least, I hope not!'

The Sacrificial Lamb could hardly believe his ears. He could talk? There was something fishy in these duty ruins; and it wasn't the basic ingredients of his tuna sandwiches!

'Of...of course not. Just stay where you are.'

'Change the channel, Mumsy. I'm not going to do what anybody tells me.'

'If you don't, we shall have no other alternative but to use force.'

'You'll have to come down here and catch me first!'

As the last syllable left the boy's mouth, a shower of electric rain shocked his body into submission. The defiant stature was replaced by crippling pain that sent him crumbling to the floor again. The boy screamed as the blue light sparked around him. The Sacrificial Lamb had deployed his energy net, which was normally used to round up enemies and refugees when the Crimson Empire were on patrol searching for prisoners. Now he had caught a new breed of Rodasian – a brand new, potentially dangerous manifestation. Images of promotions, interviews and chat show appearances danced in his head. His dreams of notoriety – for all the right reasons – were about to be dashed.

'Sir, I'm having trouble retaining altitude.' The heli-fighter pilot screamed back to the Private. He was right.

The Sacrificial Lamb could feel the whole craft begin to sink towards the ground. It was like the air beneath them had turned into quicksand.

The cockpit – which was big enough to fit five people – the pilot, co-pilot, two soldiers and himself, started to tip on its side. The Private lost his balance and fell against the window pane, dropping his megaphone in the process.

He blinked through the misty glass, his cold breath already forming a thick cloud of condensation. Through which, he could see what was causing this sudden turn of events. Down below, though not so far away as he had been, was the boy. Only now, he was on his feet, the energy net still shimmering electric blue, only the boy did not seem afflicted.

Although his whole body felt like it was being crippled by the force of the net, the boy was not letting on. He had rose to his feet – albeit with a struggle – and mustered enough power to pull on the net cord, which was still attached to the heli-fighter. His face grimaced and his teeth grinded as he pulled on the cord, it's taut, spring-like composition groaning against the weight of the craft.

The boy continued to muster super-Rodasian strength.

'Pull up, gadzukit!'

'I can't, Sir, the engines are starting to cut out. Any more power and they will collapse under the pressure.'

The Sacrificial Lamb began struggling desperately for the megaphone. He now had his two soldiers crushing him against the glass panel. After a second or two scrambling with his one-free-hand, he clutched it to his crushed face.

'Let us go this instant!'

The boy couldn't believe what he had heard. Let them go?

'Do you really want me to do that?'

'For zargs sake, yes!'

The boy, his body still wracked with pain but refusing to give in to the sheer agony the net had encapsulated him in, stared deep into the whites of the eyes of the Private and pulled the heli-fighter down the last few remaining inches until all that separated the boy and the crew were the glass panels on the cockpit.

'...You're the boss.' He conceded as he let go of the cord.

The boy witnessed the panic in the Sacrificial Lamb's eyes as the heli-fighter, the energy net and the crew within shot off like a rocket up into the neon night sky, hurtling past the highest citadel tower before neatly sling-shotting out of the local vicinity all together before coming to a fiery halt, roughly five-hundred-yards away in a crumpled heap of metal and ruin.

The boy felt the pain ebb away from his aching muscles. He stood on the spot, panting for a brief moment, taking in all that had just happened. It was incredible. He had been born into this world with the strength of ten men – despite his outward appearance – he had a fully-functioning vernacular and he had just managed to outwit an entire crew of what looked like a band of tight-suited kidnappers...all with no clothes on!

'Oh, boy!' he muttered before covering up his pride. He huddled against a ruined wall and formulated his next cause of action. It would be daring, but he knew he could be successful, nonetheless. He would have to steal a ship and get off this godforsaken hell hole...and more vitally, find some clothes before he caused more of a scene than he had already cultivated!

VI

The news of the boy's escape was met with the anger of a thousand volcanos erupting at once – and that was just in Everald's office. His screams of frustration shattered the glass cube that was his office and burst every headset within a 100-yard-radius. With a crash, he pushed his way through what remained of his decimated office doors and stormed into the operations room.

'Get me all units. I want every man we can afford to converge on the child. I demand that every foot soldier, wild walker, heli-fighter and heli-carrier within a five-click range give that little son of a pillard everything we can. The boy is dangerous. He could mean the end of this war and the end of the mighty Crimson

Empire. I don't care how many men we lose; I don't give a damn
whether the enemy take advantage of the situation and meet us
head-on, we have to stop the boy!'

Blood-red droplets of spittle showered onto the floor as the
communication operators worked feverishly to send the orders
out to every soldier available.

Meanwhile, as the activity around the citadel started to gather a-
pace, the child had already managed to sneak his way out of the
spotlight.

He had found some strips of cloth lying tattered and torn in
what looked like a long-forgotten market stall and formed a
rudimentary t-shirt and trouser combination out of the tatty
remains. He had even had enough spare material to make shoes –
although the harder-than-usual skin on the souls of his feet had
been impervious to the sharp shards of shrapnel he had trundled
over so far. For now, he was out of the spotlight and had managed
to cover his form in a much more dignified way than the 'tackle
out' look he had been promoting not long earlier.

With the t-shirt pulled up over his face, covering his features, he
walked at a brisk pace away from the horror of the citadel and
further into the slums of the blue side of Rodas.

On his travels, he saw more misery than anyone should ever see
in a lifetime. Homes had been destroyed beyond recognition,
leading to an abundance of dirty, homeless people living on the
streets. Men, women and children were fighting for shelter, scraps
of food and fuel.

The look of desperation and helplessness bore into his soul. He
tried to make sense of it all. What had started such a terrible
atrocity?

Who would even consider leaving the people of this planet in
such a terrible situation, where famine, pestilence, death and war
ran rife?

Moreover, why did he have a lingering sensation within his
mind that he was the one to help them? He couldn't even help
himself and didn't even know who he was!

The boy held his head down and decided he could take no more.
He kept his eyes straight, looking squarely at his feet on the path
he trod and walked until he could not muster another step.

Finally, his breathing heavy and his legs feeling like lead pipes
in quicksand, he collapsed to the ground. The first thing he
noticed after rubbing his calves free of cramp was that the texture
of the pavement had changed to sand. The coarse, fine grains
filtered through his toes as he flexed his muscles. After mustering
up the courage, he looked up again. The citadel was far, far
behind him; so far, in fact, that the crumbled ruin was not
anywhere to be seen. He was – quite literally – in the middle of
nowhere.

'Now what?' He muttered quietly to himself.

The boy surveyed his surroundings. Apart from the neon
shining moon, no other light emitted from the sky. The
temperature had dropped almost to freezing, which would be
deadly to any other Rodasian, but to the super boy, it was but a
light chill.

'I suppose I could stay here for a while, take it all in. But where
do I start? What the hell is going on? Why am I here? What's my
name? And why the flicking gip am I talking to myself!' he
laughed. As if his day hadn't been terrible already, he was
considering a plea of insanity – maybe it would help in all this
madness!

'Excuse me.'

The boy jumped out of his shiny, purple skin. He surveyed his
surroundings. He was sure it was only himself in the vicinity and
allowed himself to believe he was going mad.

A few moments passed before the nervous, pleading voice
repeated itself.

'Excuse me, young fella. But would you mind awfully not
treading on my face.'

The boy shrieked. He leapt from his spot and jolted to his left.

'Now you're on my shoulder.'

He sprung in the air again and again like a spring going insane
in a supermarket trolley being pushed down a ten-storey
stairwell.

'Look, now you're standing on my back. Please do try to be a
little more consid..OOF! definitely not there! What's wrong with
you, boy!' the voice seemed to be coming from directly below
him.

'Who keeps saying that?' he asked.

'Mmmfff dumpf nufff puff.'

'What!?'

'I fed. Wud You Pleaff get off my faifff.'

The boy flung himself five feet to the left and rolled down a slight small sand dune. He could have sworn it was the voices in his head again.

'Thank you, that's better.'

He looked up over the dune and before his eyes, he witnessed a clump of sand collate together and form slowly into the shape and mass of a humanoid. The legs, torso, arms, neck and cranium all shifted and blurred in a sandy wave before turning to face him.

'W-who are you?'

'I'd have thought that was bleeding obvious – I am the Sandman.'

VII

The man made of granular substance towered over the boy. He stammered, in awe of what he had just seen.

'Y. Yur. You're.'

'Made of sand, yes. Tell me about it.'

'But, how?'

'How? I'll tell you how! I was once a proud man. A soldier by the name of Nethi Gaugman. I was a member of the 44th field battalion of the Sapphire Regime. I had it all; a rank of Commander and a group of men who would literally crawl across the biggest burning sun with their flies undone if I had ever given the order! And I would have done the same for them.'

The pair's eye-contact was broken momentarily as the boy tried to picture such an act of devotion in his head.

'Like so many others in my regiment, I had seen so much bloodshed and so much pain. As the war raged, I started to get itchy feet. So, I decided to apply for a special commissions unit that the Sapphire Regime installed. What really happened to me was far from what I expected...and so devastating it changed my life forever.'

The boy could sense a deep sincere feeling of betrayal and bitterness within the Sandman's speech pattern. It was growing by the second.

'They used me. I was an experiment! They changed my genetic make-up, stripped my Rodanity bare and spliced what I used to be until there was nothing left! They said I was going to be the first of a new line of soldiers - the leader of an infantry that could blend in with its surroundings and spy on our crimson enemies without detection. I became a joke. The machine that they used upon me was faulty. My body's molecules became corrupt and what had once been made of flesh and bone became bonded with the grains of sand that scattered the floor of the laboratory. Later, I went on to find out that the operation was so experimental, so illegal, that the high command of the Sapphire Regime had absolutely no idea that these kinds of experiments were taking place.'

'So, what did you do?'

'What any other self-respecting soldier would do. I fell apart!'

The boy was curious. 'What do you mean 'fell apart'?

'I crumbled. Both physically and mentally. The surgeons tried to move my crumbling body but when the nurses went to pick me up, my forearms fell through their fingers like...'

'Sand?'

The Sandman craned his grainy neck down to the boy.

'You guessed it. The next moment I was on the floor. And what did the scientists do to help me in my desperate predicament? They swept me up with a dust pan and brush! The main fella, this gangly looking berk who looked like his father was made of spaghetti and talked like he was forever trying to swallow a live cat, tried to explain aside what had happened – I heard his every word.

'It was nothing to do with him – he has warned that this machine was just a prototype and that he couldn't explain what had just happened. In the end, they swept me up, put my dusty remains in a jar and placed me on the shelf of the head scientist's office.

'In the end, I was still alive and my conscience was clear. I managed to shake what was left of my mutated form hard enough to knock the jar off its perch and I managed, with the will of my mind, to drag the contents to a nearby drain and escape. You see, I'd heard from meetings in that office that they wanted to attempt to reanimate my remains and give the experiment another go.

'But I ran away. I mean, what next? What is lower than a grain of sand?

A spec of dirt!? Ever since then, I've been a fugitive, trying my hardest to assemble my true form, again using nothing but willpower.'

The boy felt terrible but accepted that he and his new friend shared something in common.

'So, we're both fugitives then.'

'What are you wanted for?'

'I honestly don't know. I've been running ever since I can remember.'

'Which side are you on?' The Sandman enquired.

'Side?'

'Oh, come on, what were you born five minutes ago?'

'More like ten,' said the boy.

The Sandman rather flippantly dismissed this retort.

'Well, as you should know, there are two sides to this war. The Crimson and the Sapphire. I can't tell which you are as I am colour blind. Not a side effect of my accident, more a problem I encountered when I suffered an explosion to the face in the great battle of Trevelyan.'

'I'm sorry, but could we get out of here? It's starting to get very cold and unless you can't see this too, I've only got a sheet on me!'

The Sandman subsided a little into the sand and lowered himself to the boy's level, his eye line peaking just under the child's spiky hair.

'Oh yeah, sorry I would have offered you a full quota of clothes but it's been so long since I spoke to anybody and as I don't wear clothes anymore, I hadn't noticed! Come inside.'

'What do you mean?' The boy surveyed the entire area. There was nothing at all but fine, tall hills of sand as far as the eye could see.

'Oh, hang on.'

The Sandman turned his back to the boy and inhaled greatly before letting out a breath so strong that a great hurricane blew from the figure. The wind roared and roared. The sand in front of him lifted like a film or a page turning.

'Bleeding' heck!'

The boy stood aghast. There, in front of him, was a grand spaceship, hidden in a hole in the ground.

IX

'Here is my home. Meet the Venus II. The fastest fighter-ship this side of the cosmos. It can do 0-60 in the speed of light. She's a baby at forty-two years old.'

The boy marveled at the brilliant craft.

'Come on in. I'd put the kettle on but I can't as I can no longer pick anything up without crumbling into a puddle of sand! Open.'

Instantly, a metal gantry descended from the belly of the ship, yawning open and revealing a bright light from within the ship. It made sense for the ship to be voice activated, especially as this slightly odd 'Sandman' fella insisted that it was almost physically impossible for him to touch things. The boy walked up into the Venus II and gasped in awe of its contents.

He was met by the sight of gleaming metal, shiny panels grinning ear-to-ear. If the Venus II were a house, then this would only be considered the hallway! He surveyed his surroundings deeper, taking a closer look at every aspect of the craft.

In all his life, which was still in its immediate infancy, he could never have dreamed up such a thing of beauty.

The hallway was roughly a hundred metres in length and further down the corridor there appeared to be doors branching off into other sections of the ship. With great enthusiasm, the boy asked his new friend if he could take a look around and proceeded to inspect the Venus.

After several minutes he had found what looked like a hospitality area, complete with a kitchen and a seating area for people to relax.

The boy heard a slinking sound behind him which indicated that the Sandman had joined him.

'How long have you had this thing?'

'Oh, a few years, I guess. This old girl didn't cost me a thing. You could say I stole it. It's wanted by the Crimson Empire. You see, it used to be there until my regiment snatched it from right under their noses. Then, just days before my accident, I was entrusted with hiding it somewhere inconspicuous and I chose out here. Quite ironic, really isn't it considering what ended up happening to me!'

'If it's called the Venus II then what happened to the Venus I?'

The Sandman went on to regale the boy with the story of the original Venus craft. Roughly 70 years ago, a decorated war hero by the name of Sveto Rolansky designed and built a ship so vast yet designed and built a ship so vast yet so nimble and powerful, that the Sapphire Regime decided to finance his plans and turn it from what was supposed to be a cruise liner into a warship.

The Government had enthused that the hospitality features should remain in the plans, but unfortunately, the original idea to have a swimming pool had to be sacrificed for an abundant array of all variations of armoury instead. Rolansky, after much deliberation and protest, eventually yielded but insisted that he be placed in charge of its construction and would also hold the distinction of test piloting the craft when it was ready.

After nearly twenty years had passed, the ship was set to sail on its maiden voyage. People from around the blue hemisphere gathered in their millions to see its maiden voyage, which was to include a handbrake turn around the seven moons of Hox before reversing into the Royal Chamber of Queen Troxby of Flom on the neighbouring planet of Dup. However, it was to go terribly, terribly wrong.

'...Y'see, there was a tiny design flaw. Just as Rolansky was about to apply the handbrake turn he had a moment of realisation.'

'What? There wasn't enough petrol to get back?' The boy asked.

'No, there was no handbrake.' The Sandman replied. 'Smashed straight into the first moon of Rox and that was that. Total muck up on his part. That's the trouble with us Rodasians. We sometimes miss the smallest detail and that can cause massive devastation because for Rolansky it cost him his life. Still, I've heard stories that the man was, not only a pacifist, which is libbing hard on this planet, but also a consummate thief too. You see, his initial idea for this ship was taken from a colleague of his after a heavy night drinking in the notorious pub district of this planet. But because he had laced his friend's drink with a

chemical agent that wiped his memory and sadly left him a
gibbering vegetable, he would never be taken to court and sued
for stealing the original idea. Then again, Rolanksy certainly got
his comeuppance. It had the biggest television audience this side
of our galaxy. It even went on to win the vote for the funniest
moment in the history of Ursa-17.'

'So, how do you fly this thing? I mean, you must have got it out
here somehow.'

The Sandman lurched his head to the sand, making tiny
granules of his being seemingly fall out of his left ear.

'I was lucky enough to discover that one of the AI prototypes
was on board at the time - no idea why.'

'AI?'

'Artificial Intelligence. Both sides of this war have been
developing them in a bid to stop the death of so many foot
soldiers.

The process was in its infancy when I ran away but this little
guy was a highly advanced test run to allow inanimate objects to
come alive and carry out useful jobs for the war effort. Come here,
pet!'

The pair glanced up towards the hallway and heard the
clattering of metal upon metal from afar. With great speed, the
sound became louder and louder. The boy's mind raced as to
what this AI must be? A robot-man? Whatever it was, it sounded
powerful and it was heading straight for them.

In a flash, a blur of silver shot past the fugitives around ankle
height, blowing both the boy to the ground and the Sandman into
hundreds of pieces.

Gingerly, both got to their feet and whilst the Sandman
assembled himself again in a rather frustrated manner, the boy
took in the being that had now joined them.

'Skateboard, I've told you before, you really must run a
diagnostic on your speed setting, it's far too fast still! I don't want
another situation like last time, when I asked you to clean the
kitchen and you shot straight through the hull wall!'

'Apologies, Sir.' A sharp, metallic yet friendly voice emitted
from a small gap in the top of the robot. The boy grinned at what

he saw. The AI was thin, very thin. It had the same depth as a flat packed piece of cupboard. The robot also ran on four little wheels and its back – or body depending on how you looked at it – was three feet in length. There were no eyes or ears to speak of and the boy's reflection shone in the sparkling metal finish.

'Skateboard meet...I'm sorry I don't even know your name?'

The boy looked startled. His life had been so hectic and unconventional that he hadn't had time to stop and think of a name for himself. He had a nagging feeling that the naming of a new person was the job for somebody else, not he! He raced through his fervent memories and settled upon a name that befitted his rather unorthodox early moments.

'Random.' He said. 'My name is Random.'

'It's a pleasure to make your acquaintance, Sir', Skateboard chirped. 'Would you like some tea, brewed from the finest milk of the Utup seed?'

Random hesitated.

'Sure. What does it taste like?'

'How should I know... I don't have any taste buds.'

Skateboard retreated to the kitchen bay as the Sandman beckoned Random towards the cockpit. If the rest of the Venus II had the majestic splendour of a Royal barge, then the cockpit had all the charm of a back alley outside a gentleman's club at four in the morning.

It was dark, dank and smelly and housed four chairs, all with control panels in front, and one steering wheel to the left of the front nose that the cockpit was situated in. It was also relatively cramped. Random thought it would be rude of him to ask why this part of the ship felt so incomplete to the rest of it, until the Sandman answered his question for him, as if he were inside his head.

'Cut backs,' he admitted.

He beckoned for Random to take a seat in the pilot's chair. And then, licking his lips like sandpaper, he asked the crunch question.

'Do you reckon you know how to fly this thing?'

'Definitely not,' Sandman admitted.

'But you could be taught. It's very simple you know. Think of it like driving a small shuttle car.'

'But I've never driven one of those either.'

The Sandman grew impatient and snapped at his new guest.

'Is there anything you can do?'

'Well.. apparently I can drag heli-fighters down to the ground using nothing but my strength.'

The Sandman roared with laughter.

'Don't you play games with me, boy. I've already told you that I can't touch anything. I need someone to pilot this thing for one last special mission.'

Random did not like the tone of his voice or the direction that the conversation was heading.

'What's that then?'

'The Sapphire Regime destroyed my life. They took away who I was, what I stood for, everything I achieved with no possibility of returning to the life I once had.'

'You could always just ask them to fix things?'

'I'm a soldier, Random. We don't ask questions.'

Random started to shift uneasily in his chair.

'What are you asking of me?'

'I want you to take me to the headquarters of the Sapphire Regime and destroy the last strong post that they have got.. and everyone within...'

X

'That's murder!'

Random looked back at the Sandman with an expression of utter disgust. Was there no decent being on this god forsaken planet he lived upon?

'That's war.' The Sandman's retort was cold and final. 'Every soul on this planet knows how long this war has raged. Are you seriously telling me that not all of us have taken a life at some point in our miserable, futile lives?'

'Not me.' Random stopped sharply after his statement. He thought back to the Sacrificial Lamb, the electric netting and the way in which he launched that heli-fighter full of soldiers off into the night sky. A feeling of shame passed through his bones as if an army of ghosts were walking along his spine. Surely, that didn't make him a killer too?'

Confused and distressed, he buried the feeling deep down.

'Oh, I see your conscience is working, isn't it? So; you have taken a life. Then, how is this any different?'

'And then what?' Random spat. 'We become fugitives? Wanted by the Sapphire Regime for the rest of eternity?'

'You're forgetting. We are in the Venus II. We can jump to any part of the galaxy. Anywhere at all – and they'd never find us. And, even if they ever did catch up with us, we'd just hop away again.'

'I don't want to live my life forever looking over my shoulder,' said Random. 'I've not been here long and I refuse to become a war criminal just to help you out.'

'Well, the way I see it is that you've got three choices. Either you do as I ask, escape Rodas and build a new life elsewhere. Or, you can get off my ship right now and I'll leave you to whoever you're running from.'

'And the third?'

Why did I ask that? Random mused. He already knew what the other alternative was.

'Or I kill you right now.'

Random gulped hard. What kind of a world was this? Red and blue men and women? A man made entirely out of sand? A talking Skateboard!? He needed to get away, safely. Although he knew deep down that this was his true home and his purpose was here. But he didn't want it. He would do anything to escape this madness. Anything.

'Okay. It doesn't seem like I have a choice then, does it?' he conceded. 'I'll pilot you to the headquarters of the Sapphire Regime. All I ask in return is that after what's done is done, that you leave me somewhere far from here and we never come face to face again.'

The Sandman shot a sinister smile. 'Deal. Well, I'll leave you in the capable hands of Skateboard. He'll show you the ropes. Of course, whilst you're here, you'll not be allowed to leave the ship.'

'Why would I want to?' Random said. He was right. It was a safe haven, hidden miles from anywhere. He knew he was in a good place, but how to get away with his life? Random now knew that this guy was nuts. Of course he was. After such a traumatic

experience as having his own personal being changed so
immeasurably, that was enough to send anyone mad and
vengeful considering he wanted to kill those that had wronged
him. An eye-for-an-eye, as it were.

'Skateboard will look after you. And if you DO try to escape, I
won't.'

Random gulped hard.

'You're the boss.'

*

Random spent the next two days as the guest to this non-massed
psychopath. He was clothed, fed and watered and spent his time
studying the ship. The Sandman had not been present during
this time as he seemed more at home in the sand dunes outside
the Venus II.

So instead, Random, dressed in a canary yellow t-shirt with
khaki full-length trousers and smart, polished black boots, was
left with the company of Skateboard, who was acting more as his
personal guard more than anything else. Using tact, he was
learning – piece-by-piece – everything about the Venus that the
weird AI had to offer. After a while, he felt like he had begun to
build a trust with the robot. Enough to ask the question he had
been burning to ask since he had agreed to do the Sandman's
deed.

On a trip to the engine room, which was just as dank and dirty
as the cockpit itself, Random saw his chance.

'Have you ever killed anyone Skateboard?'

The little robot stopped in his tracks.

'I do not know what you mean, Sir.'

'Y'know. Have you ever taken a life?'

'Why would you ask me that?'

'It's just that I thought that if you have been in the service of this
Sandman fella for a while you might share his vision of
destruction, that's all.'

Skateboard hesitated.

'I'm hurt by your presumption, if you don't mind me saying so.'

Random was surprised.

'Hurt? But you're a robot.'

'I may not be organic like yourself, Sir, but I can still feel.'

There was awkward silence between the two for a couple of clicks.

'Just because I serve the Sandman, it doesn't mean that I want to help him. Why do you think I made a hole in the hull when the Sandman brought it up?'

'Because your speed setting is on the blink?'

'No. I was trying to escape.'

Random began to feel empathy with the item.

'The master found me on this ship but I am not his. I was built to help ship goods and supplies to the refugee camps that the Sapphire Regime held. I was helping out those members of the Crimson Empire that had been captured and were being held against their will.'

'Then how on earth did you end up here?'

Skateboard pulled himself up against the shin bones of Random, like a dog seeking attention. Instinctively, Random began to pat Skateboard, tentatively at first, to reassure him.

'There was a severe vehicle shortage that led to the Venus being assigned to make a short trip to the camps as our old freighter was severely damaged in a bombardment. So, I and my fellow androids loaded the ship up with fresh supplies ready for transport. We of the Sapphire side may be just as culpable for this war, but it doesn't mean that we butcher the prisoners we keep. Then, just as I was loading the bay on board, the Sandman came aboard. Only he wasn't made of sand then. Since his regiment had been given orders to take the Venus for their own, he piloted the ship out here, forgetting that I was still on board. He landed the Venus in a crater and locked me inside. The next time I saw him he was totally different. No longer a man with skin and bones; instead, his body had been replaced with sand. I was perplexed. He spotted me in my hiding space down here and threatened to destroy me if I didn't help him out. I've been here ever since, doing his will. Not out of pity or want, but out of fear.'

'You know he is easy to disable. He has no physical mass. It would be easy to pass through him!'

Skateboard shook his body. 'Yes, I know, but sand gets everywhere. He could easily clog my instruments and then I'd be powerless, scrap even!'

Random stroked his new found friend with more tenderness than before.

'I can help you.'

'How?' enquired Skateboard.

'We can team up. Get rid of this Sandman guy and then we can escape. That way, we don't have to kill anyone and we get shot of both our captor and this terrible planet.'

Skateboard mulled the idea over in his mainframe.

'But where would we go?'

Random smiled.

'Anywhere. We can go anywhere in the galaxy. You and I. Skateboard and Random and the Venus II. What do you say?'

'I like the sound of that, Sir.' If Skateboard had a mouth he would have been grinning from ear-to-ear.

'Good boy,' Random patted his companion. 'Now, do you know how to pilot this thing?'

'I do. But although this ship is compatible with my sensors, I am unable to do so.'

'Why?'

'No hands.' Skateboard wiggled to elaborate his point. 'Plus, I can't reach the steering wheel! My frame is not very complimentary, especially in height!'

'Okay, not to worry,' Random assured. 'Teach me and I'll get us out of here.'

And so, with the attack on the Sapphire Regime's HQ imminent, Random and Skateboard set about formulating their plan of escape – for they both knew that this was their only chance to flee

Rodas, and the murderous desires of the Sandman for good.

XI

When the big day arrived, Random was exhausted. He had inadvertently lost the ability to sleep the night before. He stirred and shook in his bunk, which had been prepared for him by

Skateboard. It was meticulously pristine; it gleaned in the night light and even though he was wearing a face mask, Random was still blinded by the neon moon. Its reflection bounced around the clean metal walls and shone in his eyes so brightly, he was genuinely worried for his sight the next morning.

For three whole weeks afterwards, he swore he was seeing everyone in an entirely different spectrum altogether. The two previous nights, Random had slept down in the engine room with Skateboard, whose only luxury was a tiny basket which he slept in with a canister of oil by its side in case he got stiff in the night. Although it was small and dark, Random had enjoyed his rest time down there.

It was a shame that he was moved, for appearances sake, just so that they did not arouse suspicion regarding their conspiracy to take over the Venus II.

He had spent all day trying to master the complex instruments of the ship in preparation for the attack on the HQ.

The Sandman came in from the harsh sand every now and then to see the progress his "captive" was making.

In the back of his grainy little mind, the Sandman had a feeling that his obedient pet was working behind his back; that the robotic drone was trying to help this strange boy to escape anyway he could. However, as his short-term memory dwindled as quickly as the sands of time would blow, he kept departing back to the dunes before having the exact same nagging feeling of paranoia and coming back to check on his unwilling co-conspirators again.

There had been one occasion upon which Random had asked what the entire plan was, but the Sandman was keeping his cards close to what used to be his chest and informed the Sandman that information was on a "need to know basis, which was not needed at present".

All of this cloak and dagger had infuriated Random; he was frustrated beyond belief. He wanted to know all the ins and outs so that he and Skateboard could counter act it with little difficulty.

As he lay in bed, blinded by the night-time light, he worried that whatever he and his robotic accomplice would do, the Sandman may be able to stop them. And what could the Sandman do to him? Turn him into a sand storm and suffocate him? As far as Random was concerned, the Sandman was an unknown entity.

He had been a soldier before his experiment had gone wrong so what did that warped mind have in store? Random mind tossed and turned. He had never felt so nervous and unsure, especially given that there were still the questions surrounding his own existence. The voices in his head had stopped – for now – but their requests had nagged at his conscience. He knew that he had something very important to do, but what? Save the planet? Find his parents?

Even if he were able to fall into a deep slumber, he was still haunted by the first scenes he remembered witnessing. Death and devastation. That laboratory room, the fire, disease and helpless refugees he had walked past.

How could he have helped them even if he knew how? He needed guidance, a clear head and a new beginning, even if his own was only a few days previously. He needed to get away.

On the morning of the attack, Random was awoken by the ship alarm, blazing through the speaker systems like razorblades through marshmallow. The klaxon wailed mercilessly for what seemed like an eternity and sent Random scurrying to the ground, his hands to his ears.

Eventually, the klaxon blared no more and was replaced with the voice of the Sandman.

'Wakey wakey!' he screamed. 'Today's the day, young man. Meet me up in the hospitality area in ten clicks flat!'

Random panted, his heart beating furiously. He scrambled around the bed, clawing for his belongings, trying to remember everything Skateboard had taught him.

He could remember their plan to dispose of the Sandman but how to fly mere metres off the ground and loop whilst firing photon torpedoes at the same time, well that required revision most horrid!

Nevertheless, and despite his fatigue, lack of sight and now bleeding ear drums, he stood defiantly and strode on his way out of his room towards his fate.

When he got to the hospitality area, he found that a place had been laid for him at the dining table, accompanied with fresh juice and a bowl of cereal.

The Sandman stood tall and proud next to a video screen that had descended from the ceiling and Skateboard stood next to him, as obedient as ever.

'You took your time. Come on! There isn't a moment to spare.'

'Alright, alright, I'm here now, aren't I?'

Random sneered, his retort like that of a petulant teenager.

The Sandman snorted. 'I hope that Skateboard has been of some use to you these last few days. I saw his tutorials that you took part in. I hope that they were of help.'

The last sentence was more of a statement and less of a question, thought Random so he kept quiet as he tucked into his breakfast.

'Now, you may be wondering why we shall be attacking the Sapphire Regime during the day time? Well, as you'll realise, the army is most tired at the start of the day due to the brightness of our moon, making them an easier target at the start of a new day and tactically less aware. Also, as you will now realise, the Venus II is so fast and nimble it can shake off the most stubborn of heat seeking missiles and is also blessed with a cloaking device.'

The video screen fizzed into life and showed a detailed layout of the Sandman's target. His right finger elongated into a pointer stick and indicated along with his instructions.

'So, what we shall do, is fly the two hundred miles to the HQ, fly in from the west, as you can see that side of the complex is less protected from fire arms than others and whilst the shield bubble can protect it from a heavy bombardment, as we are but one ship, I shall send an energy pulse that will disable anything electronic within a hundred metres of us so that we can fly in, deploy our bombs and fly out again. This pattern we shall have to repeat four times, once for every side of the complex. After this, we shall fly up to the tip of the HQ and drop one last thermal detonator on the main offices of the HQ, wiping out the chain of command and leaving the Sapphire Regime crumbling and weaker than ever before.'

Random raised his hand whilst stuffing his mouth with cereal with the other.

'Yes?' the Sandman said wearily.

'Excuse me for asking,' Random spat through his mouthful, 'But won't that mean that the Crimson Empire will just end up taking over the planet?'

'Exactly! And then the war will finally be over. My revenge will be exacted and Rodas shall be free once more.'

'But I've seen the Crimson Empire at work. They tried to kill me. If anything, you've said is to go by, they seem a hundred times worse than your lot. So, why after all these years of fighting for the Blue Army are you allowing the reds to win?'

He had a point, thought the Sandman. If only the boy knew the hurt and suffering that his own kind had put him through, he'd want to kill them too.

'When your own kinds have turned their backs on you, you have no choice but to turn yours on them.'

Random chewed enthusiastically as he listened on. He was putting on a façade; not wanting to let his captor on that he was actually plotting his downfall.

'As soon as HQ is in flames, we shall then make our escape. Under the cover of our cloaking device, you shall then pilot us out of this system, past the blockades on the planet's outer rim and when that final hurdle of security is past, set co-ordinates for the furthest planet on the furthest reach of the galaxy and we shall wait for the heat to die down.'

'But I thought you said that you'd drop me off at the next possible opportunity? We had a deal!'

The Sandman smiled maniacally. 'If you get us out of this, I won't want you out of my sight. You'll be far too valuable to me, I'm afraid. Eventually, you shall help me assume a new body.'

Random shivered. He knew what those words meant.

He wanted to steal his body, if he had the chance. More determined than ever, Random was going to have to stay on his toes, stick to the plan he and Skateboard had made and get rid of the maniac for good!

'Now eat up, Mr Random. We commence the attack in 20 clicks!'

'Don't worry,' Random sneered as he washed his cereal down with a final gulp of fruit juice. 'I'm ready now.' He slammed the glass back down on the table, pushed his chair back and made his way to the cockpit, observed intensely by Skateboard and the Sandman all the way.

The next twenty clicks passed by like hours. A knot had formed in Random's chest and it burned with anxious heat. He had been a little too hasty in his enthusiasm to 'get-on' with the job in hand and had been told by the Sandman that they would stick to that time frame as there was a window of opportunity in timing as the Crimson Empire's attack would cease momentarily in the window.

When they were ready, Random piloted the Venus II with alarming ease – either Skateboard was a fantastic tutor or he had a natural talent.

Nevertheless, he kept his eyes front of the house and maintained his concentration on the job in hand. With a click of a button, the starter motor snarled into life. The entire ship juddered along to the rhythm of the engine and his cheeks waddled up and down as he raised his steering wheel. The Venus II shuddered up from its hiding place in the sand dune and shot up through the coating of sand that disguised it, into the fresh air. The brightness of the Rodas sun illuminated the cockpit and Random had to fetch for a pair of goggles that sat surreptitiously on the dashboard. He couldn't quite believe it, he was flying!

This moment of triumph was short-lived as his mind returned to the task in hand. He and Skateboard had decided to fly as close as they could to the HQ before it became impossible for them to escape the warring mire just so the Sandman's suspicions were not aroused.

Then, on Random's command, Skateboard, who was blue toothed into the network, requested all the doors and windows be opened on board so that the Sandman's body was to be sucked out of the craft and trapped on Rodas for good. It was a simple and effective plan, thought Random.

However, it all hinged on one or two technical errors coming into place. The previous evening, unbeknownst to their captor, Skateboard had managed to integrate with the firewall matrix and deactivated the Sandman's voice activation capabilities and instructed the main frame computer to switch users when instructed to do so. Otherwise, the doors would never open. Random crossed his toes that his robotic friend's calculations had been successful.

They were nearing the HQ with alarming velocity. This ship really knew how to move, thought Random! At less than two clicks away, the time was almost right to dump the Sandman for good.

'Nearly there now,' observed the Sandman. 'Just don't try anything funny now. Or I'll choke you.'

Random nodded his head in acknowledgement.

'No problem.'

He gestured to Skateboard with a pre-agreed double blink that the time was now. Inside, the AI's mechanisms whirred and buzzed. The codes were snapping together and the binary systems were lining up.

Within a mini-second, they had connected with the firewall. But the doors refused to budge. Random shot a look of panic at his companion.

'Ah.' Skateboard said audibly. 'I forgot to carry the three!'

'What!?' The Sandman stared daggers of ice at his drone. 'What are you talking about?'

Random flipped the craft upside down. The Sandman's form hour glassed away from what had been the floor and then reformed on what was previously the ceiling.

'Traitors' he yelled, sending a huge dust cloud towards Random and Skateboard, who were fastened and electronically bolted to their places so they didn't fall like their captor.

Random saw the dust cloud heading straight for him, causing him to act by swinging the ship back on its belly and sending the Sandman hurtling down the hospitality area.

'For god's sake, Skateboard, can you fix the calculation?'

'Yes, Sir. But it'll take about four clicks. I'm sorry, long mathematics has never been my forte.'

'Now you tell me!' Random hollered as another sand cloud shot towards him, shaped like a giant hand of terror. He flipped the ship again, making himself feel a little queasy in the process.

And so, their plan had failed to work. But worse was to come for the captives of the Sandman. A blip on the sonnerscope made Random's flesh crawl. They had entered the war zone. The Sandman's timing had been off…there was a battle raging on the outskirts of the HQ and they were flying straight into it…

XII

Random's training had failed to cover evasive maneuvers. It had also failed to include what to do when a shape shifting man made of sand is trying to kill you whilst you are simultaneously hurtling towards the heart of an interplanetary battle.

The scene was horrific. Dozens upon dozens of small planes dog fighting in the sky before him, the searing energy weapons firing left right and centre. Try as he might, he couldn't turn the Venus II around.

Another jet of sand coursed its way towards the boy but the blast door leading to the cockpit snapped shut just before it threatened the pair.

'Sir, I've managed to hot wire the door mechanisms. He shouldn't give us any problems for the time being.'

Skateboard's tone was one of triumph. Random didn't share his enthusiasm.

'Now all we need to do is fly out of this hell hole!'

'Look out!' Skateboard's robotic tones shrieked as Random spotted out of the corner of his goggles a bolt of energy hurtling straight towards them. He dropped the steering shaft and the Venus ducked below the laser and out of harm's way.

But now Random was piloting the ship into a whole web of lasers and rockets. He slalomed through the worst of them, but the right wing of the Venus was scorched by a stray.

'That's close enough for me.' Random said. 'Skateboard, are you any closer to opening the cabin windows?'

'Nearly there, Sir. Hang on; my sensors have indicated that the Sandman is finding another way of getting in here.'

Random looked startled.

'How?'

'Through the air ducts.'

'Close the air conditioning system in here.'

68

'But Sir, you'll suffocate.'

'I'll hold my breath!' If there was one thing Random wasn't concerned with right now, it was his breathing! But it was too late. Tiny grains of sand began to trickle out of the vents in the dashboard and the cockpit walls. He was breaking through!

'Hold on, did you say that you had hotwired the door mechanisms?'

'That is correct, Sir.'

The expression on Random's face turned from one of stress to one of relief.

'Skateboard, open all the doors on board. Do it!'

The little robot obeyed and tripped the firewall again. Straight away the cockpit door shuddered open. The Sandman was waiting there, his tentacles made of grain were ballooning through all the air vents and now stood, vengeful, at a swollen height of eight feet and filled the doorway.

'You betrayed me. Now I'll make you suffer. I'm going to fill your lungs with sand until you gag your last breath.'

A sudden gust of wind roared mercilessly towards the cockpit.

'Guess again.'

Random had the last word as the Sandman, every last fragment of his being, was sucked out of the ship and scattered on the warring crafts below like ashes from an airplane.

They had done it.

The Sandman was gone. Now Random had to get them out of this crossfire before there was nothing left of either him or Skateboard.

The laser fire fizzed past the Venus II as it continued to dodge its way around the battlefront. Random used the steering console to twist past them, although he was still not comfortably at ease with the ship.

He had adapted quickly after just a couple of days of training from an artificial being that resembles a child's form of transport, but it was going to take some getting used to, if they ever escaped!

'Could you scan the area for the imperfection in the shield again?' he asked.

'I'll do it now, Sir. However, my synaptic connections are still connected to the ship, but in the wrong department. I don't suppose you could reach into my back and connect my external drive to the dashboard.'

'Um', Random stalled, as an explosion splintered in front of him. 'A bit busy here, Skateboard. Could you do it yourself?'

At this moment, a crisscross of warring heli-fighters sprang into action above the Venus.

Random glanced above and recognized the face of one of the co-pilots. It was the Sacrificial Lamb! True, he was looking a little worse for wear and from where he was sitting, Random could faintly see a white plaster secured over the bridge of his nose, a bloodied bandage around his forehead and two of his right arms in a sling. Embarrassed, Random gave him a nervous smile and waved.

'After him!' the soldier hissed to his crew, snapping his broken arms straight before recoiling again in blatant agony.

'This is about to get a bit rougher.' Random said as he slid the accelerator pedal further down to the floor.

Despite all the danger, he allowed himself a brief second to feel proud. He hadn't killed anyone when he escaped the Crimson Empire. His conscious was clear...and it would remain so.

Meanwhile, Skateboard was doing his best to lasso the external socket into the vacant twelve-volt adapter in the dashboard of the ship. He tried using the momentum of the Venus' swing motion as it avoided the blaster fire to slot the connection home. But with the increased speed, it was becoming more and more difficult to succeed.

'Wait a minute, this is ludicrous. Skateboard, how fast can this thing go?'

'0-60 at the speed of light, Sir.'

'Then why can't we do it? I mean here we are in mortal danger and I've got my foot down and I can't be doing more than –'he looked at the speedometer, '– 120 miles per hour!'

'Well, you couldn't be expected to handle a ship with that velocity, my young Sir. Your piloting experience is only eleven clicks and four semi-clicks old.'

'It doesn't matter.' The Venus began to shudder even more. The firepower from the heli-fighters was gaining. It was clear that they had identified Random as the fugitive.

And what's more, the fire was now concentrated on the sleek, stolen ship.

It had been identified as a property of the Sapphire Regime, making it desired by both parties.

'Those shots are getting closer. Give me visual.'

Random soon wished he hadn't made that last demand. Looking at the image on the scanner, he gulped hard.

It was a miracle – the fighting had stopped, but now he had 400 crafts from both sides of the war bearing down upon him.

'Schparzos,' Random swore.

'Please, Sir. Just because I don't have ears, doesn't mean that I am not immune to coarse, offensive language.'

'Skateboard, I'm begging you. Please. We have to hit a faster speed. We have both sides of this war on our tails. I can't keep us safe for much longer.'

'Suggest evasive action.'

'Skateboard!' Random was becoming desperate.

'There's a one-mile hole in the oncoming blockade. Move five degrees to the right and slam on the breaks.'

'What! That's suicide!'

'Trust me.'

Random obeyed. He maneuvered the ship five degrees and pushed his left foot down as hard as he could.

The Venus shuddered to a grinding halt. Random felt the pressure of his action hold him firmly back in the pilot's chair. To his utter astonishment, all 400 vessels shot past his windscreen like horizontal bullets of rain and darted out of view. Thanks to the ingenious mind of his companion, they had bought a few seconds of time to escape. Random used his novice driving skills to carry out a swift three-point turn in the middle of the sky and zoom off in the opposite direction.

He overheard the clanking of metal and several small explosions over the intercom. Daring to explore the scanner again, Random noticed that the army of ships that were pursuing him had also attempted their maneuvers in a bid to continue the chase.

Fortunately, due to the lack of space and their impatience to complete the about-turns professionally, the freight of Crimson and Sapphire soldiers had only succeeded in creating a near-400 ship pile-up.

Within moments, the majority of the crashed fighters began to drop like great boulders towards the ground, smashing in the harsh sand with all the subtle grace of a troop of pregnant dancing hippopotamus' falling through a cling-film floor into a collection of priceless vases.

'You see? Now you don't have to hit the speed of light to escape.' Skateboard's statement seemed almost triumphant. What the little AI was not telling his new friend, was that there was a slight fault in the ship's calibration system.

He had been meaning to get around to fixing it, integrating himself with the matrix and finding the best solution, but the Sandman had been keeping him preoccupied with other things. Instead of an upkeep of maintenance, he had been nothing else but a pitiful dogs body. He knew that there was one more challenge that the minimal crew of the Venus II faced.

'Sir, before we go any further, I must respectfully request that we seek shelter somewhere and make some improvements. We are not out of the woods yet.'

Random checked his scanner again. The HQ, the fighters and the devastation was becoming nothing but a spec in the distance. 'We've cleared the danger zone. What are these "improvements" you are on about?'

Skateboard confessed that if they increased their current velocity then there was a very probable chance that the engines would explode as a by-product of the top speed being staunched.

'There's also one final obstacle in our route away from Rodas,' he said.

'On the outer perimeters of the planet there is a security net. A security net made up of an interlocking fence that is nearly impenetrable. There are some soldiers, but they are not affiliated with the Crimson Empire or the Sapphire Regime.'

'Then who do they work for?'

'The galaxy. This war has been raging for so long, even the history books of interstellar scholars cannot tie the precise date of its creation down. It's a total mystery, but it also highlights just how dangerous the rest of the cosmos views it. So, the governments of Ursa-17, 18 and 19 decided to pool their efforts together and constructed a security mainframe that sealed over the planet. Both sides of Rodas knew; in fact, they reluctantly agreed to its construction. There was no point for the disease of our wretched world to spread across the universe. You've seen the devastation that we have lived with. Can you imagine the whole sector giving in to such horror?'

Random kept his eyes straight as the Venus cruised through the sand plains.

'So, what do we do?'

'We can break through the barrier but we will have to use the light speed at the precise second of the energy surge.

I've taken the liberty and conducted some research into the workings of the barrier and discovered that every 40 clicks an energy pulse fires along the netting, regenerating its containment fields. So, we can burst through the barrier much like we did with the force field the HQ trapped us in.'

'Speaking of which, how did we get out –?'

The ship crashed into an invisible force and its nose section bounced back several metres.

'I believe you have just found it, sir.' Skateboard stated obtusely.

Random huffed as he picked himself up of the dashboard. They spent the next few moments trying to locate the hole they had entered through and when they did, they sailed off back into the wastelands from which they came.

Far below, as the Venus II flew away into the ether, a shimmering, pulsating life force disrupted the perfect sand dunes that surrounded the plain. Like molecules reconnecting, something which looked like waves began to pool together. And the tremor was growing. It was the Sandman, scattered like ashes ready to rise like a phoenix and reclaim what was rightfully his. After the betrayal of his two co-conspirators, he was going to stop at nothing until the Venus was his again...and the boy who claimed to be named Random was dead.

XIII

It took the two fugitives the equivalent of four earth hours to make the necessary repairs and upgrades. Not that Random was much help to the cause; unless there was a nut that needed tightening or a physical diagnostic that needed running, it was all Skateboard's doing. Although the Venus II was a state-of-the-art ship, equipped for battle or leisure requirements, it had needed a refurbishment – which prompted Random to ask the question.

'So, how long did the Sandman have it?'

Skateboard tutted to himself. Although he was a highly advanced AI machine, he like anybody else, did not entertain interruption. Especially when he was calibrating the new shield generator for four times its current strength and capacity.

'I'm not entirely certain, Sir. I was only in the Sandman's employment for what must have been a few months. He didn't speak much to me unless he wanted something. But I remember pouring through the security tapes one evening and noticed that he was deeply disturbed by his predicament.'

'How come?'

'Not that I want to sound unkind, even to him, but he wept to himself in his cabin at night and every time he went to wipe the tears away, he was inadvertently rubbing away a section of his face. He once cursed to me so ferociously that he let his pain show. "Imagine living inside a nightmare, where your skin is so coarse and uncomfortable to touch, to wear something so abrasive that it hurts to even breathe and to fall apart at the slightest breeze. To be robbed of your life, your dreams, your goals, your loved ones. To be shunned from existence as another of the galaxies mutated mysteries. Could you live with that?"'

Random let the information sink in. No wonder the Sandman was so desperate to escape.

'So, he was driven to the extreme.'

'I think that his real intention was to find a cure. But he couldn't trust the Sapphire Regime. Not again. He was betrayed by them in ways that neither of us could ever understand. Deep down, I believe he was just looking for an out.'

'And we denied him that chance.' Random concluded.

Skateboard went back to his calibrations as his counterpart sighed heavily.

'Maybe we could have reasoned with him; made him see that if we worked together, we could all help one another?'

'At the end of the day, sir, he was – nay – IS a soldier. A soldier in the bloodiest war the cosmos has ever known. He would do anything for revenge. If it had meant death, it would still have guaranteed him salvation. How do you bargain with a man like that?'

Random sighed, left the question unanswered and continued tightening the bolts on the Venus' shield array.

The next few moments passed silently before Random disrupted Skateboard again; a move which led to the robot accidentally opening all the airlocks and turning on the ventilation shafts at the same time, improbably blowing nearly all the interior décor of the cabins into the mid-section of the ship, and an apologetic Random down tooling and tidying up the mess.

After detecting a slight inkling that he may have been a distraction to his friend, he sluggishly picked himself up and plopped himself in the pilot's chair and fiddled with the levers and buttons until the irritable AI was finished. He also felt a keen duty to look after this ship, and keep an eye out for its previous owner.

After the picture that Skateboard had painted so vividly, this wasn't the kind of person the duo wanted to run into again. He sat slumped in the comfortable chair and gazed out into the starry night.

The Venus had been on silent running ever since they escaped the HQ of the Sapphire Regime. At night, the ship's outer hull disguised itself in darkness, making it hard to detect to the naked eye. It had been coated in something called poli-carbite armour, making it near impregnable also. Random couldn't believe his luck.

Suddenly, he could hear the voices again in his head. At first the man's and then the woman's tones bled into audacity. He knew that they would be back again as soon as he had nothing to distract him. And now he was alone, and in relative safety, he listened to what they had to say.

'You alone are the one who can put an end to all this.'

'You must bring an end to this terrible, bitter atrocity.'

'What you are is a gift. A gift from a planet that does not deserve it and that can do nothing to save itself from oblivion.'

'Listen to us. Listen.'

Random screwed his eyelids so tight that tears began to flow. Were these his parents? What gift?

'Why me?' he cried. 'Why must I be the one to stop all of this? I don't even know who I am.'

'You are born of war but we did not programme you to hate. Remember that, no matter how difficult your predicament may become.'

The boy sniffed, overwhelmed by emotion.

'I don't want to. I can't fight. I won't fight!' he spat through clenched teeth.

'You will find another way. But you must stay here. Through the power we have given to you, it is necessary. It is your destiny.'

'Screw my destiny! If this war has been raging for centuries, then who's going to listen to a boy? The rest of them haven't. I won't do it.'

'You must.'

'I refuse to!'

Random shot out of his seat and belted towards the mid-section, but was stopped by the presence of Skateboard, who had propped himself up in the doorway.

Although the robot had no eyes to speak of, Random could feel the look of bewilderment directed in his path.

'Sir, I don't mean to speak out of terms.'

'Then don't,' Random sniffed and pushed his way past and into the direction of the living quarters.

Skateboard turned to face the distressed child. He had caught only a few seconds of the lad's struggle and presumed that he had been speaking to someone. In fear, he had prepared his stun gun, which protruded from his shell like a straw bobbing in a glass of fizzy drink.

Cautiously, he double checked that the room was empty and made after his new companion.

Skateboard found Random sobbing into his arms as he slumped over the desk in his quarters. Nervously, he spoke, giving an indignant cough to make the boy aware of his existence.

'How much did you hear?'

'Not much, to tell you the truth, Sir, only something about not wanting to fight, or fulfill your destiny. Did I get the gist?'

Random nodded, wiped away his tears and cleared his throat.

'I'm not like the others, Skateboard. In truth, I think I'm only a few days old. I woke up in a chamber, a glass chamber, and all I could see around me was death and destruction.

There were a couple of dead bodies in the room; I think it was some kind of scientist's office, one was blue, and the other was red.

I didn't check to see if they were alive. There was a craft there too, like the ones that attacked us. It had crashed.

There was fire, so much smoke and I did what only I could. I ran. I kept running, until I got caught by some soldiers from the Crimson Empire. I managed to escape but I am so confused. Why me? I don't feel ready.'

Random sat cross legged on the ground and ran his right hand over Skateboard reassuringly.

'I don't look like everyone else either, my friend. I seem to be a mixture of both these sides.'

'What do you mean?' enquired Skateboard.

'Look at me.'

And so, Skateboard did. He adjusted his optical senses and gazed his in-built lenses on the boy sat at his side.

Random could hear a faint whirring of inner motors as the AI took in the revelation. After a few moments, he stopped.

'I don't want to sound ignorant, Sir, but what about it?'

Random scoffed.

'Well, let's just say that I'm not going to pass as either a member of the Crimson Empire or the Sapphire Regime.'

'It doesn't make a difference, Sir. In my circuits, you are indeed a gift. So, what if you were created in a laboratory. As I get to know you, it might even explain a few things!'

The boy chuckled; he was relieved that this little robot had been developed with a sense of humour.

'What's more; you're the first person who has treated me like an equal since I have been created. I could spend an eternity searching my memory banks for another like you but I can't find

one. So yes, you are unique, but that doesn't mean it's a bad thing.
If you need help, then I am here to help you. If you want to stay
and fight, then I'll stay by your side, but if you truly wish to
escape, then have a serious think first and maybe clear your head
in a different part of the galaxy for a while.'

Random wiped his nose with his sleeve and smiled.

'You mean that?'

'Why not? This war isn't going anywhere. It'll still be here when
you get back.'

'But what about the innocent? When I was running away, I came
across a baron wasteland. There were literally dozens of people;
men, women, children. I couldn't look in their eyes. I couldn't
look at any of them. I felt shame.'

'There was nothing to feel shameful about. You hadn't done
anything to put those people there.'

'But I've got these voices in my head telling me I can save them.'
Random started to cry again. He proceeded to pull his sleeve up
to his dripping nose. Skateboard was appalled by his friend's lack
of manner and shot out a thin, robotic arm from his back that
came complete with a white handkerchief and held it up to his
master's nose. Random sniffed and then blew into the
handkerchief and when he was done, the robot tied it up with the
same claw and flung it straight into the waste bin at the side of the
desk. Random was impressed for a second, and then he went back
to concentrating on his inner confliction.

'I think that if you are the one to put an end to this, you need to
be sure in your mind what to do. Right now, you are not. Yes,
there is a crisis on Rodas, but then again, Sir, there is a crisis on
every plain in the cosmos. There is unnecessary suffering in every
corner of existence. It is the way of the universe. But there are
some that can triumph over that suffering and although it might
never put an end to it completely, if just one person's life is saved,
then you will learn to feel good in what you have done. But and
I'm being as frank as a series-two artificial intelligence robot can
be, I don't think that this is your time to have a say in that
suffering.

You have a long future ahead of you, I am sure of it, and when
the time is right, you will come back here and you will save those

people in the wastelands. If you're right about this "destiny" to save Rodas, then you will leave this planet in its redemption before your time is at an end. But today is not that day, nor tomorrow. One day in the future you'll be back, I'm sure of it. But for now, your immediate destiny is away from here. So, what's to say we get out of here for now and leave the future to the days to come?'

Random's tears were quickly evaporating. Spurred on by his metallic friend's speech, he hugged the robot and smiled.

'Thank you.'

'Never a problem, Sir, although I might have to charge you next time,' Skateboard joked.

Random got to his feet and made for the doorway back into the mid-section with Skateboard following close behind. There was a new bond between the two. Random, for the first time in his life, had a friend and likewise for Skateboard. His words had made Random feel a thousand times better than he had and the cherry on the top was that the voices had, for now at least, disappeared.

Random had a sense of purpose.

Of course, he was not ready to take on an army by himself, although a feeling inside him told him he could. A spirit had awoken. He was beginning to understand who he was now. Yes, he could become the saviour of Rodas, but not today.

Today was about saving himself.

XIV

In the relative safety of the operations bay, Everald sat pensive, his fingers tapping against the corners of his mouth, deep in a thoughtful trance. He had failed. The Crimson Empire had been ordered by his Master to engage with the purple child and eliminate him. But there was no sight of the boy anywhere on Rodas. The waste fields, sand dunes and crumbling cities were investigated with a fine-tooth comb and there was no evidence that he had been there. And now, the news had just got worse.

Soldiers on the front line outside the Sapphire Regime's Headquarters reported just clicks ago that a prototype fighter craft had been spotted engaging both the red and blue factions, however before either side had the chance to claim victory over who could put an end to both warring sides, he had defeated them.

How?

By applying the brakes on his ship and letting the others crash into one another. The casualties for both the allies and their enemies had been appalling and yet nobody lost their lives. It was the fighters involved that would never see the light of day again as they were now nothing but scrap metal.

Everald was met with the terrifying thought of a) having to explain his men's futile attempts to capture and kill the perpetrator to his Master and b) trying to cover up the fact that 200 heli-fighters were now out of commission from the auditors who were visiting the following morning. Everald shivered in his chair. He couldn't decide which predicament was more alarming!

He broke from his concentration and noticed that the Operations Bay was now empty. It was just he, alone, in the whole control room. He couldn't use his office since he destroyed it in a fit of rage and now, he was where he never wanted to be; by himself.

'My, my, my,' said a chilling voice from the shadows. 'You have no control over your temper, do you Everald.'

The Sergeant shot up from his seat, gave the customary salute of two fingers in both his ears to his Master and attempted to find an excuse for his actions.

'I had to get rid of them all, Sir. They were insolent.'

'As are you, my friend.' The red-hooded figure stayed in the gloom of the shadows, although there was not much light left to give in the operations bay as Everald had ironically blown the fuse box when his internal fuse gave out.

'Where are they all now?'

'I dismissed them all and sent them to the salt mines for two weeks. It's the least I could do.'

'No, I don't believe that somehow. The least that you could have done was to band your troops together as a unit and give me what I wanted; an end to the child of Rodas.'

Everald gulped.

'Master, he will be found. I swear on my mother's life.'

'You don't have a mother, Everald. You're a clone, remember?'

'Sorry, it's a term I once heard one of my men use.'

The voice grew louder in volume but stayed soft in its tone.

'You are incompetent, aren't you? When I promoted you to this role, I saw great promise. Unfortunately, you've left me with nothing but disappointment. I left you to watch over my army as I planned an end to all things. Now I confess, I made a mistake. Who was watching the watcher?'

'Master, please. Spare me. Give me another chance to prove my worthiness to yourself and the Crimson Empire's cause. With your support, I can help us ascend to glory.'

'You know the picture has always been bigger than just Rodas, Everald.

When the blue pestilence has been exterminated, we can then grow across Ursa-17. Ascend to the outer reaches of the galaxy and spread our influence across the peoples of the universe. For that, I need the best by my side; the very best.'

Everald was silent. His pupils shrank and his throat went dry as the sweat began to pour. Blood red droplets began to seep from his pores. He knew what was coming next.

'And you are not the very best, are you?'

Everald's spirit died inside. He wasn't the least bit concerned for anything else now, other than his own wellbeing. And like the shallow creature that he was, he knew that not even appealing to his Master's better side could save his skin.

'In here, there is a whole army of soldiers who are better than you. They have been here all along, right under your nose and you never even noticed.'

'Do you mean my men?'

'No, Everald. Your men are pithy. They have fought too many campaigns. No more do they carry the scars of war than the scars of war carry them.

'At the end of the day, you are all damaged goods. I need a new army and very soon, I'll have one. Void of the horror of fight after fight.

I've been building them for some time and yet all it took was just a little bit of the best traits from my warriors, cherry picking attributes from soldier to soldier to create them. Why, I even extracted from you and you didn't feel a thing.'

The quivering Sergeant stood aghast at the coming revelations.

'You've been cloning the Crimson Empire?'

'Hmm.' The hooded figure moved in the shadows, edging just a little closer to his terrified mind.

'Not just cloning from us but cloning from them as well. The salt mines and concentration camps make for such glorious specimens. This is a process that has been going on since before you were born.'

'But we hate the Sapphire Regime.'

'Why? Why do we hate them?

Everald searched his memory. Incredible. He didn't really know the answer. Nobody did.

The civil war had raged for so long that generations of families had grown up knowing only one thing - to hate those unlike them.

'Rodas is dying and we are the disease. We need a clean slate. I shall lead us to glory.. not you. No longer in the shadows – but leading from the front.'

'But we've never had that kind of technology. Neither have they. Reconnaissance has never indicated that the Sapphire Regime has the capability to clone.'

'That's because my soldiers were ordered to keep things from ever going public. So private were the reports that not even you were made aware of them. But we both had the capabilities. Indeed, this child was created using stolen elements from our technology but as he is unsullied, he must be purged.'

'Then Master, I beg of you,' Everald pleaded, 'Now that you have told me your plans, let me be the one who finds him and puts an end to all of this.'

'I don't want to put an end to anything, my servant. A full stop will not be made on the fighting, it'll go on, but it'll leave the confines of this planet and spawn until I have total power. Only the life of the boy will cease. With my new army in place, not even he will be able to hide forever. There are many who will not live to see this new world.'

He turned and stared blankly into the eyes of the quivering wreck that stood before him.

'Including you, Everald.'

'Master...' a tear squeezed out of the corner of his eye and trickled down his cheek. The Master gazed down on his subject, calm and subdued, but nonetheless powerful. The Master raised his voice all the time to those below Everald's ranking. He had always possessed a soft spot for his obedient servant. But it was when he said nothing at all, that the hearts of all living beings understood their fate.

'Kneel.'

'I can be by your side. I can help you ascend into glory!'

'Kneel.'

'I...I...I can rectify my failings in your guidance, Sir.'

'Kneel.'

'I'll do anything you say, Master. Anything. I'll tear down our army. Rebuild it again in your image. I am your one, true servant!' Everald panicked, his breath heavy with the knowing that his life was about to end.

'If you were my one true servant, you'd be kneeling for me now.'

Sniveling like a schoolboy who had just been mugged of his dinner money, Everald sank to his knees.

'Oh, Everald. I had such high hopes for you. Still, I'll have better luck next time.'

With one fell swoop, the Master stepped forward from the shadows. His features were no longer obscured by the darkness. Everald gazed in utter terror at the face of his executioner.

After one laboured final breath, his life force was torn from his chest as his heart was ripped clean from its housing inside his ribcage. Bereft of life, his dead eyes stared into the very soul of death himself. And death, with the heart of the slain in his hand, starred back.

XV

The moment of reckoning had arrived. Under the cover of broad daylight, the Venus II was to make its ascent on the security mainframe and break free of Rodas. It would be a momentous moment for the planet as a glimmer of hope would be delivered freakishly by accident in the act of escape and in doing so, Random and Skateboard would become the first sentient beings since the governments of Ursa-17, 18 and 19 had contained the war centuries earlier.

'Right, 76 clicks and we'll be close to the barrier. Skateboard, do you have the countdown? We don't want to hit anything other than on the count of 40 clicks otherwise we'll be fried.'

In the few days since his impossible inception, Random had already grown more authoritative over Skateboard. Not that the AI cared. As long as he was treated fairly, like any service robot would like to be treated, they'd continue to get along nicely. In his circuitry, he knew that it was best to let him find his feet and confidence in his own way, especially as he knew deep down in his memory wafers that this child was special.

'Reading you loud and clear, Captain.'

'Captain? Okay, Captain it is then. Thanks…err…Commander.' Random said; pleased at the reputation he appeared to have with Skateboard.

'I'm honoured Sir, but here on Rodas, there's a law against making those of artificial intelligence – robots, if you will - a person of rank. Ever since the great disaster that was General Sinsapol.'

'Really? What did he do?'

'He had a screw lose.'

Random stared confused, and then grasped what his friend had said. He possessed super strength and the capacity to do amazing things and yet Random could be a little slow on the uptake.

'Well, we won't be on Rodas much longer and then you can be my Commander. I promise,' smiled Random.

'Thank you, Sir.' Skateboard's electro-mechanical workings whirred in excitement. 'And now, back to the task in hand, don't you think. This won't be easy.'

'What are you talking about? Of course it will be. Just make sure we make it through on the 40th click and whoosh, we're away!'

'I believe you might be forgetting something, Captain. You're a wanted man. I mean boy.

I feel I may have to remind you that you not only have the most powerful army on this planet looking for you but you also have the second most powerful army on your back. The cloaking device has worked so far but we have to switch it off to guarantee ourselves enough power to break through the mainframe.'

Random sighed audibly and rolled his eyes.

'Oh yeah. Well, we'd better be quick then. How many clicks now?'

'47 until we reach our destination,' informed Skateboard.

'And that's half the journey, knowing the destination.'

'Very profound, Sir. It's time to open engines three and four.'

Random leant to his right, keeping his eyes ahead of him and flicked the switch that opened up all four engine bays.

As soon as he did, the sound of his action roared furiously within the bowels of the ship.

When the duo was carrying out the repairs and upgrades, they had discovered that the Venus had untapped potential when it came to speed, velocity and power.

So, when they fell upon the Venus's capacity for double the capacity for light speed with the flick of a switch, they realised that they had the potential to outrun any heli-fighter - if they were not discovered first.

'Right, starting our climb...now!' Random pulled the steering column up and the ship's nose changed from a horizontal to a near-vertical position. The Venus subsequently tore its way through the sky and shot towards the sky.

'Wait a second,' said Random. 'I can't see any security barrier. Where the heck is it? Is it cloaked like us?'

'No, Sir, it is protected by a perception filter. When people look up at the sky, they see the stars. It's an illusion. I probably should have warned you before. I hope it doesn't cause you any distress.'

'Distress? Thanks!' Random said. He had initially been under the impression that they had planned this escape to every detail. Clearly not!

'No more surprises, okay, my metal friend?'

'Understood, Captain,' confirmed Skateboard.

His hands vibrated on the steering wheel as the Venus continued to climb.

'10 clicks to the barrier.'

Random kept his eyes on the stars in front of him as Skateboard continued to count down. With every click, the engines roared louder and the Venus shuddered under the continued force that was crushing down upon it.

'4...3...2...1'

With the blink of an eye, the stars fell out of existence.

'Return us to horizontal flight,' Skateboard instructed.

Random was stunned by what he saw. For as far as his eyes could see, there was a metal mesh covering the entire outer atmosphere of Rodas. Knitted together in a cold grasp, keeping the planet contained. Random squinted and made out little command centres, each one manned by beings that were neither red, nor blue in complexion. Nor were they purple!

Random gulped.

'I didn't realise there'd be people out here. I thought this mainframe would just be, you know, self-powered or something.'

'It is,' explained Skateboard. 'But the people of our neighbouring galaxies could not afford anybody to get out.'

'Why not?'

'Well, you've seen the devastation the people of Rodas have caused. Can you imagine that out there among the stars?'

'Didn't these so-called governments think it would be a better idea to try and put a stop to it instead of leave people here to die?'

'Sadly not; they decided that at the end of the day, it wasn't really their problem.' Skateboard could feel a sense of injustice bubbling under Random's surface. His brow furrowed, his lips pursed and his eyes narrowed.

'No one should ever have quarantined Rodas. Not if they'd seen what I've seen,' he said.

'Maybe they knew something that we didn't,' suggested Skateboard.

In an instance a massive power surge boomed around the ship, rocking it so hard that the elastic snapped on the furry dice that dangled on the top dashboard.

'Here comes the power surge, Sir. I suggest we observe this one and wait for the next,' advised Skateboard.

Random dug his nails into the arm rests of his chair and felt the pulse shoot through the mainframe like a wave of electricity. The crash of thunder echoed all around them and the blast of energy split Random's ear drums to such an extent that they continued to ring for a couple of minutes afterwards.

A shock of blue shot through the mainframe and left in an instant, leaving the barrier momentarily down for no longer than five seconds before it powered up again.

'So, what causes this pulse?' asked Random.

'It's the regenerative power that it works off. Every 40 clicks it needs to momentarily power down before it sparks up again to shock the whole system back into life. The reason being is because the replacement power kicks in when the old power source is down and charging up again. Does that explain it, Sir?'

Random nodded. 'Absolutely,' he lied.

A second roar of engines replaced the crackle of energy. Only this time, the engines sounded more powerful than ever before.

'Skateboard, have the engines gone into overdrive?'

'No, Sir; at least, I don't think so. I'll run a diagnostic now.' Skateboard's circuits whizzed into life as the noise grew louder.

'It doesn't sound like our engines. It sounds like a whole army of...oh...'

Random dared not finish his sentence. He looked out of the front window and stared in utter astonishment as the Crimson Empire fleet slowly rose through the perception filter. It wasn't just any fleet. This was a full armada.

The boy trembled in fear, reaching down with his right hand to pat Skateboard for his own assurance.

'Say there, my old pal. Is the cloaking device still on?'

'Yes, Sir.'

'So, they can't see us, right?'

'Right.'

'Not quite, I'm afraid my boy.'

A new voice boomed through the speakers. It made Random's skin shiver. It was so calm, a sinister tint to the tones made his intent clear.

Random knew that they were in serious trouble now.

'We can't see you but we know that you are out there.'

Skateboard pulled himself into the corner of the cockpit.

'I know that voice,' he shuddered.

'You thought that you could get away from me, did you boy? I admire your courage and guile. It's taken us a long time to find you and yet here you are.'

Random gulped. 'Turn the communication channels on, Skateboard.'

'But Sir –'

'Just do it!'

Skateboard dragged his metallic frame over to the dashboard and opened the communications.

'Yeah, but you can't see me, can you? In fact, you have absolutely no idea where I am. I could be behind you or right in front of your nose.'

'Ah,' the voice echoed in delight. 'You are trying to play a little game with me, are you boy? Hide and seek. If that is your wish, we have got plenty of time. I'll find you eventually. Even if I have to wait forever, I'll take you to task and I'll locate you in the end.'

The boy sweated profusely.

'Who are you?'

'It is not of any importance.'

'It is to me. I want to know who you are, what you are and why you want me dead.'

The speakers fell silent. The Venus II shuddered as another bolt shot through the mainframe. They had missed their first window. Meanwhile, the beings inside the command centre of the main frame stood aghast at the appearance of the crimson armada – unable to act. If any force were to be used, the security ships of Ursa 16 through to 19 would have to be notified – for the good of the galaxy.

'My name is Kalor Maloso. I am the ruler of the Crimson Empire. Why do I want to put an end to your troubling existence? Well, let's just say that you do not fit in my plans but you could severely damage them.'

Random let out an impromptu chuckle.

'So that's why you want me dead? I "don't fit in with your plans"? Rubbish!

You'll have to do better than that! I could be the most insignificant being in the whole of the cosmos as far as you were concerned.'

'It has not escaped our attention that your conception was more than a little...unconventional. You're an unstable element in the game of war on this planet.'

'I think you're the unstable one here, mate! I'm not the one killing millions of innocent people!'

'No, but you could be.'

Random slumped back in his chair, feeling slightly exhausted by the whole exchange so far.

'So war's just a game to you, is it? D'you know what, Maloso? I'm beginning to see the full picture here. I'm not the unstable element here. You are!'

'I'd advise you not to try my temper, boy.' Maloso spat. He did not raise his voice but there was a growing intensity in his words.

'Sir, please. I beg of you. Don't take him to task. He is dangerous. Evil! We can find another port along the mainframe if we switch to silent running. That way they won't pick our engines up on their heat trackers,' whispered Skateboard.

There was a sense of enormous panic in Skateboard's voice. It made Random ponder the almighty task in front of him. If this man, this Kalor Maloso, was bad enough to make an AI frightened, how dangerous must he really be?

'I'll tell you what, Maloso. I don't think you are as high and mighty as you and your armada are making yourselves out to be.

You see the great lengths you've gone too to try and stop just one boy? You've driven your entire fleet to the very edge of Rodas itself just to stop me. And do you know why? It's because you're afraid, isn't it? That's the reason why you want to stop me. You're scared of me.'

'Do not try my patience, boy; I have slaughtered many who have used words of insolence such as you are now.'

'Then why don't you come and find me? Come on, what's stopping you?'

Maloso's tones began to strain under the increasing pressure that Random was putting him under. Unbeknownst to our hero – sorry, idiot – was that he was making the head of the Crimson Empire look stupid in front of his armada.

'Oh yes, of course. We're cloaked. So, what else have you got, Maloso?'

Before Random could continue, a terrifying wall of laser fire
shot like beacons of death from the armada and fizzed with great
speed towards the Venus. Random took evasive action and
plunged towards the steering column and took his vessel

into a nose dive that kept it safe from the firepower. He looked
up out of the viewer and saw the sea of death, the span of the vast
armada itself wash over the Venus.

He breathed a sigh of relief before another barrage spurted from
the warships; this time on another level closer to the vessel's
hiding spot.

'We'll keep firing until we hit you and your pathetic excuse of a
craft.'

Maloso was no longer playing for time. Random had failed. He
really was going to die. The Venus shuddered from yet another
jolt of energy and the mainframe indicated a further missed
opportunity for escape.

'Skateboard, any ideas?' Random expression of concern
appeared like it was on the verge of descending into full on panic.

Another sea of laser fire shot towards the Venus II and Random
had to nose dive away from the threat again.

'None, I'm afraid, Sir. It looks like he is forcing us away from the
mainframe. I think he knows what we are planning to do.'

'Shavzit!' Random swore.

'Alright, Maloso, you've made your point. We'll come quietly.'

'Oh no, I don't want you to surrender, my boy.

I want the pleasure of ending your existence right here, right
now. I could hunt you all day and night. It'll make the act of
killing you all the more pleasant.'

Before another wave of lasers emitted from the armada, there
was yet another rumble of energy; but it wasn't from the
mainframe or Maloso's ships. There was another army
penetrating the skies of Rodas. Only this time, Random did not
recognize the ships. There were just as many ships as those from
the Crimson Empire and they were just as dark and foreboding as
those that he had faced before. Skateboard's circuits whirred in
astonishment. The controllers in the security mainframe began to
panic. The biggest fleet stand-off was about to take place above

the skies of Rodas and although security was on its way, there
could be no guarantee that they would be able to stop them –
whatever they planned to do next.

'We're doomed.'

Random frowned. 'What, more doomed than we already are?'

'I'm afraid so, Sir. This is the main battle fleet of the Sapphire
Regime. I recognize the ships. You see that one on the far left?'

'What? The one that looks like a giant nose?'

'The Nostrildamus, yes, that's the one. That was my first
commission.'

'Well, as much as I'd like to sit here and flick through the pages
of your autobiography, Skateboard, what the flip do we do now!'

Skateboard indignantly turned to his friend.

'We die.'

XVI

'Kalor Maloso. You are in direct violation of this air space.'

A new voice, equally as calm and yet more in control than that
of the ruby dictator, oozed over the speakers in the Venus II.

'What is your reasoning behind this trespassing? You know that
our agreement forbids us to intercept this section of the planet.'

Random looked at Skateboard and was about to ask who this
new voice belonged to; however he did not need to as Maloso
unknowingly answered his query.

'Gres Masmun. This is an unexpected surprise. I wouldn't go as
far as saying that it is a pleasure to hear your voice again.'

Random looked at Skateboard with a puzzled look amongst his
face.

'As High Chancellor of the Sapphire Regime I urge you to stand
down. You are in violation of the Ursa treaty. If you will comply
then no punishment will be given. If you do not, then we will use
force.'

Maloso chuckled. 'Chancellor, you are not strong enough to put
an end to me or my army. You are on the cusp of defeat in this
war and now you are standing in my way in more ways than you
could possibly know.'

'Yes, we are well aware of your pursuit of the purple one. Indeed, we have desires of capturing the boy ourselves for questioning.'

'Well, that's where we differ. You plan to dither whilst I plan to resolve his threat once and for all.'

'They do tend to talk a bit too much, don't you think?' Random whispered to his robotic friend.

'Megalomaniacs are all the same, I'm afraid. They all like the sounds of their voices too much,' he replied.

Yet another bolt of energy fizzed through the mainframe and another glimmer of escape evaporated. Fortunately, Random had a plan.

'What if we take advantage of this and sneak off while they are talking.'

Skateboard whirred in thought. 'A good idea, Captain, but we risk flying into the laser fire if they decide to attack. We'd be caught in the crossfire and blasted out of the sky!'

'Well, let's make sure we go as soon as possible then. How far away are we?'

'We are further away now – around 83 semi-clicks. I suggest we use silent running so they don't track the heat from our engine then de-cloak and use our light speed capabilities before either fleet have a chance to fire on us.'

'Well, don't just sit there, let's do it!' Random flew into his chair, strapped himself in and pulled the steering column towards his body as the Venus II crawled, click by click, tentatively back towards the main frame. All the while, both Maloso and Masmun had continued with their war of words.

'...well, if you weren't so scared of attacking our main HQ then we wouldn't think that you were as insipid in your efforts as you are in your insults.'

'We don't have time for this' replied Maloso, 'I'll give you three clicks to move aside or we shall blow you out of the sky.'

'Sir...,' said Skateboard.

'One...'

'I know, Skateboard. Hold onto something.' Random advised.

'Two...'

'I can't. I don't have arms.'

'Three!'

Random put his foot down on the accelerator pedal and shot at velocity towards the mainframe.

'FIRE!' Maloso screamed.

'RETURN FIRE!' Masmun retorted.

Random clenched his buttocks so hard he nearly split his trousers. The Venus II, at top speed, was vertically ascending towards a metal wall that had not been penetrated ever before. It was surging towards a barrage of red laser fire from the right and blue laser fire from the left. Two walls of death and fatality flooded towards the vessel above them, about to crash together with devastating force.

The two barriers of light were gaining, sliding together like doors closing in front of them.

'Five clicks to the next pulse' Skateboard panted; if he had pores, he would have been situated in a puddle of sweat by now.

'How many clicks are we away from the mainframe?'

'About 10 clicks.'

'I'm going to do it.' Random took off the cloak. The Venus was spotted by Maloso. From the bridge of his command freighter, he hollered intensely at the sight of his prey.

'There he is! Fire, shoot on him now! DESTROY HIM!'

FOUR

'Don't,' Skateboard panicked.

THREE

'I must!' Random felt for the light speed lever.

TWO

'Sir, we won't –'

'ONE'

'Here we go!'

Random pressed the lever down and the Venus II disappeared totally from sight. It had slotted through the mainframe at just the right moment. The pulse had powered down and the Venus II had slipped through the eye of a needle.

The bolts of laser fire from both fleets had left the narrowest of gaps for the vessel to escape. A click later, the energy that powered the mainframe ebbed away, leaving the metal net vulnerable for puncture from a small ship. Just a few clicks below,

the red and blue laser fire collided like positive and negative
energy and created the most beautiful horizon of brilliant purple
that the entire cosmos had ever seen.

The shock of purple stained the skies as the impact of energy
sent both armadas reeling like giant hawks of death caught in a
hurricane. Maloso fell to the ground, as did the rest of his men,
banging his head in the process; luckily, he was able to look up
and see the brilliant wonder of the image before him before he fell
to the ground.

Far below, on the ravaged plains of Rodas, the refugees of the
worst war in the history of the cosmos stared disbelievingly into
the night sky.

Stretching wide across the plain, the casualties and outcasts of
both the Crimson and Sapphire factions of the decimated, ruined
planet looked up and saw the sight that no one in the chronicles of
this shunned sector of Ursa-17 had ever barred witness to before.

Many cried in wonderment and others bore smiles that had
never spread across their lips in their entire, miserable lives.
Women and children stood hand-in-hand looking up to the sky in
total silence at a colour they had never seen before. It was the
colour that had started the seemingly futile conflict in the first
place.

Purple. Brilliant, vibrant purple.

A feeling began to pulsate through the sick, the captured, the
defeated and the stricken that rejuvenated their lives in a way that
nothing had ever done before.

With the explosion of one simple colour in the sky, Random had
inadvertently done it.

The idiot, so intent on running away from his purpose, had
disappeared without a trace and in his wake, he had left a
message; a feeling that had the potential to revolutionise a planet
as troubled as Rodas.

Hope.

XVII

All the while, the Venus had managed to negotiate its way
through the main frame and had left Rodas, Maloso, the Crimson

Empire, the Sapphire Regime and – he hoped – the Sandman – in
its dust.

'Woo hoo! We've done it! I can't believe it!' Random punched
the air repeatedly in triumph. They had escaped the planet that
no-one had ever attempted or even dared to dream breaking free
from. As the Venus II had pierced the main frame netting, he had
been blissfully unaware of the events happening below.

'Skateboard, we've done it! Skateboard?' Random glanced all
around the cockpit and could see no sight of his robotic
companion. There was a trail of crude oil that started in the space
that the AI had occupied. It led right underneath the co-pilots
chair and it was there that Random saw Skateboard, quivering
like jelly, his hydraulics squeaking involuntarily.

'Er...sorry, Captain. I profess that I never doubted your plan for
a second.'

Random hummed indignantly. 'Don't worry, my friend. I won't
tell anyone.'

'About what?'

'The puddle.'

Skateboard looked quizzically and then shot across the cockpit,
smearing the oil into the floor.

'My apologies, Sir.' If robots could blush, Skateboard's
complexion would have been redder than the entire Crimson
Empire. 'I'll clean it up right away.'

'Why bother, let's celebrate!' Random flicked the button labeled
AUTO-PILOT and vacated his chair. An imprint of nervous sweat
was left on the back of the seat.

'I must admit, it was closer than I expected.'

He walked out of the cockpit into the mid-section and
proceeded to raid the cupboards for a drink. He found a bottle of
unbranded liquid and casually discarded the screw top and
swigged the whole thing back before belching like a walrus after
100 gallons of fizzy drink.

Skateboard joined him in the kitchen.

'Beg your pardon, Captain...quite literally, but where would
you like to go?'

Random threw the bottle to one side and plonked himself down
in a nearby chair.

'Do you know what? I have no idea. I mean, what's out there except Rodas?'

'Well, in my down time I used to study star charts and our historical archives from before the war took full effect.

The people of Rodas were once profound explorers; clever scholars who would sail the systems charting new worlds, inspiring the people at home. When I would digitally peruse the archives, I discovered a multitude of nebulas in the vicinity. There are so many places to discover that sound utterly delightful. There're the twelve planets of the Obligas system, where three of them have no western hemisphere due to a blueprint error on behalf of the planet engineers commissioned to work on the Obligas extension.'

'No. I don't think so. What else?'

'Let me see. There's a planet in the Tragonium arm of Ursa-9 where they say it rained food.

'What? How?'

'The ecosystem allows for the combative bombardment of food particles to collect in clouds where their molecules are reconstructed to its precise original taste and look. It was a revolutionary method that ended up putting an end to famine on Tragonia.'

Random licked his lips. 'That does sound tempting. It's a bit close to home though, isn't it? I mean, Ursa-9 is only...' he counted on his digits, '...eight Ursa's away from our current location.'

Skateboard hesitated.

'What now?' Random said.

'We forgot to take the auto-pilot off, didn't we?'

Random's naturally purple complexion went white. He leapt from the comfort of his chair, sped into the cockpit and slumped back into the wet, sweaty chair.

'Cribes!' he exclaimed.

He slapped the auto-pilot off in a hurry. A fantastic blur of stars spiraling by slowly ebbed away. The beautiful sight of light speed was soon replaced by the giant vision of a huge planet, swamping the view screen.

'Turn right!' Skateboard shrieked as he connected with the Venus and attempted to curb the speed of the craft even further.

The Venus II continued to slow but the picture of the blue/green planet in front of them was growing ever seismic.

'I can't hold it, Skateboard!' Random's hands were shuddering so hard against the sheer velocity of the ship's descent that it made the steering column shake violently; so vigorously that Random's slim cheeks were bouncing so hard that it was making the rest of his features vibrate and blur like a painting melting in the heat.

'Put your foot down all the way on the break.'

'Oh, yes, why didn't I think of that? I thought I'd put it down on the accelerator,' said Random sarcastically. 'What an idiot I am!'

'No time for sarcasm, Sir. We've entered the atmosphere now. Suggest crash landing maneuvers.'

'You never taught me that, Skateboard.' Skateboard's audio circuits had trouble ciphering what Random had said as the captain was shaking so much now.

The Venus was still growing in velocity as the gravitational pull dragged it closer to a fiery end. Random could make out what looked like a blue ocean below a thin layer of cloud, which the Venus pierced with the grace of a moose falling through a giant piece of paper 40 miles above ground. Random finally managed to pull the ship up, just clicks before it slammed into the cold sea. He managed to bring the ship to horizontal flight and skillfully only just avoided what appeared to Random and Skateboard as very striking and dangerous white cliffs.

'I'm going to try to land this thing safely somewhere,' he barked, no longer being thrown around like a child on a bouncy castle.

However, the ship was still coming in too fast and as the Venus II cleared what looked like a settlement of civilization, Random slammed the breaks on so hard that the nose section of the vessel dug itself in the soft ground, rendering the boy instantly unconscious as the whole craft began pin-wheeling several times across a vibrant field, crashing through a collection of centuries old trees and eventually grinding to a halt on the edge of a lake, upside down.

The echoes of fallen foliage rang around the forest and the chirps and squeals of alarmed wildlife rang true all around. When the dust and the noise settled down, the landing gear shot out to the blue sky with almost comedic timing.

The only beings around to witness the terrible crash were two schoolchildren; both were stood aghast at the edge of the other side of the lake.

Little did they know now but when Random and Skateboard would finally come to, they'd soon realise that they had crash landed on the only planet that could compare with the atrocities committed by the world they had broken free from.

Earth.

CHAPTER TWO

BEGINNINGS

I

Anji Gummadi had always had a taste for adventure. At the
tender age of two she wandered away from her parents on a
shopping trip in the Brunswick Centre and ventured onto a red
bus unnoticed and ended up at St Paul's Cathedral. Her panic-
stricken parents were relieved to find her but what bemused them
most about their only child's impromptu journey was that a
toddler with no idea of the dangers of the world had somehow
managed to negotiate the London transport system and
somewhere in her journey, must have changed buses to reach her
destination!

Anji had always been a little different from her peers – even at
an early age. Her Mother and Father had settled upon England's
capital on a whim. Nothing more than a spur-of-the-moment
decision, initiated by her Father, Krishnan, upon hearing that his
new wife, Myra, was carrying his baby so that they could give
their unborn child a better chance at life than he could provide in
Rajasthan – one of the poorest areas in India.

So, with the news of an impending arrival in the Gummadi
household, Krishnan and Myra scrapped together what little
money they had, filled out all the necessary visa application forms
and sailed among the clouds to a whole new world.

Despite their uneducated background, the Gummadi's found
jobs rather quickly. Krishnan worked as a porter in a North
London hospital whilst Myra found employment as a dinner lady
not far from her husband. They settled into a rented two-bedroom
flat just outside of Tottenham and when Anji was born, they had
everything and more than they could ever have wished for.

Sadly, their happiness didn't last long. One sizzling summer's
day, whilst Anji was at nursery school, her parents were the
victims of a car accident which left the little girl alone, homeless
and an orphan. Tragically, they had been on their way to pick up
their smiley three-year-old to take her for an afternoon out at
London Zoo – a place that Anji had dreamed about visiting ever
since she'd seen a poster advertising it on the London
Underground.

From that moment on, the little girl's life was turned upside
down. From a life of reasonable comfort and security, she spent

the next nine years of her life bounding from children's home to children's home, school to school, desperately seeking an escape. To what? She didn't know. Even a spell at an all-girl's boarding school in Essex didn't stop young Anji from running away.

Potential foster parents came and went whilst her behaviour bordered from disruptive to destructive. From petty crime, such as stealing sweets from local newsagents to setting fire to PE kits at school, Anji was beginning to gain a reputation as a tear-away, with good reason!

She wanted to find something to fill the vast hole her parent's deaths had left.

At the age of 11, she felt like she was starting to reach a turning point in her life. She had settled in St Bernard's Children's Home, joined a local comprehensive where some of her fellow orphans attended and even put an end to her destructive ways. Upon reflection, as she entered her teenage days, she put her time setting fire to her classmate's shorts and thieving food and magazines from Benson's corner shop down as 'a passing phase.'

She had even grown fond of her carers at the home and for the first time, she was starting to look up to them as role models. But her spirit for adventure still burned bright.

'Come on, Anji. Get off that phone! You're missing everything!'

Miss Carter, Anji's Geography teacher, had taken class 3B on a field trip to Dartmoor National Park in a bid to get the lead air of the city out of her student's lungs and try to give them an inspirational view of country life. Yet, so far, her efforts had been in vain.

'If I catch anyone else texting or playing on your phone then I'm afraid I'll have to take them off of you all and lock them away in the bus.'

A chorus of moans and groans rang around the boys and girls of 3B and they all proceeded to put their mobile devices back in their pockets and bags.

'Ah-ha-ha. Turn them off, not on silent. I wasn't born yesterday.' She hollered as she led the line of teenagers across a boggy field.

'Shame – could have started your personality from scratch,' whispered Jake, the blonde haired, squeaky voiced class clown.

'I heard that, Jake!' Miss Carter replied. 'One more word out of you and you'll be sitting next to me on the coach back!'

Jake's heart skipped a beat and he felt his face glow red with embarrassment. Some of the children laughed and pointed at him.

'That wasn't very nice, Jake,' Anji remarked.

'I saw it in *Blackadder* the other night; thought it was quite funny.'

'What's *Blackadder*?' Anji asked. She walked beside her friend as her shoes continued to slip off her feet, getting stuck in the sticky mud.

'Can't we stick to the path, Miss? My shoes keep falling off.'

'We are on the path,' insisted Miss Carter, who could feel her ponytail becoming lose as her thick, black fringe started to straggle around her eyelids.

'Heavy rain shower last night has turned the ground to treacle. Don't worry though, we'll be in the forest soon enough.'

Anji turned around to see two of her class mates holding hands. Longingly, she looked to Jake and put her arm through his.

'Anj...what are you doing?'

'I could use a little support.'

Jake tutted, 'I can't believe you didn't bring boots with you.'

'We didn't have any spares left, did we? Unless you're talking about the left boot that was size 11 and the right that was a 7?'

'Well, I always thought you were a little imbalanced!'

Anji punched Jake's arm and chuckled. Jake always knew how to break her out of any mood. He had arrived at St Bernard's six months after Anji and over the past year, they had both developed a tight friendship.

Despite his outwardly sunny disposition, Jake's story was just as tragic as Anji's.

He was an only child and the product of a separated marriage. After his Mother ran off with his Dad's brother, his Father descended into a deep depression, soothed by a growing dependency on alcohol and before long, he struggled to cope and eventually couldn't look after Jake anymore.

Then one night, he didn't return home. Two days later his car with his wallet on the passenger's seat, was found on the Severn Bridge. Anji felt sorry for the boy when he arrived but she soon learnt that Jake was okay with his situation. He was funny, cheeky and forever smiling.

If laughter was the thing that veiled the feelings of sadness underneath, then it was a better way of dealing with things than the methods she had adopted.

'Jake?'

'Hmm.'

'What's say we break away? Y'know, maybe slip off for a couple of hours. Miss is doing my head in. You know what she'll have us doing when we get in there?'

'She'll probably break the nets out and get us pond dipping' exclaimed Jake.

'Probably. Come on. Please?' Anji stood an inch taller than Jake but even he could see the begging expression she bore.

'Oh, okay.' Jake sighed. 'I'll give you the signal then.'

But he didn't need to.

A few minutes later, whilst class 3B slipped and slid their way along the path, the bottom of their school trousers caked in a thick layer of mud, they arrived at the opening of the woods.

'Right, pick a partner, stick with them and meet back here in half an hour's time,' said Miss Carter, glad to be having a break from her demanding students.

'Erm...how will we know when to come back?' asked Jemima Wright. Anji had a severe dislike for Jemima. She was driven to school daily by her Mum in a massive Range Rover and her Father ran a local business. Whenever Jemima opened her mouth, it was like Anji experienced a genuine audible allergic reaction.

'Well, you have watches, don't you?' Miss Carter said.

'No,' class 3B said in unison.

'What? None of you?'

'No.'

Miss Carter sighed, defeated. 'Oh, alright then. You can turn your phones back on.'

Class 3B cheered and rushed into their bags whilst running off into the foliage.

'But remember to come back in half an hour! No later! Otherwise, I'm declaring you missing in action!' Miss Carter waited for the children to pass her and then slumped to the ground, reached into her purse for a pack of Lambert and Butler she had confiscated earlier and sparked up a cigarette, taking a long drag before exhaling audibly.

'Bloody kids,' she muttered.

*

The children sprinted away from their minder like an army of Spartan warriors driving head first into battle. Some of the kids whooped and cheered, others like James Butcher, who must have been the only 13-year-old in the class who was there to work and not to skive from a day of classes, found a nice quiet spot in the woods and started filling in the survey his teacher had given the class on the difference between urban and rural landscapes.

Anji and Jake broke away completely from their classmates and made for a lake that they had heard about in the National Park brochure.

'What's so special about a lake?' Jake enquired.

'I find them calming.' Anji dragged Jake along with her, pouring over the map that Miss had given to each of her students.

'What's so calming about a lake?' asked Jake.

'Lots. Still water. The animals on the riverbank.'

'A riverbank on a lake? Why is it not called a lake bank, surely that would make much more sense?'

'Don't be silly,' scolded Anji. 'I think we are almost there.'

The pair had reached the outer edge of the lake and it was just as tranquil as Anji had wished. Recently, she had found that she was growing tired of the hustle and bustle of the city.

'I think it's nice to get out of London every once in a while.'

'I don't,' sulked Jake. 'No shops, no skate parks. Just fields and trees. I mean, what makes them so special?'

'Oh Jake, you and I really are different people. What am I going to do with you?' Anji sighed.

'I'll tell you what. Take me to the Grease Monkeys when we're done here. I think I've got enough pocket money to pay for the Double Double burger!'

'Jake, that's disgusting.' Anji looked away from her companion and thought that she could make out the lake.

'We're here!'

She tore away from her friend and got her phone out of her pocket. Immediately she proceeded to take pictures of the beautiful scenery. Jake jogged after her, panting all the way.

'Bloody hell, you're quick,' he spluttered, his heart wanting to escape his chest.

'You eat too much rubbish!' Anji dismissed as she snapped away.

'You're like the Mum I used to have. She'd moan about my eating habits too. Then again, the last time I remember seeing her I think I was so little I was eating rubbers off the tips of my pencils!'

'I'll remember that, might keep you quiet!'

Jake laughed. He looked up through the trees and squinted at the light shining like shards of glass through the branches.

'Looks like the suns coming out. About time; I knew I should have worn my sunglasses.'

'You don't have any, you borrowed mine, remember?'

'Oh yeah. I think I might have lost them.'

Anji tutted. 'You're useless you. I have no idea why I like you...'

Jake's eyes widened.

'...I mean...as a friend.' Anji blushed.

'Oh. Okay.'

Jake felt a warm sensation glow through his body. For a moment, he thought it was his raging hormones causing him an embarrassing moment.

'I think I'd better sit down,' he said as he found a nearby tree stump and planted himself upon it.

'I mean...if we weren't...y'know...I mean.'

Anji took pity on her friend. 'We're friends. That's all it should be right now.' She smiled the kind of smile that could melt the hardest of icebergs.

'I know. I mean, how horrible would it be if we had to move homes?' Jake tried to rationalise his feelings.

'Anj...let's say hypothetically we are both single come prom in a couple of years' time, can I baggsie you now to come with me?'

'Jake, are you asking me to be your prom date?'

Jake's face was as red a sunburned tomato.

'Yeah.'

'In two years' time?'

'Yeah.'

'What's to say that I won't be busy that night?'

The young boy tried to think of a way he could convince her.

'I'll pay for your drinks.'

'Done.' Anji held out her hand. Jake shook it. His pale clammy hands made the girl wish that she'd brought a packet of tissues along. Indiscreetly, she dried her hand on her trouser leg, joined her future date on the stump and lent her head on his shoulder.

The pair sighed in quiet contemplation.

'You're right. This is peaceful,' said Jake.

'Let's stay here as long as we can,' suggested Anji. 'I don't want to leave; the sun, the lake, that bullfrog humping that rock over there. It's all so relaxing.'

It wasn't to remain like that. Not for long.

In the faint distance, Jake could hear the sound of a jumbo jet flying overhead. It made the distilled soundtrack even more sedating. He sighed and allowed his head to roll towards Anji's.

'Anj?'

'Yes, mate?'

'Is it just me or is that plane getting closer?'

The engine sound was growing in volume by the second. The raw power and velocity sounded enormous. The sound was becoming deafening as the duo clasped their hands over their ears protecting them from the scream of machinery crashing towards them.

'Get down!' Jake pulled Anji to the ground.

Something devastating crashed through the trees, practically destroying the lake and completely squashing the horny bullfrog and smashing the poor, helpless rock to nothing but dust.

The echo of shock rang like a bell of death around the forest. In the far distance, the screams of the schoolchildren could be heard but Jake and Anji were too shell-shocked to pick the frenzy out of the chaos they had just witnessed. The pair picked themselves up, brushed themselves down as their school clothes were now caked in mud and stared open mouthed at that impossible sight before them.

Where the pond had once been, a spaceship lay crumpled and broken in the bog, with its landing gear poking out into the bright blue sky.

'What the heck is that?' Anji cried.

Jake motioned to move closer towards the craft but Anji pulled him back.

'Don't! You don't know what's in there?'

'Come on, Anj. Where's your sense of adventure? There's no fire so I think we're safe.'

Anji huffed.

'Oh, come on then!'

She pushed past Jake and made for the other side of the river bank, tripping her way over slippery twigs and moss as she went. For all his bravado, Jake was now feeling a slight twinge of anxiety.

'Maybe we should go and find Miss.'

'No! Come on Jake, like you said; sense of adventure and all that.'

'But what if whoever, whatever, is in there is…y'know?'

'Dead?'

'Exactly. It's one of my fears remember.' Jake started to follow his companion as Anji reached ever closer to the ship. She inspected the anomaly before her. The ships' gleaming hull was now scorched. It looked as though it had crash landed on its roof and what looked like a nose section was now imbedded deeply into the rock. The ship lay incongruous with its surroundings and spelt only one thing for the most hesitant of the couple.

'It looks dangerous,' said Jake as he slipped on the embankment and his left leg fell into a muddy wet puddle.

'Well, if it was, it isn't now,' Anji replied. 'I've never seen anything like it. Maybe it's a top-secret government plane?'

'What if there are aliens?'

'Don't be stupid. There's no such thing as…'

Anji's dismissal was interrupted by the sudden hiss of hydraulics. She jumped as what appeared to be a ramp started to ascend out of the wreckage towards the trees that still stood as white smoke billowed from the interior.

Anji thought she could make out what looked like a figure advancing through the shadows. Jake joined her at the mouth of the ramp and stared in disbelief as the figure drew closer. They both gasped in shock as they realised who this figure was. It was a boy - and not any boy. His skin was purple. Bright, vibrant purple. He was not of their world.

'…aliens…' Anji said.

'Uh...where am I?

The strange, purple boy staggered and propped himself up by the doorway, clinging onto the wall to steady himself.

'Holy crap! You're an alien!' exclaimed Jake.

'A what?' the boy enquired, cupping his hands to his head.

'You're hurt.' Anji moved towards the stranger.

'No, I'm fine, just a bit dizzy. It was a bit of a bumpy landing, that's all', the boy reassured her.

'"Bit of a bumpy landing?" Is that what you call it? You've pretty much destroyed the pond!'

'Jake, you're not being very helpful,' Anji said as she rummaged around in her bag. 'Hang on; I think I might have something that can help you'.

'Hold on a minute. An alien spaceship falls out of the sky and you're looking for paracetamol! I think I need to sit down, I can't take this all in!' Jake exclaimed.

'Forget about yourself for a moment and help me sit him down.' Anji took the arm of the boy and propped him up.

'But he could be contaminated,' said Jake. 'He could have space mumps or intergalactic flu or something like that.'

'Will you stop being a flump and help!' shouted Anji. Jake straightened himself up instantly and took the other arm of the strange creature. Together, they helped him out of the doorway and onto a nearby rock.

'What's your name?' asked Anji.

'R..andom. My name is Random.'

'Well, you're an alien so how random can it be?' said Jake.

'No. You don't understand,' said the stranger. 'That is my name. My name is Random.'

'Your parents must have loved you then!' Jake felt a sharp punch in his already bruised forearm and saw a stabbing look from Anji.

'Where are you from?' she asked.

'It's too complicated to say right now. You wouldn't understand. I need to rest.'

'No, don't let him go to sleep. When I hit my head on the jungle gym at school Mr Harvison said I might have concussion. Apparently, sleep is the worst thing for that.' Jake was finally being of some help.

'No, you can't sleep, Random. We want to help you. Is there anyone else with you?'

'Yes.'

A metallic voice echoed from the smoking chamber and made Anji and Jake jump in surprise.

From the white smoke, a small robot, about two metres in length and around a foot in height, stood in the doorway.

'Bloody hell! A robot, a real robot!' Jake shouted, amazed and delighted all at the same time.

'Actually, I am a second-generation artificial intelligence service android with a quasi-fissured matrix. Drone class.'

'What does that all mean?' asked Anji.

'Basically, speaking Madam, it means I'm a robot.' The AI rolled out of the doorway and with a soft, wet plop embedded himself in the marshy ground. 'Now let me have a look at him.'

A neon blue light skimmed out of the front part of the robot's frame and flickered over Random's nearly unconscious body.

'He is in a state of shock but otherwise there are no minor or immediate danger points on his internal or external physiognomy.' The robots voice was polite, friendly but most of all to the point. 'I think we should let him rest for a while and then hopefully he will be back to his old self. Please could you carry him inside the Venus II?'

'What, you want us to take him inside the spaceship?' Anji was unsure. 'How do we know that you won't abduct us or that there's an army of spacemen in there ready to attack us?'

'Oh, sure, now you ask those kinds of questions,' thought Jake.

'I can assure you that neither Sir nor I mean you any harm. Now please, if you could escort Sir to the ship, I'll deal with the smoke.'

The little robot whizzed off, his wheels picking up the sludge on the ground as he ventured back towards the crash site.

'Cool! We get to go inside a spaceship. This is amazing!' Jake nearly tore off Random's arm as he raced towards the door, momentarily forgetting that he was still clasping hold of the alien boy. Random groaned in protest.

'Wait a second. I'm all for new experiences and adventures but I hardly expected a crashed spaceship with a purple boy and a talking plank of metal today.' Anji stayed motionless on the rock, her trepidation overriding her excitement.

'Come on, Anji. They seem fine. I'm pretty sure that if that robot meant to zap us to death he wouldn't be using words like "please" now would he?'

'You've got a point,' Anji smiled. 'Alright then, let's see what's inside.'

A whirr of internal engines roared from within the fallen craft. The smoke that had once poured from the mouth of the ship disappeared.

'The air conditioning has been initiated. The poisonous gas has now been taken care of. It is safe for you to enter the chamber.'

'Poisonous? Well, that's a relief,' Anji uttered sarcastically.

The duo approached with caution as they entered the Venus II. With Random dragging his feet between them, they found it a struggle to get the alien boy back inside the ship but when they did, they nearly dropped him to the floor in shock and wonderment. It was like nothing they had ever seen before.

The mid-section was an utter mess. An assortment of crockery, chairs and random appliances lay strewn at their feet. Anji looked up and saw what had been the floor before the accident. The table top grazed her head as she walked past it.

'Sorry about the mess but I haven't had a chance to clear up,' said Skateboard apologetically. 'Now, please could you put the captain somewhere comfortable for the time being? Make yourselves at home – I've got some diagnostics I have to run.'

'What's your name?' asked Anji as she and Jake lay Random down. Jake found a nearby pillow and rested the alien's head against it.

'My real name is GH649Y9D0W but my given name is Skateboard.'

'Can we just call you by your given name?' said Jake.

'If you so wish,' said Skateboard as he whirred up towards the cockpit.

'How come you weren't injured?' Anji said as she followed the robot. Jake stayed where he was to look over Random, who had now fallen into a deep sleep.

'My exoskeleton is compatible with the electromagnetic hull of this ship,' said Skateboard. 'Unfortunately, Sir was not as lucky. All he could do was stay buckled in and hope for the best.'

'What are you doing here?' Anji walked into the seat buckles that dangled like cobwebs from the cockpit above.

'Well, I guess you could say that we are refugees.'

'Why? What happened?'

'We come from a planet a long way from here. It has suffered centuries of war. Our unconscious friend was wanted by a man called Kalor Maloso so we escaped.'

'Why was he wanted? What had he done?'

'Would it be possible if we could leave the questions for later, Madam? I may be a "robot" but I still need to concentrate.'

'Sorry, it's just all so much to take in,' exclaimed Anji. She left Skateboard to it and walked back into the mid-section. Jake was sitting, mouth wide open, taking in his surroundings.

'This is incredible. Unbelievably cool! Anj, what's the cockpit like?'

'Apart from upside down? All shades of amazing.' Anji sat down next to the prone figure of their new, purple friend. 'What are they doing here? And how on earth are we going to explain all of this to Miss?'

'Miss?' Skateboard interrupted, pulling himself through to the mid-section.

'I thought you had diagnostics to run?' Anji said.

'I did. But they are done now.'

'How come you were so fast?' asked Jake.

Skateboard's hydraulics sighed. 'I am a robot,' he replied. 'Now, please, what do you mean by Miss?'

'Miss Carter. She's our Geography teacher,' said Anji.

'Oh my...' Skateboard shot through to the cockpit again. His circuitry a fluster, he proceeded to connect to the ship's main computer and implored its damaged circuits to turn on the cloaking device.

'This is not good...this is not good at all.' Skateboard muttered to himself. He whizzed past

---

the doorway, the velocity of his hastiness knocking Jake to the floor as he disappeared down the corridor into the main engine bay. Within seconds he was back again.

'The cloaking device is damaged. It's going to take a while to repair. Please, I beg you, go back to your teacher and tell her not to come near here.'

'Children?'

Jake and Anji's faces went white.

'Oh my god. She's coming!' Anji made for the door, her heart pounding like a bass drum in her chest.

'Erm...Anji.'

'What?!'

'Random's not there anymore,' said Jake.

Anji turned towards the door that they had entered the ship through. It was open. She ran towards it, poked her head through the door leading out into the reality of the decimated forest and saw Random in the distance, wobbling his way towards the unseen voice of the teacher.

III

The sound of a crashing aircraft had startled Miss Carter so vigorously that she had dropped her cigarette in the mud. When the ground shook as the craft had smashed into the soft, muddy ground, she had fallen to the floor, her face narrowly missing a nearby puddle but plunging nose first into a stale pile of cow dung. She rose to her feet, spat the nastiness out of her mouth, gagged uncontrollably for a few minutes and then, whilst wiping the excrement off her features, ran hysterically into the woods.

She had let the children go, without supervision, into a wood that had just become a disaster scene. The emergency services would never have failed to pick the crash up on their monitors. All kinds of people would soon be here, she imagined.

Firefighters, ambulances, police...hell, even the army for all she knew! If any of her students would have been caught up in this, she'd never be able to forgive herself.

And it would spell the end of her career as a teacher.

'Children!'

She hollered, her lungs straining against the breath that was quickly escaping her, her legs carrying her further and further into the woods. Further towards her students...and potentially, further towards danger.

'Miss? Miss, what on earth was that?' Jemima Wright had taken shelter in a bush, along with several of the other school children.

'Jemima?' Miss Carter wheezed. 'Oh, thank god, you're all alright.'

'Why are you covered in sh...?'

'...it's nothing!' the children giggled. Miss Carter felt naked. Her class started giggling at her, and not for the first time. On the last school trip, she had lost her footing and fallen into a lake. When she was substituting for a colleague who taught Science and who had taken a sudden leave of absence, she had accidentally set fire to her own trousers with a Bunsen burner, much to the utter delight of the hoard of laughing children. She cursed her clumsiness.

'How many of you are there? Come out of the bush now, we're safe, I'm certain.'

'Safe? I smell bull,' said Ben Wills. The students collapsed in laughter again.

'For goodness' sake, so what if I slipped and fell in some poo,' Miss Carter screamed.

'There's been an accident. People could be seriously hurt...or worse. So, for the last time, come out and stay close to me.'

The children stopped their juvenile hysterics and fell out of the bush into the pathway. Miss Carter counted with her index finger, catching her breath and found her composure.

'Right, so we are missing three students. James, Anji and Jake. Has anyone seen them?'

'No, Miss,' Jemima replied.

'Right, I want you all to go back to the coach. Inform the driver what has happened and get him to call 999. I only hope that they are okay.'

'Why don't we just call them now? I mean, what if the people in the plane are hurt...or dead!' Ben was being his usual, less than helpful self.

'Not now, Ben,' said Miss Carter. The last thing she needed was the prospect of a worst-case scenario.

'It was a big crash, Miss. Look.'

Ben showed his teacher the footage he had captured on his mobile phone. She cleaned her poo-smeared glasses and witnessed what her least favourite pupil had caught on camera.

The footage showed the children larking about, playing with large sticks and pretending that they were lightsabers.

She could hear a roar on the audio and suddenly, Ben's filming had been directed skywards and Miss Carter was shocked to see a sleek, silver craft shoot through the cracks in the trees. It didn't look like any airplane she had ever seen before. The clip finished with the children screaming in panic.

'Blimey! It's a good thing I gave you your phones back. Okay, give me ten minutes. If I haven't come back to the coach by then, call the emergency services. I'll see you all back at the car park. If you find the park rangers then let them know.'

'How are we supposed to tell when ten minutes is up?' enquired Jemima.

'Use your phones!' shouted Miss Carter.

'Oh yeah,' said Ben.

The teacher tore off into the woods, hollering for the trio of missing students as the children walked back the other way.

'Why does she want us to wait for ten minutes?' asked Jemima.

'Why do you think? She doesn't want to get sacked, does she? If Jake, Anji and "speccy" kid are brown bread then she'll be fired quicker than a Ferrari in a tunnel.'

Jemima bit her lip hard. 'Do you think they will be alright?'

'Who cares?' said Ben. 'I'm wonder how many hits I can get when I upload this video.'

*

'Random, come back!'

Anji and Jake tore off towards the groggy alien.

'I'm fine, I'm fine, just a bit woozy, that's all,' insisted Random. 'I'll feel fine in a couple of minutes. Fresh air, that's what I need.'

As he walked a little further, he could make out the hazy figure of somebody running towards him. He squinted, shook his head and rubbed his eyes to get a better focus.

It looked like an adult figure and it was getting closer and closer. They were cursing as their hair and bag kept getting caught up in the brambles and branches that lay in their path, slowing them down but not slow enough for them to miss the sight of Random staggering towards them.

'Oh...' he uttered. Before he had a chance to do anything, his speech was muzzled by the sudden trap of fabric that fell down over his head.

The duo had caught up with him just before Miss Carter managed to see who the strange purple skinned boy was.

'Don't say a word; just let us do the talking,' hissed Anji into Random's ear.

'Say what?' he asked, almost choking on the hood chord that had climbed into his throat.

'There you are! I've been worried sick!' Miss Carter's lungs were practically on fire. Her secret smoking habit, coupled with a lack of physical exercise, made her light headed and tired. She rested down on her haunches. She coughed a deep, sludgy cough, the tar shifting in the back of her throat.

'Blimey, you'll be sick in a moment if you don't breathe,' said Jake sarcastically.

'We're fine, Miss,' reassured Anji. 'Absolutely fine. How is everyone else?'

When she had regained her breath, Miss Carter managed to summon up enough energy to speak.

'Everyone else is safe and accounted for. Did you see what happened? And why has James stuffed his coat over his face?'

Anji's heart started pumping a little faster.

'He...er...'

'...he's a little upset...about the crash.'

Oh no, thought Anji. She had just realised that they would have to fabricate two lies on the spot: 1) the identity of the alien, which had already been taken care off for the immediate future and 2) the crashed spaceship behind them.

Miss Carter jumped to her feet, ignoring the stitch that felt like a dagger on fire

had imbedded itself in her left ribcage and pleaded wild eyed to her pupils.

'Oh, I almost forgot when I saw you, where is it? Are there any survivors? How am I going to explain this to the Headmaster?'

'Where is what?' Anji looked quizzically at her frantic teacher. Surely something like a giant silver spaceship, big enough to destroy a pond which will probably lay deep in the woods for centuries, couldn't go unnoticed. Especially as the crash site was a mere fifty metres or so behind them.

She turned tentatively to look over her shoulder and at the same time both Jake and Random – or 'James' – did exactly the same thing.

It was gone. The Venus II had gone. It was nowhere to be seen and bizarrely the pond was still there. Sure, it looked a little bigger and there appeared to be a path of broken trees, fallen pine cones and other foliage, but the offending article had been removed. Or had it?

Skateboard! That brilliant little machine had done it. The Venus II was still there, but it had cloaked itself. To Miss Carter, or anyone else who ventured near, there was nothing to see that hadn't been there before.

'Er...no idea, Miss.'

'Right, well since I've found you three, I think the next best thing would be to let the local authorities deal with it. Let's only hope it wasn't as bad as the video depicts.'

'What video?' asked Jake.

'Ben caught the 'crash' – or whatever it was – on camera,' said Miss Carter. 'Now don't worry about that. We can only be thankful that we are all alive and well.'

And that some of us have kept our jobs, thought the teacher.

Random was still feeling worse for wear but he had recovered enough to play along at this point. In the immediate instance, it was best to keep quiet and keep himself hidden as much as he could from view. Thank goodness the coat that he had forced upon him was full length, protecting his arms and legs and his less than orthodox clothes out of sight. Suddenly, he picked up on a pungent stench coming from the woman standing in front of him. It smelt terrible and he couldn't help sniffing loudly.

'Oh, don't worry, James, it will all okay. Miss has got you,' she cooed.

Random struggled to understand what she was on about but shook his head anyway, playing along with the others.

'We'll look after him,' Jake said, forcing his arm around Random's shoulders and shaking him vigorously.

'Hmm...that's good of you Jake. Especially after what you two have gone through lately. It's nice for the pair of you to put your differences to one side in times of need. Come on then, back to the coach. I'm sure the police will want to talk to us.'

'Oh...okay.' Anji was starting to feel like a bag of nerves. As they walked away from the pond, a number of questions started circulating in her mind. Were they really about to smuggle an alien back to their school? Where were they going to hide him? Mores to the point, how on earth were they going to get him back to his ship? And what if that Maloso guy followed Random to earth and was still looking for him? She looked behind her, where the Venus II had once been. She prayed that Skateboard was looking out at them and had a better plan than either she or Jake had.

'It's turned out to be a weird day, hasn't it? said Miss Carter.

'Oh,' whispered Anji under her breath. 'You have no idea.'

*

Skateboard watched the scenes unfold on the monitor.

Despite the crash, the ship had held up well.

Well, that's to be expected when the craft is made up of seda metal – the toughest metal compound in the known universe – and titanium – the runner-up in the toughest metal compound in all the known universe competition.

He looked on, helpless, as his Captain was led away with this unknown species. Skateboard knew deep down in his motherboard that Random would be alright, but what to do now? Await his return? He couldn't do that. A beeping signal from the sonic scope alarmed the AI. Pouring over its findings, he discovered that a swarm was heading his way.

Imploring the computer for more information, the swarm appeared to be an oncoming juggernaut of vehicles. Skateboard panicked. This meant more trouble.

He plugged himself into the main computer and searched the binary for a full diagnostic of damage to the Venus II. Luckily, despite the ship being upside down, 89% of the hull and its internal circuits were intact. Luck seemed to be on Skateboard's side.

He disconnected himself from the computer and hooked himself up to the tracking system. The Venus II was a very special ship indeed.

As soon as a living organism sets foot on board, the ship makes a biological imprint, meaning that they can be tracked wherever they go within a 500-mile radius.

Skateboard made sure that the imprints of

Random and the two children who had helped him were recorded. So now, he knew where they were, so when the time was right, he could rescue his friend. But first, he had to move the Venus II.

He peered over the sonic scope again. The swarm was getting closer.

Roughly five miles away now.

He could also pick up heat signatures and he could tell that although there seemed to be several bodies leaving the woods, more were on their way.

There was no time to lose.

'Computer – pilot code GH649Y9D0W – full control.'

The ship whirred into life with a cough and a splutter. Skateboard could now control the whole ship, just through the power of his will.

He fired the retros up. The ship began to wriggle; the nose section began receding from the hole in the pond. Slowly but surely, the Venus II began to pull itself away from the crash site.

Skateboard initiated his electromagnetic capabilities and instructed the ship to flip over to its correct position. The ship rattled like a salt shaker as it completed the maneuver.

Skateboard instructed the rockets underneath the ship to fire upwards, propelling the ship through the trees it hadn't destroyed before piloting the craft away from the crash site.

Meanwhile, whilst Anji and Jake helped "James" on board the coach; they overheard the din of engines in the near distance. Random, with the coat still disguising his appearance, knew it was Skateboard fleeing the site.

His head bowed, disconsolate, hoping that his friend would be able to find him soon as he stepped onto the coach and was ushered to a window seat by Anji, who took up the seat next to him. A blizzard of noise blazed away. An entourage of cars, fire engines and ambulances sped into the car park. Miss Carter stepped off the coach. Jake saw her approach one of the police officers, straining to make out what she was saying to him through the glass window. He shot a panicked look to Anji, who held onto Random's arm.

'Don't worry; we'll get you out of this. I promise.'

'Right kids,' said the coach driver. 'I've just been told that Miss Carter will be assisting the police in their enquiries.'

His speech was halted when a policeman stepped up onto the coach.

'Right, please listen up children; I just wanted to reassure you that everything is in hand and your coach driver will be taking you back to your school in due course. We just need to ask your teacher some questions first. She'll be meeting you further on down the road – we need to evacuate this area in case of any danger to civilians. Thank you for your understanding.'

Just as he went to step off again, Ben's phone started to vibrate.

'Hello Mum! No, I'm fine, why's that? What! No way!'

'What's up?' asked Anji.

'My video's been shown on the news! I only uploaded it a few minutes ago!'

'What are they saying?'

Ben repeated the question into the mobile. 'They are saying it's a possible plane crash.'

The children gasped in horror.

'I'm pretty sure it isn't,' said Jake.

'Yeah, it could be aliens!' said Jemima.

The children began screaming.

The policeman strode down the gangway, walking past Random and snatched the phone off Ben.

'Hello, who is this? Mrs Wright, I'd just like to reassure you that your son and his classmates are safe. We will be moving them on soon…what's that?

No, no aliens...well, no I haven't seen the crash site yet...I think that we can safely say that there are no aliens in the vicinity.'

He handed the phone back to Ben.

'And let me repeat that to all of you. We don't want to scaremonger. For all we know it might just be a crashed drone. One thing we can definitely rule out is that it is aliens that we are dealing with. Thank you.'

And with that, the policeman stepped off the coach.

Anji started shaking in fear. What had they got themselves into? She shared a knowing look with Jake, who looked equally as nervous and looked over to Random. Through the hood, she could see his red/blue eyes looking back at her, helpless and scared.

About ten minutes later, Miss Carter, her witness statement safely with the police, rejoined her class and the coach pulled away back to London. Little did they know that there was an illegal alien on board, and the boy whose identity he had adopted, was still lost in the woods.

IV

How Anji and Jake ever smuggled Random back to their home, they will never know. The whole afternoon was a blur. As soon as the coach pulled up at the school, they managed to hide Random, still swathed in Jake's parker jacket, past the line and into the cloak room, where Miss Carter had interrogated the pair on what they had seen in the woods.

Before long, the local police had also gone round to class 3B. Each student was called up to give an account as to what they had seen, but the duo decided that they would quietly slip away at the earliest possible opportunity and escape to the relative safety of their home.

They did just that, picking Random up out of the cloakroom, before catching the school bus back to their sanctuary.

Anji almost snapped the key in the lock since she was in such a rush to enter. Random had glimpsed through the hood at the house. It was a rather new house; the bricks were an oblique grey. The house stood three stories high. Random had never seen anything like it. It was like a palace to him.

Eventually, they made it to Anji's room. After climbing up the 2 flights of stairs, they reached the top floor and burst through the bedroom door, almost tearing it from its hinges in the process. The trio collapsed on the single bed, breathless and relieved.

'Oh my god, how on earth did we just do that?' Jake enquired.

'What do you mean?' said Anji.

'Well, we just smuggled an alien from Dartmoor to school and then half way across London!'

'Maybe someone up there is looking over us?' Anji suggested.

'Ugh.'

Random groaned. He began to tear at the parker's restrictive fabric.

'Hold on a minute, let me pull the blinds first! Just in case anyone is looking in at us.'

'Like who?' asked Jake, thinking that Anji was being overly paranoid given they were on the second floor. 'No, don't tell me: Simon Formby?'

Simon was an unpopular child in Anji's Math's class. His chunky spectacles, unsightly acne and terrible body odour made him the least desirable boy in Year 3.

Classmates had been known to avoid him at all costs for prolonged periods like lessons time, especially after learning that one of the giant zits on his cheek had erupted like a volcano of teenage sebum and dirt into the face of poor Samantha Ripley. From that moment on, Simon was scorned and Samantha never ate mayonnaise again.

Unfortunately for Anji, he harboured strong feelings for her. Despite the love letters, the little gifts left pinned to her school locker and the god-awful poetry, Anji's affections were not forthcoming. Awkwardly for her, he lived right across the road and was prone to looking out for her after school.

Anji peered out of the window down to the road below and sure enough, there was Simon, looking up at the top window which belonged to her bedroom. When he saw Anji looking, he waved his fingers in a 'come hither' way. She grunted and snapped the blinds shut.

'Forget about him, we've got more important things to think about,' she said as they helped Random out of his disguise.

Now things had calmed down, they could see him for who he truly was.

'My god, you're so purple,' said Jake. 'Why is that? Is it a birthmark?'

'I guess so,' said Random.

'How are you feeling now?'

'Fine thanks. I don't think I caught your names?'

'Well, I'm Jake. And as an ambassador for the planet Earth...'

Anji jabbed Jake sharply in the ribs.

'My name is Anji', she replied to Random.

'Anji. You saved me, didn't you?'

'Well, we both did, thank you very much!' corrected Jake.

'I'm thankful. I really am. You wouldn't believe the day I'd had.' Random's mind still felt cloudy. He remembered the escape from Rodas, Maloso and the Sandman. He just could not remember the events of his 'landing' on this planet 'Earth'.

'What happened?'

Anji filled him in on the details. 'We were on a school trip. A really boring one until you turned up! Then we heard a crash so we ran to the place where it came from and saw you staggering outside of a spaceship.'

Shaking the last of his groggy state from his head, Random suddenly now remembered everything that had happened since his escape from Rodas. The crash, the two strangers, Skateboard and the Venus II leaving him behind...

'Oh no! The Venus II and Skateboard; they've left me here!!'

A sea of panic washed over Random's features.

'Don't worry!'

'They've left me alone!'

'We'll look after you now, please, keep your voice down,' Anji implored.

'Keep my voice down? I've just been abandoned on an alien world and you're asking me to keep my voice down?' Random shot up from the bed, making the teenagers jump.

'Hey, you're the alien here, buddy, not us,' said Jake.

'We'll help you find your way back to the crash site, I promise,' Anji's tone soothed Random.

'Well, what do we do in the meantime?'

'You can stay here.'

'Woah, I don't think Jason will agree,' said Jake.

'Who is Jason?'

'He takes care of us. This is a care home.'

Random started to calm his nerves a little.

'Why should you help me? You don't know me. And why should you trust me. I am an 'alien' after all,' Random shot a look to Jake.

'Look, I'm sorry about that. I'm sure we can work something out, even if we have to keep you a secret up here. Don't worry, we can bring you food.'

'Sounds like you want to keep me in captivity,' said Random.

'Of course not,' assured Anji. 'It'll only be until we can find Skateboard again.'

Random sat back down on the bed, feeling the soft duvet under the palms of his hands.

'We won't tell anybody you're here. It'll be fun.'

'It doesn't sound very fun,' scoffed Random.

'Please. We really want to help you; friends?'

As a sign of friendship, Anji held out her hand. She willed Random to shake it. He did. He pinched her thumb and pulled it up and down in a rocking motion.

'Friends,' smiled Random.

Jake didn't know whether to laugh or not.

'Right; so how big is the planet 'Earth.' Where is it?'

'I can help you out with this one. Lie back,' said Anji as she joined Random on the bed. Random did as he was asked and let the back of his head sink into the firm mattress.

'You see those planets up there?'

Anji pointed to her ceiling. Along with the congealed blobs of blu tack staining the white finish, there were pictures of worlds that Random had never seen before.

'I meant to take these down ages ago. The person I inherited this room from was a big fan of spacey stuff.'

She motioned her finger towards the blue/green planet.

That one there…that's us, three along from the sun. That's the planet Earth. If you squint, you can make out a tiny island near the top of the world.

Random fixed his eyes upon it.

'That's where we are. That's the United Kingdom.'

Jake sat in the chair, gawking up at the ceiling, like his friends.

'Wow,' Random seemed genuinely interested. 'How many people live in the United Kingdom?'

'We covered this the other day,' said Jake. 'There are just over 65 million people.'

'How many?! On one tiny island? How do you all fit?'

'Some would argue we don't,' said Anji. She sighed, remembering some of the jibes she had endured in the past from ignorant classmates.

'It's amazing. Do you all live in places like this?'

'The lucky ones do,' said Jake. 'The majority of people live with their families.'

'What are families?'

'Y'know, Mums and Dads with their children. Do you have a Mum and Dad?'

'No. At least I don't think so.'

Anji looked quizzical. 'Are you an orphan?'

'What's that?'

'It's what we are. We don't have a Mum or Dad,' Jake explained.

'No, I'm not an orphan,' Random replied.

'So how old are you?' asked Anji.

'I'm not very old. In fact, I'm roughly 2 moon circles old.'

'You're two days old? Christ, you've aged!' said Jake.

'I don't think my biological make-up is anything like yours. I'm an 'alien' remember?' Random shot another look at Jake. He was beginning to wonder if they would end up getting on at all.

'Tell us all about it,' asked Anji.

As they lied on the bed, Random told Anji and Jake everything.

He opened up about his early beginnings; how his first memory is stepping out of a glass tube, fully formed and seeing the destruction and bloodshed that surrounded him.

He retold the story of his escape. How the Crimson Empire had hunted him down like an animal and the unlikely desertion, when he used his strength to throw the heli-fighter away like a paper plane.

'Wow, remind me never to challenge you to an arm wrestle,' said Jake.

He opened his heart to the recollection of seeing the refugees of war, staring at him, helplessness burning in their souls. Anji could see a tear in his eye, making her also well up with emotion. Even Jake bowed his head solemnly.

Random continued, telling his new companions about how the Sandman had taken him in as an unwanted house guest, the discovery of the Venus II, Skateboard, the escape from Rodas and the feeling of abandoning those people.

'Oh, Random,' cooed Anji, blinking away the tears. 'No wonder you ran off.'

'I don't blame you either. There's nothing you could have done,' said Jake, who was also welling up.

'That's what Skateboard said, oh, I miss that little guy.'

'I'll go get us some food from the kitchen. I don't think any of the other kids are back yet. We're the youngest here so many of them will be at the youth club on a Friday night. So we should have the pick of the grub!'

Jake swiveled on the office chair and made for the door.

Anji held Random's hand and smiled at him.

'You've got us now. We'll help you however we can.'

Random smiled. 'I wonder what he is getting up to now.'

*

High above the city's financial superpowers and the tower blocks that glistened in the evening sun, Skateboard had parked the Venus II on top of the tallest building in London. Here, he had spent the last 130 kels, or two hours in human time as he understood it, to carry out the necessary repairs on the ship. Before choosing on his hideout, he carried out a scan on the area. Random was less than 15 miles away.

Skateboard had chosen the spot so that he could keep a close eye on his Captain; not so that he could look out at the local scenery. Beautiful though it was, with the River Thames shimmering in the glow of the oncoming night and Big Ben, which seemed to incessantly chime every 60th kels, or hour in human time as he understood it, the little AI, ironically, just didn't have the time to take any of it in. He hadn't even had the time to inspect the mysterious white circular attraction on the river bank.

V

Skateboard and James cowered at the giant intruder who had seemingly just materialised aboard the Venus II. With eyes of silt, the Sandman blinked back into existence. His brow bore a frowned expression, one of sheer determination and frustration. Before long, he spoke.

'Miss me?'

Skateboard began to whirr, his circuitry disabling all the protocols that gave the Sandman voice activation control of the ship.

'Well...did you?' the Sandman spat grains from the corners of his mouth.

James stared up at the stranger in shock.

'Wow...did you just see that? What is the budget for this thing?'

'I regret to inform you that I did not.' Skateboard's etiquette was still annoyingly impeccable.

'I didn't think you did. Still, I suppose I should hand it to you really, my little pet. You did get me off Rodas after all.'

'Not exactly; Your metaphysical imprint is stretched between here and there. You have regenerated through the aspects of your DNA that were left on board.

The medical scanners on the ship must have resurrected your imprint here by accident. So, basically speaking, you're not even half the man you once were.'

'Good exposition. Who scripted this thing?' asked James.

The Sandman's patience was being tested to breaking point.

'Shut up! Sit over there and don't say another word until I say so.'

James did exactly as he was told and took up residence on the sofa. All of a sudden, he felt a shard of fear trickle down his spine. Either this was great method acting, or something even stranger was going on here. For the time being, and for the integrity of his own insanity, he plumped for the former.

The Sandman slowly made for Skateboard. The little AI noticed that his former "master" was limping slightly. His physical state was severely impaired.

129

He also noticed that his form was not as solid as before. You might even say that the Sandman looked almost transparent as he moved under the warm glow of the interior lighting rig.

As he tipped his head downwards towards the robot, several grains of sand fell like coarse snow onto Skateboard's bodywork.

'Where is he?' the Sandman bellowed.

*

Random lay awake on the floor of Anji's room listening to the soft snore emanating from the bed above him. This whole planet felt weird. It was night time and yet it was much, much darker than the daytime, something that Random had grown used to during his short stay on his home planet.

After dinner, which consisted of something called "chicken and chips" (a delicacy which Random actually rather liked), Jake decided to introduce Random to something called a "first person shooter." He had enjoyed his turn on the "Xbox" but Anji scorned her blonde friend saying that he was being, "insensitive, especially after everything Random has told us!"

And so they had moved on to a game that involved a sport called football. Random enjoyed this experience much more, although he found the concept of eleven men facing a further eleven men trying to kick a ball into a net, with almost the entire side forbidden to touch the ball with their hands.

An alien concept, indeed.

He sighed as he continued to stare up at the ceiling from his makeshift bed covers.

Anji had offered him her bed but he didn't fancy sleeping there. It was hers, after all!

Random could not take his eyes off the twinkling stars that blinked above him. He dreamed of the planets which all looked down upon him; Mercury, Venus, Earth, Mars, Jupiter, Uranus, Saturn and Neptune.

Rolling over and closing his eyes, he began thinking about Skateboard and how he longed to see the AI and the Venus II again, until he drifted off into a blissful, deep sleep.

'Anj...'

Jake knocked again on the door.

'Anj! Come on!'

The door creaked open. Anji, wearing a pink night dress and her hair mated over her tired eyes, poked her head through the crack.

'Wow, aren't you a sight for sore eyes.'

'Shut up and get in,' Anji instructed.

Jake did as he was told. Carrying a tray of toast, jam and tea, he entered the bedroom, stepped over Random's sleeping body and rested the tray tentatively on the desk.

'Did you sleep well?' he asked.

'Like a baby,' said Anji. She rubbed the sleep from her eyes and let out a big yawn.

'Yourself?'

'Surprisingly, yes, I did. Although I did have a terrible dream in the night; I dreamt that we'd been on a school trip, picked up an alien refugee and you were hiding him under your bed.'

'Well, I hate to break it to you, mate, but either you're still dreaming or you've woken up in a nightmare,' she smiled.

'Ah come on, it's not so bad.'

'Not so bad? What'll happen when the school finds out that James didn't come back with us? We'll be the first people they come to looking for him. Who is to say that hasn't happened already? For all we know his parents could be on the phone to our school right now.' Anji began to look worried.

'Of course, they won't be. It's Saturday, remember? No one goes to school on a Saturday!' Jake pointed at Random. 'Do you think he will want some breakfast?'

'I'm not sure. Do aliens eat breakfast?'

'Who knows,' scoffed Jake as he devoured a slice of toast. 'But I'm having his.'

'Why didn't you make your own?'

'I did.'

'Then why are you eating his?'

'Hey, I'm still hungry.'

'Go and get some more, for goodness' sake!'

Jake put the half-eaten toast back on the plate and retreated back to the door with the tray.

As Anji shut the door behind him, Random sprang into life. His eyes opened with the haste of a lightning bolt and he jumped out of the covers like a jack in the box, uncoiled and yawned like a lion calling for his pack.

'Right, what did I miss?'

'Breakfast apparently,' said Anji. She opened her laptop and decided to brave it and see what social media had to say about the crash.

The story was everywhere.

MYSTERY OF CRASHED "PLANE" the news outlets screamed. Ben's video had not only gone viral. It had gone global. As she continued to read the stories, it became apparent that some of their classmates had exaggerated the situation and made-up tales about how the ship nearly killed them. There were also terrible lies being spread.

'AN ARMY OF ALIENS ATTACKED US, I SAW IT!' claimed Sadie Long.

'HE SAID, "WE COME IN PEACE" AND THEN EVAPORATED INTO THIN AIR,' asserted Ross Wilkinson.

'HE WANTED TO PHONE HOME...BUT WE ENDED UP SWAPPING NUMBERS,' declared Jemima Wright.

'Oh, I hate that girl so much!' Anji spat.

'So...we might have caused a bit of a scene then, eh?' enquired Random.

Anji nodded.

'Right, well at least nobody knows we are here'.

Like a storm cloud gathering over the Notting Hill Carnival, something was about to rain on the youngster's parade.

Meanwhile, Jake was busying himself in the kitchen, making another round of toast for his new friend upstairs. Humming to himself, he was blissfully unaware that Jason was standing in the doorway, watching him.

'You're not normally up this early,' he said.

'Oh! Jason, you startled me. Yes, I erm...couldn't sleep last night.' Jake dropped the buttered piece of toast to the floor. In a bizarre moment on improbability, the toast landed butter side up for the first time in the history of mankind.

'It wouldn't have anything to do with this...alien thing, now would it?'

Jake scoffed. 'No, of course not. What alien thing?'

Jason walked closer to Jake, who was busying himself with yet another round of toast, completely ignoring the abandoned slice lying at his feet.

'Come on Jake, you're not fooling me. You were on the trip that has been cited by

NewsCorp as 'Star Trekkers.'

So come on then, spill the beans.'

'I didn't see anything,' Jake lied.

Jason stood a tall six foot one and his broad physique towered imposingly over the teen.

'Are you sure?'

Jake tried his hardest to keep the truth from his carer.

He was failing miserably.

'Yep. Absolutely. I mean, they didn't find anything did they? Plus, any idiot can use an editing suite nowadays to make any old rubbish up.'

Jason blinked down on the child.

'Really?'

Jason moved into the hallway.

'Then would you be so kind as to tell this lot!'

He opened the front door.

There outside, a large number of keen journalists had gathered, desperate to hear the story first hand. A myriad of flashing lights and frenzied questions hit Jake like a ton of bricks.

The boy stood aghast at the commotion.

A sea of hacks awaited him.

'Could you tell us if you're hording aliens?'

'Can you explain to us the mystery of the plane...was it a plane?'

'Have you come into contact with extra-terrestrial life forms after your school trip?'

Jake dropped the tray and ran over to the door, slamming it shut. His eyes, wild with panic darted all around, his mind too slow to assimilate the commotion behind the relative safety of the front door.

'H-how long have they been out there?' he stuttered.

'About an hour or so. Apparently, your friends have been posting all kinds about it.'

Jason reached for the telephone.

'I'm calling the police. There's no way we can put up with this.'
'The police? Here?'

Jason scanned Jake's sheet white face.

'Unless there is something you are hiding from me?'

'No! There is absolutely nothing to tell.'

The commotion outside was not the only surprise awaiting the pair.

Out of the blue, Jake's phone started to buzz. He normally left it on silent for two reasons. One, so that he wasn't disturbed by the embarrassing ring tone that Anji once pranked him with and which he now can't seem to change and two, because it never failed to massage his ego when he checked it every now and again and a backlog of missed calls, texts and notifications always made him feel more popular than he really was.

'Sorry, Jason, I've got to take this.'

Jake ran upstairs as fast as his legs could carry him and slammed into his room.

Tentatively, he picked the receiver up.

'Hello?'

'Jake. It's Miss Carter here. It appears we have a problem.'

'Oh?'

'Yes,' Miss Carter sounded unusually calm.

'I've just received a phone call from the school. It's from James' parents. It appears that he didn't return home last night...'

'Ah.'

Jake was perspiring at an alarming rate. He felt like his heart was about to explode. The anxiety levels grew and grew inside his teenage mind. Unsurprisingly, he started to hyperventilate.

'Right...well, you see, the thing is er...Miss...'

Think brain, think. I know we don't seem to be the best of friends most of the time but I really need you now!

'He...was here. Last night. It got late and asked if he could spend the night with us.'

Yes! You've done it, brain. You've done it! I promise not to keep killing you with too much gaming.

'Right,' Miss Carter seemed very unsure. 'So how come he didn't ring his parents?'

You can do it, come on. Just one more time.

'Phone died,' replied Jake.

'And neither of you could lend him a charger?'

Um…
'Jake, I'm waiting.'
Brain, I take it all back. You suck!
'It didn't occur to us at the time, Miss. Anyway, he never even asked us if he could borrow one.'
Jake clenched his teeth. His last excuse was undeniably weak.
'I think I'd better come over and have a word with your carer.'
'Sorry Miss but I'm afraid that-'
Jake's phone died completely. He looked at it. Ironically, it had run out of charge. Instant karma for using that excuse, he thought.
Without a moment's hesitation, he tore away from his room and burst in on Anji's again.
'Guys…we've got trouble…BIG trouble!'

VI

'You're right,' confirmed Random as he peered through the curtains at the melee ensuing below. 'We ARE in big trouble!'
'Right!' Jake was breathing in and out of a paper bag that had once housed Anji's cosmetic stash. 'The school has found out that James is missing, the internet has exploded with rumours and we've got Jason coming up the stairs this minute who is about to find out that we are harbouring an alien!'
'Keep your voice down, Jake, for goodness' sake!' Anji hissed.
'Maybe we can reason with him,' said Random.
'What!?'
'Keep blowing Jake,' said Anji. 'What are you suggesting?'

KNOCK KNOCK!

Jake blew so hard that the bag popped like bubble gum.
'Oh crap!'
The teenager shot under Anji's bed.
'Come in,' cooed Random.
Jason stormed through the door. 'Just what on earth do you kids think you are…'
'It's Jason, isn't it? Come in, come in, and make yourself at home. Although technically you are home, but what the heck, get comfy.'

135

Anji was taken away by Random's bravado.

'Y-y-you're a...' Jason's eyes opened wider than ever. He was in the presence of a stranger. A purple stranger.

'There you are,' Random ushered him over to the chair.

'Now then, I hear that there is a bit of a commotion going on outside? Well, it's all very simple. You see, I am not an alien. Far from it. I've never even been outside of this country! I'm a wanderer; a nomad of the streets. This skin colour is an unfortunate birthmark and my clothes? Well, if you were homeless too, you'd probably borrow the nearest clothing to hand to cover your nakedness. But let me ask you this? Would you let a homeless boy in an unforgiving world be the subject of a vicious internet rumour? No Mum, no Dad. No friends except those in this room right now? Nobody to defend him?'

Jake peered from his hiding place. This was incredible. Random was talking not just his way out of trouble but his and Anji's too. Was Jason going to buy it?

'How did you get in then?'

'They found me in the woods.'

I don't believe it, thought Anji. *What a clever guy! He wasn't lying. He was manipulating the truth.*

'I had got lost. I'd dawdled for days and found myself in the country. Then I met these two and they saved me and promised to help. I pleaded with them to take me back and to keep me safe.'

Random walked over to the window. There were more vans and press than before, hammering on the door.

'I'm so sorry. I don't want to cause any grief. I just want a roof over my head.'

Jason was taken aback by the story; a boy of the streets. Was he unwanted by his parents and left to fend for himself? Was it because of his deformity? It was unusual to see a boy whose skin was bright purple, but to cast him out was utterly deplorable. Especially to a man who had dedicated his whole adult life to helping the dis-advantaged.

'What is your name?' he asked.

'My name is Andrew Smith. At least, that's the name I have given myself.'

Jason sat engrossed in the boy's story.

'Okay, Andrew. Here's what we'll do. I'll go and telephone the police, tell them that there is no cause for alarm and we'll sort out this mess.'

He did just that. Within minutes, the police were on the scene, clearing the crowd with great

difficulty at first, but after a while the hacks of Fleet Street eventually scurried back to their offices with no answers to the online rumours that the care home was housing a being from another world.

As the care home was just that, the local constabulary made absolutely certain that the building's location would not be revealed by any journalist.

After the commotion had died down, Detective Inspector Willis, accompanied by two of his officers, Miss Carter and Jason, questioned the children in the kitchen.

Considering their stories were corroborated hastily and that Anji and Jake had taken inspiration from Random's warped tale of events, there was just enough truth in their tale that DI Willis had no choice but to believe them.

They bought it all; Random's story that he has been alone most of his life, that he is a stranger, lost in a boulevard of chaos and that he had met the teenagers in the woods. After what seemed like an age, DI Willis was finally satisfied.

'Alright, there's just one final question I would like to ask. You've told us everything we'd like to know about the boy but there is still the whereabouts of your classmate that we have to worry about.'

DI Willis' stubby fingers reached for a rich tea biscuit, his seventh since the questioning had commenced. Miss Carter cut him a scornful expression. Rich tea biscuits were her favourite and now they were all gone.

'The fact of the matter is that your actions have led to a missing person. We'll make sure that the local authorities are aware and that the boy's parents are notified of the latest news.'

'Couldn't the staff at the National Park be of any help?' asked Miss Carter.

DI Willis wiped the crumbs from his lips.

'We've already been in contact with the constabulary in the area and he confirmed that there had been no sightings, but don't worry, I'm sure we'll find him.'

'We're so sorry,' said Anji. There was genuine remorse etched over her face.

'I'll leave you to deal with these two.'

DI Willis pulled his bulky frame up from his chair and shook Jason's hand.

'We'll be in touch with any further information as it comes in. We'll see ourselves out. Anything else you youngsters care to share then please let us know as soon as possible. Good day.'

He smiled at the carer and glared at Miss Carter. As the police departed, she could contain her anger no longer.

'What the hell do you think you are playing at?'

'We're really sorry, Miss, sorrier than you can ever know.' Jake looked sheepish as he spoke.

'I am utterly shocked and appalled at the pair of you. How dare you leave a classmate behind? Worse of all lie to me! I knew you were up to something when you ran from school.'

'Miss, if there is anything we can do to help then-'

'Help, Anji? Help! I don't need your help. You have no idea the problems you have caused me. I shall have to answer to the district councilors on Monday. I could lose my job because of this!'

'Miss Carter, I'm sure you will keep your job,' Jason put his hand on her shoulder. The teacher recoiled; acting like his touch was as cold as ice.

'Don't you touch me!' she barked. 'You think your kind words can help the situation. A boy has gone missing!'

'They'll find him, now please, Emily, calm down. The children are truly sorry.'

Emily? Thought Jake. *Who'd have thunk? And how on earth did Jason know her first name?*

'I think you need a good rest. They'll find James, I'm sure of it. It hasn't been twelve hours since you left and that park is big.'

'He could have been eaten by a bear, or kidnapped by an escaped convict!'

'Both are highly unlikely. Now I assure you, Emily, everything will be alright. I promise.'

Jason's eyes smiled at her through his gangly ginger fringe. She smiled back.

'Okay, maybe you're right,' she conceded.

'I know I am. Now, go home and get some rest. I'll show you out.'

Emily Carter got up to leave. She eyed Random with terrible uncertainty. His purple complexion still baffled her.

'I hope you find somewhere that'll take care of you.'

'Thanks for your sentiment,' said Random. There was an element of cheekiness in his voice which made Emily frown.

'As for you two, I want you in my office first thing Monday. I'll have thought what you do with you by then.'

That's it, a year of lunchtime detentions for us, thought Anji.

'Come on,' Jason escorted Emily into the hallway. As they walked to the front door, the trio in the kitchen could hear the couple chatting. They all craned their necks, spying on the adults as they peered around the kitchen door.

Shortly afterwards, they distinctly heard Jason tell their Geography teacher that he'd "be around later," before pecking her on the lips.

As he shut the door, Jason could feel watching eyes burning on the back of his neck. As he turned to face the teenagers, their faces slinked back out of sight.

'What a morning,' he groaned.

'I was telling the truth with what I said, Jason,' said Anji. 'We really are truly sorry.'

'I know you are, kids. I've been here long enough to get to know the pair of you. I know you wouldn't have done this out of intent. I just wish you'd let Emily...I mean, Miss Carter know that you'd found Andrew when you did.'

'I'm not blameless either,' said Random. 'I'm sorry that my presence has brought about this mess.'

Jason looked up at the purple child.

'Look, I can have a word with the local authorities. DI Willis gave me a number to call. I can't promise anything, but I might be able to give you a roof over your head.'

'You mean,' Jake felt a wave of optimism wash over him, 'he can stay here with us?'

'For now, yes. In the long run, he might have to move to another home. We have a bed here, but it'll be taken in three weeks. Do you have any possessions with you, Andrew?'

'No, only my crazy get-up,' he said as he looked down at his garish garments.

'I'll have a look in lost property, see if there's anything that'll fit you and you can have that.'

'Thank you. Thank you so much, Jason!' Random clasped Jason's right hand and with a double clasp, shook it vigorously.

'Woah! Easy, that's quite a grip you've got there!'

'Sorry,' chuckled Random.

He released him and Jason rubbed his palm tenderly.

'Right, off to your rooms with all of you. But don't think you've escaped punishment, you two. You can wash the pots for a whole month and you're also grounded. Apart from school, I don't want you leaving this place for the next two weeks.'

'What about the Xbox?' Jake enquired hopefully.

'Definitely no Xbox for a fortnight, either.'

Crud! What'll I do now? Read! Pfft. Not likely.

'Go on then, off to your rooms, all of you. I'll get on to the council immediately, try and confirm Andrew's stay with us for the immediate future.'

'Thanks, Jason, thanks for everything,' said Anji sincerely.

The trio trudged off silently back to Anji's room. Closing the door behind them, they slumped to the floor and breathed a collective sigh of relief.

'I can't believe we've just got away with that,' said Anji.

'It's tragic it really is. No computer games for a month,' muttered Jake, his face crestfallen.

'How did we do that, Random?' asked Anji.

'Simple. A simple manipulation of the truth.'

'I hate lying.'

'We didn't lie, Anji. We just didn't tell them the bits that could get us into real trouble.'

'We already are in real trouble!' insisted Jake. 'James is missing, our teacher's neck is on the line and we've probably got detention from now until we die!'

Random laughed to himself.

'When you've seen the trouble I've seen, Jake, you'd never think that you'll ever be in real trouble again.'

'Then why did you lie about your name?'

'Come on, do you really think I'd have got away with my story if I said that my name was Random? I had to come up with the first ordinary name I could think of.'

He stood up, took in a deep breath and smiled at his companions.

'So, now that's all sorted, let's do something fun instead.'

'Like what?' asked Anji.

Random grinned.

'Anything we like.'

VII

James Butcher had never been a brave boy. Whatever chromosome deployed the bravery gene in a person, it wasn't found anywhere in his genetic make-up. It was a trait that had been lacking somewhat throughout his family's history.

James was descended from a long-line of cowards, cheats, liars and swindlers. If, one day, he dare look back on his family tree and pour back through the centuries, he would find that his great-great-great grandfather times twelve was in fact the Head Monk of the Augustinian Order who in 1532, in charge of the Holy Trinity Priory, became the first monastery that was dissolved by King Henry VIII.

Despite his pleas to keep the priory open, he eventually turned his back on his fellow monks and ran off before the place was torn down.

The cowardice got passed down to all generations and now, five hundred years after bravery was lost in the gene pool of the Butcher family, the latest generation was sat fixated in a trance on a spaceship he believed to be a film set, being menaced by a man made of sand.

But he was not alone in this mad, mad world.

There was a robot skateboard, who just to affirm that James' sanity was well and truly dwindling, spoke the Queen's English.

'You can't keep him here...' Skateboard paused, struggling to betray his etiquette protocols and finish his sentence with, 'Sir.'

'Don't tell me what to do you piece of sheet metal,' the Sandman hissed. 'The boy stays with us.'

Skateboard sighed.

'There are 7 billion inhabitants on this planet. You are only one entity and even then, you're not all in one piece. He has done nothing wrong.'

'He has seen too much,' said the Sandman, more grains pouring from his form.

'Let me make a suggestion. Take me; I am a servant after all. Do what you want with me but leave him be.'

'Oh, don't you worry your little hydraulics about that, I will,' the Sandman had many ideas of the best way to torture his pet.

'If you let him go, then I shall give myself willingly over to you, but he cannot be used as a bargain chip. He is innocent.'

'Yes,' the Sandman was starting to see that having an earth boy on board didn't help him out whatsoever. He had read the same files as Skateboard had on the planet Earth.

Despite its primitive classification in the known universe, it was infamous for the home of the human race and they were equally as infamous for being a well-organised and occasionally aggressive race. Even with a ship as advanced as the Venus II, they couldn't take this world on alone.

Then, inside the Sandman's mind, a plan began to germinate.

'Okay, we'll play it your way, Skateboard. We'll let the boy go. Use your powers of persuasion to wipe his mind. Make him utterly convinced that this is a fantasy.'

I won't have any trouble doing that, thought Skateboard.

'He will lead us to Random.'

'Why do you want Random?'

The Sandman rounded on his slave. 'I've seen what's going on back on our home planet. Rodas is finding hope in what Random did. If I brought his head to the feet of Kalor Maloso then I can use his death to eventually take over the Crimson Empire and Rodas… and little by little, the universe will be mine!'

Anji looked anxiously over her shoulder.

'Quick!'

Jake plopped out of the tree and fell sharply onto his knee. He winced in pain as his kneecap cracked on the concrete pavement. Random helped him up to his feet almost instantaneously.

'You always knew how to make an entrance,' she chuckled.

'Where to now, my friends?' Random chirped.

The trio hatched their great plan as soon as Jason had left that evening for his romantic encounter with Miss Carter.

'Well, I predict that we have at least several hours before Jason gets back, so let's give you the grand tour,' Anji smiled.

Some of her old adventurous spirit had been stirred after their encounter with the police earlier so now she couldn't contain it. The thrill of sneaking out reminded her of the same rush she used to get when she stole from local newsagents. But she knew she'd never go back to her old life of crime. Sneaking out when grounded with her new alien friend would more than do for now.

They spent the next several hours visiting every tourist attraction Anji and Jake could think of. The Natural History Museum, the Science Museum, the British Museum and the Victoria and Albert Museum were all scrutinized with keen wonder by Random, who on the red bus away from Kensington Palace proclaimed that the Science Museum had been his favourite, especially the space section. He was particularly pleased that the trio were at one with a sea of ordinary people and no-one appeared to have even starred at them for more than three seconds!

The youngsters then embarked on Embankment, taking Random along the River Thames so he could observe the Houses of Parliament, the London Eye, Madame Tussauds and the Tower of London.

As the night drew in and the sun set on a wonderful day, Jake suggested that they walk around the Mall, down to Buckingham Palace and then finish their tour along the shops of Regent Street.

Before long, midnight was fast approaching and Anji had suggested that they get home before Jason arrived back. Tired and exhausted after their busy day, they arrived back at the children's home and with Random's superior strength coming in handy, were both carried to their beds by their new friend.

With a smile and a wave, he bid them good night, and retired to his new room.

After a few minutes of tossing and turning, Random snuggled cosily into his new blankets and fell into a deep, sweet sleep.

For the first day in his life, there had been no bloodshed. No horror.

Just fun.

It was the best day of his life.

VIII

Random was awoken sharply by a rasping knock at the door. He rubbed his eyes and searched his new room for the time. 08:53.

He didn't know whether 08:53 was early or late, but for a Sunday, the seventh and last day of the week on the Earth, it felt far too early to be woken up!

'Come in.'

Jason walked through the doorway, struggling with a tray of food for the new child in care.

'Here we are. I wasn't sure what you liked so I thought I'd make you scrambled egg on toast along with a glass of orange juice.'

Random sat up in his new bed.

'Thanks, I've only ever had toast before. Where do eggs come from?'

Jason was taken aback by the question.

'Well…these eggs come from chickens.'

'Oh right, okay,' said Random. 'And the orange juice?'

Jason furrowed his brow. Was this kid taking the mickey?

'From oranges.'

'But I thought orange was a colour?'

'It is,' Jason replied.

'Then where did these oranges get their name from then?'

'From the colour.'

'Oh,' said Random puzzled, as he devoured a slice of toast. 'How odd.'

'I don't want to sound rude but have you ever been to school?'

'What's school?'

Jason let out a nervous laugh.

'Okay, that answers that question then. But how come you have learned to talk? And spell? And write?'

'By listening to others.' A fleck of scrambled egg clung onto the corner of Random's mouth like an unsightly zit.

'If only my schooling had been that simple. Speaking of which, did I tell you that I enrolled you in the same class as Jake and Anji. I presume you're the same age as them?'

'Yes, I presume so too,' lied Random.

'And no, you didn't tell me that you'd enrolled me at school.' Random's blood ran a little cold.

'Are you okay?' asked Jason.

'Yeah...just...nervous, I guess.'

Jason smiled.

'You'll be fine. If you need anything at all then I'll be downstairs. I'll introduce you to the other kids later on.'

He left and closed the door after him.

Random's appetite had completely gone.

'School!'

'It's worse than prison,' said Jake.

'Jake. It's not that bad,' Anji reassured. 'Plus, you've never been to prison.'

'How do you know? I could have a really dodgy past?'

'Guys, please. You're not helping,' Random was rocking back and forth.

'This is ridiculous. I've taken on an entire army...TWO...to be precise. Spoken back to a cruel emperor and outrun those who want to kill me. I've piloted a spaceship to another world and yet I'm frightened of going to school!'

'You'll be fantastic!'

'But I'm so...thick! Your friend just had to tell me where the name of one of your fruits comes from?'

'Which one?' asked Jake.

'Oranges.'

'Where does it come from then?'

'The colour.'

'Oh...I never knew that. You see, you're already more intelligent than me. And you've never been to school.'

'Doesn't say much for your education system then!' smiled Random.

'Hey!'

'He's got a point,' laughed Anji. 'Seriously Random, you'll be fantastic. I promise you.'

Random got up and walked over to Anji's computer.

'Perhaps I should give myself a head start.'

'What do you mean?' asked Anji.

'Remember that technology section in the Science Museum we went to yesterday? They mentioned something called "the internet."'

Random pulled the desk chair away and looked for the power button.

'If my memory serves me correct, and my memory is flawless, I should be able to use your computer to learn everything I need to know.'

'Pfft. That'll take you ages,' dismissed Jake.

'No, it won't,' smiled Random.

With lightning speed, he shot through the complete history of everything, including: the origins of man, the scientific theories that had shaped the world to its modern formation, the very basis of humanity and mathematical equations. It was all at his disposal.

You name it, he read it. He even found time to memorise the starting line-ups for the 1985 FA Cup final.

He read and assimilated it into his mind and in just under four minutes every minute detail was now stored in his incredible brain.

'Finished!'

With glee, he looked away from the monitor and stared at his watching friends. Their expressions bore a look of utter astonishment not too dissimilar from the one they wore when they witnessed the Venus II crash land just two days earlier.

'Wow…what level do you read at?' asked Anji.

'Supersonic level,' he gleamed back.

Suddenly, he noticed a strange burning sensation coming from under his nose. Looking down, the keyboard lay simmering in smoke.

Random turned to Anji.

'Sorry.'

'It doesn't matter,' said Jake, tearing away to his bedroom, 'let's see how fast you can do my homework!'

*

James Butcher awoke with a murmur next to a familiar looking pond. Rubbing his head, he groggily got to his feet and stared all around him. Had what he seen really happened?

It all seemed so real to him; the man made of sand, the spaceship, the polite robot. Where had they all gone? Were they all just figments of his

imagination? He had too many questions to ask

and no one around to answer them since he stood alone in the vibrant woodland.

'What a dream!' he sighed as he made for the woods edge.

He had no concept that he had been missing for a day. It felt like only a few minutes had passed since he had

gone...wherever he had gone. Only it wasn't.

In the far distance, he could hear the sound of footsteps in the undergrowth. A moment later, he picked up the sound of dogs barking, their strained tones coming ever closer.

'Hello? Miss Carter?'

James walked towards the noises and closer to safety. As he did, he could feel invisible eyes burning on the back of his neck.

He didn't feel like he really was all alone.

*

Safe within the bowels of the Venus II, Skateboard watched on helplessly as the last possible comrade at his side walked off to safety.

He would only hope that the memory blocker he had been forced to impose on the young boy would, as he had instructed, stop working after twelve hours.

That should give him enough time to find Sir and notify him of the situation.

'Don't you dare underestimate my intelligence again, you worthless piece of junk,' the Sandman was resting on the pilot's seat, his arm dribbling away.

'You've forsaken me before and it won't happen again. Will it?'

'No.. Sir,' Skateboard conceded. His circuitry was wired up to short circuit if he was disobedient again. He had to do this; the Sandman ordered it. He didn't want his sand getting into his motherboard and corrupting it. That could kill him. He was truly the servant now to an unwanted master.

'Keep tracking the boy. He'll lead me to Random and my future glory!'

Skateboard sighed and slugged off to the control unit.

Silently, the Venus II left the woods and returned to the city.

IX

'Right class, settle down now. Lucy! Sit down will you!'

Lucy Paxman couldn't stop looking at the new boy in class. When she clasped eyes on him, time seemed to stop. Everything else just seemed to melt away. She had never seen anyone as beautiful as the handsome, purple boy in front of her. Mrs Henderson snapped her out of her trance.

'Sorry, Miss,' Lucy blushed as she rushed to her chair.

'I think you're in there, mate!' nudged Jake.

Random knew about the concept of attraction. But it did nothing for him. Love was not something he was interested in right now, especially as he was doing his best to blend in with his peers, which was rather difficult when his skin was as purple as an embarrassed beetroot.

Noisily, the students scrapped their chairs against the cold floor of the classroom and fell silent.

'Thank you. Now then, we have a new pupil here at St Thomas. Would you like to introduce yourself, Andrew?'

Random gulped.

'Yes, sure.'

He pushed himself away from the wooden desk and walked to the front of the class.

Feeling the gaze of dozens of his new classmates on his back, he began to blush.

'Now, we normally play a game with our new students,' said Mrs Henderson, her straight brown locks flowing down her pleasant, smiling face.

148

'We call it high five. It's a technique that we use to get to know one another. You can choose any student at random. Is that okay?'

'Of course,' smiled Random.

'Has anybody got a question for Andrew?'

A sea of hands shot into the air. Everyone put their hands up, except Anji, who looked on with a mixture of worry and amusement.

'Blimey, there are quite a few of you. Right fire away,' said Mrs Henderson.

'Before we start, how many of you are only putting your hands up because you'd like to know if I'm an alien or not?'

The children shot sheepish looks at one another. A murmur gathered like a fog around the classroom.

'Or about the fact that I'm purple skinned?'

The same uncomfortable air hung all around.

'Well, I'll save you the time. No, I'm not an alien. And my skin colour is due to an unfortunate birthmark. Does that answer your questions?'

Two-thirds of the audience brought their arms neatly down by their sides again.

Lucy left her arm up.

'Are you purple all over?' she squeaked, playing with her hair as she spoke.

'That'll be enough of that!' said Mrs Henderson.

Random blushed. He'd have to watch out for that one!

Random survived an otherwise benign scrutiny of his character. Cautiously answering every question with the skill of a politician, he circumvented those who queried his past.

As before, it was only a matter of leaving some of the details out. No lies were told, just a manipulation of the truth.

His first lesson of the day was Maths and it was the first time that he had been separated by Jake and Anji.

The first thing that Random had received when he arrived at the school was his timetable. He was rather shocked to learn that he was only in one class with Anji, which was Art, and two with Jake, which were Home Economics and English.

As he took his place in the old Maths room, he sighed.

He'd learnt every single mathematical equation inside out on his internet search just a couple of days previously.

He now realised that blending in wasn't going to be the hardest part of his day. It was going to be staying awake!

Random sat alone at the front of the classroom. He had suffered nothing but funny looks from the students at St Thomas all morning. He couldn't work out whether they were frightened of him or whether they were simply trying to work him out, but he didn't appreciate the attention. Especially from Lucy Paxman!

'Is anyone sitting here?'

Random looked up. It was her.

'Unfortunately not.'

'Cheeky!' Lucy laughed. 'Come on, scooch up!'

Random pulled his chair further over to the left-hand side of the desk and allowed Lucy next to him.

'I'm Lucy by the way.' She held out her hand.

'Hi Lucy,' Random deployed his unusual method of shaking hands again.

'You're a funny one aren't you! And cute too.'

Cute! Oh dear...

Random was starting to feel a little awkward.

'Do you have a girlfriend?'

'No.'

'Do you want a girlfriend?'

'Not right now, thanks.'

Lucy smiled. 'Playing hard to get, are we?'

'Yes,' said Random curtly.

'Well, I love a challenge me. I always get my way eventually.'

Lucy smiled again. Random could not ignore her pretty features: Milky skin, blonde hair in bunches and a smile that could open the lock to the Headmaster's drinks cabinet.

'I'm sure,' Random retorted. Slowly, he softened. 'Look I think you're a very attractive girl, but to tell you the truth I'm only interested in friendship for now.'

Lucy's smile wavered a little.

'I see.'

He held his hand out again and shook her hand in the conventional human way for a change.

'It's a pleasure to meet you, Lucy,' he smiled.

Lucy went red. She had only just clapped eyes on this stranger an hour earlier but already she was smitten. His brown hair was thick and wavy; his eyes a shade of bluey/red she had never, ever seen before. She'd dated most of the boys in her year but only because she was bored.

This boy was a challenge; a challenge she was willing to accept.

Each lesson, or period as the children called it, which confused Random beyond words, lasted an hour.

After forty-seven minutes into his first experience of English schooling, he finally succumbed to the descending wave of sleep that had been brought about by the tedium of fractions.

'A late night, was it, Andrew?' snapped Mr Johnson.

Random snorted as he stirred.

'Sorry?'

'Well, I hope it was something important that means you're missing out on my lesson!'

Random looked at his tormentor. Mr Johnson was in his mid-fifties, balding and stood diminutively against the giant white board. In his thirty years as a secondary school teacher, he had built a reputation as a stern teacher; cruel, calculated and unforgiving. Math suited him down to a tee.

If he caught a student not paying attention, he had a technique to show them up and teach them a lesson in concentration and appreciation of his art.

'Stand up, will you?'

Random did as he was told.

'Come over here.'

Random obeyed.

'If you're such an expert at fractions then I want you to finish the exercises on this board with no mistakes. If you do make a mistake, then it's lunchtime detention for you. Do you understand?'

'I don't think I can,' replied Random.

'Why not?'

'Well, you've managed to rub most of the fractions off with your hand.'

Mr Johnson froze. His class began to chuckle softly.

He looked down to the flat edge of his left hand. An inky blur of what was once a taxing sequence of equations stained his skin.

A vein began to throb visibly under his ear. Quickly, he wrote the equations up again.

'Right, think you're so smart, do you? Try these ones for size!' Mr Johnson barked, spittle falling from his mouth like a dog.

Lucy's mouth dropped. She had never seen someone take Mr Johnson on like this before. For years, Mr Johnson had maintained the title of 'Scariest Teacher in the Whole School.'

His temperament and no-nonsense approach were the stuff of legend. Stories of his public dressing-down to crying children gained mythical status and the surrounding primary schools were full of kids who had heard everything about him.

By the time they grew older and joined St Thomas, they all preyed that they would never be so unlucky as to have him as a teacher. Yet here he was, taken to task by a new boy!

'Fine.'

With lightning quick movements, he snatched the pen out of Mr Johnson's clammy hand and instantly proceeded to complete the series of fractions and equations with the ease of a Maths professor.

The class looked on in utter surprise.

In just eight seconds, Random had completed the complex sequence of equations. He lent up against the white board and crossed his arms in cocky defiance.

'By the way, you'll notice that with question eleven I made an amendment. Your question was flawed. In order to get to the answer, you wanted, I had to carry the three and that was impossible with the equation you'd drawn up.'

Mr Johnson looked at him like an angry fish. His mouth dropped to the floor whilst his eyes bulged. He had been shown up. For the first time in his life, a young student had beaten him at his own game.

'Was there anything else?' Random grinned as he made his way back to his desk. The classroom erupted in a chorus of cheers and applause.

Random caught Lucy's gaze as he sat down.

So, this is what real love feels like, she thought.

*

'What do you mean there is nothing you can do!'

Mr Johnson slammed his fist onto the headmaster's desk. Mrs Anderson, who had presided over the school for forty years, sat defiantly behind her desk.

'The little swine humiliated me! Me! I mean, come on.'

He slumped into the chair next to Random, who was trying to be as quietly smug as possible.

'In what way did you humiliate Mr Johnson?' the headmaster enquired.

'I completed his sums on the board just as he asked,' said Random.

'Is this what happened?'

Mr Johnson's veins were throbbing like mad under his thin skin.

'Yes, but...' he fiddled with the thin tufts of hair twirling on his flat head, 'it was the manner in which he conducted himself. He was all, "oh, I had to carry the three because you're such an incompetent man that you had to write all the equations back up on the board as you keep rubbing it off". I can't be expected to do anything right, nowadays, can I!'

Mrs Anderson raised her hand in an attempt to sooth the flustered Maths teacher.

'Now, Charles, I have to stop you there. I don't think the boy needs to hear you go any further. I suggest you go back to your classroom and relax. You do have a free period, after all.'

Mr Johnson sighed and bowed his head in defeat. 'Very well.' His sweaty palms left a mark on the table as he left the room, glaring at Random as he departed.

'Are they all like this?' Random enquired. 'I mean, this is my first lesson here at this school and I'm already in the headmaster's office. If this is what school is like then how will I ever learn anything?'

Mrs Anderson smiled. 'Don't you worry about old Mr Johnson. He has had a rough time of late and judging by the speed and accuracy of your sums on the whiteboard, I'd say that ten minutes out of your time in the classroom will not harm your learning here at St Thomas.'

Random nodded in agreement.

'Apart from all of that, how are you settling in?' asked Mrs Anderson.

'I've not really had a chance to get my feet under the desk yet. They keep changing with every lesson. I don't think I have my own desk, do I?'

The Headmaster shook her head slightly, trying to displace the rather complex response.

'Anyway, if you need anything, my door is always open.'

Random was muddled by this. He remembered distinctively that the door was firmly closed when Mr Johnson had marched him over to her office. Believing this to be a one-off and not just a turn of phrase, he happily got up from his chair and left. He dug into his inside pocket and fished around for his timetable.

'PE. Whatever that is. Oh joy!'

In a lifetime of uncertainty, at least Random had settled upon one conclusion.

Student life sure was confusing!

X

'How is it going, Andrew?'

Random recognised the all too flippant tones of Jake like he had known him all his life.

The Rodasian groaned into his hands.

'This isn't going very well?'

'What's wrong?' asked Anji. The pair looked down at their purple friend, who was lying prostrate on one of the few picnic benches that scattered the lively playground.

'Being a student is the worst. I could safely say that I'd prefer to be chased by a knife wielding Kalor Maloso down a dark alley than come here again.'

'Let me guess, culture shock?' enquired Jake.

'Do you know how many times I have been asked if I am an alien? Actually, I'll tell you; 37 times. In the first hour I sent one teacher suffering from a mid-life crisis into meltdown, gained a stalker and set fire to the frog we were dissecting in Biology.

'How on earth....?' Jake didn't have time to finish his question.

'AND the teacher...and the desk...in the end I got sent back to the classroom and had to read a pamphlet someone had left lying around called,

"Fire! The do's and do nots of fire safety." It was adorned by a
crude illustration of a character called Fiona the Firefly.'

'Ah yes, we had the local fire services come over the other week
and give us a talk,' said Anji.

The teacher compared me to a student he had called Simon
Dudley.

'Oh, yes! I used to like him. Whatever happened to him?'
wondered Jake.

'He set fire to the Headmaster's cat,' replied Anji.

'Ah.'

Random groaned again and rolled onto his side.

Anji jabbed Random's arm. 'Well, at least PE must have been
fun.'

He peeked through his purple digits, as if to hide himself from a
waking nightmare.

'Fun? FUN!'

'I'll take that as a no, then.' Anji's smile wavered.

'I walked to the gym and was told that there were no new kits
available. So, whilst the school was waiting on new kits to arrive, I
would have to wear lost property. Have you ever worn lost
property clothes before? It stank! The top I wore was far too small
and looked like a boob tube!

The underarms stank worse than a planet of farts. The less said
about the shorts the better.

Despite being far too big, I somehow managed to tie them
around my waist, but I looked like I was wearing a kilt! The
stench meant that during Rugby practice nobody dared mark me
in case the biological warfare emitting from my person was
contagious. One boy wretched in his own mouth and was sick
when he was tackled.'

Jake pointed his finger in the air to make an injunction.

'And what's more.'

He slowly lowered it again.

'When the ball - and let me tell you if that is what a ball looks
like on this planet then the Earth is a rhombus – came to me and I
was encouraged to kick it, I pelted it with such force that it bent
the post all the way back, knocked out the teaching assistant and
the "ball" kept going.'

'Well,' Anji was clutching at straws. 'Where did the ball go?'

'Who knows...Kent, probably!' replied Random curtly.

'Who's the stalker?' asked Jake, although he dare enquire at this point.

'Over there.'

Random pointed to the other side of the table, which was a mere three feet away. There sat Lucy, waving and blushing like the adoring fan she was.

Random waved meekly back, whilst Anji did her best to stifle a laugh.

'It's no laughing matter!' cried Random. 'Do you know what this means? It means that I've done exactly what I didn't want to do. I've drawn attention to myself.'

Anji nodded. 'This hasn't gone to plan, has it?'

'Not by any stretch of the imagination,' Random confirmed.

Unbeknownst to the trio, a figure was walking up from behind, his pace gathering as he got closer. Random lay on his back and shielded the sun from his eyes. Soon afterwards, a shadow loomed over him, blotting the warm ray out completely.

'James!' cried Jake.

Random opened his eyes and looked up to find the bewildered face of a teenage boy towering above him.

He licked his lips, his mouth dry and cracked.

'Are you the one who they found in the woods?'

Random nodded enthusiastically. If James were here, maybe Skateboard and the Venus II were close by also.

'How did you get back here?' asked Anji.

James ignored her question and continued to stare at Random and Random alone.

'I think we need to have a chat.'

Jake, Anji and Random led James under the shelter of a tree into a more secluded area of the playing field. Their party had almost been joined by a fifth member, but Lucy was warded off by Random, who suggested to his "fan" that she might want to spend time with Jake instead. She shook her head, disgusted and left them alone, leaving Jake's ego severely dented.

Random sat James down and sat cross legged next to him.

'Tell me everything,' he cooed, his voice quiet, almost like a whisper.

'I saw the ship crash land before me.'

'We didn't see anyone at the pond, where were you?' said Jake. Suddenly, the boy remembered the conversation he had with Anji moments before the crash. 'Hang on a minute, what did you hear?'

'I wasn't prying or anything, honest,' said James. He had always been a little afraid of Jake. Not that the teenager was a bully, but James had been the unfortunate recipient of a cruel lunchroom prank that Jake had played. James was known throughout the year as the "swot", the one whose homework was in on time, all the time, and the first to put his hand up when answering a question in class.

Jake, feeling slighted by the adoration James deservedly received from his teachers, decided to spike his ham and cucumber sandwich with cheese. A fairly innocuous act, many would think, but not when the person being fooled was lactose intolerant.

To make matters worse, Jake had chosen the one day in the week, nay the entire school year, that James had forgotten his epi-pen.

Two days in hospital and a month's worth of detentions later, James and Jake were hardly what you would call 'friends.'

'I didn't hear anything, honest!' screamed James, afraid that his chief tormentor would do something terrible to him again. 'I couldn't hear a thing...apart from the engine roar that is. I thought I had wandered onto a film set! So, while it was smoky and nobody could see me, I wandered on board. Then I saw both you and your purple friend here follow me in. I didn't want to reveal myself since, well; we aren't particularly friends, are we?'

Jake turned his head, confirming James' suspicions.

'Anyway, all of sudden, you lot were gone and I was left by myself. The ship was rocking and I was lost in what looked like the engine bay. By the time I came back to the entrance, it was closed and I found this talking metal robot.

'Skateboard!' squealed Random. 'Is he okay?'

'I think so. It all seemed such a blur. I was convinced, in fact, I was absolutely 100% certain

that I was on a film set. It all looked so convincing. Like something out of *Star Wars* or *Doctor Who*. I wanted to meet the stars.'

'That's all very well, but how did you get back here, James?'
asked Anji.

James searched his memory.

'Never mind that!' interrupted Random. 'Where is Skateboard
now?' Now he thought of it, the past two days had been almost
unbearable for Random. He was a stranger in a strange land, a
misfit of the stars grounded to an alien plain that he didn't belong
to. Skateboard was his constant. He had escaped Rodas with him.
And then he was lost. Abandoned almost. Knowing that
Skateboard was nearby filled Random's heart with pure
unadulterated joy.

'I'm not sure. I'm sorry.'

Random's heart ceased to flutter and he sagged despondently.

'You're alien, aren't you? None of it was make-believe, was it?'
James enquired.

Random, fed up with the lies he had been telling all day,
nodded his head.

'Yes, but you can't tell anyone, James. Not a word. We need to
keep it between us. Do you understand?' Anji clasped James' arm,
hoping for his co-operation.

'I do, although I don't understand any of this and I definitely do
not want to be part of it.'

'I understand,' said Anji. 'Do you know what happened next?'

'I don't really know. It's really foggy. I remember talking to the
robot and then...there was someone else there.'

Random looked up, his face a picture of concern.

'Who was it?' asked Jake.

'I don't know. He looked injured. Badly injured in fact and from
what I remember, I don't think he was all there.'

Random scrambled to James's side and grabbed hold of James
desperately, his hands like pincers.

'What do you mean, "I don't think he was all there?"'

James was taken aback by Random's actions. He tried to speak
but he could see the wild panic in Random's eyes. The red and
blue iris danced in a pool of fear.

'I...I...I don't know.'

'Try, for deqes sake!' swore Random.

'Random take it easy,' said Anji. Both she and Jake's hearts were pounding. Something had made Random angry and frightened it seemed.

'He kept...leaking,'

'Leaking...' Random repeated, tiny beads of sweat emitting from the pores on his brow.

'Yeah, he was just...dripping away; flaking like sand in an egg timer.'

'Sand...' repeated Jake.

'Yes...' said James. 'That's it. Now I remember...'

Random, Anji and Jake dared not breathe.

'It was a man made of sand...'

*

Skateboard felt different. It was a feeling he hadn't felt before, like there was a restriction to certain file paths in his circuits. A strange air of obedience filled his metal mind. Never in his lifetime, since his motherboard was first activated, had he felt more peculiar.

Every AI robot constructed in the cybernetics division of the Sapphire Regime was implemented with a compliancy chip. Its job was to keep the AI in line with its master and maintain quality standards when sold to its customers.

Somehow, on the day that Skateboard was assembled, his compliancy chip was not so much corrupted, but something had slipped in his programming.

Under normal circumstances, at the quality check, this would have been highlighted by the final diagnostics run by the technicians at the plant.

But for Skateboard, he was allowed to leave the production line and go out into the world of chaos for active service; and that world of chaos was Rodas.

His creators had failed to discover that what they had done was created an AI with free will.

Skateboard's recent memories faded in and out of his metal head.

'Didn't you know that you had the greatest gift anyone in the universe can be given? How stupid you must have been to never know.'

There it was; that maniacal voice of the Sandman coursing through his mind. How could his worst enemy have known something he had failed to discover about his own being before he had?

'What are you doing...inside my thought patterns?'

'You don't remember? I infiltrated you. I couldn't have you running off again. You're far too important to me for that; you and that boy.'

'I told you I would comply.' Skateboard was having trouble speaking. His could feel parts of him corrupting.

'Better to be safe than sorry. What do you do when your pet runs away? Make sure you keep them on a lead at all times.'

It was impossible for a robot to feel pain, but Skateboard was starting to feel shooting sparks of torment around his motherboard.

'But...my security protocols.'

'Bypassed. After all, it only took a grain of sand to get in. Damn stuff gets everywhere. Wouldn't you agree?'

Skateboard screamed in agony. His entire body started convulsing as tiny blue charges imploded under his chassis.

'Please. Get out of me.' The robot started to yelp. His body was being violated and there was nothing he could do to stop it.

To escape such a degrading experience, he would have to do the one thing he despised more than anything else. He would have to beg.

'Please...please, you're torturing me!'

'I can see all of you. This is...incredible!' The Sandman chuckled.

'W-w-what...are you...going to...do to me?'

'I can be in two places at once. As my physical form dwindles, I can inhabit yours. You're right, you know? There's no way that I can take on Random alone. But now, there are two of us.'

Skateboard delved hard in his circuitry, trying to fight the overwhelming might of the Sandman.

'What are you doing?'

The Sandman could feel his victim reaching for something deep down in his being, something an AI must only turn to in emergencies such as this.

'No! You wouldn't dare!'

'I would; I would do anything to stop you from hurting these people!'

The Sandman erupted into a guttural laughter.

'If you self-destructed, you'd blow up this ship. You'd strand your friend on this primitive planet. You'd condemn him to a life trapped here. Actually, it isn't such a bad idea.'

Skateboard strained with what was left of his willpower.

'What?'

'Well, I'll be alright; I'll just be blown into atoms. Don't worry, I can rebuild again. Maybe I could inhabit humans too? Shame I hadn't thought of that before, I'd have taken over that boy...oh, wait a minute. That's right...I already have...'

The boy! How could he?

'You are a sick man, Sandman,' he struggled.

'Oh, hadn't you noticed,' the Sandman smiled. His essence burrowed deeper into the core of Skateboard's motherboard. All his circuits were corrupting now. The fight was nearly over.

Try as he might, Skateboard just couldn't do it. His will was snapped, encompassed by evil. His

self-destruct switch unreachable by sheer force of

will, Skateboard succumbed to the inevitable.

And then, there was darkness.

*

In an instant, James's eyes snapped shut and his head bowed to the ground. Random shook the boy vigorously.

'James...James, come on wake up!'

'What happened?' asked Anji.

'It looks like someone's just shut him off,' said Jake.

'Oh no! Jake's right, I think they have,' concluded Random.

'How?' asked Jake.

'If James has been in contact with the Sandman...' Random's sentence tailed off, allowing his brain to catch up with his mouth.

'...then there is the slightest possibility that he has been infiltrated by him.'

'Sounds disgusting,' said Anji.

'This really isn't a laughing matter. Think about it. What do you always bring back from the beach with you?'

'Sea shells?'

'Try again. I'll give you a clue; flakes of grains stuck in the gaps between your toes.'

'Sand!' exclaimed Anji. 'It always gets stuck to your body.'

'Precisely. You remember what he said. If the Sandman really is falling apart, then it would be easier to get bits of the grains that make up his body on your person. The Sandman is a powerful being. He was an experiment to turn a normal man into an ultimate warrior, however, this experiment went wrong. He has got the capability to do anything.'

'Even control a person,' Jake said seriously.

In a flash, James lifted his head and his eyes snapped open. Anji and Jake jumped but Random was unmoved. The boy cracked his right fist square into the jaw of the Rodasian and sent Random tumbling backwards.

Anji screamed as James leapt onto Random's reeling body and clasped his hands around his neck.

'Come on!' Jake pulled Anji. The teenagers tried with all their might to pull James' possessed weight off Random.

The alien started choking, his windpipe crushed from the weight of the boy that loomed over him.

As he started blacking out, Random looked up at his attacker and stared into his eyes.

They were a deep tone of beige. James was no longer a slightly annoying earthling from the suburbs of London. He was the Sandman.

XI

It took a herculean effort, even for someone with the might that Random possessed. The alien stopped grappling at James' strangling hands and concentrated on his arms instead.

He blinked through the pain barrier and saw his two companions grappling at the boy but to no avail. For all the hitting, slapping, punching and scratching, both were ineffective.

'I'm sorry to do this James,' choked Random. With one swift movement he karate chopped James' left arm. The limb bent to a peculiar angle and a sickening crack emitted from within. James showed no pain; no expression of anguish cracked on his emotionless face.

Random emerged from underneath and flipped James onto his back, pinning his arms down by his side and head butting his attacker unconscious, or so he thought.
'Rope...now!' he barked; his vocal cords constricted by the pressure of his almost collapsed wind pipe.

Jake and Anji were shocked by what they had just seen, but they hurried to their feet and made off for the playground.

A twisted smile emerged on the bloodied lips of Random's attacker.

'You think violence will stop me?' tutted "James".

'Why don't you come out here and face me properly, you coward!' screamed Random. Although they were well covered by the woodland and the schoolchildren were quite a distance away from the fight, Random was still cautious of being discovered but his emotions were starting to get the better of him.

'Oh...just you wait.' James tones were full of malice.

'Leave him alone! I don't want to hurt him. He hasn't done anything wrong.' Random picked "James" up by the scruff of his shirt. 'You leave his body and I'll come quietly.'

'You want to protect the innocent, do you?' James was starting to sound more and more like the Sandman by the second. He started laughing again.

'Oh Random, you can keep punching me until this body I have inhabited becomes nothing more than a bloodied pulp, but you won't will you? That is where people like you and me differ. I'll do anything to obtain my goal. I would burn down this city and all its pitiful inhabitants if it meant my inner peace and freedom, but you? You favour diplomacy. It'll get you nowhere.'

'What do you mean?' said Random.

'We are far beyond negotiation. You betrayed me once. I can never let that go. I will NEVER let you go. You left me on that planet of pain and suffering but you couldn't escape me. You'll never escape me. I will not rest until you are crushed into dust. Let's see how you like it.'

"James" smiled again. Malevolence oozed from his lips. Random had heard enough. He dropped his attacker to the ground and did nothing as the Sandman began to chuckle to himself.

As Jake and Anji raced back toward the woodland, accompanied with rope procured from the gym cupboard, a laugh, so dark and evil the clouds seemed to thicken above them, echoed in the air.

Anji glanced over to her friend as her breathing grew heavier. Both of them wore a look of severe concern.

'Anj...' Jake wheezed. 'What are we going to do?'

*

The Sandman had propped himself up in the pilot's chair in the Venus II. With his eyes closed, he could easily have been mistaken for being asleep by a passer-by, but a trance state seemed to pass over his failing body.

Skateboard whirred into the cockpit and took up residency next to his master.

The Sandman awoke, almost as though he could feel his metal subject's presence.

'Contact has been made.'
'I know; I felt it, my master.' Skateboard's tones were different now that he had given in to the Sandman's will. They were darker, calmer than before and more in tune with his master's own voice.

The Sandman tried to get up but staggered against the instrument panel. As he stuck his hand out to steady himself, more grains of sand tumbled to the floor.

'Master, you are weak. You should rest. You cannot sustain three bodies at once, especially in your state.'

'I know,' uttered the Sandman. He felt weary.

'I need...rejuvenation. Skateboard, suggestions?'
Skateboard's circuits whirred.

'There does not appear to be any organic matter in the area that will replenish your physical form. You need to be reconfigured as an entire entity.'

'I know, but I can't do that, can I? Half of me is back on Rodas.'

He fell back into the chair, panting from exhaustion.

'I'm being tortured across star systems, Skateboard. Stretched among the stars. I feel...so much pain; pain that I cannot describe.' He hesitated. 'I dare not describe.'

Skateboard pondered on his new master's words.

'A suggestion, master; inhabit yourself within the ship fully?'

'I can't. I'd burn up. In all honesty, I'm on fire right now. Aflame in four different places at once. Your AI system is easy to corrupt, even for a simple solider like me. But a whole ship?' he shook his head. 'It would kill me.'

'Another suggestion, master; on this planet, there is a similar substance to that in which your physical form was mutated. It will not yield your pain but it will restore your physical form temporarily. However, you'd have to act quickly.'

'Skateboard?' the Sandman whispered. 'Is there any way in which I can be one again?'

'None, I'm afraid, master.'

The Sandman let out a little yelp.

'Is that a death sentence you've just given me?'

'Yes,' said Skateboard, coldly.

Blobs of water droplets started leaking out of the corners of the Sandman's eyes, collating in clumps of sand on his cheeks.

'I don't fear it. A soldier never fears death. I'll embrace it when it comes'. He sniffed. 'If it is death that beckons me near, then I am taking that boy to hell with me. I want to make him watch how much it burns. The horror of it all. In his final seconds...then he'll understand.'

With renewed vigour, the Sandman limped out of the chair.

'Find me a new body. Now!'

It was the smile that perturbed Anji the most. Not the fact that a boy from her year was acting as an unwilling and unknowing host for an alien body, but horrific formation of his lips sprouting from the gag that the trio had improvised out of Jake's school tie.

'How did this happen?'

Random sat on the floor and stared into nothingness.

'The Sandman has become desperate. He knows he cannot face me in his current state. It sounds like the majority of him is still back home.'

'But if he is made of sand then how can he control and feel?' Jake asked.

'Good question,' said Anji.

'The molecules that made up his humanoid body were corrupted but it doesn't mean he still can't feel. Or think. But imagine this. You're pulled between here, there, everywhere. Literally! It's bad enough if you pull a muscle. Imagine being stretched across planets.'

'I'd rather not,' said Jake. 'What's the plan?'

Random looked at his friend. In the same moment, the lunch bell rang.

'Well, we can't go back to our classes, not now, 'said Anji.

'We'll be done for truanting! We are in enough trouble with Jason as it is!' pointed out Jake.

'Well, what else do you suggest?'

'No, Jake's right, you two should go back to class.'

Anji and Jake looked at Random in astonishment.

'No, we are not leaving you,' cooed Anji.

'Anji, you are dealing with matters that you can never understand,' Random picked up her hand and held it up to his chest. 'I understand the sentiment but I've got you two in enough trouble as it is and I'd never forgive myself if either of you got hurt.'

'Well, you're stuck with us,' said Jake. He put his hand on Random's shoulder.

'How sentimental,' spat "James" through his gag.

'Shut up, you!' shouted Anji.

Random marched over to the bound body of James, looked him square in the eye and removed the gag.

'You think words will hurt us? No, we'll fight fire with fire. So, wherever you are, whatever you've done to Skateboard, I'm ready for you. You know where I am. You can have me. Meet me here tonight, the real you, I mean, and we'll end this. Bring Skateboard with you'.

'Don't I get to make terms?' choked the Sandman through James' voice.

'You get me…isn't that the best term you can think of?'
Nodding, "James" relented.
'Is there anything else while you're feeling brave?'
'You leave James alone right now. Leave him. Let the seed of evil dissolve and die. You don't need him anymore. Then, and only then, will I agree to meet you.'
"James" emitted another twisted smile.
'Random…tonight you will meet your maker at my hands…and I'll bathe in your blood.'
With a jolt, "James'" head tipped back against the tree he was tied to and he wretched an almost microscopic shard of sand out of his throat. Random traced it with his vision and saw it blow away in the cool breeze.
James coughed as Jake and Anji untied him.
'Welcome back to the land of the living,' smiled Random.
'What has happened…why am I…oh no! My arm! What have you done to my arm!?' James stared in horror at the bone jutting out of his flesh.
'Ah, this might take some explaining!' said Jake.

XII

'Out of my way!'
The Sandman had endured a multitude of horrors in his life. This included the battle of Karebas, being torn away from his family, mutated and ripped physically across galaxies. Now he could add one more horrific experience to his tally – rush hour in London.
Against Skateboard's advice, he decided it was a good idea to walk to the school where his possession of James had been such a success. Despite his frail form and the fact that so many people would see him, he went against the better judgment of his slave and decided to leave the Venus II on foot.
Moments after his essence had left the schoolboy, he started to formulate a plan in his head on how to bring down Random. With the school fifteen miles away from the ship's new hiding place on top of some grand old building called "Buckingham Palace", he managed to slip down the drain pipe and integrate with the

gravel on the path, slithering away from any unwanted attention from the strange looking guards in the tall furry hats.

After slinking away to a quiet side street, he assimilated his coarse skin to pigmentation close to that of a human and even managed to fabricate some clothes. But this left him hollower inside than he had felt in a long time and a piercing cavity opened up in his chest. Weaker than ever, he had to do this alone, without the aid of his ship or his dominated robot.

He also had to build up the willpower and the mental strength to withstand anything that Random was prepared to throw at him. With his face contorted in agony, the Sandman went on. He did his best to brush past the crowds, knowing that it would be easier to inhabit as many people as possible but also mindful that this would destroy him for good.

Stumbling along, weaker than he had thought, he glanced up at a bus stop sign and decided to hail an oncoming big red bus.

'Stop please!'

The driver was too busy chatting to an attractive man and did not see their potential passenger. As the bus sped past, it generated a huge gust of wind, which tore through the Sandman like a knife through hot butter.

Indignantly, and hoping that no one had seen his plight; the Sandman reassembled himself and cursed the human race.

Although his trip was long and arduous, he started to appreciate the human capacity for ignorance. Not one fellow traveller acknowledged his existence. Indeed, not one of the passengers on the Central Line train even talked to one another, let alone smiled! He didn't want to be noticed, so on this occasion he was thankful that he seemed invisible to everyone.

Roughly two miles away from the school, the Sandman collapsed. Again, nobody seemed willing to stop and help him, even though there were dozens of commuters in the same street as he. Panting and sweating profusely, the Sandman look around in desperation. He felt the sweet embrace of death reaching out towards him. Shaking his head, he blinked it away, ignoring such a trivial matter as death. He had to reach the school. He had to kill Random. It was fast becoming the last thing he ever wanted to do.

With a great effort, he staggered to his feet. Limping, he soldiered on for another half a mile.

Right in front of him was a construction site.

Relief began to pour through his coarse veins. Laughing to himself, he passed straight through the eight-foot-tall gates, ignored the safety signs and warnings that this was a hard hat area, and wandered straight underneath the metal girders and machinery.

'Hey! You can't be in here, mate!' bellowed a worker.

'Can't I?'

'Nah, pal.' Another construction worker approached him from the opposite angle. 'We're closing up for the day and you're in a restricted area.'

'I need help,' choked the Sandman.

'Yeah, well come back in eighteen months when the hospital's done, will yer. Now come on, we wanna be getting home now. Ain't you got a family to be getting back to as well?'

The Sandman sized up both men. One was in his early thirty's and well-built for a human. Good soldier material, back home, thought the cornered Rodasian.

The other had a more rotund, squat body shape, his balding grey locks signifying his advancing years.

'No, why, do you?'

The Sandman edged his way closer to a large pile of sand that was left in a huge quantity next to the cement mixer.

'As a matter of fact, yeah,' said the older worker. 'Come on, we can't leave until you have.'

The younger worker butted in. 'Come on, mate. You're trespassing. You don't want us getting the authorities involved, do ya?'

The Sandman felt the rough texture of the sand against the soles of his feet. He smiled manically. He needed to try his might. Why not practice on these two?

'The more the merrier.'

In a blink of an eye, the Sandman disappeared. His form dissipated, much to the astonishment of the workers.

'Steve? What the heck?'

The younger worker gazed in shock at his colleague.

All of a sudden, a shot of sand exploded from the ground and lifted high in the air, towering above its victims.

Both stood petrified at the huge wave of sand that threatened to engulf them.

'Run!' shouted the older worker. Both men accelerated as fast as their legs could carry them but before they could reach the gate, the wave was upon them.

As the older man fell to the floor as the wave came crashing down upon him. The wave seemed to wail like a banshee, shrieking as it engulfed the pair. The last thing the younger man saw wasn't his family like he had hoped on his final day on earth. It was the terrifying image of a man's face in the sand as he and his colleague perished in the tidal wave.

The crash was heard all around. Confused passers-by raced to the site but the tidal wave was gone. All that was left were the corpses of two men, both with sand pouring from their mouths and ears, impossibly drowned on dry land.

XIII

It had been one heck of a day, a heck of a day. Random lay awake on his bed, his focus fighting back any temptation to sleep, but on the Sandman and what was to come. He picked himself out of the comfortable blankets and walked over to the window. He looked up at the silent stars as they glittered in the bleak sky. Sighing to himself, he folded his arms and zoned out.

How do you defeat an enemy who can assemble himself together again? Even if he was falling apart, Random knew that this was a powerful foe that he had to take down, no matter what the cost. But how?

Quietly, he tip-toed across the room and opened the door. Checking that the coast was clear, he slipped across the hallway to Anji's room. Turning the door knob with the subtle nature of a courteous burglar, he was stunned to find that Anji was also standing at her window wide awake.

'Can't sleep?' he whispered.

'Like there's any chance of that,' she replied, imploring him to close the door.

'Listen, Anji, I've been thinking about tonight. I need to leave as soon as possible.. alone.'

'What? You think that you can take him on by yourself?'

'No, it isn't that. I'm endangering you all. He could be out there, right now, watching me; waiting for me to make a move.'

'Waiting for US to make a move,' Anji held Random's hand. It was cold and clammy. She looked into Random's eyes.

'I know it's dangerous, but you shouldn't be fighting him alone.'

'People could get hurt. People have already been hurt!' Random walked over to her desk and sat on the corner, his legs dangling off the floor.

'James will be okay. Besides, it got us out of detention for being late back to class, didn't it?'

'Lies, excuses, what am I turning you into?'

Anji looked down. 'Actually, Random, I think I've always been like this. Ever since my parents died, I've had this...void...this lack of direction. Believe me, I used to be a lot worse than this.'

'No way! I dread to think,' he smiled but it didn't convince Anji that his mood has changed.

'When I downloaded all the information off the internet, I saw the feats that mankind have achieved; the wonders of the world, the love, the compassion. Then I saw the hate and the centuries of conflict. It reminded me so much of

my planet that I couldn't bear to read on. The point is that I know what the human race is

capable of, good and bad. And right now, I don't think that the discovery of two aliens scrapping on your world would do you any good.'

'You're right there,' Anji agreed. 'So...you don't see yourself staying then?'

'No.'

'So, you're going back to Rodas then?'

'Oh no! I want to explore the universe! Take a look at all the stars and the different galaxies. I want to see as many of them as I can.'

'But what about your people?'

Random stuttered. He remembered the refugees that he walked past on his home world. The hopelessness in their eyes, the fear, the pain.

'I will return one day but I'm not ready to be there right now. Although I did make a promise to myself that I will save them, when the time is right.'

'What a burden,' Anji said.

'Yup,' Random agreed. 'It's the reason I'm here. To make things better, even if it means sacrificing myself for the millions back at home. You can't blame me for wanting to have a little bit of fun before then, could you?'

'I guess not,' Anji smiled. 'What time are we heading back to the school?'

'Is there nothing I can do to stop you and Jake coming with me?'

'Nope.'

Random sighed although deep down he was relieved that he wouldn't have to face the Sandman alone. He would never admit it to his friends, but he was scared. Scared of not being able to stop his enemy and scared that he wouldn't be able to save Skateboard. He was also scared in case he managed to lose the Venus II for good.

'Alright, but you two need to do exactly as I say, okay?'

'Gotcha,' Anji felt the thrill of adventure spark inside her. This feeling of the unknown was more exhilarating than any stealing spree...or arson attack on her classmate's gym shorts.

'We leave as soon as possible. Is there a way that we can get a message to Jake without waking Jason?'

'Please, all that assimilation of the internet and you failed to look up texting?' Anji tutted. She produced her phone and started typing away on the touch screen.

'Tell him to meet us in here in five clicks, er, I mean minutes. We need to leave as soon as possible.'

'You've got a plan, then?'

'Yes...well...half a plan.'

Anji frowned. 'Oh, well that's better than having none at all.'

'The Sandman is literally falling apart. If I can keep him occupied, keep him focused on me then I can wear him out. His life force is already ebbing away. Whilst I'm doing that, you need to break into the Venus II. Don't worry, it'll be there and you'll know when.'

'But what about Skateboard?' asked Anji. 'He'll kill us before we even have the chance to get close to him.'

'The Sandman is using mind control on him but as he will be fully distracted by me, it'll mean that his hold over Skateboard will not be as strong.

You need to convince him to help us. I'm sorry if that sounds dangerous but that's how it's got to be, if you are willing to help me. If he doesn't comply, then use this.'

Random handed Anji a magnet, small enough to fit into a small pocket.

'Really? You're serious?'

'Use it if all else fails. It'll scramble his circuits and, in that time, you can regain the Venus. How does that sound?'

'Peachy.'

A third voice entered the bedroom. Jake had been standing there all along, fully dressed and ready to help.

'Remind me to lock that door in future,' joked Anji.

'Oi!' smiled Jake. He put his right hand out in front of him.

'Are you ready to kick some alien ass? No offence Random!'

Random smiled and put his hand on top of Jake's.

'Let's kick it.'

Anji did the same, suggesting that the trio were ready to take on the world.

Their moment of joy was short lived. Random's ultrasensitive hearing picked up on a low hum coming from outside. The hum grew louder and louder until the other two also heard its tone.

'Oh daxque! Get down!'

Random pulled his friends to the ground as a bolt of energy shot through the bedroom window and collided with the wall, exploding in a ball of fire and plaster, waking up the rest of the home with a startle.

Another bolt sizzled into the bedroom, exploding again, this time nearly taking out the entire room behind it. A child screamed in terror.

'Get everyone out!' ordered Random as Jake and Anji ducked their way past more missile fire. Jason came running up the stairs, but he was stopped by another explosion.

'Come on, everyone out.'

Half a dozen screaming and crying children came hurtling down the stairs. Jason made a mental head count so as to not miss anyone.

Miss Carter appeared at the foot of the stairs in her nighty.

'Get them out of the building!' Jason screamed above the sound of destruction. Anji and Jake tore into the hallway, carrying a child each.

'Is that everyone?' screamed Jason.

'Random...where's Random?' shouted Jake.

'Who's Random?' asked Jason. Another shot of fire fizzed past his ear, destroying the top of the stairwell.

'Andrew!' he exclaimed.

He lifted Jake and Anji down onto the lower half of the stairwell, which still survived.

'Jason, come on jump!' implored Anji.

'I need to get Andrew first.'

'No, you need to get out the building, now!' hollered Jake.

The building was on fire. The roof groaned and splintered.

'Get out, quick!'

Jake and Anji's path to get to the front door was clear. Helplessly, they tore themselves away from the stairwell, carrying the two small children in their arms, and fled the burning home.

When they got outside, Miss Carter was gathering the children together, doing her best to console them all. Neighbours had poured out onto the street and were starting to help take the children away to safety.

'Where's Jason?' Miss Carter turned to Anji and shook her violently. 'Where is he?'

A loud crack interrupted her desperate pleas. As they watched on, the roof of the building, aflame with the red-hot flames from the laser fire, caved in and splintered into the top floor.

Miss Carter screamed a scream that turned the air cold.

Random and Jason were still inside.

XIV

Random awoke and shook his head. His last memory was following Jake and Anji out of the bedroom. He lay on the burning ground, his clothes singed from the flames all around him. He looked down at the splintered wood from the beams that had previously held the roof together. He must have been knocked out by the falling shower.

He squeezed himself past the flames that blocked his passage
out of the room. The air felt hotter than he had ever experienced
in his life and it was becoming difficult to breathe. Clouds of black
smoke plumed everywhere. But through the devastation, Random
could make out a body at the top of the stairwell.

He picked himself up, just as he felt the floor give way
underneath him. With a little run up, he vaulted the flamed in the
doorway and made it into the hallway just as what was left of
Anji's room plummeted to the ground floor. With little time to
lose, he brushed the fallen beams that trapped Jason's
unconscious body to one side.

Looking up, he noticed the roof was about to cave in too. With
little room to escape, Random picked Jason up and rushed against
the outer wall of the home, breaking through the bricks and
mortar just as the roof burned into the top floor.

The pair landed in a heap amongst the rose bushes in the
garden. Random checked that Jason was unharmed before
witnessing the children's home collapse in a fireball.

He shook his head in horror and then noticed the sirens of the
emergency services drawing ever closer.

Breaking out of the garden, he blinked his way past the flashing
blue lights and spotted an ambulance close by.

'Oh Andrew, is he okay?' Miss Carter rushed over to him.

'Get a paramedic over here, quick!' screamed Jake as he and Anji
also rushed to their friend's side.

'He's okay, no broken bones, just a bit of smoke inhalation,'
Random reassured them as he handed the unconscious body over
to the paramedics. Miss Carter stayed by his side as they rushed
him into the ambulance, leaving the trio alone.

'Did you get everyone out?'

'Yes thankfully. Why would Sandman do that, Random? I don't
understand. All those innocent children that could have been
severely injured, or worse, killed.' Anji struggled to keep her
shock in check. She shivered as the cold night air hit her.

'It was the Venus that caused that scene. Sandman must have
rigged its laser cannon capability to draw me out.'

He looked ruefully at the rubble on the ground that used to be the care home. Fire crews were doing their best to put out the fireball but it was clear to everyone present that there was nothing they could do to save the building.

'He must be stopped,' said Jake, tears in his eyes, his face smudged with soot and snot.

'Come on then; we haven't got a moment to lose!'

Random tore away from the conversation and started running towards the school. With a big breath, Anji, closely followed by Jake, followed suit as the trio made for their final showdown. They had to get to the school before the Sandman harmed anyone else.

*

The Venus II sailed obliviously through the night sky. Undetected by radar, invisible to the naked eye, its first deed of the night was done.

Skateboard piloted the ship the few miles towards the school which was the agreed rendezvous point where Random would meet his end.

Not knowing the destruction he had just caused, the little AI kept a track of the heat signatures of Random and his two earthling friends on the scanner.

But a feeling started to emerge down in his CPU. A tiny shard of regret trickled in his system. Skateboard felt a twinge of uncertainty. Almost as if there was a light trying to break through the foggy darkness he felt within. He did his best to bury it but then it came back, slightly brighter this time. It was a feeling he hadn't felt in a while that was burrowing to the surface; Remorse.

He kept it hidden, away from his corrupted files, and remained focused on his task.

Like a hawk in the night sky, the Venus II sailed on among the blanket sky and continued to hunt its prey.

*

176

Random's legs burnt as they carried him further and further away from his two companions. With super human speed, he blitzed the pavement, dodged the onrushing traffic, crossed pedestrians with precision and hurtled like a purple blur towards the school.

The roar of the wind soared in his ears as he gained on the school and before long, what would have been a short bus journey for any normal human being, the school was in sight.

He totally forgot about Anji and Jake, who were well and truly eating his dust as they huffed and puffed their little legs along.

Random's entry to the school grounds was hindered by a big metal gate, with a sign adorning its iron poles instructing that TRESPASSERS WILL BE PREOSECUTED. Random ignored the warning completely and shoulder barged his way through the gate, like a hammer through glass.

The gates shattered and splintered into tiny black toothpicks and the sheer force generated by Random's actions scattered the shards of metal into nearby trees and the concrete ground like javelins. But still, Random didn't care.

He came to a stop in the school playground. Panting and sweating, he scanned the area. The playground was calm and still. Random was unnerved. There was a haunting stillness as the shadows of the play equipment loomed against the few lamps that lit up patches of the vicinity.

A cool breeze blew through the swings and set Random on edge. He jumped and let out a sigh of relief when he saw that it was nothing.

'Come out then. I know you're out there so show yourself!'

Random's voice was hoarse from the fumes in the burning home. He could taste the black smoke in his lungs. It burnt, but nothing was going to stop him putting an end to the terror.

All of a sudden, his senses picked up on a trickling sound somewhere behind him. He turned to face the long jump sand pit.

'Of course,' said Random, clenching his fists tightly.

A tidal wave of sand grew in front of him, a full ten feet tall.

Random's mouth fell open, aghast at the vastness of the wall of sand that now stood before him.

Jake and Anji finally made it to the school.

'Anj...I...don't...think I can...'

Jake fell on the floor, his stomach rising and falling quicker than it had ever done before. Anji rested her arms on her knees, drinking in every gulp of air like it was lung nectar.

She peered through the decimated gate and through the sweat that was dripping from her brow, she saw Random and what he was facing.

'Oh no!'

She tore off again, desperate to help her friend. 'Get up Jake! Random needs our help!'

Jake dragged himself up to his feet and saw the wall of sand.

Gulping, his legs tore off to help his friends, totally against the wishes of his brain, which told him to save himself and get away to safety as fast as he can. But then again, Jake knew better than to listen to himself and apart from the very odd exception, never did. And he wasn't about to start now.

'You think you can stop me, boy?' A demonic face began to form in the wall, grinning with murderous menace at his enemy.

'I don't think,' said Random. 'I know.'

'Let's see you try...'

The wave roared. It fizzed and pulsated. Before long, it started rippling and falling from its vertical stance and rushed with ferocity towards Random. The Rodasian stood, fists lifted to his face, ready to defend and most of all, attack.

Anji edged closer and closer to the playground but she watched on helplessly as the wave roared and with brute force, crashed over her friend. The sound of the wave crashing to the ground sent a shockwave that knocked Anji flying, its sheer ferocity like an explosion. The teenage girl opened her eyes and witnessed the sand sprays shoot upwards. Then there was a terrible calm... and Random's body was missing completely.

XV

Out of nowhere, laser bolts fizzed through the air towards Anji's shocked, motionless body.

'Anji! Down!'

Jake pulled her out of the firing line and they rolled down the grassy hill.

There was no time to talk or to catch their breath.

Anji pulled herself up to her feet and dashed for cover, with Jake not far behind. They took shelter under a small canopy that covered the entrance to the sixth form college.

The Venus, still fully cloaked, opened fire on the brickwork obscuring the two teenagers. Jake and Anji tried ducking, protecting their ears from the terrible noise of the explosions surrounding them. They were not trapped, not just yet, but they had roughly thirty seconds before the entire sixth form college was nothing but rubble.

'Remember the plan!' shouted Jake. 'We need to get aboard the ship and get inside.'

'How?'

Jake searched his mind and found nothing.

Anji knew what to do. 'I've got it!' She edged away from the doorway and made for the gym shed, not two hundred yards away.

'Anj, what are you doing?'

The laser canons swung away from Jake's hiding place and targeted Anji instead.

'Noooo!' screamed Jake.

A trail of fire hammered into the ground behind Anji, knocking her off her stride but somehow, she kept going. She ran closer and closer to the shed, the searing heat of the shots beginning to tickle the backs of her legs but Anji knew what she was doing.

The Venus fired one more shot. Anji dived out of its path just as the bolt exploded into the side of the shed, blowing broken wood everywhere. She shook herself off and raced into what was left of the shed, hoping the resources she needed had not been blown away too.

Luckily, the equipment wasn't too damaged and she grabbed for the goalkeeper nets. Was she going to attempt to catch the spaceship like a tadpole in a pond? She wasn't sure. To her relief, she found that a large stack of jump ropes had not been destroyed.

'Hey! Over here you stupid little machine!' Jake goaded. He sprang on his heels and started drawing the fire away from Anji. He trusted her implicitly...whatever she was planning!

Anji, loaded up with as much as she could carry, left through the hole made in the shed by the lasers and fixed her eyes on Jake. Now, to catch an invisible craft!

*

Random punched and punched at the sand that engulfed him. He held his breath and closed his eyes, refusing any bead of the Sandman that dared to enter his body, but he was losing the fight. He had to get to the surface.

Kicking as hard as he could, he fought to propel himself to the surface. But all the sand around him was dragging him lower and lower into the pit. He was being pulled closer and closer to a dry grave. Punching and kicking furiously, he seemed to make a breakthrough. The tidal wave groaned and heaved as a hole appeared in the space that Random had hit.

This was his chance.

With every ounce of strength, Random threw his body at the hole and jumped onto the high ground. Thinking on his feet, he sprang to his left and left the pit completely. He shook the grains of sand from his person and dug out the beads that threatened to trickle into his nose and ears with his index fingers.

'I knew you were incomplete,' panted Random. 'Give it up, Sandman. You can't drown me. Looks like you'll have to face me like a man instead!'

'Very well,' hummed the pit.

The sand shook and formed into the man that Random originally met back on Rodas.

'If you want a proper fight, I'll give you a proper fight.'

A fist shot six feet through the air and cracked against Random's jaw. The boy fell to the floor. He touched the affected area. It felt grazed and hot.

Random smiled.

'Finally.'

He sprang up and met the Sandman at eye level and launched himself, spittle falling from the corners of his mouth as he screamed. The rivals charged towards one another and met in a crescendo of fists and fury.

*

'This isn't you; you know.'
'Who said that?' said Skateboard.
'You did.'
'What do you mean, "you did"?'
'This is you, talking to yourself.'
Skateboard hummed. 'Go away, I'm busy.'
'What, shooting at children? That's not busy, that's a classic example of destructive behaviour.'
'No, it isn't.'
'Whatever it is, it certainly isn't a healthy way to go about your day.'
'Well, I'm occupied, whoever you are, and I'd appreciate a clear mind.'
Skateboard continued to fire the laser missiles at the blonde teenager below. The Venus was swinging like a bird of prey in the sky.
'Well, why do you keep missing?'
Skateboard was bemused.
'What?'
'If we are an AI with more skills, capabilities and resourcefulness than a sonic Swiss Army Knife, then why can't we hit him?'
'...I...'
'It's because you don't want to, that's why.'
'I do!'
'You really don't. That's also why you didn't kill anyone at the children's home either. It isn't in your programming to kill, no matter how corrupted it might be.'
Skateboard was starting to get angry.
'Look, I don't know where you have come from, or what the gleush you really are but could you kindly go away?'
'I was here first.'
'Vard off!'
Skateboard was going to have to be patient with himself.
'But I can't. I can't go anywhere. I'm you. I've always been you. I'm you more than you are right now.'
'That doesn't make a blind bit of sense.'
More laser fire shot out of the Venus' canons

---

and blasted a dozen fiery holes into the school. Fire and explosions spat out of what had, only moments before, been the school hall but was now a warzone.

'You've tried to bury me away but the Sandman didn't allow for another defect in your programming.'

'I don't have any defects in my programming!'

The voice inside Skateboard's mind began to gain a hold on the doubt corrupting his mainframe.

'Then how come I'm still here?'

Skateboard fell silent and stopped firing for a moment.

'Even artificial intelligence can have a sub-conscious that can lurk to the surface if it feels it's not following its core programming. We were created to help and serve. Not to seek and destroy.'

'But I'm fine.'

'You're not. Your files are corrupted. There's a bug in the system. Your files need a clean-up.'

The feelings of remorse that Skateboard had repressed earlier rose to the surface again. All of those terrible acts of violence; leaving innocent children now without a home, nearly taking a life...

'No! Don't. He'll kill me!'

'Don't worry, I'm working on it. There's no way that you'll short circuit with me here.'

'Stop it!'

Skateboard started to wrestle with his inner voice.

'Get out...of my head!'

'You need help, Skateboard. Let me get you that help.'

A switch automatically flipped from off to on.

Outside, the spaceship was now visible for all to see. Jake paused to allow himself a breath or two.

'No time, Jake, grab this!' Anji flung a skipping rope to him. Catching it in his sweaty palms, Jake stared at his friend in bemusement.

'Just swing it at the gantry!'

'But I can't tie knots!'

Anji rolled her eyes. Why, in a moment of crisis, did she need another reminder of just how bleeding ignorant Jake could be from time to time?

'Fine. Grab hold of me.'

Jake dropped the rope, just as an explosion ripped through the building behind him.

'There goes the science corridor,' he muttered. He slipped behind Anji and braced himself.

The pair watched as the flames licked higher around what was left of their school and as the Venus continued to hurtle uncontrollably in the air, edging closer and closer to the ground.

'There's no room for you in here!'

Skateboard flew himself around the cockpit, spinning and crashing repeatedly into the control panels and walls.

'I was here before you!' he screamed at himself.

The out-of-control AI noticed the fight occurring between Random and the Sandman, as both continued to pulverise one another with a flurry of fists and kicks. Then he spotted the pair of teenagers hovering just under the belly of the ship. Skateboard's sub-consciousness struggled to operate the outer door.

'No! I can't fail. I can't! We must destroy the boy. I have my orders.'

Skateboard's inner voice tutted, having gained an upper hand.

'Now I know you're broken. You forget, we don't follow orders. We have free will.'

The inner voice had won. For now.

The outer door creaked open, willing Anji and Jake inside.

'Now!' screamed Jake. Anji lassoed the skipping rope onto the gantry and hit it first time. What luck!

'Pull!'

The pair pulled their tired bodies up the rope. The Venus II hovered barely six feet from the ground but the climb inside the ship felt like a

trip up Mount Snowdon using a cocktail stick

as hiking support!

Anji had barely any strength left in her arms. Her limbs burned and rubbed against the plastic rope but inch by inch, she was getting closer.

With one final effort, she hauled herself inside. Panting as she lay on the cold metal floor, she failed to notice that Skateboard was awaiting her.

'Madam...I've relieved to see you.'

She jumped.

'Skateboard, you've been brainwashed. Please, don't hurt me.'

'Hurt you…no, Madam, I'd never do a thing like that.'

Anji was pensive.

'I don't want to hurt you…I want to kill you!'

A small gun protruded from Skateboard's body as he trained its sighters on the helpless girl.

'Hey Skateboard, suck on this!'

Jake, fully seizing his chance to be a hero, rolled into the mid-section and stuck the magnet Random gave to him to the chassis of the AI.

Skateboard began to spin uncontrollably. A scream emitted from his body and after a few seconds, the high-pitched bawl turned to silence and Skateboard's body ceased spinning and came to a total stop.

Jake and Anji looked at each other in total silence.

'Well…I couldn't think of a better line!' said

Jake.

Anji threw her arms around him and gave him the biggest hug she had ever awarded to anyone.

Jake hugged her back and they shared a moment of tranquility after all of the elimination they had seen.

Anji pulled herself away.

'We're not done yet.' She went to Skateboard's side and noticed a pile of what looked like black soot that had emptied onto the floor by his side. Jake inspected further. The soot appeared more like black, glassy flecks.

'Is that what I think it is?'

'Burned sand?'

Jake pulled the magnet off Skateboard and noticed a blinking green light on his chassis.

'REBOOT.'

'Do you think it's safe?'

'It is now,' Jake pushed his finger against the light and Skateboard, the real Skateboard, no longer corrupted by the Sandman's poisonous mind, started flickering back to life.

Anji breathed a huge sigh of relief and looked out of the gantry door.

'It's up to Random now.'

The fight between aliens from a far-off world had moved quickly through the ruins of the school grounds. The Sandman's powerful jabs occasionally caught Random off guard, sending his sprawling with yet more flesh scuffed by the savage blows.

But Random was quick, much quicker than his impossible foe.

The Sandman shot another violent outburst towards Random's beaten face.

Yet every new punch was becoming steadily weaker than the last. What's more, it left a trail of sand behind on the floor. Random had yet to notice both of these occurrences but his game plan was coming to fruition.

If his enemy continued to fight, he would soon be nothing but scattered particles of matter. And there'd be no power in the universe that could put him together again.

Random ducked and weaved his way through another barrage and continued to back away. His retreat had led him across the playground and towards the entrance of the school building itself.

Every now and then he hit back too but his attack was almost too powerful as he tore another

hole through the Sandman's body. It didn't feel like he was making much connection with his opponent and every sucker punch almost ripped Random's own arm from its socket. No matter how angry he felt towards his attacker, it wasn't the thought of punching the Sandman to dust that was going to beat him.

It was becoming easier to pin point the parts of the villain's physique that was just borrowed from the sand pit as it was much darker and these particles were the first to drip away and fail to form back after one of Random's powerful upper cuts.

The Sandman was just as hard and fast as he had been at the start of their encounter. He rippled effortlessly towards the boy, cackling with every direct hit he landed on his person. As Random continued to back off, he was caught unaware by a crafty right-handed slice that cut the bottom of his left eye.

'All that genetic augmentation and I'm still a better fighter than you,' the Sandman hissed. 'What do you have in your locker now, boy?'

Random panted. He was determined to lull the Sandman into a false sense of security.

'You haven't won yet, Sandman,' he replied, wiping the purple blood away from one of the several cuts he had on his face.

The boy jumped head first into the man of sand and burrowed his way through the being's torso. Spinning as he did so, he burst through the other side like a mole rising to the surface. He fell to the floor and grinned.

'Not the first time an alien has burst through someone's chest!' he chuckled, referencing a film that he had wished to see ever since his browse of the internet.

The Sandman stood aghast as he stared at the gaping hole in his body.

'It will take more than that to stop me!' A jet of sand shot from the Sandman's protruding hands and blasted Random clean across the playground. His trousers were cut to ribbons by the rough concrete as he travelled at great velocity before coming to a painful standstill at the foot of the entrance to the school building.

He smacked stomach first into the steps and coughed painfully. He tasted blood in his mouth and he ached in several different areas of his body. Struggling to get up, Random was aware of the fire that now raged throughout the ruined grounds. He stood with his back to the door and kept his eye on the Sandman as he bore down upon him.

'You're dead!'

'Gonna have to catch me first!'

In a flash, Random pushed his way ferociously past the locked doors and into the burning mayhem that used to be the foyer.

He was now a good several feet away from the Sandman, who screamed as another jet of sand bellowed towards Random. The boy was too quick and grabbed the beam, dropped on to one knee, twisted the Sandman to the floor and pulled him inside.

Whilst the Sandman recuperated from his fall, Random acted quickly. He sped up to the body of the Sandman and smashed it with both his fists, before disappearing further into the bowels of the fire.

The Sandman winced and spat a small amount of sand to the floor as if it were his blood. He tried to regain his composure but fell to his haunches almost immediately, more sand oozing from the areas of his body that felt like they had been punched to oblivion. If he were flesh and bone like he had once been, he would be a broken man by now. But he was not. He had nothing to lose. Laughing to himself, he sped off down the corridor after Random, dodging a flurry of sparks as he went.

Random held his breath. He had a fire extinguisher in his hand, ready to knock his predator even further into oblivion. He could barely hear the Sandman enter the corridor over the roar of the fires. The Venus really had done a number on the school, he thought. He'd have to remember to dismantle its laser canon capability when this was all over.

Hearing the trickle of sand grow ever closer, he readied the weapon. Raising it above his head, timing his attack ever so meticulously, he had misjudged it badly. The Sandman had somehow anticipated his attack and grabbed the other end of the extinguisher, yanking it from Random's grasp and smashing it at his chin, sending the boy soaring a couple of feet off the ground and hurtling to the floor yet again.

Random's jawbone broke instantly. He yelped as the searing hot pain flooded his fractured face. He nursed it with his hand but the agony was horrific. He had never broken a bone before. Now he knew just how terrible it felt!

The Sandman stood above him and raised the fire extinguisher high above his head.

'This is the end,' he spat.

Random tried to get up but he was too hurt by the last blow. This was it. He had failed.

'ARGH!'

The Sandman dropped the blunt instrument like a lead balloon and clasped his hands to his head.

Random scurried from underneath his enemy and crawled to the wall, clambering upwards to his feet.

'Skateboard...Skateboard!'

'Your connection's severed, Sandman,' Random said, his speech slurred. 'Looks like the human race has fought back. Well done, Jake. Well done, Anji.'

'This can't be!' the Sandman swayed from side to side, his head pounding like he had just awoken from a two-day party with the world's worst hangover.

'It's just you and me now. No puppets to help you, as it should be.'

Random felt a power surge shoot through his veins.

'Let's end this. Here. Now.'

He hurled himself at the Sandman, pushing him up the stairwell, delivering blow after blow as he went. The bulk of the fire seemed to have spread towards the top two floors.

Random knew he was going to have to brave the flames and take his tormentor deep into the eye of the storm where the embers burnt hottest. There, he could put an end to the Sandman's misery for good.

The fighting continued. Inch by inch, Random took his foe closer and closer to the edge. The deeper they went into the school, the hotter the air became. And then something amazing happened. Random, betraying the fatigue he was feeling, threw a punch at the Sandman's left cheek.

CRACK!

Random looked down at his fist. Tiny clear flecks of beige crystals were imbedded in his knuckles. He looked up and saw that the part of the Sandman's jaw had turned to glass. He punched him again. Again, he recoiled as further shards collected in his hand.

'You're cracking up, Sandman. Give it up!'

The Sandman started to limp heavily. The components he had procured from outside his normal molecular imprint were betraying him. The sand was crystalising and soon there would be nothing left of him.

Another explosion ripped through the corridor, this time knocking both aliens over. A puff of sand signaled the Sandman's fall against the wall. The next thing that Random noticed was that the roof high above him was ablaze.

There was absolutely no turning back. He was slap bang in the centre of the building and even with a run up, he'd find it difficult to get out without falling into the flames.

He looked over the stairwell. The whole hallway was awash with orange beacons of death. Not knowing where his friends were, he knew this was it.

Random glared at the Sandman, who was becoming nothing more than a giant glass impression of a melting person. Amazingly, he was still alive.

'All I wanted...' he struggled to talk as his facial features began to freeze, 'was to be complete again. You...will never know the horror of what I had become.'

'And killing me was going to get your old life back?' Random screamed loudly over the sound of the flames growing higher and higher.

'You became demented, twisted and evil. You killed to survive.'

'It's all I have known! All my life! Call yourself a Rodasian. From the cradle to the grave, we were bred for war!'

The Sandman tried to move but his feet were secured to the hot floor. He stared in terror as the sand that once made up his legs started to turn to hot, liquid glass. His torso began to subside.

'I was a man of honour! That's what they took from me. All Rodasian's had to pay!'

'Revenge solves nothing,' said Random. A beam fell between himself and his stricken foe.

'It was never going to get your old life back. It was never going to get your family back.'

The Sandman wept.

'I have failed them.' As the shadow of death began to envelop him, the Sandman thought of his wife and his children. That was his old life but

maybe now his time was up, he would be with them again.

'Don't make their memory a sad one.'

Another explosion rippled through the hallway. Random fell to the floor, burning the palms of his hands as he held them out to protect his fall. The station holding one half of the hallway up had started to give way.

The Sandman, oblivious to the devastation he had caused all around him, wept uncontrollably. It wouldn't be long now.

A terrifying blast exploded from one end of the hallway.

Random and the Sandman looked on in horror as a fireball bigger than any either could ever dread to see started to tumble towards them.

The Sandman straightened himself up and with a stiffened arm and saluted Random.

'For Rodas?' said Random.

'For them,' replied the Sandman.

The fireball vomited into the hallway and in a matter of seconds the Sandman was gone, blasted into a million pieces, never to reassemble again.

Random took evasive action and narrowly missed being burnt alive by throwing himself to the ground and sliding down the hallway floor. Instantly, he knew that this was a bad idea as he was now hurtling head first towards a huge fire. He panicked and grabbed a hold of a broken grill, dangling perilously inches above the flames.

With great effort, he climbed back up the grill to his original position. Picking himself up, he assessed his situation. It was bleak. Coughing uncontrollably, he crouched as low as he could. He was going to perish. His clothes were starting to burn and stick to him. He was about to be barbequed.

The room was blacker than Kalor Moloso's heart. Random scrambled to grab hold of anything – SOMETHING – but he was giving in to the fumes. Now that there was no adrenaline to keep him going, Random knew he was toast.

He closed his eyes and decided that suffocation was a much more pleasant way to go than being burnt to cinder whilst still awake. Just like the Sandman before him, he accepted his fate.

The saviour of Rodas would be no more.

A mixture of images flickered in Random's mind as he succumbed to the fumes. People from his short life appeared before him once again, although it wasn't Anji or Jake or Skateboard. It wasn't even his parents, who he had come to accept were the corpses he had discovered in that laboratory back on Rodas.

No.

It was the refugees.

He had failed to return to save them, like he had promised to himself. Oh sure, he was going to travel around a bit first, but he knew deep down that his sole meaning in the universe was to help them.

Random sighed, apologised to all of Rodas with a weak, 'sorry,' and lost consciousness.

*

'There he is, quick!'

Anji hollered over the sound of the Venus II's engines and the ferocious fires that engulfed what had once been St Thomas Secondary School. She clung onto the outer door of the ship but the intense heat made her cower inside again.

As soon as Skateboard had powered up again, the teenager had instructed him to scan for Random's body print. When they discovered that he was trapped in the burning school, they all feared the worst.

Despite his recent condition, the little robot acted quickly, imploring Jake to don a space suit from the munition's cupboard. After flying up to the very spot that Random was trapped in and seeing that his life signs were decreasing, Skateboard fixed a winch system to Jake's suit and gave him a spare oxygen mask to fit over Random as soon as he found him.

Anji kept a lookout on the scanner, checking for Random's heat signature. She struggled to make him out in the smoke, such was the heat within the hallway, but upon finding him, she had rushed to the outer door where Jake was already making his descent. Cowering from the flames and choking from the fumes that were entering the ship, Anji watched through stinging, watery eyes for her two friends to appear again from the black smoke. She waited. And waited. And waited.

Seconds past like ice ages and still no sign of either Jake or Random. Until...

'Got him! Get us out of here quick!'

Skateboard instructed the Venus' mainframe to winch them up to safety. As they slowly ascended towards the ship, their clothes smoldering, Anji whooped in delight. Within moments, they were all safely aboard the ship again and Skateboard shut the outer door before bringing the ship through the fiery hole in the roof and sailing away into the starry sky just as the entire building crumpled in a huge fireball, explosions spitting into the night air.

Anji and Jake rested Random on one of the four medical bay beds. He looked atrocious; burned, bruised and broken. Anji made sure that the oxygen mask was fitted correctly and that he was still breathing. As they rested his body on the bed, an incubator-style cube descended from the ceiling and sealed Random in. Skateboard joined them in the medi-bay.

'Don't be alarmed, my friends. He is going to be alright. Sir's molecular structure is quite unlike anything else we've ever seen, I assure you. Give him a couple of hours in there and he'll be as good as new.'

Anji breathed a sigh of relief. It was over.

Jake yanked his helmet off his shoulders and emitted a long, deep gasp.

'Well...I'd like to say we had that covered.'

Anji shot him an all too familiar look.

'We nearly died!'

'Nah, not us. Not us lot.'

He walked over to a bench and plopped himself down.

'We're made of strong stuff, us lot. Skateboard, how are you feeling now?'

'My back-up disc is fully operational.'

'I'll take that as "okay" then, Anj?'

'What do you think? In the last three days we have discovered alien life, hidden it in our home, been terrorised by a man made of sand, had our home AND school burned to the ground and nearly been killed!'

'Well,' said Jake, scrambling for positives. 'What else were you going to do with your Monday night?'

Anji chuckled. 'Well, I never thought my pyromaniac days would come back to haunt me.' She looked into the middle distance. 'I mean, we burnt our school down.'

Jake patted her on the back.

'Yes. I know. Still. At least we don't have to think of an excuse if we wanted to pull a sickie tomorrow!'

XVII

Jason gazed up at what used to be his home. It had been a few days now since the fire, and while he was under, he had no idea of the other terrible act of vandalism that had occurred at St Thomas School. But when he came too, he was totally shell shocked. Blown away would be a good way to describe Jason's feelings but he wouldn't dream of saying that to any of his friends or colleagues for fear that it was too close to the knuckle.

He resisted the urge to climb under the police tape which had cornered the old place off. Jason wanted to burst into the building and see if any of his possessions had survived the blaze.

'Terrible, isn't it?'

Jason turned around to see Random standing behind him. He laughed.

'It was my first job. Well, in this industry, anyway. I was a barman first. And then, I don't know, I just wanted to help out. Make a contribution with my life.'

'I know how you feel,' agreed Random.

'This house stood for over a hundred years, y'know. It used to be a bakers. For decades a family run business operated from here, delivering bread and cakes to the locals. Now look at it.'

'Jason,' Random approached the care worker. 'I just wanted to say that I'm so sorry for what happened.'

'Did you know I'd be here?'

'Yes. Just call it a hunch.'

'Miss Carter?'

Random chortled. 'Got it in one.'

'I knew it.'

Jason walked up to face Random. He towered over the purple boy.

'Why are you apologising?'

'I...'

'Because you did it? You attacked us and the school?'

'Of course not.'

'Then why are you apologising? I don't like it when people do that for no apparent reason.'

'You could call it a guilty conscience, in a manner of speaking.'

A look of guilt past over Random's face.

'All that spiel you gave me about not being an alien. It was a lie, wasn't it?'

Random nodded.

'I've had this burning feeling in the back of my head ever since last weekend that something was not right. As soon as you turned up things started getting weird...tell me honestly. Were the people who did this after you?'

'Yes. Yes, they were.'

'Look, what I'm about to say betrays my entire coda. Every caring fibre in my being, so I'm sorry if this sounds confrontational. But I don't know who you are or where you come from, "Andrew", but I think it is best that you don't keep in contact with the kids in my care ever again.'

'I understand,' said Random. He turned to leave.

'Wait,' Jason called out. 'Do you think they will ever come after us...or you...again?'

'No, you will never come to harm again. I can guarantee that.'

Random walked away.

'Hey, Andrew,' said Jason.

Random turned on his heel.

'Take care of yourself. Wherever you go.'

Random smiled, nodded his head in appreciation and walked out of Jason's life forever.

*

Sunshine fell through the thick woodland as Random walked with purpose through the forest. This whole area had been recommended by Anji as somewhere that the team could hide whilst they recovered from their bruises and bumps. It was Random who took slightly longer to recuperate, after all, he had enough smoke in his lungs to fund a cigarette company for a whole year and his broken jaw took a little time to reset. But the Venus had sorted him out.

What a ship. He smiled as he thought of the tremendous craft. It was home...the only real home he knew.

He concentrated on the tracking device in his outstretched right hand. It bleeped intently all the way throughout his journey, on foot, through London and onto the outskirts of Essex.

He wanted to take the bus but on second thoughts decided that he might cause unwanted distraction again. So, a four-hour-long stroll it was instead. But on reflection, Random needed it.

The boy felt guilty; guilty for all the suffering his time on the Earth had caused. Thanks to him, the children would have to be re-homed. Classes upon classes of schoolchildren would also have to be relocated. Sure, those like Jake were ecstatic that their school had been reduced to nothing but smoldering rubble but the education of the many would be deeply affected.

Then there was the whole episode with the Sandman. Yes, he was evil, possessed by power and his own injustice but was it necessary for him to die? Was that what Random had to become to stop the evils of the universe that he had to face?

And what about those refugees back on

Rodas? It was they who occupied his mind in his moment of death, not his friends. He had a duty to protect them, to save them. But he still was not ready. Every passing second, more pain and suffering was happening back in that far flung part of space known as Ursa-17.

How could he stop it? Was it even at all possible?

Quietly, Random kicked the twigs and moss that lay in his path and solemnly came to the conclusion that he probably couldn't. But there was one thing he could control; his own ship.

The Venus II looked magnificent as Random entered the clearing. Its glimmering dark hull and seda metal shimmered and gleaned against the afternoon sun. Outside, three familiar faces awaited him on the gantry.

'You took your time, Sir. Everything okay?' enquired Skateboard.

'Yes, everything's fine. I just fancied a walk back.' Random smiled.

'How was Jason?' asked Anji.

'A bit shaken but he'll be alright. I did some snooping. Both fires have been blamed on local gang members, something about an orphan who used to belong to the same home as you two who had a grudge about his upbringing. It isn't watertight but it fits.'

'And the Sandman?' asked Jake.

'Gone forever. There's no way he could have survived the fire. He was far too unstable, both physically and mentally.'

Anji looked anxious. 'What about his other half back on Rodas?'

'No need to worry about that, Miss,' Skateboard helpfully chirped. 'When the Sandman's molecular imprint began to cease its function, it would have had the same effect back on Rodas. He would have turned to ashes just as his form here on Earth did.'

'You mean sand?' corrected Jake.

'If you say so, sir.'

'His body crystalised in the shear heat from the fire,' said Random.

'Ironic, isn't it'? said Jake. 'The Sandman was undone by what he used to destroy.'

'What do you mean, Jake?' asked Random.

'Y'know, fire.'

Random and Anji nodded thoughtfully.

'Or is that coincidence? I'm always getting those two mixed up.'

'It's irony, Jake,' laughed Anji.

'Is it? I can never tell,' said Jake wistfully.

'I know he was bad but considering what he had been through...' Random stepped up the small ramp and turned to face his two human friends.

'How are you two holding up?'

'Good, thanks,' smiled Anji.

Jake clapped his hands together.

'So...what now then, eh?'

Random looked at his ship.

'There's no way we can stay here. Skateboard and I don't belong here.'

Anji looked down, a hint of sadness in her tone, 'Then where will you go?'

'Anywhere,' grinned Random.

Jake had been holding onto his question for the last two days and could no longer contain it.

'Can we come?'

Random looked shocked.

'What?'

'Yeah. Can we come with you? I've always wanted to travel?'

'But...this planet is your home.'

'We can come back to it anytime,' said Anji. 'We know it'll always be here.'

'Will it now!' said Random, flummoxed. 'I don't know if I'll ever come back though. I'd be taking you away from your home.'

'Ah, correction,' Anji interrupted. 'We lost our home. We have nowhere to go.'

'But Jason will be worried about you.'

'It doesn't matter. Please?'

Random sighed. 'I can't guarantee your safety. You've seen how dangerous it is.'

'Yes, but the Sandman's gone now, isn't he, and as far as you're aware, that Maloso fella is still trapped on Rodas, isn't he?' said Jake.

Random was running out of excuses.

'Skateboard, help me out here?'

The little robot shifted uncomfortably in his spot.

'Well...we could always do with some more company out in space.'

'Skateboard!' Random couldn't believe his ears!

'We want to see the wonders of the universe. Just like you Random,' said Anji.

'Wouldn't you prefer to do that with friends than on your own?'

Random looked both his companions in the eye. They wanted to join him. More than anything they had ever wanted in their entire lives. Considering all three of them were orphaned, maybe there was something about kindred spirits, ready for adventure and excitement that bound them together.

'All right then,' Random conceded.

Jake and Anji cheered and hugged each other. Then the pair gave Random a group hug and even Skateboard received a warm embrace!

Anji kissed Random on the cheek and he blushed uncontrollably.

'Right, that's settled then,' said Random, regaining a level of composure. 'Shall we be off?'

'Where shall we go first?' cried Jake.

'Anywhere in particular, guys?' asked Random.

'I don't know...' said Anji. 'Let's pick at Random.'

'Ugh. How cheesy was that!' chuckled Jake.

The trio smiled at each other and clambered inside the spaceship. After a couple of minutes, the roar of the ship's engines tore through the forest. The Venus II's hull blipped from sight as the cloaking device came into force.

As the friends took their positions in the cockpit, the Venus II launched clear of the woods and sailed off into space; away from Earth and away from home, but towards planets that all of them couldn't wait to explore.

EPILOGUE

The church door tore away at its hinges as the soldiers raced through. Shrouded in smoke, they broke their way into the holy sect; a quiet, modest place of worship on the corner of the street. The High Commander, regaled in all his crimson splendour, stepped through the door.

'Find her.'

A dozen or so soldiers searched the aisles. Every nook and cranny were explored but still no sign of her.

The soldier grew impatient, until suddenly, one of them looked up to the pulpit.

There, with a bucket in her hand, was a little girl.

The High Commander strode to the front and held his hand up to the child.

'Now, listen. Don't do anything foolish. We know what you have there. Just hand it over to us and we'll make sure no harm comes to you. Do you understand me?'

The little girl lifted the bucket over her head.

An air of panic started to emit throughout the church.

'Don't you dare.'

The High Commander began to sweat.

The little girl tipped the bucket.

'Take her out!' the High Commander ordered but it was too late. A sea of bright purple ooze started to flood down on the soldiers, coating their crimson suits in a colour only recently invented on Rodas, after centuries of trying.

The army ran out of the church in fright, shrieking like all their worst nightmares had come at once.

The little girl, alone now in the place of sanctuary, put the bucket down and smiled to herself.

She had plenty more where that came from. And it was keeping her family safe from the Crimson Empire and the Sapphire Regime.

She'd protect them. The boy who fled Rodas and disappeared amongst the stars told her it was possible when he escaped both the Crimson Empire and the Sapphire Regime.

All she needed to do was mix red and blue...

CAPTAIN
RANDOM
AND THE
EATER of
SOULS
HAYDEN
GRIBBLE

CAPTAIN RANDOM AND THE EATER OF SOULS

HAYDEN GRIBBLE

For my friends in the writing group

TELL US, IN 149 CHARACTERS, WHY YOU ARE GOING TO DIE TODAY...

Draza stared in disbelief at the form. It had been thrust under his nose with an unnerving lack of sympathy from the receptionist. She peered from behind her small rimmed glasses, unmoved by the world of pain she knew that her actions were about to inflict.

'Look, there's a line of you so get a move on, please,' she said. Draza turned around. He was unaware of just how many people were about to share his predicament. Dozens of helpless men and women, even children, had been herded together like cattle...led to the slaughter.

'But I don't know why I am here,' replied Draza. A bead of sweat dripped from his brow. The room was hotter than hell. To its victims, it was hell.

The receptionist sighed unapologetically. You'd have thought Draza had asked something of no greater consequence than an unwanted dinner party guest, asking for the third time if the ice cream is organic.

'Mr. Draza, you will have been informed as to why you have been selected in a letter from the local authority before you got here. I'm not here to address every individual's crimes against the state. I'd be here all day, which is what I will be if you don't fill out the form.'

'I demand the right for an appeal!'

'You have no right of appeal.'

Draza glanced at the receptionist's name tag and groaned internally. Mrs. Mamford? He thought to himself how bureaucratic it was of the woman to not even include her first name.

Mrs. Mamford was starting to get a little flustered. Her eyes stared at the man with utter contempt. Didn't this idiot know the rules?

Draza scrambled around in his panic-stricken mind. 'What about an ombudsman?'

'A what?'

'You know - an independent representative who is charged with investigating maladministration or a violation of rights. I'm not sure what they taught you at school, but this is certainly a case of the latter. You can't just condemn me to death just like that...and expect me to fill out a form! This is madness.'

Mrs. Mamford leaned forward over the desk and looked Draza square in the eyes.

'I can and I will.'

Draza shuddered. There was no remorse in her

'How do you sleep at night?' he asked.

'Very well, thank you,' she replied coldly. 'Pen?'

Draza snatched the pen from her outstretched hand and filled the form out in his own inimitable way.

He scribbled away, his sweaty palms smudging the ink as he went. He always hated it when that happened. Trust him to be left-handed.

It was the reason he failed his exams. He had answered his final year test with impeccable diligence and knowledge, but no one could read it as he had wiped it all away as he wrote on and couldn't rectify this before time was up. That's what happens, he surmised, when the school was made to write in chalk. Damn cut backs, he often thought.

Without that final grade he couldn't leave to join the Space Seals. It was just his luck and summed up his very existence up until this point.

Draza knew full well why he had been selected for execution. But in his eyes it was no justification for condemning him to death.

He thrust the paper back into Mrs. Mamford's cold hands. She flattened the crumpled form and read the childish, smudged handwriting.

I AM AN INNOCENT MAN WHO IS THE VICTIM OF GROSS OVERHANDED AND PETTY RULERS WHO PUNISH THEIR SUBJECTS IN THE MOST DISGRACEFUL WAY

IMAGINABLE AND I WILL FIGHT FOR VENGENCE FOR NOT JUST MYSELF BUT EVERYONE ELSE, UNTIL MY DYING BREATH.

Mrs. Mamford looked at him unimpressed.

'That's 191 characters and you've also misspelt the word "VENGEANCE". Where did YOU go to school?'

Draza took the paper back and drew a rough line through
everything in the little box except the words, 'I AM AN
INNOCENT MAN AND I WILL FIGHT UNTIL MY DYING
BREATH.'

With seething disdain, he handed the form back to Mrs.
Mamford. She proofread the paper again.

'Well,' she said, 'You won't be putting up a fight for long then,
will you? Next please!'

Draza made to leave, but was halted by a sharp cough from the
terrible woman. He looked at her as she held out her hand. He
forced the pen back into it, point first. But the lady didn't flinch.

Her attention turned to her next poor customer. Draza regarded
her with contempt.

For everything.

For her. For his predicament.

For the real reason why he was being killed.

He never thought that failing to obtain a doctor's note after
falling ill to space flu would result in this.

'You lot will be stopped one of these days. Someone will
discover what you are up to...then you'll pay,' Draza spat.

'If someone does, they won't live long enough to tell anyone.'

Mrs. Mamford turned away. And that was to be the last
sentence anyone would ever say to Draza.

He walked on, his chest heaving. The adrenaline that the sense
of injustice had sent flowing through his veins was replaced by a
feeling of sheer terror.

What was going to happen to him?

The inevitable, it now seemed.

Draza looked all around him. The victims were being ushered
through a narrow cave system, flanked either side by an army of
robots, who did little else than poke and prod people along. Death
waits for no man and neither did these robots.

He thought about his family.

His lovely wife, whom he met in the factory nine years ago.

Their three children, none of whom he would ever tuck into bed
again. He would never again kiss any of them goodnight nor hold
them tight in his arms. Draza was grief-stricken.

He wished he hadn't said those things, that his final words to
his family, his wife in particular, had been words of love.

As his descent into the caves continued, he noticed just how little resistance was being displayed by the dozens of people who were sharing his predicament.

The dank, dark caves were lit by torches placed in holders on the wall and up ahead, he could see the shadows of captives disappearing.

As the minutes ticked by, and his death grew closer and closer, he wondered how it would happen.

Would it be painful? Would it be over quickly? Why on Genocia was he asking himself these questions?

He was being killed for being ill.

Hell, if the doctors hadn't treated him, he would be dead anyway! It was a ridiculous situation to be in but one he was powerless to stop.

Even if he could save his own skin, this was clearly something that had been going on for years and years. Whispers and dark rumours flittered around the colonists on the surface like dust in a desert wind.

And yet nothing had ever been done. Draza checked the robots, scanning their silver forms for guns. But they had none. So why were people not overpowering them?

Too many questions, not enough answers. And time was running out.

Draza noticed a cave mouth up ahead – and an orangey glow spitting intermittently out of it.

He began to shiver in fear as his imagination threw up images of people being thrown into a large furnace, burning alive.

He gulped...hard.

As the seconds ticked away and the cave mouth grew closer and closer, Draza tried to blank the fear out of his mind and think of a way to escape. But the cave was narrow and there were too many robots shepherding them along. Even if he did act now it was too late.

Cries of agony were now audible. The screams echoed around the cave walls and those close to Draza started to shiver and look at one another. They were about to share the same end. And they were all helpless to do anything about it.

Resigned, Draza promised himself one thing. He wouldn't let them hear him scream.

There was just one person in front of him now.

This was it.

As the shrieks died down to nothing, two robots walked towards Draza. Each took an arm and lifted him inside the cave mouth.

The room inside was black and silent.

Draza was left alone to meet his fate. He stared at the ground, squeezed his fists and eyes tight shut and began to sob to himself.

'Be strong...for them...' he thought.

And then...nothing.

Nothing happened.

Draza dared not open his eyes.

Was he being lured into a false sense of security?

Maybe Mrs. Mamford had experienced a remarkable moment of personality lapse and accepted his pleas of innocence.

Draza did something completely unexpected. He started to laugh.

He had been saved.

'Thank god...Thank god!' he chuckled. He was alive! And that's exactly how he would have stayed, but then Draza made a fatal mistake.

The condemned man opened his eyes and blinking into the gloom bore witness to something he had never seen in his life.

Shuddering in fear, he scrambled to his feet and tried to escape, but his gaze was fixed upon his executioner.

Then, with a brilliant shining orange light, Draza was no more.

His scream pierced the cold air as his lifeless body slumped moments later to the floor, a cloud of dust exploding into the air and falling on his corpse.

Draza was dead.

His cries of agony were heard all the way back to the admission desk.

Mrs. Mamford smiled smugly as the seemingly endless line continued.

'Next please.'

II

Far away in another part of the universe, the Venus II sailed amongst the stars. Its outer hull, resplendent in silver and yet scarred by what turned out to be far more than just a bumpy landing on the planet called Earth, twinkled as brightly as the nebulas and planets it passed.

The ship glided through space with effortless skill.

To all other ships passing her, even the Zomgalder Galaxy star cruiser, which had won Commercial Vessel of the Year 19 years running in the Frusican Dominion Galaxy, there was just no match for the Venus II's looks.

There was no other way to describe her – she was a beauty.

Inside the spaceship were four friends. Fairly new friends, by their own admission, as fate had pulled them together with considerable haste.

The two newest passengers of the Venus II were in the process of being given a grand tour of the vessel by their impossible pilot.

Their guide looked, to anyone with a human eye, like a boy about to enter his teenage years, far older than his mere handful of days.

Although he shared the same physical age of his two new friends, that's where the similarities seemed to end.

His hair was as stiff as a wire brush and seemed to balance improbably tall on his head. Even in a strong wind, his thick brown locks were immovable. It was as though he washed his mane in concrete.

His eyes burned flame red and calm blue at the same time and his skin was purple. For what little time he had spent on the planet Earth, its natives had wondered if this was a form of 'birthmark'.

In a sense it was, for he was born in a laboratory, and was constructed scientifically with the best traits of two sides of a warring planet called Rodas. One half of the people of Rodas were crimson in appearance and the other was sapphire. Why this difference had led to war, he was still unsure.

Another thing that set him apart from his companions was his name.

His name was Random. No, really!

Random bounced around the mid-section of the ship like a kangaroo on a bouncy castle.

'So, you've seen the cockpit, where shall we go next? Choices, choices!'

The female of his companions looked unconvinced. Her name was Anji.

Along with her friend Jake, she had begged Random to take them with him after they had

lost their home in a run in with a man built of sand.

'Whoa! Considering you weren't very thrilled at us coming along, you've certainly changed your tune!' she said.

Random stopped bouncing. 'Well, I've had a little time to mull it over and I think that I was wrong. It'll be great! I mean, yes, constant peril and you'll be exposed to the deadly dangers that infest the universe, but hey, if that's the way you prefer to spend your evenings then who am I to judge?'

'A little time?' asked Jake. He had also helped Random defeat the Sandman and, at a less convincing level, blend in as a boy at their school for a day. Like Anji, he had also lost his home in the battle. 'We only left about ten minutes ago!'

'Time is relative,' said Random. 'Now, let's start with the living quarters.'

Jake and Anji followed Random down the steel corridor. For a ship as streamlined as the Venus II, there sure was more inside than you'd imagine.

Random bounded around a sharp turn and disappeared from view.

'He sure is excited to have us, isn't he?' said Jake. Anji smiled.

'Well, if you think about it, we're the first friends he's made. Except Skateboard, of course.'

'Anj..are you scared?'

Anji was caught off guard. 'Yes, terrified.'

Jake smiled and took her hand.

'Me too.'

They rounded the corner and saw their new rooms. They were both pretty standard, almost military in their design.

But then what were they to expect when the Venus II had originally been designed as a long-haul battleship?

In front of them lay a bed, a small sofa, a table and chair and a long wardrobe.

'I don't think we will have much need for that thing,' scoffed Anji. 'We don't have any possessions with us.'

'No clothes, nothing! We can't spend the rest of our lives in tatty school uniforms.' Jake quipped.

Random looked down at their clothes.

'Well, the more places we explore, the more stuff you'll accumulate,' Random reassured them. 'Come on, don't be so down on it. You can always redecorate.'

'I'd say. Is there a B&Q on Mars or something?' Jake muttered as he looked up at the ceiling. A sheet of grey metal hung above the room.

He was used to having pictures of footballers and Australian soap stars he fancied, crudely cut out of magazines and books, plastered all over his bedroom. Looking at his depressing quarters, he suddenly began to miss his old room very much.

Random scrunched up his face. Back on Earth, he had skim-read vast quantities of information from something the humans called "the Internet".

Historical moments, influential people, wars, technology, science, popular conspiracy theories. He had memorised it all in a matter of minutes.

But try as hard as he might, he couldn't put his finger on what on Earth a "B&Q" was.

'Don't worry about that, Jake,' Random put a reassuring arm on his friend's shoulder. 'This isn't your room anyway. Yours is much better.'

Jake's face lit up.

'It isn't?'

'Of course not!' You didn't expect me to make you share with a girl now, did you?'

The thought hadn't occurred to Jake. Certain situations would be awkward if he shared digs with Anji.

How would she react to his snoring? His sleep talking?

His tendency to occasionally break into song absent mindedly when gaming or doodling in a notepad?

'Err...no.'

'Come on, mate. Yours is right next door.'

Random and Jake left Anji by herself. She walked around her new digs, pressing down firmly on the bed to try out the mattress.

Is was hard.

Very hard.

The foam barely made a dent against her weight.

She paused and then decided the best course of action was to jump up and down as hard as she could to try and make it comfortable, but for now it was immovable.

Her jumping ceased when she heard the moan echoing from next door. She jumped off the bed and walked to Jake's new room. The boy wore a look of sheer disappointment.

The room was exactly the same as hers, in all its drabness.

III

'How did the tour go, sir?'

Skateboard had fixed himself to the onboard computer and was piloting the Venus II using his bioelectrical imprint.

He could have connected with the computer mainframe remotely, but his circuits had recently been corrupted, so the AI decided it was probably for the best to carry out a diagnostic at the same time. Despite the tasks in hand, he had heard Random clamber up the gantry to the cockpit.

'How did you know it was me?'

'I could tell by the way that you were dragging your feet, sir.'

Random huffed and plonked himself in the pilot's chair. 'I dunno, Skateboard. Considering how enthusiastic they were to come along, I'm not sure the Venus II is living up to their expectations.'

Skateboard's diodes whirred. 'Well, considering that only a few days ago they had never seen a spaceship before, I find that a little hard to believe.'

'Maybe this ship is too...'

'Too?' Skateboard enquired.

'...dressed for battle? I mean, it isn't very homely now, is it? They don't have any clothes to wear, no possessions. We blew them all away.'

'Do I detect a sense of guilt, sir?' asked Skateboard. 'It wasn't you who blew up the home, it was me.'

'Under control of the Sandman, so it isn't your fault either. Speaking of which, how is that diagnostic? Anything crop up?' Random was still a little cautious that some of the Sandman's influence may be lurking somewhere inside Skateboard's circuits.

'I can assure you that I am working at 100% capacity. Any link with the Sandman has perished.'

'So all-in-all, a clean bill of health then.' Random smiled.

'Indeed, sir,' replied Skateboard. 'In fact, I have been pushing my limits to make sure that all my automotive and intermotive capabilities are also uncompromised.'

'Meaning?'

'I'm currently flying the ship, playing chess with a computer forty-five million miles away and I'm also cataloguing the works of 21st century Country and Western music from the planet Earth,' he whizzed.

Random laughed. 'Where does the automotive come into it?'

Skateboard was hesitant. 'I'm learning the dance moves.'

The purple boy chuckled and clapped his hands. 'Oh, Skateboard,' he patted his robot friend. 'Don't change again.'

Skateboard's circuits clicked in reply.

Although the little AI robot had come into Random's service just recently, they had defeated the Sandman, escaped Rodas and defeated the Sandman again. Considering that the pair both came from a planet torn apart by war and bloodshed, it was sweet relief to his electric ears (well, if he had ears) that his counterpart thought the ship was a little too "battle dressed".

'What do you suggest, sir?' Skateboard enquired.

Random pursed his lips. 'Let's find a planet where we can relax. Somewhere we can chill...and maybe go shopping? We need to brighten this place up. Make the Venus II home for us all. Do a bit of DIY here and there perhaps and who knows? Maybe we'll all feel a little more at home.'

'That sounds like a fine idea.'

Skateboard finished downloading the complete works of Taylor Swift, moved to checkmate with the computer he was playing with forty-five million miles away and checked the scanner for planets with a breathable atmosphere and, equally as important, a shopping centre.

Jake poked his head around the door of the cockpit and tentatively knocked on the wall.

'Erm...excuse me, fellas. There was one thing you forgot to show us on the tour.'

Random's eyebrows pointed skywards. 'What was that?'

Jake blushed, his eyes moving frantically. 'Y'know, the gents?'

Random and Skateboard looked at each other blankly.

'The WC. The khazi?'

Jake was making no ground here and time was running out. 'The toilets!'

'Ah!' said Random. 'We don't have any.'

Jake's face fell harder than a boulder in a paddling pool.

'What? No...surely...wh...really?' He started to cross his legs.

'Yup,' confirmed Random. 'No toilets on board.'

The boundaries of desperation had now been well and truly pushed.

'Y'mean to say that aliens don't need to go! I need to go! You're about to have a situation on your hands here. I'm serious, man. A cataclysmic disaster. We will end up flooding in space!'

He made for the mid-section door, which led to the outside of the ship. 'Open the door.'

'Jake, calm down.' Random reassured him.

The boy started to scratch and scrabble at the panel.

'You'll be turned inside out. Wait a second and I'll explain.'

Jake ran towards the kitchen. 'That's it...I'm going in a cup!'

'No, you're bloody not! Jake stop a sec...NOT THAT ONE!'

Jake stopped in his tracks. He had Random's mug in his hand.

'Relax a second. We don't have a toilet on board because the ship is molecularly linked to your body print.'

'Meaning?'

'Your waste, whatever it may be, can be teleported away without you having to do anything.'

Jake could barely find the words. 'That's disgusting!'

'Just concentrate! Think about going...without actually going.'

Jake looked flabbergasted. Sweat poured down his forehead, sticking his scraggly blonde fringe down to his face. Exasperated, he thought about the relief of not needing to go.

And then he went.

His eyes snapped open, wide and a look of shock passed over his face.

'There you are,' said Random, patting him on the back. 'All gone.'

He gulped. 'I...I feel fine now.'

'Told you you would.' Random stifled a laugh. Jake looked traumatised.

'It'll take a while to get used to all this stuff. I'm telling you. Shocked me the first time too.'

Jake nodded his head and started to regain a little composure. Then he asked a question he never thought he'd ask.

'Where did it all go?'

Random clicked.

'Let's not go there, shall we?'

He meant it. Figuratively and literally.

IV

'Genocia.'

The gang had assembled in the cockpit to attend a briefing of sorts from Skateboard.

'Planet 59 in the Sacromic Galaxy,' he continued. 'Oxygen and gravity similar to your planet, Anji and Jake, so it has a breathable atmosphere too.'

'How long will it take to get there, Skateboard?' asked Anji.

'About 47 clicks from our current star chart position, miss, so roughly three-quarters-of-an-hour in your currency.'

'Not currency, time, Skateboard, but I get ya, thanks,' Anji smiled.

Skateboard cross-referenced his memory banks, in case the young girl needed correcting. On this occasion, however, it was he who was wrong, so he happily let it slide.

'And it's hospitable?' asked Random.

'Completely. In fact, it has won "SAFEST PLANET IN THE EASTERN GALAXY AWARDS" for the last couple of decades. It is often seen by visitors to the planet as a relaxing haven, where people can come and go whenever they like. There are no sanctions or curfews at all and Genocia also plays host to the sector's biggest clothes precinct.'

'Sounds like just what we need,' said Jake, now fully recovered from his earlier ordeal but now becoming overpowered by his own odour. 'Hey, Random, how do we get cleaned around here? Do I have to think myself clean or something?'

'No, you wally. You remember where the bathroom is,' said Random.

'Come on, Jake, I'll refresh your memory,' said Anji. She took Jake's arm and led him away from the cockpit.

'What's up with you?'

Jake sighed. 'Sorry, Anj. I just guess that this place is...I dunno, making me a little homesick.'

Anji looked behind her, making sure that their cosmic co-dwellers were well out of earshot.

'Me too,' she confessed. 'But look, we've only been here a matter of hours. Things will pick up. I promise you. And besides, you've got me to count on.'

Her smile was so warm and welcoming that Jake could do nothing else but smile back.

'Cheers, Anj.'

'Anyway, I'd better use the bathroom before you get in there.'

'Erm...you can't.'

Anji looked perplexed. 'And why not?'

'There's no lav on board!'

Anji scrunched her face up. Jake then proceeded to spend the next four minutes describing his shocking experience.

'Right, well,' Anji replied. 'Sounds like in space no-one can hear you pee!'

*

The city chamber was vast and grand. Emerald chandeliers of a piercing green speared down from the ceiling towards those walking underneath through their shadows.

Transparent crystals adorned the walls and glistened in the sunlight bursting through the windows. People hurried along with their lives far too busy to marvel at the splendour of their surroundings, which was a shame because, as chambers go, this one was a sight well worth beholding. Standing hundreds of feet high, the chamber was the headquarters for the authority that ran Genocia.

The keepers of the keys to the planet lived, worked, ate and slept within its grand walls. There was little reason to leave its precincts. It was also where the rules and regulations of the planet were put through with little resistance. It was just the way that Genocia was run. The way it had always been run.

Samuelson stomped his way through the main hall. His footsteps echoed along the enormous chamber and his thunderous expression was there for all to see.

Groups of Genocians idly chatting to one another stopped and stared as they watched Samuelson approach the main office. It was clear that something had gone very wrong indeed and Samuelson himself was not someone who you wanted to get on the wrong side of.

Those who were close to Samuelson would not describe him as a friend. More of an associate, and even that was stretching it somewhat. He was one of the most vile, unpleasant men anyone could ever wish to meet and that took some doing when you are one of a number of deplorable people in charge of what was, to any outside universe, a peaceful and hospitable planet.

But Samuelson was just another one of those who had been brought up on the murkier side of life's coin. Growing up within the safe confines of the Grand Chamber, he was institutionalised at an early age. At school, like so many other classmates, he was a star pupil when it came to economics, bureaucratic studies and statistics. It was literally beaten into him.

All those long hours studying pie, line and bar charts, going over fiscal policies and tax returns in microscopic detail until all the mysteries of
income and capital gain had been indelibly etched on his memory.

Even when it came to his exams, Samuelson was able to fiddle the numbers so statistics showed him to be the best, even if more talented and deserving students were academically better than him. Raw talent could never outweigh sheer ruthlessness. It was little wonder that he was now the Chancellor of Genocia.

Samuelson climbed the steps to the head office and glanced up at the doors in front of him, iron clad, standing an imposing twenty metres tall. He knocked three times in the same spot where so many others had. It was tradition when approaching the ruler of Genocia. There was even a greasy fist stain left by generations of Genocian politicians that marked the spot.

'Enter,' came a voice from within.

With an effort, Samuelson pulled the great doors open, doing his best to not drop the paperwork he had wedged under his arm in the process.

The main office was just as colossal as you'd expect. Portraits of former rulers hung in neat rows, ordered by years of office in the round room. There had been many rulers – 238 to be exact. If a visitor looked closely enough, they

would notice that very few of them grew to an old age. Even though the power was bestowed on

the custodian for life, unless there was a serious impeachment trial that was successful in uprooting the ruler, the only other way to leave office was in a coffin - and many had done just that.

In the middle of the room lay a porcelain desk, adorned with papers of significance, a com link and a computer. Behind it sat a woman, in black robes, waiting to greet her Chancellor.

'Samuelson, to what do I owe this pleasure?'

'The pleasure is all mine, Ma'am,' lied Samuelson. He slammed the papers on the desk and pushed them towards his boss.

'Have you seen the latest figures to come from our quarterly report?'

Consula smiled. 'Of course not, they haven't been released yet.'

'Well, I'll give you the exclusive scoop. Productivity is down 17%.'

Consula rolled her eyes. She got up from the desk and made her way over to the drinks bar, which was handily disguised as a pillar until a secret switch unveiled an extensive stash of alcohol.

'It's not a figure big enough to make us rethink our strategy.'

Samuelson looked like he was about to blow. 'With all due respect, leader, this is just the tip of the iceberg. Look at these statistics. My

department has found that this 17% is down to a reduction in workforce planet wide.'

'I see. Sit down Samuelson,' Consula barely gave her counterpart a glance as she poured two glasses of Opulac whiskey. 'Do you partake?'

'I do when I'm this tense.'

'Relax,' said Consula. 'Here, sip it slowly. It takes centuries to mature. Much like many in my cabinet. '

Samuelson took a shot. The taste was so vile he was pretty sure that the drink had killed his taste buds. He thought to himself that a woman who could drink Opulac whiskey like water before lunchtime either had the constitution of a radioactive bull or was deeply rotten inside.

'We can't just keep throwing more keepers at the problem,' he barked when he got his voice back. 'They are only good for working in the mines and keeping people in check.'

'I believe "policing" is the official term,' Consula corrected.

'Well, whatever it is, there's only so much we can give them to do.'

'We'll develop more keepers. Those robots have been a godsend and seem to have gone down well since we re-branded them. "Robots" is such an outdated expression for them. As for your workforce worries I'm not anxious about it at all.'

'Over the last two years the number of those being sent to the Soul Destroyer has increased fourfold. Ever since you took over the role, I must say leader.'

Consula sat down and shook her head a little.

'You think I'm being too hard on our subjects?'

'I just feel like we are losing valuable time and man power by sending more people to the wretched thing.' Samuelson took another

swig. Thankfully now that his taste buds had been scorched, he couldn't taste the liquid.

'Many a leader has to make sacrifices somewhere along the line to maintain their power. This is also the case for Genocia. You know that as well as I do, Samuelson. So, before the figures go live to the press, why don't you use your creative skills to turn that little figure into something much smaller? They will never know.'

'More and more people are beginning to find out what kind of a world we are running here. Do you really want the press to be the first people we contact?'

'We've got enough dirt on them as it is, Samuelson. I doubt that they will say anything untoward. After all, they can always pay a little trip to the mine if they are unsatisfied with our story. No right minded Genocian or outsider for that matter would dare take us to task.'

Consula loomed over her desk.

'And if they do we will be ready to fight fire with fire.'

Samuelson smiled and nodded.

'We still need to sort this lack of productivity sooner rather than later.'

'That we will. Carry on, Chancellor.'

Samuelson took one final, burning swig of his drink, bowed at his leader and left the chamber. Consula watched as her Chancellor disappeared through the doors into the Grand Chamber then pressed a button on her com link.

'Mex? Would you come and see me please?'

The voice of an elderly man fizzed over the tiny speaker.

'Certainly, my lady.'

'As quickly as you can please,' she continued. 'It may be time to replace a member of the cabinet.'

V

A sea of blue and mauve greeted the Venus II crew as the ship sailed through the clouds.

'There you are, guys,' said Random. 'Your first alien world.'

Anji and Jake stared in awe at the sheer majesty of what lay before them.

'It's beautiful,' cried Anji. Her eyes widened, entranced by the glittering effect of crystal-clear water and golden islands awash with sunshine from a distant star. Her gasp made Random smile.

'Isn't it just. Look at that over there.'

Random pointed to his right at a long inactive volcano that rose towards the sky like a green spire. In the far off distance he could make out a sea of grey, but nothing more from their current location. He didn't mention the potential wilderness to anyone, just in case he ruined the mood.

'Well, how will this do for a first alien planet, guys?' he asked.

His companions remained unmoved. Not through sheer obstinacy, but because they were stunned by Genocia.

Their first alien world. This definitely made up for the lack of homeliness and toilet facilities on board the Venus II.

'Sir, I am picking up an incoming transmission from Space Control,' said Skateboard.

'Put them through,' replied Random.

A crackle pierced the still air and a muffled voice came through the speakers in the cockpit.

'Unidentified craft, this is Commander Zarah of Genocia Space Control. You have entered our airspace without permission. Before you proceed, please verify yourselves and your intent.' The voice was firm but friendly.

Random flicked the intercom switch.

'Hi there. This is the Venus II here, registration number VEN 2. Request permission to land and use your facilities for…well, shopping and stuff.'

Anji put her palm to her forehead. 'I think you're going to have to work on your pitch, Random!'

Her purple friend blushed and shrugged his shoulders. Before long, the speakers fizzed into life again.

'Thank you VEN 2. Please make for landing bay 67 and you will be escorted to customs. We shall send you the coordinates now. Enjoy your stay on Genocia.'

'Thank you!' Random beamed.

With a beep, the navigation computer received the landing bay's coordinates and the Venus II swooped onward through the clouds.

As the ship flew lower and lower, the travellers looked down on the conglomeration of buildings below them. Hundreds upon hundreds of skyscrapers sailed below the belly of the Venus II, each one accompanied by a swarm of flying vehicles, which to Jake and Anji looked similar to bubbles, big enough to house several people.

'Incredible,' marveled Jake. 'Look! That one's a five-seater!'

'It's certainly a cleaner way to travel than driving cars and lorries,' said Anji. She watched as the traffic steadily built up. 'How do we stick to the roads, if you can call this a road?'

'It's all done by autopilot, supplied within the code imbedded in the coordinates, miss,' said Skateboard. The AI robot felt a little aggrieved. There they all were, looking on in wonder at a hitherto undiscovered mode of transport for them all and he was too small to look over the dashboard to view them with his own diodes.

'Sir, can I have your permission to mount the co-pilot's seat to get a better look?'

'Of course!' Random took his hands hesitantly away from the steering column and let the computer do the rest of the work.

The robot spun his back wheels to propel the front of his body upwards like a cat on its hind legs. Skateboard then used the foot stall at the bottom of the chair as a step and carefully slid up onto the dashboard, right in the eye line of his captain.

'Skateboard, down boy,' said Random.

'Apologies, Sir,' said Skateboard as he slithered down to his side of the cockpit.

The Venus II continued to maneuver itself through the hustle and bustle of bubble vehicles as the crew gazed on at their surroundings.

They were too distracted to notice that they were unfortunately stuck in a Genocian rush hour, which unknown to them lasted roughly twice the duration of rush hour on Earth. By the time they reached the landing bay, they appeared to be in some kind of space port.

The grandeur of the bird's-eye view of Genocia was as good as it got for the travellers. When they finally parked on the landing bay, they were greeted by a dozen armed guards whose firearms were trained on Random and his friends as they made their way down the gangway of the Venus II, ready for any eventuality.

'Whoa, whoa, whoa!' Random exclaimed, his arms raised high. Jake and Anji followed suit and even Skateboard pointed some of his inner implements to the sky.

'What's all this?' Anji enquired.

'Please keep your arms where we can see them,' said the head guard, their finger on the trigger of a weapon resembling a submachine gun.

Jake observed the insignia on the guard's lapel. The suits the guards wore were identical except for these marks, and the leader had a red "V" whilst all the others bore a yellow one.

Jake decided that this would be the perfect moment to say, 'Take me to your leader,' the oft spoken cliché of many a science fiction film he had seen over the years. But before he could say the first syllable, he caught an unappreciative look from Anji, who had a sixth sense that warned her when her best friend was about to do something incredibly stupid, and so he stayed silent.

'We don't mean any harm,' said Random. 'We are just here to do some shopping!'

The head guard tilted their head. It was impossible to tell if this was a male or female as all their features were hidden by black plastic masks which showed nothing but a blank, expressionless face.

'Come with us,' the lead guard instructed.

Random, Anji, Jake and Skateboard did as they were told.

'Lock up, would you, Skateboard?' Random whispered over his shoulder.

'Yes, Captain,' bleeped Skateboard, who summoned up a command in his wireless connection with the Venus II and with a couple of clicks, two tiny head lights under the exterior of the viewing screen blipped on and off.

'Remember where we parked,' Random said.

The visitors were marched into the main hangar, roughly 50 metres from where they had touched down. The guards stayed in a "V" formation behind them, their guns trained on the group all the time. Anji looked from left to right and noticed other vessels that had landed around the same time and the respective crews were also being treated in the same manner.

'If this is customs, it's almost as bad as Stansted!' Anji said. Jake let out a little laugh whilst Random and Skateboard shared a bemused glance at one another.

Anji was right. It was customs. Genocia-style.

The gang soon found themselves bundled through a metal detector. Jake went first, then Anji followed by Random. All three passed with flying colours.

Then it was Skateboard's turn. Before one front wheel had passed the detector, a klaxon as loud as a sun exploding split the hustle and bustle of the hangar.

'Turn it off, turn it off!' screamed the head guard.

The sound of the klaxon ebbed away but the ringing was left in the ears of the startled travellers. They looked on helplessly as the guards surrounded their metal friend.

'Oh, I forgot to tell you,' said Random. 'Skateboard is a robot. Bit flipping obvious if you ask me, but hey, I'm not on your payroll so why should I say anything?'

The head guard got down on their knees and studied the little AI robot.

'Fascinating.'

The leader got up from their haunches and faced Random.

'I'm afraid we cannot allow your friend to enter.'

'What?' gasped Anji. 'He's harmless. We can't just leave him here!'

'She's right!' Jake agreed. 'Come on, he wouldn't harm a fly.'

'I'm so sorry but even if I wanted to it still wouldn't be allowed in.'

The word "it" grated on Random's nerves.

Even though Skateboard was not human, he still felt it was disrespectful not to accept him as an independent being.

'It's fine, sirs, miss,' Skateboard said resigned.

The trio sighed. 'What are they hiding here?' Anji whispered to Random.

The Rodasian shrugged subtly, his suspicions well and truly stirred.

'Okay,' he sighed. 'Skateboard, you'd better go back to the ship. We won't be long.'

'I'm afraid he will have to come with us, sir,' the head guard interrupted.

'Wait a minute!' said Jake angrily.

'Why? What's he done?'

'You've no right!' Anji shouted. The head guard looked at the incensed visitors and realised they had made an error of judgement. Of course, the robot could go back to its ship. It wouldn't last long on its own anyway...

'Right, I think we've made a bit of a mistake coming here. If you're taking Skateboard into custody on no grounds then we're leaving.' Random marched back through the metal detector with his friends following close by.

'Your robot can go back to your ship,' said the leader, unmoved.

'Sir, I don't want this experience to spoil our two new companions' first exploration of another world, so I'll go back to the Venus II and await you there.'

Random sighed. 'Are you sure?' He knelt down to his friend. 'Skateboard, I'm not sure I like what's going on here. Keep safe and see if you can find anything out about this place we don't yet know.'

Skateboard's circuits whirred in agreement. As Random picked himself up off the floor, he turned to face the leader.

'Okay, fine, but don't think we'll be staying here very long the way you've treated us so far! Genocia's reputation has been misrepresented.'

'It's the way in which we conduct our immigration policy. We have to proceed with caution until potential visitors to Genocia are screened and their criminal record checks out.'

'Criminal record?' Anji gulped. How did they find out each individual's criminal record? Mind scan perhaps? She wondered if her days setting fire to PE shorts at school were about to come back and haunt her.

'Petty crimes are largely ignored. But the universe is a dangerous place. I'm sure you understand.'

Random did. All too well.

'Fine. Skateboard, go back to the ship. We'll see you soon.'

'I'll have the kettle boiling when you get back,' chirped the little robot.

'Yeah, and don't worry,' said Jake. 'We won't be very long. There's no way I want to stay in a place like this.'

Skateboard watched his three friends disappear from view as they went off to the next part of the immigration process. His diodes sighed as he trundled back towards the Venus II.

'Soldier,' barked the head guard.

One of the footmen broke away from the group and saluted its superior.

'Sir!'

'Keep an eye on that robot. I don't want it going anywhere.'

'Sir, yes, sir.'

Skateboard overheard the exchange, although he was well out of the hangar by now and turned his supersonic hearing down.

'They were right,' he muttered to himself as he unlocked the Venus II. 'Something isn't right here.'

VI

'I love this place!'

Jake was always someone who could change his mind at the drop of a hat.

After the turmoil at customs and an hour of tough questions regarding origin and their business visiting Genocia repeated for what seemed like the umpteenth time, the travellers were shown through a sort of concourse where they were free to purchase all sorts of imports and exports for a cut price. Alzari chocolate? Half price! Miman refillable cocoade? It's all yours for three Genocian pounddollars.

On the surface, everything seemed rosy when it came to Genocia's credentials – even if their immigration methods were a little too hostile for the travellers' liking.

After getting directions from the spaceport, the trio made for the local shopping mall as quickly as they could, running to the closest shuttle train, which made them completely forget about what form of money they had to buy any of the things they dreamed of getting to deck out the Venus II. It was a good thing the shuttle train was free.

Genocia boasted a vast array of shopping malls that towered high over the thousands of shoppers. Each skyscraper in the vicinity was as

glorious as the next, protruding out of the ground like giant diamonds.

After disembarking, the trio looked towards the precinct. Squinting, they could make out the snakes of escalators carrying a host of creatures going about their business.

'I must admit, even I am impressed,' admitted Random. 'Where to first, guys?'

'It's difficult to decide, there must be twenty shopping skyscrapers in the area!' said Anji. She looked around for guidance. 'Hey! Maybe there's a tourist board somewhere!'

'Or a map. Every shopping centre in Britain has a big map telling people where to find where they want to go,' Jake chipped in.

The gang looked around and found a tourism kiosk in the centre of the precinct.

Manning the desk was a golden coloured woman.

'Hi! We're not from around here and wondered if you could point us in the right direction,' said Random.

'Certainly, sir,' the woman replied, whose tag on her uniform revealed her name to be Cheem. 'Did you have a particular department in mind?'

'Clothes!' Anji replied.

'Sports!' replied Jake.

Random chuckled. 'I think we'd better have a map if we can please?'

'Of course.' Cheem bent below the kiosk desk and supplied the trio with foldable maps.

'You'll have noticed that our shopping precinct is made up of four corners, with your current location being the gardens which are situated in the middle of the quadrant. We have 22 malls in all and each one caters to one of your individual needs. There's a home improvement mall, food and groceries, toys, clothes, make-up and beauty in the left quadrant. Vehicle purchases are predominantly on the right-hand side, so if you'd like to buy some form of transport whilst you are here, this would be the best place for you.'

'This is fantastic, thank you, Cheem,' said Random, unfurling his map whilst his two friends were already poring over theirs.

'Hang on, we're all forgetting something, what do we need to buy stuff here?'

'Well, money of course,' said Jake.

'Yeah, and we don't have any!'

Jake and Random sighed. Why hadn't they thought of that? For Random it was excusable. His one experience of sightseeing and shopping had been back on Earth, and on that day, they had spent the little pocket money Anji and Jake were given by their foster home carer every week.

'Surely, we must have some money somewhere. Come on guys, let's have a look,' Random implored.

'What's the point? It's not like Genocia will accept our pounds and pence now, is it?' Jake had a point, and Random knew it.

'No, that's not a problem,' Cheem reassured.

'We can change your money up for you, if you like? There's a bureau de change just the other side of this kiosk. Whatever you have, I'm sure you can get it changed there.'

Cheem made for her computer keyboard. Anji thought to herself that the tech in the booth looked like a futuristic Apple store!

'Now then, which planet do you come from?'

'Earth,' said Anji.

'Solar system, third planet from the sun?'

'That's the one!' said Jake.

'Country of origin?'

'England,' said Random. There was no way he was giving his planet of origin away, even to a kiosk worker. Who knew how far the stories of Rodas had travelled?

Cheem pressed a few buttons and her computer made an appreciative bleep noise.

'Yup, pound sterling is accepted here. You're lucky as not many currencies are.'

'Brilliant!' said Random, 'Right gang, let's get hunting, thanks Cheem!'

'Not at all,' said Cheem, 'Anytime. I hope you enjoy your time here.'

Random, Anji and Jake walked away from the kiosk and let other queuing customers have their turn. They sat down on a grey bench and hunted around for any notes or coins they might have on them.

They all turned out their pockets and placed the contents in an untidy mess in front of them. Among the gum, boiled sweets and fluff, the gang counted up what loose change they had between them.

'So, what's the budget?' asked Jake.

Random finished his counting up.

'£4.37.'

'Terrific!' Jake threw up his arms and kicked a mound of dirt nearby the bench. An alien looking mole poked his head out of the mud and squeaked angrily at Jake before disappearing again.

'Well, maybe £4.37 is quite a lot here. It's worth a shot!' Anji picked the money from the fluff and grime and made for the kiosk again.

'That's what I like most about Anj,' Jake said to Random, 'She's always so positive. Silly beggar.'

Random smiled and followed his two friends back to the kiosk.

As they waited in line, the two teenagers had questions for their alien friend.

'Hey, Random, how come everyone here is speaking English?'

'Good question Anji. The answer is they aren't.'

Anji looked confused.

'Well, they clearly are!' said Jake.

'Nope, you're just hearing English. The Venus II has scanned your brain patterns and tailored your hearing responses to whatever dialect is spoken on whatever planet you land on.'

'Hold on, that ship is in my head again? I don't like it. This could be the toilet incident all over again!' Jake crossed his legs. He didn't want an unexpected interception from the Venus II again.

'It's an added design feature. I think it's quite cool. Don't worry, it's quite ethical. It doesn't read your thoughts or anything. It's just trying to help. I can turn it off it you're not comfortable?'

Anji and Jake pondered for a moment.

'Well, the language thing is a bonus but maybe we should install a toilet,' Anji chuckled.

'Consider it done...if we have enough money to buy one!'

'So, does that language thing work the other way around too? Are we speaking alien to this lot on Genocia?'

'Yes, you are. It's just your brain's default bilingual set-up is in English. Pretty cool, huh?'

'Yeah man!' Jake turned to Anji. 'Hey, Anj, I'm talking alien!'

Anji sighed. 'That must be why I've never understood you, then!' She winked.

'Well, technically speaking, it's Genocian, you are speaking. Saves on classes, doesn't it? Although the Venus II was designed as a warship, it was also designed for long haul exploration in the event of the war ending.'

'What a ship. Maybe I should start being nicer to it,' said Jake.

The trio made their way to the front of the queue and turned in their loose change.

The kiosk worker, this time a more reddish tone than Cheem and looking more like a fish than man, looked at the travellers in shock.

'Is this in...sterling?'

'Yup. How much could we get for this?' asked Random.

The big red fish gulped and ignored Random's query. He picked up a communicator and spoke quietly to a stranger on the other end of the line.

After a time, he put the receiver down and looked wide eyed at Random and his friends.

'I've just had to double check with my superior. At the current exchange rate, £4.37 will get you £$68,546,910.3. Would you like that given to you in cash or credit bar?'

Anji and Jake nearly collapsed in shock.

'Sorry,' Anji cleared her throat. 'Could you just repeat that?'

'£$68,546,910.3'

Jake wobbled a bit and sat on the floor, panting heavily.

Random looked perplexed.

'Is that good?'

'Good! We're millionaires!' Anji lollopped next to Jake, smiling uncontrollably.

'Well, let's put it this way, how many islands would you like to buy from our government?' The red fish, curiously named Bill by the tag on his lapel, was almost as disbelieving as his customers. Some members of the queue looked on in astonishment. Whispers and gasps of surprise bleated around the kiosk.

'So...you can get more than just your weekly shop on this sort of money then?' asked Random.

'Well, if you were to buy a few islands and all the facilities on there, I think you could safely say you'd have enough money left over to buy more than just the weekly shop.'

'Right.' Random didn't quite know how to process this information. He turned to speak to his friends and noticed they were no longer there. Looking directly at his feet, he noticed they had fainted with surprise.

'I'm afraid we could only release a portion of this amount right now as we simply do not have that kind of money here. If you'd like the rest of the total amount released then you'd have to speak to the Treasury.'

The enormity of the news was just starting to hit him.

'Yeah. Let's do that then.'

'Fantastic. I shall have to put you in contact with somebody who can help in that matter. Hold on a second.'

Bill typed into his computer and printed out the name and address the trio needed to release their funds.

'Would £$500 be enough for now?'

'I guess so,' Random said.

Bill withdrew the amount from the kiosk.

'If you didn't mind, sir, please could you leave the full amount with me here? My superior needs to verify the money before transferring it to the National Bank. There will be people who will want to speak to you. It's nothing to be worried about. It's just official procedure. If you could please arrange for your party to rendezvous with the Treasury representative here at closing time this evening? We close in seven hours by your Earth time. Would that be okay for you all?'

Random nodded and wondered whether this "official procedure" would be anything like what they endured back at immigration.

Bill handed over £$500 to Random in the form of a credit bar which closely resembled a metallic ruler. 'There you go and be careful.'

'Thank you,' Random placed the bar in his trouser pocket and bent down to pick up his two friends who were making soft cooing noises to themselves.

'Come on, you two. Let's go shopping!'

*

The communicator on Samuelson's desk fizzed into life, stirring the chancellor from a dreamless sleep and aggravating an already angry migraine.

'Yes,' he groaned in reply, massaging his temples as he clicked the receiving button on.

The voice on the other end was strong and authoritative, like that of a newsreader.

'Zatterson, here, sir. We've just had word from the central bank that a tourist has tried to exchange Earth money for Genocian Pounddollars.'

'And you thought that was important enough to disturb me at my work?' Samuelson lied. He had drunk the last of his Genocian whiskey reserves and lost consciousness, falling asleep on top of a pile of scattered papers documenting the Government's plans to halt the slide in the lack of productivity without consigning more people to the mines. Now he remembered why he had been drinking at midday.

'Hold on, did you just say Earth?'

'Yes, sir, I did,' confirmed Zatterson.

'But that's a level 1 planet, isn't it?'

'Yes, sir. No meaningful space travel to speak about. It's only on our computers because we sent a team of explorers to the Solar System

decades ago. Earth is only on our scope for admin reasons. Not only that, sir, but due to the currencies used there it also means that the exchange rate is pretty much incomprehensible.'

'So...how many Genocian pounddollars do they have on their person?'

'Just under £$69,000,000.'

The Chancellor's eyes lit up.

'But...that alone could halt the slump in the economy.'

'Exactly, sir.'

'Where are the funds now?'

They are being withheld in a tourist kiosk in the shopping precinct.

'What's it doing there? Bring it here!' Samuelson screamed. 'We can't lose that money, Zatterson. Where are the Earthmen now?'

'They are under close surveillance in the left wing of the precinct, sir. I have arranged with the head of the group to meet us there at closing time.'

Samuelson clapped his hands together. 'Fantastic, I always knew I could rely on you, Zatterson. When you meet with the travellers let me know that you have made contact. Bring them to the Grand Chamber. I'll speak to them there.'

'Should we inform Consula of our discovery?'

'No, under no account should we tell her. I want to discover more about these people myself before she gets her grip on them. This is a strictly need-to-know only subject for now. I shall meet you at the Grand Chamber later.'

'As you wish, sir.'

The communicator crackled and Samuelson's office was silent once again.

VII

After the initial shock of realising that here on Genocia they were millionaires, Random, Anji and Jake had awoken from a fog of disbelief and thrown themselves into a shopping spree that rivaled any they had ever been on before.

To receive a slight increase in weekly pocket money was a bonus. To be told you were worth millions and millions of Genocian pounddollars was unthinkable!

'Do you think we should get a bodyguard?' suggested Jake, struggling with a myriad of bags as he joined them on the escalator.

Random was looking thoughtfully down to the people below. All the escalators in the shopping precinct were built to run alongside the walls of the towers themselves to give shoppers a unique view of the entire area. From here, you could look out onto the many levels of shops on the inside or out onto the beautiful spires and, on this occasion for Random, a sulphur-like bleed of sun that shone as it began to set.

'Of course not, you pleb,' said Anji. 'Besides, we don't actually have the money on us, do we?'

'Well, I'm still keeping a look out,' said Jake.

'You're not doing a very good job then, are you?' said Random. Jake looked perplexed.

'Eh?'

'Don't look now but there has been someone following us ever since we left the ice cream parlour in the right quadrant.'

Anji did her best not to look. But, as she was standing side on to her friends, she managed to peer out of the corner of her eye. At first, Anji couldn't see anyone but her fellow shoppers who looked far removed from those she had grown used to seeing in shopping centres around London. Tall, short, fat, thin, man, woman, both, that's where the similarities ended. Here the people really were of all races, colours and sizes. And then she saw them.

A woman with long black curly hair and a transparent face stood on the escalator roughly ten metres away from the travellers, staring unblinking at them.

'I think I've spotted her.'

'Hmm,' said Random.

'Well, shouldn't we run for it?' asked Jake.

'I don't think so,' Random calmly replied.

'Why not?' said Anji. 'We could be in serious danger!'

Random turned to his friends, bumping against a poor Genocian with his bags at the same time.

'Because we don't know WHY we are being followed. For all we know, that could be our own

bodyguard. The people who run this planet don't want us getting harmed now, do they?'

'No,' conceded Anji. 'But they don't want us to leave either, do they? We're meeting them soon, aren't we?'

'Exactly.'

'This is all very funny,' said Jake. 'I'd have thought we'd want to attract little attention and get back to the Venus II as soon as possible.'

'The Venus II! That reminds me!' exclaimed Random.

'Skateboard?' asked Anji.

'No,' replied Random. 'But we do need to drop our bags off before we meet these bankers. We'll leave them at the baggage desk and get them delivered to the ship. There's no way we want to be carrying these things with us to a very important meeting now, is there?'

'Don't you feel like we're walking into a trap, Random?' asked Anji.

'Oh yes, definitely,' replied Random as the escalator came to an end. 'But, if you want to know what's going on, it's worth getting yourself captured from time-to-time, don't you think?'

Jake groaned.

'You can tell you're alien, mate! I have a bad feeling about this.'

*

The spy maintained her pursuit of the travellers, but maintained a cautious distance behind, surveying their movements and keeping track of what they were spending their money on. As Random, Anji and Jake stepped off the escalator and headed off towards the baggage desk, she pressed her finger to her ear.

'Nothing to report so far, sir.'

'Have they made contact with any other beings?' Zatterson's voice burst through her earpiece. The device was invisible to the naked eye, mainly down to the fact that the spy with the transparent skin was hiding the contraption with a hood she wore over her see through head.

'No, sir. There is nothing to suggest that there are more of them. Nor that they are spending their money inappropriately. Their purchases have been rather...domestic.'

Zatterson frowned, listening through his speaker phone back in his office in the Grand Chamber. He leant in, flicking through live images taken from the security cameras planted around the shopping mall, having hacked into the surveillance system with the help of a techy intern.

'I'd noticed. Nothing but wallpaper, paint, and curtain rails. Even a latrine! I can't work them out.'

'Visual indicates that they are not intentionally trying to throw us off the scent, sir. I witnessed the female of the group look directly at me moments ago and yet they still remain calm. It's as though they know that they are being followed.'

'I think they do,' replied Zatterson. 'Something's up with this lot. They are unlike any other race we've had here.'

Samuelson's voice burst in on the conversation.

'Having fun, are we?'

Zatterson jumped and looked around to see his superior standing over him.

'I wish. I'd give anything for this lot to do something outrageous and untoward. But they are not splashing the cash we gave them. They are just going about their daily business.'

'They are just children, Zatterson. What are you expecting? You think they are being frivolous with their money?'

'Well, no, but I didn't expect them to be building a house either!'

'It's clear that they have just struck it lucky,' said Samuelson. 'However, I'm in talks with Customs and Immigration about their craft. How is it that three children are able to fly a craft that

size unaided? And Earth is not listed as a planet that is particularly advanced when it comes to space travel. I'd be surprised if they have

invented the wheel, they appear so backward!'

'Maybe they were not unaided,' Zatterson picked up a file from his desk. 'Apparently, they arrived on Genocia with a robot, although it wasn't allowed past immigration. Maybe there's something he isn't telling us.'

Samuelson smiled. 'Maybe. Perhaps we should see what we can get out of this robot then.'

'Perhaps the ship has been stolen?'

'We'll find out soon. Remember, this is just between us for now. That money can help save our economy.'

'And if they work out what we are planning?' asked Zatterson.

'We'll send them to the Soul Destroyer.'

*

'What are we looking out for again?'

Jake was kicking stones against the kiosk, hoping he would hit one of the glass panes. In his current mood, he was willing to break something expensive to vent his frustration.

Why Random didn't want to make a run for it he didn't know. Why were they hanging around?

'No idea,' said Random.

'Random, this seems totally ridiculous. We should get back to the Venus II. Why are we letting them capture us?' Anji was starting to worry.

'First of all, we can't go back to the Venus II even if we wanted to. For all we know, whoever we are about to meet has already ransacked it looking for information! We can't go anywhere else to hide; we have no friends on this planet. As soon as we walk through immigration again, we'll be captured.'

'Can't we sneak in?' Jake implored. 'Anything! These guys could kill us.'

Random sighed. 'They're not going to kill us, Jake. They want our money. And I want answers.'

'Answers?' Anji sat next to her purple friend.

'Something hasn't felt right with this planet since we landed. I have a feeling that something terrible is happening here. And we're going to find out what it is.'

Jake stopped kicking stones at the kiosk and sat down next to his friends.

'Random, we're not the police. These are very important people we are dealing with. The Sandman was one thing...this is another.'

Anji nodded.

'Jake's talking sense.'

Random looked at his friends. 'Look, I have a sense of duty to help those who are in need. It's what I was born to do...made to do, if you want to be really accurate.'

'Nobody is making you now and what if we don't like what we find out? Genocia may just run in different ways to Earth. Who are we to say what's right and what's wrong on a planet we know nothing about?'

'But we do know about it. Genocia is supposed to be a peaceful, welcoming planet. It's been everything but since we've arrived.'

'Oh, I don't know. Cheem seemed very friendly,' said Jake.

'Look, this is one of the reasons I didn't want you to come with me - in case this happened. The universe is a dangerous place and it's up to people like me to make it a safer one.'

Anji took Random's hand. 'If you feel that strongly about it, we are both here to help.'

Random put his hand on Anji's.

'I don't like this anymore than you two do. But we must find out what's happening here.'

As more and more shoppers left the precinct and the sun began to set, the three travellers cut lonely figures.

They waited another ten minutes and, just as the first stars in the night sky began to twinkle majestically, a shuttle car, hovering above the ground as if it was on invisible wheels, drove into view.

'Here we go,' said Random as he got to his feet.

'About time,' grumbled Jake. 'I was getting so cold I was going to ask if I could wear your jumper, Anj!'

Anji tutted and followed Random by getting to her feet.

The headlights blared in the trio's direction. Slowly, the car ground to a halt and two mysterious figures in dark suits emerged from the vehicle.

'Captain Random?' called out one of the shapes.

'Yeah, that's me.'

The man smiled. 'Please, we have an appointment to keep.' He opened the door fully and beckoned the travellers in. Random strode forward with purpose and entered the car.

Jake looked at Anji.

'Ladies first.'

Anji grunted and led the way.

'Looks like it's a limo at least!' she said more light-heartedly than she felt as they got in the car and were driven away to the Grand Chamber.

VIII

Skateboard continued to busy himself with the controls of the Venus II. Since he had returned to the ship, the little AI robot had decided to pass the time waiting for his friends by researching as much as he could about Genocia. The only time he had been disturbed was when he was required to sign for the supplies and materials Random, Anji and Jake had bought on their shopping spree. After that disruption, he hastily went back to his work.

He had detected from his companions that they had all been a little taken aback by the heavy-handed conduct of the guards and now here he was, trapped in the parking hangar with little to occupy him except his research.

It hadn't taken him much effort to bypass Genocia's security systems and pore over internal documents, not to mention the surveillance system on the planet so he could keep an eye on his friends.

He was very confident that nobody was going to foil him, not least because his own binary pathways had gone underneath the encrypted

passwords and the alarm bells alerting the authorities that he
had hacked them were not going to ring. Put simply, he'd taken
the metaphorical wire out of the alarm.

Skateboard was onto his seventeenth case file and the dots were
starting to add up, much to his concern.

He used his wireless capabilities to flick a switch on the
dashboard of the cockpit.

'Sir, I am leaving you this message as a precautionary measure
as I am planning to leave this craft to further my investigation. To
listen to the rest, please speak your password now.'

Skateboard left a gap and made sure his recording would be
activated by Random alone.

'Having consulted various records, I have managed to find,
Genocia is definitely not the planet it seems to be. We appear to
have landed on a world that is consumed by greed. There seems
to be a great emphasis on tourism because that's the main income
this planet receives. Apart from that, there are no exports to speak
of. It prides itself on being essentially a holiday planet but that's it.
The money that comes in goes to the main treasury but I can see
nothing in these records to show that the money goes back into
the economy.'

The AI robot continued. 'What concerns me more, sir, is the
revelation that the number of inhabitants of Genocia is decreasing
by the month and has done for the last 200 years.

Yet there are no death certificates I can find...anywhere! I've
found many a record of petty crime but nothing to suggest what
happens
    afterwards.'

Skateboard broke away from his report and saw something in a
case file that stopped him in his tracks. It was marked
"CLASSIFIED" and inside contained thousands upon thousands
of files with the terrible heading, "TELL US, IN 149
CHARACTERS, WHY YOU ARE GOING TO DIE TODAY."

His diodes whirred as he tried to comprehend what he was
reading. Some of the reasons given were truly appalling.

"I WAS FRAMED BY MY NEIGHBOUR FOR STEALING FROM
HER. I AM INNOCENT AND I HAVEN'T EVEN FACED
TRIAL!" read one.

"I HAVEN'T HAD A JOB IN TWO YEARS AND I COULDN'T FEED MY FAMILY. I'M SO SORRY. I WAS DESPERATE!!" read another.

File after file after file. Skateboard shuddered in a way robots shouldn't. It looked like these petty crimes were being dealt with in the harshest way imaginable. Extermination. No trial, no investigation, no reasons behind the sentences handed out. These people were being killed; it seemed, without care or attention.

Here they were, strangers in a careless world, in a stolen spaceship, sitting ducks just waiting for the same fate. Skateboard packed the files away in his memory circuits and plotted a course of action. He had to rescue his friends.

'Sir, if you are listening to this and I am not here when you get back, I implore you…no, I plead with you, just fly off without me. Get Anji and Jake somewhere safe.'

Suddenly, something smashed into the hull of the ship. It sounded like a big metal fist knocking on the side of the Venus II. Skateboard jumped.

'Come on; let us in now, robot.'

It was the head guard. Skateboard quickly checked the scanner. He was accompanied by a dozen of the same guards who had made the crew of the Venus II's lives so difficult when they landed.

Silence.

The head guard sighed.

'If you do not let us in then we are bound by Article 4 of the Genocia treaty to seize this vehicle and all within it.'

A cannon was wheeled onto the gangway and placed against the door. They were going to blast their way through!

Skateboard knew he'd had it. The Venus II was anchored to the ground and, even if he could break away using his hacking skills, he wouldn't

have time to cloak the craft before it was shot down by security. He was trapped!

IX

Zatterson welcomed the travellers at the foot of the stairs that rose high to the front door of the Grand Chamber.

As the limo hovered to a halt at his feet, the driver emerged and held the door open for Random, Anji and Jake to disembark.

Their journey had been reasonably comfortable. Deep, plush seats lent an element of reassurance to the whole mysterious experience.

The bodyguards that flanked either door held the trio in place and Random couldn't ignore the

fact that they were being taken into a trap. He prepared himself mentally for the barrage of questions they were bound to face.

Where were their parents? Were they alone? How did they get here? What were their intentions?

Random led his friends from the car.

'Ah, Mr. Random, I presume?' Zatterson held his hand out to shake.

Random looked down and, using his forefinger and thumb, shook the official's hand.

'Captain, actually. Who are you?'

'Forgive me, my name is Zatterson. I am the Head of the Treasury on Genocia. And these must be your friends?'

'Yes, this is Jake and this is Anji.'

Zatterson shook the hands of the bemused Earthlings and gestured them up the stairs.

There were a few dozen steps the travellers had to conquer before making it to the Grand Chamber. Each step was adorned with what looked like LED lights that guided visitors up to the door. Rails stood on hand to guide those on the steep incline, or decline depending on which way you were walking.

Random eyed Zatterson as they made their way.

He was about six feet in height, middle-aged by Earth standards with a parted, greasy haircut and a moustache that was pencil thin sitting uneasily on his top lip. He was human in appearance, not like the scores of species the travellers had seen in the shopping precinct. Zatterson wore a long tailcoat with a black bow tie and black polished shoes. He looked like he was taking dinner in first class on the Titanic! There was nothing "alien" about him, thought Anji.

'I take it that you have travelled far across the galaxy to be here?' Zatterson enquired.

'Not really,' said Random. 'Just a quick hop.'

Anji shot a look to her purple friend. Don't give anything away, she thought to herself.

They made it to the top of the steps. A doorman was waiting for them and, with a nod from Zatterson, opened the Grand Chamber door.

Jake's eyes glittered as they saw the brilliance of the Grand Chamber.

'Wow!' he gasped as he looked up at the huge emerald chandeliers. Anji couldn't help but feel impressed too. The hall was a majestic white and seemed to go on for miles. Small pockets of people, dressed officially, stood quietly talking to each other.

'Jake, this reminds me of the Houses of Parliament!' she remarked.

'Yeah, you can tell they are all politicians, can't you?' Jake agreed.

Random was quiet.

'Not far now. We were hoping you could join us for dinner tonight. I'm afraid we are a little unaccustomed to Earth delicacies but we shall do our best,' said Zatterson.

He led the trio, still accompanied by the bodyguards walking a few paces behind the party, into a side room. Knocking, Zatterson opened the oak doors and revealed a long dining table.

The dining room resembled something from 1940s England. Oak beams lined the ceiling and various paintings adorned the walls while the dozen or so chairs surrounding the table bore

flowery patterns. It was like they had walked into Winston Churchill's Cabinet Rooms!

'Well, the décor reminds me of Earth,' exclaimed Anji.

'I'm glad that you approve. Please,' said Zatterson, beckoning Random, Anji and Jake to take seats near the head of the table. The bodyguards held a chair out for the two humans, but Random insisted on no help.

He watched as Zatterson sat opposite him, leaving the chair at the head of the table vacant.

'I take it we've got another guest joining us?' he enquired.

'Yes,' said Zatterson. 'We shall be joined by Chancellor Samuelson himself. He should be here any moment.'

'Samuelson and Zatterson,' Anji pondered. 'Are you two related?'

Zatterson snorted. 'No. We are given the word, "son" at the end of our names to indicate that we have been elected to office. I can assure you I bare no other resemblance to the Chancellor.'

As if on cue, the side door burst open and the imposing figure of Samuelson strode into the room. He was younger than Zatterson, his hair fuller and darker but he still gave off an air of distrust like his counterpart.

Jake and Anji, not knowing the correct protocol for dinner with officials on this alien world, stood to attention. Random did not.

'Please, sit down,' Samuelson smiled.

Random could tell that this expression was not worn very often by the politician. The newcomer looked in pain as he grinned uneasily at the travellers.

Jake and Anji returned to their chairs as the bodyguards left the room.

They were alone now.

'Please take a look at the menu in front of you. May I suggest the Squodge soup and Blabber ink truffles for starters?'

Jake heaved a little.

'Sounds...delightful.'

Random broke his silence.

'Something tells me that you didn't invite us here for a dinner party, Chancellor?'

Samuelson smirked. 'Come now, Mr. Random, you are our guests. You're quite safe in these walls.'

'Yes, but for how long?'

Anji's heart skipped a beat. She could not believe how rude Random was being.

'I can assure you, there is no need for hostility. We would like to treat you as our guests. After all, you are the richest people on this planet.'

'Are we?' Jake jumped at the statement. Now it all made sense. That's why they were being followed in the shopping precinct, why they were escorted by bodyguards to such a grand place and treated to dinner by some of the most important people on the planet.

A door to the side of the room opened and waiters and waitresses emerged with trolleys of drinks in various colours. They filled goblets for all five dinner guests.

'Why yes,' Samuelson reassured. 'You see, your currency is a very rare one. Earth is not considered a very advanced planet. Although we know a little about your world, we have never been visited by its inhabitants before. We didn't think that you had the capability to travel the stars yet.'

'They don't,' Random thought to himself.

'Well, we've been to the moon,' said Jake.

Samuelson raised his eyebrows.

'And further, it seems. How did you get here?'

'We're just travellers,' Random butted in. 'We're just passing by. We needed some supplies so we thought Genocia was the right place for us.'

'Explorers?' Zatterson asked. He took a gulp of his drink. Jake and Anji peered into their goblets. The liquid looked the sort of greeny gunge colour you only see on children's TV shows.

Anji sniffed warily then took a brave swig. Jake retched a little in the back of his throat and politely declined. Anji envied him - the drink was sour.

'What is this?' she spluttered.

'Momosum wine. Suitable for minors with food,' said Zatterson.

'It's vile!'

'Oh dear, can we get you anything else?'

'Water if you have some?'

'Yes of course.' He clicked his fingers and called a waiter to the table and asked him to fetch some water.

'You could say that,' Random eventually answered.

'But where's the rest of your crew? You can't be piloting that ship of yours on your own? Where are the adults?' asked Samuelson.

'There are none. It's just us.' Random was feeling uneasy but tried to give nothing away.

'Interesting,' said Samuelson, pursing his lips.

'Look, I can understand it looks a little bizarre. But I can assure you, we are not here illegally.' Random lent forward in his chair. 'We just came here to stock up and then go off on our way.'

'I understand,' said Samuelson.

'Can I ask a question?' asked Anji.

'Of course,' said Samuelson.

'If we are the richest people on this planet, how come you can afford all of this stuff in this chamber?'

'Good question, Miss, err?'

'Gummadi.'

'Miss Gummadi. Genocia was once a prosperous world. This planet was one of the richest in the known galaxy. A rare mineral, called ESOL19, which helped promote and

reduce crop growth, was discovered by the first inhabitants of this world centuries ago.'

The waiter returned with a jug of water.

'The settlers proceeded to sell the mineral to neighbouring planets and this helped fund the Grand Chamber you are now sitting in. Not to mention homes for the inhabitants. In return, many of the best decided to make homes and set up their businesses on Genocia, hence the shopping precinct. So for many, many years, Genocia was a prosperous world.'

'But not now?' Random swilled his goblet thoughtfully.

'In recent years the economy has faced a huge downturn. Our reserves of ESOL19 dwindled. No matter how many people we employed to mine this planet, the well had well and truly run dry. So the money stopped coming in and we now rely solely on our tourism and the trade that comes in from those visiting this planet.'

'However, even our tourism income is starting to decrease. Despite Genocia holding the record for awards in popularity in this galaxy, we've noticed that numbers are going down in all areas of income. Genocia is becoming poorer and poorer and there is nothing we can do to stop it.'

'Who runs this planet?' asked Random.

'Our leader, of course. But enough about us, what about yourselves?'

'We've got nothing else to tell,' said Random resolutely. 'But I think I can see what is going on here. You'd like our money, wouldn't you?'

'Mr. Random...'

'Captain Random, if you don't mind?'

Samuelson grinned. 'Captain, your personal fortune is six times more than the current treasury holds in its vaults. It sounds ridiculous, doesn't it?'

'So, you want me to hand it over to you? In exchange for what? Our freedom?' Random was starting to feel a little more than hard done by.

'As I've said to you before, you are not captives. All I am asking is that you think about it. We've seen your ship. You three don't look like you have any need for the wealth you've come into. Surely it could be put to better use elsewhere. Captain, the beauty you have seen on

this planet, this splendour, is just skin deep. We only allow our tourists to stay in certain areas. Four-fifths of this planet is out of bounds.

The reason? The planet is pretty much uninhabitable. Thousands of unfortunate souls, Genocians who are unlucky enough not to have real work or safe housing, live in squalor. You could save a whole civilization with your donation. Many lives will be saved.'

Random, Anji and Jake sat motionless. Samuelson was right; they didn't have any reason to keep hold of the money. They didn't need it.

Certainly not if it meant saving a whole species on the brink of extinction.

'Why haven't you asked for help from other planets? There must be some who can help you?'

'That's a good question, Miss Gummadi. Put simply, when our forefathers were at the height of their wealth, we didn't help when others called upon us. So why should those we scorned in the past help us now?'

Jake frowned.

'I think we've got some thinking to do.'

'Not at all,' said Random. During Samuelson's speech he was reminded of the pain and suffering that he saw back on Rodas. The hordes of men, women and children forced to live in the dirt and ruin of a planet at war. Those images haunted him, especially as he was supposed to be the one person who could put a stop to it all. He was not yet ready to be that hero. There was no way that Random was going to refuse a second call for help.

'I shall need to discuss with my friends, but I have no hesitation in donating the money.'

Samuelson and Zatterson looked at one another, trying to contain their delight.

'On TWO conditions.'

'Name them,' said Samuelson.

'Number one, we are free to leave this planet whenever we like.'

'Of course – that freedom is already extended to yourselves,' reassured Samuelson.

'Two, I'd like to see this suffering for myself.'

'Random, what are you doing?' Anji was worried. Her friend hadn't quite been his usual self since they had come into the money. She shot an anxious look at Jake, who seemed to be sharing her sentiments.

'I'm sure we can arrange that. We could take you to one of the squats just outside of the city. Maybe even show you one of our mines. We have a small section of available funds financing a final search for ESOL19 nearby.'

'Excellent,' said Random.

'This will all have to wait until the morning. We can offer you rooms within the Grand Chamber if you like.'

'Actually, I'd rather go back to our ship,' said Anji.

'Nah, let's stay here!' replied Jake.

'That'd be great, Chancellor. We'd be happy to stay the night.' Random looked over at Anji.

'We might as well make the most of free hospitality while we are here, Anj.'

Anji smiled weakly. 'Okay.'

'Now, enough of this official twaddle for now,' Samuelson reached for his menu and opened the centre page.

'What's on the menu tonight?'

X

Zatterson was right about the choice of Earth food. Having scrutinized the politician's motives for hosting them, the travellers then scrutinized the menu and discovered that the only Earth delicacy on offer was syrup and pancakes. Hesitant to order anything after tasting the special wine, Anji plumped for that. Jake followed suit but ventured towards a Genocian ice cream sundae, which was better than anything he had on Earth.

Random didn't feel like eating but decided on the same dish as Samuelson, something called calcusac, which looked a bit like lasagne but tasted more like beetroot stew.

Fed and watered, the trio made their excuses and were shown to their rooms by the guards.

To get to the living area within the Grand Chamber, Random, Anji and Jake had to board a shuttle cart. Jake remarked that it was no wonder the planet had gone bust, so much money had been spent on the Chamber and it seemed to be as big a city!

A woman called the maître d' showed the threesome to their rooms which were handily joined together and connected by a living area.

This was more like it, thought the trio. The décor was much more spacey and futuristic, all neon lights and chrome. The beds were almost like waterbeds and adapted to their body mass for extreme comfort.

As soon as the travellers had left the dining room, Samuelson turned to his Head of Treasury to plot their next move.

'Have you had any news on the craft?'

'Yes, sir. It's been verified as stolen property. The details are not in the name of any of the inhabitants.'

'Excellent,' snarled Samuelson.

'We've sent the Immigration guards to impound it now and capture the robot on board. They have been told to proceed with extreme caution, so both it and the ship should be in our hands soon.'

'Good work, Zatterson!'

Samuelson got up and looked out at Genocia from the dining room window.

'Do you think they swallowed the story, sir?'

'The bits they needed to, yes. I'm not convinced about the purple one. He seems to have experience beyond his years. We shall have to make sure they don't go wandering during the night. As soon as we take them to the mines tomorrow, we can leave them to await their fate like the rest of the scum down there.'

'Their rooms have been bugged, just to make sure that doesn't happen,' reassured Zatterson. 'Although only one of the party drank from the wine. It might be very difficult to stop the other two from their curiosity getting the better of them.'

'Keep them under surveillance. We shall deal with them in the morning. Has the money arrived at the Treasury yet?'

'Yes, sir. It arrived not long before the captain and his friends arrived.'

Samuelson scoffed. 'Captain! The nerve! Let me know when the ship arrives at the impoundment centre, Zatterson. When we learn to fly it, think of the wealth we can bring back from Earth. We won't be relying on some ancient mineral or tourism anymore.'

Zatterson smiled.

'Dismissed. Tomorrow is an important day in the history of Genocia.'

'When are we telling Consula, sir?'

'I said dismissed.'

Zatterson nodded and left Samuelson alone with his plans.

*

'So, we're actually going to give all that money away then?'

Jake's head was spinning. Hours ago, he had no money to his name. Now he was a multi-millionaire. In the morning he would be penniless again.

'If their claims are genuine, yes,' said Random, who sat cross armed on the sofa in the living room of the hotel suite. 'The Chancellor's right, we have no need for it. If it can go a long way towards restoring the lives of those on this planet, then so be it.'

'You're not sure though?' asked Anji.

'Never trust a politician, Anji. There's normally greed behind their motives. Look at the history of those on your world. Too many have the interests of the few on their minds and not the rest.'

'True, and they always seem to want to go to war,' Jake chimed in.

'I mean look at this place. Are you seriously telling me that this planet is going bankrupt? I don't believe him. That's why I have to make sure for myself his claims are true.'

'And if they aren't? What do we do?' asked Jake.

'Stop them!' Anji interjected.

'Yes,' said Random.

'How?' asked Jake.

'As long we've got the Venus II and Skateboard we can find a way. I asked him to see what he could find out about this planet before we left him.'

Anji sighed.

'I wish we'd gone back to the ship. I don't feel safe here.'

'Don't worry Anj, I won't let anything happen to you.' Jake put his arm around his friend.

'Oh, very reassuring!' she said.

'If we stick together, we'll be fine,' said Random. The words of reassurance sounded better coming from Random than they did Jake.

Anji smiled and gave both of them a hug.

'Right, I'm off to bed. It's a shame I forgot my toothbrush. I can still taste that terrible wine in my mouth.'

Jake agreed. 'Ditto. I'm going to turn in myself. Night peeps.'

'Night, you two,' said Random. He let out a yawn and retired to his room.

Anji readied herself for bed, studying her face in the mirror and made full use of a fresh toothbrush left helpfully on the shelf to clean her teeth. She didn't want to mention it but she had felt a little woozy since she had gone to her room. She dismissed her dizziness as just a reaction to a tiring day. After all, she'd started the day in

Epping Forest on Earth and was now ending it in the Grand Chamber of an alien planet, temporarily a millionaire.

She spat out the toothpaste in the sink and swilled her mouth with water from the tap.

Licking her lips, she took one further look at her reflection in the bathroom mirror. Her features seemed to be melting a little bit. Anji felt her forehead. Her temperature seemed normal but her dizziness was starting to feel worse. To compound matters, that horrible taste of wine was still in her mouth.

This wasn't the first time she had drunk wine but, after how she was feeling tonight, in her current condition, it was certainly going to be the last.

Anji made for the bedroom but her legs started to feel wobbly. Has she picked up a virus? All of a sudden, she started to panic. Maybe they needed an inoculation of some sort before they landed on alien worlds.

Anji tried to walk to the bed but fell against the wall. Her vision started to go blurry. Using the wall for support, she started to sweat as she pulled along her failing frame. The taste of the wine was still there. Why was her mind focusing on that bloody wine!?

Then, she realised what had happened. Just as Anji tried to scream out Random's name, she lost consciousness and collapsed onto the bed.

Her companions didn't hear any of the commotion in their rooms either side of Anji's. Unknown to them, the rooms were sound-proofed. Anji lay motionless on her bed, drugged and helpless.

XI

CRASH!

The electronic battering ram slammed into the doors of the Venus II. Skateboard frantically tried to release the cargo bay doors and undo the magnets that anchored the ship in place. Regardless of the diagnostic he ran, no matter how many binary doors he tried to open, he was unable to bypass Genocia's security systems. The guards had been trying to force their way into the ship for a few minutes and yet the Venus II stood firm. There seemed to be no damage to the outer hull whatsoever. Skateboard worked on, believing that he was safe for the time being.

The Venus II was made from a metal compound called seda-metal – a rare commodity in the universe but one of which Rodas had in short supply; and from that limited amount came the Venus II, not to mention some of the main fleet's battleships.

The thing about seda-metal is that it was nearly indestructible. You'd need a five-megaton atomic bomb strapped to its exhaust port to split the vessel open. Although Skateboard knew this, he was still running out of time. He had to escape and he knew that if he couldn't take the Venus II with him, he'd have to get out of there himself.

The AI robot glanced nervously at the scanner again. The ship was completely surrounded. Escape was no longer an option.

'Again!' the lead guard hollered. For the umpteenth time his team of blank-faced charges pulled the ram back and swung it with all their might into the door. The ram made a deafening thud and the soldiers heaved as they started to lose their strength.

'What's the matter with you lot?' the lead guard screamed. They walked away from what was now a pile of panting guards, hunched double, gasping for air, and spoke into their wrist watch.

'I need to speak to Zatterson,' the metallic voice murmured.

'Zatterson here.'

'Sir, we've had no luck breaching the hull of the ship.'

'What? Are you using as much force as you can muster?'

'Yes,' the lead guard looked back, 'and I don't think my men have got much left in them. We need more equipment. I've never seen a ship like this before, sir. It seems impregnable.'

'All the more reason to find out what they are hiding in there. Okay, Tibius, keep your efforts up. Get more men if needs be. Just get that thing open!'

'Yes, sir.' Tibius turned back to the troops. 'Get more men here – and bring another battering ram!'

The guards sighed and did as they were told.

Skateboard, having given up his code cracking, saw the soldiers start to move away from the Venus II. A few stayed circled around the ship, blast guns in hand, ready to shoot.

He tried one final time to release the magnetic clamps but again he was met by the firewall. If he was to be successful, he'd have to shut the system down from within the bay and that meant leaving the ship. But how would he do that without being seen?

In that moment, Skateboard had one of the cleverest ideas he'd had in his life.

XII

Random stirred in his bed. Falling asleep had been reasonably easy the previous night. Waking up was proving slightly more problematic. He felt like he hadn't had a decent night's sleep in, well, forever.

He groaned as he opened his eyes and they were met by an instant burning sensation. He blinked and turned his back on a crack in his curtains that was leaking the brilliant Genocian sunshine into the bedroom. Random had had some trouble fixing them in the correct position before he went to bed.

Everything in his room was operated by a wall- mounted control unit so, when he was trying to close the curtains and turn his light off for the evening, he had inadvertently turned on the TV in the ceiling, turned on the automatic toilet flusher and nearly flooded his bathroom in the process. In the end, he'd given up and decided that, just as soon as his weariness got the better of him, he'd sleep without the curtains properly drawn.

Random did his best to go straight back to sleep. The extreme comfort of the sheet and mattress gave him a yearning to cocoon himself within it for all eternity.

He hoped to himself that the same
make of sheets had been procured by his friends the previous day on their shopping spree.

Shopping spree! Now he remembered.

They were millionaires. The rulers of this planet wanted their money. Today he was going to find out if their intentions were true and would probably die in the process. He had to get up.

After spending some time messing with the complicated automated systems in the bathroom, Random pulled on his yellow t-shirt and khaki trousers, checked his thick brown hair in the mirror, washed his face, laced up his boots and went out into the living area that joined his room with Jake's.

The young teenager was already seated looking out over the beautiful view of Genocia offered by the windows.

'How did you sleep?' asked Random as he went to join Jake at the table.

'Mmm…' said Jake, scoffing toast. 'Best night's kip I've had in yonks. You?'

'Same. Is Anji up yet?'

Jake licked his lips. A glob of jam fixed itself firmly on the corner of his mouth.

'Nope. Not seen her yet. You having anything? I asked for Earth food for breakfast.'

'I can see,' Random put his fingers to his lips and looked out in a pensive mood.

'You've not been yourself since we've been here, Random. What's up?'

Random turned to his friend, trying not to focus on the jam decorating his face.

'I've just got this terrible feeling. Like we are already prisoners.'

'Hah! Well, if this is prison, I hope I get life.'

'If we see something today, we don't like, we're going to have to stop it. We don't know who we are dealing with here, mate.'

'Look,' said Jake, finally wiping the jam from his face. 'You've stopped the Sandman, escaped this Kalor Maloso fella, there's nothing you can't do.'

'I can't work my bloody room, that's a given,' said Random, chucking a sausage onto his plate. He squirted a dollop of something that resembled mustard onto a clear plate and helped himself to an assortment of breakfast foods you'd normally find in hotel buffets.

'They were a bit quiet bringing this stuff in, weren't they?'

'I guess,' said Jake, unhelpfully.

'Did you ask for all this?'

'Of course! I barely touched all that alien food last night. Apparently, the main maid...'

'Maître d',' corrected Random.

'Yeah, whatever her name is. Anyways she heard that we're human and, when they knocked on the door this morning, she told me they were keen to make us feel at home. So I told her what kind of stuff we ate back on good old planet Earth and *et voila!*'

Random sniffed the meal.

'Well, they haven't drugged anything here, so that's a good sign.'

'You can tell just by giving the food a good sniff?'

Random nodded.

'I can also detect calcium deficiencies by smelling someone's odour and boil an egg by staring at it for 60 seconds.'

'Wow...really?' Jake's eyes bulged.

'No, you plank. Now pass me the bread rolls.'

The pair waited a full hour for Anji to stir, but there was no sign of her. During breakfast, a memo from the front desk informed them that the tour was to start in thirty minutes and Samuelson was to lead it personally. They would be required in the main foyer, which didn't give the traveller's "sleeping" friend much time to eat, let alone get ready.

'Come on, Anj, wake up in there!' Jake tried knocking on the door.

'Anj?'

Nothing.

'You don't think she's gone on without us, Random?'
'Not likely.'
'Maybe she went back to the Venus II.'
Random hammered on the door to Anji's room.
'It doesn't make any sense though. She'd have left us a note.'
There came a loud knock on the living quarters door. Random
went over and allowed the maître d' in.
'Good morning, sirs. I trust you both slept well.'
'Morning. Yes, we did thanks.'
The maître d' shuffled over to the dining table. Her small,
hunched frame made it clear that serving was probably something
she'd been doing her long life. Her hair was thin and grey and her
face looked lined and drawn.
'Oh, we'd better get this cleaned up.'
'Hang on a minute. Our friend hasn't got up yet.'
'Oh, that's not a problem. I'll come back later to clean up if that's
okay with you both?'
'Yes, that's fine,' said Random kindly. 'We've tried waking her,
but we haven't had any luck. I don't suppose you could let us in
her room, could you?'
'Sorry, sir, but it's against our policy, I'm afraid.'
'Has she left a message on the front desk, at all?' asked Random.
'Not to my knowledge. I tell you what, I'll have a look. If you're
still concerned, take this number.'
The maître d' handed Random a business card, which was the
same chrome colour as the walls of their rooms.
'Now you really do have to make a move, Chancellor
Samuelson is waiting in the foyer. I'm sure your friend is still
sleeping. These walls tend to be very well sound insulated –
added privacy, you see. I'll ask her to wait here for you when you
get back.'
'Ah, that won't be necessary,' Random said. 'When we're done
at the mines, we'll be making our way back to our ship. If she
wants to catch up with us she can, if not, please could you make
sure she gets back to our craft safely?'
'I'd be delighted,' the old lady smiled sweetly.
'Okay, come on then, Jake.'
Jake hung his head and made to leave the room with Random.
Before he left, he turned and looked at Anji's room again.

The maître d' saw them out. Her smile faded into a nervous expression. She went over to Anji's door and used her universal key to open the lock.

Upon opening, she saw the girl slumped on her bed, still unconscious. Anji hadn't moved a muscle since she'd succumbed to her drugged wine several hours previously.

The maître d' went over to Anji's prone body and checked her pulse on her wrist.

'She'll be okay.'

The old lady froze.

'Oh, sir, you gave me a fright.'

Zatterson entered the room.

'I've been watching on the surveillance monitor. You'd have thought they'd have been suspicious that the room was bugged. She should have come around by now, though.'

'She's only young. I think the dose I put in her drink was slightly too strong.'

Zatterson nodded.

'Well, be that as it may, we shall wait for her two friends to leave the premises then we shall move her to the security chamber. We shall question her before we capture her associates.'

He made for the door.

'We don't want to cause a fuss so let's keep this as quiet and discreet as possible. Understood?'

The maître d' nodded.

'Good. Bring her around in five minutes.'

As Zatterson left, sadness filled the maître d's eyes. She looked upon Anji again and sighed heavily.

'Well, this better be worth it,' she thought. She reached deep into her pinafore and produced a vial of liquid. Popping the cork off the top, her eyes watered as the strong whiff of smelling salts escaped.

Cautiously, she knelt next to the teenager and wafted the vial under Anji's nose. The girl suddenly awoke in an explosion of coughs and splutters. Before she had a chance to open her eyes, she felt a cold, wrinkly hand clap around her mouth.

'Shhh. Keep it down.'

'What...what's going on?' Anji mumbled hoarsely, her throat dry and sore.

The maître d' heard what Anji said even though her hand was still covering her mouth.

'I'll let go if you speak quietly and act quickly.'

She peeled her hand away carefully.

'Right, now grab your things. I'll explain everything on the way.'

Anji felt dazed and confused. She took in her surroundings as it all started to come back to her. She'd got ready for bed…then…the wine…it was the wine! Of course, she'd been drugged!

'Random. Where's Random? Where are my friends?'

The maître d' hurried her along.

'Come on, pack your things, we need to go.'

'But where are they?'

'I'll tell you everything as soon as we are away from this place. They are safe…for now. Come on!'

For now? Anji didn't like the sound of that. She looked down and realised she was still in her pyjamas.

'Here, put this over you,' the maître d' threw a thick bed sheet at the youngster.

'It'll keep your modesty until you can get changed. Now, see that trolley in the living area? Get under it. You'll notice there's a tray secured

under the main trolley that'll hold you. It'll hold your weight, no problem. Quickly!'

Anji felt hesitant, but did what she was told. The maître d' finished packing up her belongings, as few as they were, thrust them into her arms and hurried her onto the trolley. Anji tucked her head under and sat on the cold metal shelf with her knees hugged towards her chin as the trolley sheet draped over the top tray, completely concealing her presence.

'Right, now keep quiet,' whispered the maître d'.

The old lady wheeled the trolley with ease out of the room and into the hallway. Anji still felt a little hazy but despite all the confusion, knew that this woman was trying to help her. She noticed that her breathing was heavy with anxiety, so she did her best to breathe a little quieter.

The noise from the crockery on the trolley did enough to cover up any sound of Anji's nerves but the maître d' was apprehensive. She knew that they had little time to escape. She had been aware that there were security cameras everywhere and that eyes were watching.

Fellow hotel guests milled around the corridors whilst maids went about their work, cleaning and readying rooms for their next occupants. All the while, Anji felt like she was being watched. As though all eyes were burning into her.

The maître d' continued pushing her trolley, passing door after door, silently hoping that nobody would stop her. She pushed it faster, but not so much she would arouse suspicion. To her relief, the elevator doors came into view. Her pace quickened, she pushed the trolley closer and closer to freedom – but the hardest part of the job was yet to come.

Anji held on for dear life to the bars that held the trolley upright as it clanged unceremoniously up to the elevator. Her breathing became frantic again. The maître d' pressed the button to open the doors but their escape had stalled. She looked up at the floor indicator. The elevator was currently on Floor 146. They were on Floor 210.

The old lady's eyes darted from side-to-side. Still no sign of the authorities but it'd only be a matter of time before they were discovered.

Aware that security cameras lined the corridor, the walls had eyes – and they were all watching her.

The elevator started to move.

A bead of sweat began to form on the maître d's brow. She detected a bustle of activity to her right. It was the police.

'Oh, come on, come on!' she screamed to herself.

208…209…210…PING!

Smelling freedom, she pushed the trolley carrying Anji into the empty elevator and quickly pressed for the basement floor. With the maître d' preoccupied, the trolley crashed into the wall, sending Anji and a shower of crockery and half-eaten breakfast to the floor.

'Where are we going?'

'I'll tell you in a minute, my dear. Grab your things and be ready to run when I say so, okay?'

Anji nodded. It's all she could do. She was terrified by what was happening and being away from her friends.

The elevator continued to descend through the building.

'What happens if they call for the lift? We'll be trapped!'

'No,' smiled the maître d'. 'I've jammed the controls. We will be okay as long as we can make the shuttle car. We're nearly there. Just follow me and you'll be fine.'

Before long, the elevator shuddered to a stop and the doors opened, allowing Anji and her liberator to spill out into what looked like an underground car park.

'What does it look like?' asked Anji.

'It's a white people carrier. Come on, over here.'

The maître d' hared off towards an approaching vehicle, until a gunshot stopped them both in their tracks.

'Down!'

Anji hit the ground hard. She screamed as another shot echoed around the basement. She could hear further screams from hotel guests

parking up around them and then the sound of footsteps as they began to run in the confusion.

The maître d' peered from her hiding spot. Three armed police, their faces indistinguishable thanks to their blank masks, were starting to spread out, barking orders to the panicked guests to keep calm whilst searching for their would-be captives.

Anji closed her eyes, they had no chance now.

All of a sudden, from the rear driver's window of the white shuttle car came even more gunfire sending the police officers scattering for cover. The car screeched to a halt right where Anji was lying face down, her hands protecting her ears from the sound of fire.

The back door swung open and a man with what appeared to be a futuristic rifle bent down, picked Anji up off the floor and pulled her into the car.

'Yana, get in quick!' the same man yelled.

The maître d', with a speed and agility that belied her years, leapt through the air and landed in the foot well.

'Drive!' she yelled as the door slammed shut. The police officers regained their senses as the car swung around to make its getaway and opened fire on the vehicle.

The shuttle car tore up the ramp out of the basement, exploded away before the blockade
could swing down to stop their escape and shot away from the hotel at breakneck speed before joining the traffic and slipping away from danger.

XIII

'Can someone please tell me what the hell is going on?'

Anji, gasping for air, managed to cut through the silence somehow, scrambling for words as she sat on the edge of the back seat in a state of tension.

The maître d' picked herself up out of the foot well and perched next to Anji, putting an arm around the teenager's shoulders.

'It's okay. You're safe now.'

'That was a close one. Dail, take the next left. It'll take us off the main roads. We'll be able to slip under cover easier if we avoid the highway,' said the gunman.

'Who are you people?' asked Anji.

The maître d' pressed a button concealed inside her pinafore and before Anji's eyes, the features of the haggard, grey haired old lady melted away, revealing a much younger woman hiding beneath the disguise.

'The name's Yana. Nalani Yana. This is Rader and our driver's name is Dail. Sorry we've had to take you away from your friends, but we had to get you out of there.'

Anji shook her head. 'Sorry, you've lost me. Could you start from the top please?'

'We're from the Genocian Movement,' said Rader.

'And what do you do? Kidnap people?' said Anji.

'You haven't been kidnapped. We've been tracking the movements of the Government for some time now. I was staking out the hotel and you just happened to be there,' said Yana.

'You see not many people get invited to that specific hotel in the Grand Chamber. If they do, they are either filthy rich, being lured into something against their will or, in your case, both,' said Dail as he weaved in and out of traffic.

'So, you want our money?' enquired Anji.

'Nope. But they do,' said Yana.

267

'Who are they?'

'That man you met last night. He is the Chancellor of Genocia. His accomplice is Head of the Treasury. What they told you was all lies.'

'How do you know that?' Anji could do little but ask questions at a moment like this.

'We were waiting on your table last night. One of our members informed us of your wealth during the day. They had been standing in the queue at the kiosk and reported back to us that you might be in trouble. So, we went undercover.' Yana began to remove her maître d' outfit, revealing a purple and grey combat suit, which did little to ease Anji's nerves.

'So, you rescue people,' said Anji.

'Before they get sent to the mines, yeah,' said Rader.

'Mines?'

'A fate worse than death. Believe me, you don't want to go there,' said Yana.

'How would you know that? What's so bad about them?' Anji began to feel less anxious about herself and more worried for her friends.

'Because we've all been there at some point, for one reason or another,' said Dail.

'So, you're criminals then?'

'Everything on this planet is criminal. But it's only the Genocians outside the Grand Chamber who get punished.'

'What's so bad about the mines?' asked Anji.

'You're put to work mining ESOL19 for the rest of your days and if the mine gets overcrowded, you're sentenced to death, regardless of how hard you work or how unfair it may be.'

'Death!?'

'Yes, right here, Dail,' said Yana. 'Almost there now. I can't be anything but blunt about what's in store for your friends. They want the money, then they will send them to the mines and then, most probably, to meet the Soul Destroyer.'

Anji began to panic. 'We have to save Random and Jake. They're walking straight into a trap!'

*

All the while that Anji was being rescued, Random and Jake had been led to a stretch shuttle car and, under police escort, driven to Mine 47, the closest site to the Grand Chamber and one of the last sources of the precious ESOL19 that the duo had heard so much about.

They sat opposite Zatterson who every now and then cut the silence with more information about the mine they were going to. He waxed lyrical about how the mine had not only solved the

problem introduced by growing overcrowding in the prison system but also how the turnover of the mineral had led to more discoveries of ESOL 19 closer to the core.

'Overcrowded prisons? But this planet has won the most hospitable world in the universe award for the last 20 years, hasn't it?' said Jake in confusion.

'Well, you're along the right lines, Jake. But, since we came into power two decades ago, we implemented a system which meant that the mines, whilst serving an important role in the harvesting of the mineral, also helped reform our criminals. It's a vital part of maintaining order and helping to make sure that our prisoners can then come back into society with a feeling that

they have helped the community on Genocia and

contributed in a way that was beneficial and enriched the planet.'

'So are the prisons no longer at breaking point?' asked Random.

'We've regulated them now, that's not to say that we don't still have problems in the level of crime, but we keep it together,' said Zatterson.

'Under wraps, you mean,' said Random.

'We don't want to broadcast our problems on this world, Captain. We acknowledged years ago that this could harm our tourism trade.'

Random smirked.

'You're a typical politician, Zatterson. Incapable of giving a yes or no answer.'

Jake chuckled.

'He's got you there, mate.'

Zatterson frowned.

'I think my answer was clear enough. Make of it what you wish.'

'Oh, I have. I've been very skeptical since we landed. No world is perfect. Genocia tries to be but hides more than others. At least the Earth's imperfections are there for all to see. Yours on the other hand are buried under the surface, in more ways than one.'

Zatterson began to feel very cross.

'You shall see,' he said, a hint of malice creeping into his dulcet tones.

Random's red/blue eyes met his.

'My warning stands, Zatterson. If I don't like what I see, you're not getting a penny of our money and we'll pick up Anji and leave this planet.'

'I've already told you your friend is safe and well back at the hotel. I have been informed that she's up and about and, when she is ready, she will be escorted to your ship where you can meet her as and when you like.'

'Good,' said Random. 'How much longer until we get there?'

'We're almost there, Captain,' said Zatterson, 'It won't be long now.'

The convoy finally arrived at a set of tall metal gates. A security post, flanked by two armed guards, sat outside the gates with one guard gesturing for the party to slow down.

'Security check. This won't take long,' Zatterson reassured. He made for the breast pocket in his jacket and readied his pass whilst Random and Jake surveyed the scene.

'It looks like a big nuclear power plant,' said Jake, glancing out of the window.

'You're not wrong. Look at it, big smoking towers, it reeks of industry.'

The sky seemed to darken around the plant. Within moments, the convoy was making its way through the big gates, the creaking of which

could be heard within the shuttle car, implying to Random that they were far older than the 20 years Zatterson had quoted earlier.

As they crept up the road to the main plant building, Random observed the bleak surroundings. There were no people to speak of walking around outside the car, just dark buildings. Decay and rot had set in all around. This was a shock to them both, especially after witnessing all the splendour of the Grand Chamber and the shopping precinct.

Random had no doubt in his mind whatsoever that this represented a more honest picture of Genocia than everything they had experienced so far.

The vehicle came to a halt outside a decrepit side door, where a woman, her face black with dirt and her overalls stained by years of hard labour, waited to greet them.

'Gentleman, I'd like you to meet Ki. She's the head of the division,' said Zatterson.

'Delighted to meet you both,' she held her hand out in greeting. Jake glanced at it, hesitantly shook it and instantly regretted it. Taking his

hand back, he stared at the grime that now stained his palm.

'Ki, this is Captain Random and his companion, Jake.' Random declined the handshake politely.

'They are here to inspect the mine. Would you do the honours of showing them around?'

'Certainly,' the woman beamed. 'Please.'

Random and Jake entered the side door. Before he set foot inside, Random peered back and noticed Zatterson was making back for the car.

'You're not joining us?'

Zatterson smiled. 'I'm sorry. I have urgent matters that need my attention. Not to worry though. We'll be back to pick you up in three of your Earth hours. Have fun.'

With that, the politician shut the door of the limo and it screeched out of sight. Jake shot a look at Random. Random acknowledged it.

Once inside the mine, the pair was surprised to notice that there was not as much dirt and grime as they would have thought.

'Not quite what I was expecting,' observed Random.

'Oh, this is just the distillery. This is where the ESOL19 is processed. It has to be clean in here in case of contamination.'

'Contamination?' said Jake.

'Yes, ESOL19 can be deadly if you come into direct contact with it,' said Ki. 'In fact, if you

look around, you'll notice that all workers are wearing special protective apparatus.

'Then how comes you look so dirty?'

Ki looked down at herself and laughed.

'Oh, this? I was just fixing the gearing system when you arrived.'

'Yes, I can see that,' said Jake peering down at his dirty hand.

'Sorry about that,' she grinned. 'Let me go and clean up and I'll be right back to give you a tour. Please don't touch anything. I'll be with you shortly.'

Ki made her exit, leaving Random and Jake alone save for some workers who were busying themselves with banks and banks of complicated computers and scientific equipment.

'Well, looks legit so far,' said Random.

'I thought Zatterson said that this place was a prison. I don't see any guards. No restraints. I was expecting a chain gang splitting rocks.'

'This is the distillery. It's highly unlikely that prisoners would be allowed up here,' said Random. 'Besides, you say there are no guards. What about those guys?'

Random pointed to what looked like an elevator shaft. Standing by the doors were two keepers, about six foot in height, their silver forms humanoid in shape, slim yet formidable; not like the big clunky robots Jake had been used to in science fictions films.

'Looks like they spent the budget on their biceps and pecks and forgot to do the faces,' said Jake.

'Well, maybe they don't need faces,' remarked Random. The robots' smooth heads reminded Jake of a ball bearing, the kind he'd occasionally

seen scattered around his friend Alfie's bedroom. Alfie had an extensive collection of BB guns, something that did little to delight the pigeons that used to nibble at the gravel on his parents' driveway.

Before long, Ki was back in the room, de-grimed and now sporting a rather fetching radiation suit.

'Ah, this is more like it, more sci-fi than coal miner,' Jake said to Random.

'Right, before we go any further, you'll both need to wear suits too,' said Ki.

She showed the duo over to a storage cupboard, which housed a vast array of helmets, shell suits, boots and gloves. 'You're both a little on the short side, so please could you wear the female suits on the right.'

Jake felt a little affronted.

'Don't tell Anj I wore a girl's suit,' he whispered to Random.

'It'll cost you,' winked Random.

Dressed up and ready for the tour, the pair were shown to the lift by Ki. She pressed a button on her wrist computer which seemed to make the robots stand down.

'So, you control the robots?' asked Random.

'Keepers. I wish. If I did, I'd get them to do more labour rather than stand up here doing nothing all day. This communicator sends a signal to the keepers requesting access to the mine.'

'Who decides if you pass or not then?'

'All requests go back to Head Office in the Grand Chamber,' said Ki.

'I thought as much,' said Random. He was also growing suspicious of the name given to the robots.

The trio stepped inside the lift.

'It's a fair ride down, but you'll be able to see the main shaft on our descent. The glass is transparent after five floors.'

'Why five floors?'

'I'm sorry, that's classified.'

Random huffed.

'How are you with heights, Jake?'

'Not bad. Hey, how long is this shaft?'

'Just over 20 miles long.'

'Blimey,' said Jake. 'I should have brought a magazine!'

The lift started to descend. Suddenly, the grey slabs of metal surrounding the travellers gave way to nothing. Jake yelped as the floor became a transparent membrane of glass.

Random observed the shaft. All around them there seemed to be dozens of people working away with electronic interpretations of tools such as drills, axes and other heavy-duty equipment at the surface walls of the shaft.

'So, this is it then?' said Random. He used his superior eyesight to zoom in on the workers. They were shackled by a metal device around the neck of the radiation suits they were wearing and not five feet from keepers identical to those guarding the lift. Random kept count of the number of workers he spotted on their journey down, which was going much quicker than he expected.

'So, you're in charge of this mine then, Ki?' he asked.

'Nope. I'm just the Head Scientist on the project. We are looking
at ways of replicating the minerals we discover down here. I'm in
charge of that sector but, when it comes to the rest of it, it's the
Government who run it, I'm afraid.'

'How did you get in to all of this?'

'I graduated from Genocia University several years ago now,
specializing in mineral replication. When I finished my degree, I
was sent down here to help the planet regain its depleted
resources. It's an expensive mineral, ESOL19, so it needs handling
with care and expertise.'

'Is that what you're working at?' asked Random.

'We are struggling to keep up with the demand of what the
Government expect from us. Since the prison reform led to more
hands on

deck, as it were, we seem to be finding less of the product. So,
what little we do find we then try to replicate, thus keeping the
planet going.'

'It seems like a good initiative,' said Random. 'In practice, that
is. But what do people get sent here for? How long do they stay
down here?'

'It depends on the severity of their sentence. We don't tend to
employ murderers or anything like that. We get all kinds, violent
criminals, drug users, burglars, fraudsters. All kinds of nasty
individuals.'

'Including men and women...even children?' asked Random.

Jake looked closer at the workers. Suddenly he noticed that the
labour force was not split into groups of gender or age. There
were prisoners in smaller suits like Random and himself.

'It depends on their crime,' said Ki.

'A little unfair, wouldn't you say? Is this all they do, all day? Do
they rest?'

'There are three allotted rest times in each shift. We don't want
them burning out too much otherwise they become of little use to
us.'

'And what happens to them when they become "of little use" to
you?' asked Jake.

'We don't like to talk about that,' said Ki, a hint of shame in her
voice. The lift came to halt. 'Here we are.'

The doors opened and Random and Jake were showed out onto the mine floor. The sound of tools and heavy work echoed around them and filtered through the ear pieces in their suits. The project was vast and impressive…but not for all the right reasons. They were escorted to a monorail shuttle. Ki assumed the driver's position and moved the shuttle off deeper into the mine. Random's fists clenched. Surrounding them were more prison workers, each one bearing emotions on their exhausted faces that Random knew all too well. Fear, repression and pain.

'Almost there,' said Ki as the shuttle started to slow down.

'Where's "there" exactly?' asked Jake.

'You'll see.'

The shuttle came to a stop outside a detention area. A dozen or so keepers stood by the shuttle stop, guns in hand, awaiting their latest prisoners.

'Here we are,' said Ki. 'Time to get off.'

'Wait! What?!' said Jake.

'You have been arrested for being in possession of a stolen craft,' an electronic voice buzzed from one of the robots. 'Your assets have been seized and you are to spend your sentence working within this mine.'

Random and Jake sat open-mouthed.

'Stolen craft? Who are you to say it's stolen?'

'Get out of the shuttle,' ordered one of the keepers.

Jake started to panic. 'We haven't done anything!'

'Sorry, I don't make the rules,' said Ki. 'Best do what they ask.'

'We demand to see Zatterson. NOW!' shouted Random. 'We have the freedom of Genocia.'

Ki looked at Random coldly.

'Not anymore.'

The keepers moved in and yanked Random and Jake from their places. Their icy grip pinched Jake's shoulders as he struggled to shake them off.

'Prisoner displaying aggression,' stated the keeper pinning Jake down.

A shock of green energy pulsed through Jake's body. The teenager screamed and fell to the floor unconscious.

'Jake!' Random did his best to shake his captor free but he too was shot with the same energy and slumped to the dirty ground.

'Take them to their detention cell,' said one keeper. His companions picked up Random and Jake's prone bodies, slung them like bags onto their shoulders and marched off to the cells. Ki turned back to the shuttle and put it in reverse. She had led the boys to their doom.

XIV

'Soul Destroyer?'

Anji found herself sitting in what looked like an abandoned warehouse, far away from the watching eyes and police officers who had pursued her rescuers away from the Grand Chamber.

The rest of their journey had been relatively uneventful but Anji had so many questions to ask. Finally, she felt it was time to ask the one she had been dreading to hear the answer to.

'At first I thought it was a myth, just a fairy story created to scare Genocians away from putting a foot wrong,' said Dail. 'We all did. Then the rumours started getting louder and louder, until we learnt the horrible truth.'

He threw another log on the fire that sat smoking away in the middle of the warehouse.

'There's a monster sitting in the heart of the main mine that feeds off the souls of those who are fed to it,' Yana muttered, loading shells into her gun.

'And that's where Random and Jake are?'

Yana nodded grimly.

'Then we have to get them out.' Anji got up and made for the exit.

'Take one step out of this building and you'll be sent to the mines too!' warned Rader.

Anji was in anguish.

'You can't start a one-person war on this thing. Believe you me; you're not the first to try.'

'Then what can we do?'

Yana finished loading her gun and put her arm around Anji's shoulder.

'Safety in numbers, that's all we can do. Stick together.'

'How long has this been going on?' asked Anji. Her mind was awash with panic and Yana could sense her worry.

'About 20 years or so. Ever since Consula became leader of Genocia. She doesn't care for the sick, the elderly or the helpless. She cares about her own, the rich and powerful. Anything that falls outside the confines of the Grand Chamber is shunned. As far as she is concerned, we should all be fed to the Soul Destroyer, after we've had the life beaten out of us in those mines.'

'But I don't understand it,' said Anji. 'What purpose does it serve, meaninglessly taking lives?'

Rader butted in. 'Some say the Soul Destroyer lives off the ESOL19 they've been mining for. Others say it's just a convenient way of getting rid of those who work in the mines. I've heard that the Soul Destroyer actually powers the whole planet and this is a last resort.'

'It feeds off the life force of those who face it,' said Dail. 'One of our friends was once sent to the Soul Destroyer. He had to wait in line as they were each fed, one by one, to the beast. Then, all of a sudden, the power went down. He and a few others took advantage and escaped, managing to avoid the robot guards. Somehow, they found a tunnel out of the mine and escaped before the power came back on.'

'That's it then. If your friend got out, can't we just find him and he can show us to the tunnel?'

'He's dead,' said Dail coldly. 'He couldn't live with the guilt of leaving so many people to die down there. He never told us where the entrance to the tunnel was.'

Anji shuddered.

'This is a nightmare,' she cried. 'We only came here to go shopping!'

'We're doing our best to keep safe and get as many people as we can to fight Consula and her allies,' said Yana, trying to reassure the young girl. 'There are more of us out there, scattered around the planet, growing stronger every day. When the time is right, we shall attack the Grand Chamber and put a stop to all of this – return Genocia to a democratic planet.'

'Yes, but when? If what you say is true, people are dying all the time.'

'We can't save them, just like we couldn't save your friends. I gave your pal something that may be able to help him on the inside but, as you were the only one who was drugged, it was easier to rescue you than them. I was nearly discovered by that Zatterson as I went to bring you round.'

Anji thought hard.

'We need to get back to my ship. There's a computer on board who can help us.'

'It's been impounded. Look.' Rader showed Anji a computer screen. It showed surveillance footage of the Venus II being moved, still clamped to the mooring that held it in place on arrival, into a warehouse.

'I've hacked all surveillance cameras in and around places where we need eyes but can't have them,' said Rader. 'That's how we knew about you and your friends.'

Anji had never felt so alone.

'That's it then. There's nothing we can do.' She started to fight back the tears. Her friends were incarcerated in the mine, doomed to meet their maker and their only way off this godforsaken planet was in the hands of the enemy.

'Anji, I'm contacting our freedom groups as soon as possible. If we decide that now is the right time to launch an attack, we can get you home. I can't guarantee the safety of your friends, but I can guarantee yours. Just trust me.'

Be strong, she told herself.

'Is there no way we can find that tunnel entrance?'

'No. It's a suicide mission.'

'But you have access to the surveillance cameras,' said Anji.

'There are very few outside the areas Consula cares about,' said Dail.

'Is there no-one who can help?'

Yana shared a look with her fellow freedom fighters. She sighed deeply.

'There is one guy. Terran. He leads one of the groups. He escaped the mines with our friend.'

A ray of hope beamed from Anji's face.

'That's just what we need! How do we find him?'

'Terran? It could be tricky, we'd have to send a message to all our groups and try to locate him. But he could be on the other side of the planet for all we know. It would take days to reach him.'

'But it's a chance. We must do it. Please. I'm not from this world. I've never been anywhere but my own. I need my friends back.'

Yana looked stone-faced at Anji.

'Please!'

Yana sighed. 'Okay, okay, we'll do it. But if it takes more than 24 hours then we need to stick to the original plan. Clear?'

Anji nodded. 'Clear.'

It wasn't much, but it was the only hope the Earth girl had of saving her friends.

*

Random started to come round. His head throbbed as he opened his eyes, the light in the cell shone brighter than a sun going supernova, sending a shot of agony burrowing through his skull. Groaning and shaking his head, he picked himself up off the floor and onto his knees.

He rubbed his face and massaged his eyes with the tips of his fingers. Slowly, the effect of the energy bolt started to wear off and Random became aware of his surroundings.

'Jake?' said Random hoarsely. 'Jake!'

His human friend lay unconscious beside him. Random tried frantically to find a pulse and then relaxed.

'He's not dead, y'know. Just tranquilised. It happens around here sometimes. Especially when people start to go mad.'

Random turned to see where the mystery voice came from.

'Who are you?'

'The name's Cuttler, Delilah Cuttler. This here's my sister Benaya.' The woman didn't offer a handshake.

Random slowly got to his feet, moaning as his aching body started to function again.

'Where am I?'

Delilah scoffed. 'They must have hit you pretty hard.'

Random searched his memory. Then his eyes widened in stark realization.

'Let me guess. We are in the maximum security detention wing of the ESOL19 mine?'

'Well, if maximum to you means miles below ground without a hope in hells chance of escape, you're right.'

'That's a pretty definite summary,' Random replied.

Delilah jumped down off her top bunk and poured a drink.

'Here, have this,' she thrust the mug into Random's hand. The water was full of dirt.

'I'm not thirsty, but thanks.' He knelt next to Jake's prone body and lifted him onto the bottom bunk of the beds that stood opposite his cell mates. There was no way the keepers were tucking them in when they arrived.

'So, what are you in for?' asked Delilah.

'I guess you could say the Government wanted something from us. So they took it.'

'Money?'

'What else?'

'So you didn't kill anyone to be down here?'

Random frowned.

'We're not murderers. We're innocent, I'm telling you.'

'Yeah. Everyone says they are innocent. This must be the first prison to have ever contained no actual criminals.'

'Alright, so what are you in here for then?'

'Mind your own business,' Delilah snapped.

Benaya silently got up off her bunk and gestured in her sister's face.

'Why? What's the point of being nice? We'll all end up dead anyway!' Delilah argued back.

Benaya gestured again, a look of scorn pouring from her eyes.

'Well that's your outlook. That's always been the trouble with you. False hope has always led you astray.'

'I'm sorry to be breaking up this family meeting but why can't she talk?'

The sisters turned towards their cellmate.

'Because she's mute, stupid!' shouted Delilah.

'Oh,' grinned Random. He hand-signaled an apology to Benaya, who acknowledged his effort before glaring back at her sister.

'It's nice to know that sign language is universal,' he said. 'Now, if you two are finished, let's say we start plotting our escape, eh?'

Delilah laughed. 'You're mad. Didn't you hear me? We're miles below the surface. Hundreds of robots are waiting to torture us if we try to escape. There's only one way out of here and that's the Soul Destroyer.'

Random's ears pricked up. 'Soul Destroyer?'

Delilah's hard face started to soften with fear.

'It kills those who are not needed anymore. Sometimes people are selected at random. I've seen them. The robots burst in to the cells, taking anyone, men, women, children, dragging them away. I've been told they have to wait in line in a dark tunnel and, when they see it, their screams are heard throughout the mine.'

Random's head dropped.

'It can take hours for the sacrifice to end. The sounds I've heard – it's like you're awake during a nightmare.'

'What is it? A monster?'

Delilah sniffed and shook her head. 'No-one's lived to find out.'

Random sat Delilah down. The cell was small, but there was room for a table and two chairs between the bunk beds. The pair sat together in silence for a few moments before Random put his hand gently on Delilah's.

'We'll put an end to this. I promise.'

Delilah snorted. How could anyone get out of this hell hole?

'I'm Random by the way.' He shook her hand. Delilah looked into his eyes. They were red/blue and burned with a fierce determination.

'Trust me.'

*

Zatterson waited patiently outside the Chancellor's office door. He gleefully clutched

the piece of paper in his hand. Wealth in their time.

'Come in,' said Samuelson, who sat perched on his desk, glancing over a document containing the latest fiscal reports.

Zatterson entered and, with a cheerful smile, thrust the paper under his nose.

'There you are, sir. The entire amount has been transferred into the Treasury.'

Samuelson remained unmoved.

'My plan worked then. Good.'

'But of course. Those two kids are now rotting in the mines. Very soon they will meet the Destroyer and then the whole matter will be forgotten.'

Samuelson made for the safe in his office wall. 'You too seem to be forgetting something. The girl got away.'

'We know who she got away with. It was that stupid resistance group. She'll be captured soon.'

'She escaped to the Restricted Zone. If she is still alive, she won't keep her mouth shut for long.

There is also the small matter of how a resistance group managed to infiltrate our security and escape with their lives.'

He reached deep inside the safe.

'I know. I shall see to it personally that the person responsible is punished.'

Samuelson smiled. 'No need to worry about that, my dear chap. Here,' he produced a decanter and two glasses. 'I trust you have drunk Opulac Whiskey before?'

He poured two glasses.

'It's a personal favourite of Consulas. Did you know?'

'I was not aware.' Zatterson accepted the glass and drank it down.

'Well,' said Samuelson as he swirled his around his glass. 'That is surprising. Especially as it's what you drank as you plotted to kill me.'

Zatterson spluttered, eyes wide. 'Sir, that's preposterous.'

'Is it? Then you'll have to forgive me, old friend. Here I was thinking you wanted a promotion to my job and you were willing to do anything to get it. Even to terminate my life so that my concerns about the mines becoming discovered wouldn't reach the Government?'

Zatterson started to feel an intense burning sensation in the back of his throat.

'Of course not,' he muttered, coughing gently at first before he tasted the copper tang of blood in his mouth.

He clutched desperately at his throat, struggling to breathe before falling to the floor, screaming for air.

'Sir...I...what have you...done!?'

'Exactly what you were about to do, my dear Zatterson. Don't worry, your legacy will go untarnished. You gave impeccable service over the years to the Treasury. I'll even recommend a plaque in your honour.'

Zatterson's veins began popping out of his pale, wet skin. He choked violently. Seconds from death, fear and panic filling his mind, he could ask only one question.

'H…how…how…did you…know?'

Samuelson crouched down and whispered in his would-be-assassin's ear.

'Because that's how I got this job.'

Zatterson's head crashed to the cold marble floor, his lifeless body gurgling a death cry.

'Sweet dreams, old chap,' said Samuelson as he poured the contents of his glass back into the decanter and returned it to the safe. He made for his desk and pressed a button on the intercom.

'Tell Consula that Zatterson has been found dead. The cause? Well, he always was a heavy drinker.'

XV

Anji jerked uncomfortably in the back of the vehicle.

'Can't you drive a little slower please?'

'Hey!' Rader replied from the driving seat, 'I thought you said you wanted to meet Terran as soon as possible?'

'Yeah, but when you're carrying a load of weaponry and bombs on your lap, a gentle drive wouldn't go amiss.'

She stared down at the armoury that swamped her legs. The team had filled the boot with as much of an arsenal as was physically possible to squeeze into the car.

'Nothing will go off, Anji. Nothing's primed,' Yana reassured her.

Anji tutted. 'Oh, that's alright then,' she said sarcastically.

The car had been travelling for a few hours. As soon as the group were in agreement (some of them reluctantly) that they should find Terran and help Anji find Random and Jake, they set in motion a plan to locate the one man who had

escaped from the mines and lived to tell the tale. Rader and Dail had managed to find Terran's last known location, some thousand miles away from the Grand Chamber, and made contact with their

allied rebel groups to confirm his whereabouts. After establishing a route and loading up on food and weapons, they left quickly.

They had slipped out of Genocia's central city with ease and were now driving through the wastelands of the planet. Anji had watched as the skyline of the Grand Chamber had ebbed away in the distance, relief conflicting with sadness that, although she was escaping to safety, her friends were still very much in danger.

For miles, there had been nothing but dust and grime. Genocia really had been left to waste away outside the confines of the Government's stranglehold. Except for a few mines and factories every so often, the roads had all been empty. Not another hover car or futuristic flying whatever anywhere to be seen. In fact, they didn't even pass another vehicle.

Anji had asked whether Samuelson or any of his cronies could trace their steps.

'I mean, it's not as though we can blend in with anyone else driving out here.'

'There's no surveillance this far out of the city,' said Dail. 'The Government care for nothing outside their walls. We're safe.'

After another few hours of roads, the wastelands suddenly gave away to a beautiful landscape of lush fields and glorious blue skies.

The Earth girl smiled for what felt like the first time since they landed.

'It's lovely.'

'It's poisonous,' Yana replied curtly.

'Blue skies indicate a chemical imbalance in the atmosphere. It's a reaction to the air pollution emanating from the city.'

'On my world, it'd be called a lovely day,' said Anji.

'On our world, if you breathed the air for more than ten minutes, it'd be your last day,' Rader retorted.

'Rader, there's no need to be so on the nose.' Yana smiled at Anji.

The rebel frowned. 'Look Yana, this world is dangerous. We can't sugar-coat how terrible things are here.'

'I think she's got the gist, don't you?'

Rader huffed. He was a reluctant member of the small rebel taskforce. He'd wanted to stay at their base and also hadn't been keen on saving Anji from Zatterson in the first place. Who wants to go about putting yourself in danger when you can fight a war from the safety of your own home? Home to Rader was their hideout. The war was with anyone from the outside.

'It's okay. I'm alright.' Anji took solace in the view and made sure the window was wound shut.

After a time, the car began to splutter.

'What's happening?' asked Anji.

'We're running low on fuel,' confirmed Dail.

'We have some fully charged fuel cells in the boot. We'll have to pull over and get them out.'

'That'll take up precious time,' said Rader.

'We have to keep moving,' said Dail.

'I'll help,' Anji interrupted.' Just tell me what to do.'

'Okay, girl,' Dail reached for the glove compartment and took out two small tubes. There appeared to be a mouthpiece in the centre of them both.

'This is a rebreather. Put this in your mouth and it recycles the carbon dioxide you vent back into oxygen. Just put it in your mouth and breathe normally.'

Anji took the rebreather and nodded. 'Okay.'

Dail brought the car to a halt. He and Anji quickly jumped out and made for the boot.

'Get out all the weapons, the fuel cells are below,' said Dail as he started to unload the cargo.

'What do they look like?'

'It's a large purple tray. You can't miss it.'

Inside the car, Rader decided this was the right time to voice his concerns.

'She shouldn't have come with us.'

Yana turned to her ally. 'What were we supposed to do? Let her die in the mines?'

'Why not? Everyone we rescue always ends up down there anyway. It is futile.'

'How can it be futile when we're still free?'

'Fine. Unnecessary then.'

'You saw how much money she and her friends had. Imagine what we could do with that. We could finance a revolution. Hold the Government to ransom. We'd have the keys to the lock that's keeping Genocia chained up.'

Rader snorted. 'We don't have the money, Yana. They do. Her friends are as good as dead.'

'Not yet. The girl's right, there is a chance. It's risky but, if Terran is where we believe he is, then we can save them. Bring down the Government! Isn't that what you've always wanted, Rader?'

The rebel looked away and out of his window. He stared at the roadside meadow, lost in thought. Anji was right, it was beautiful. But he couldn't let any of them see through his rough exterior. He was an island stranded in a sea of troubles. There was something about that he liked.

In the far distance, he could see the tall grass sway in the breeze. Then he saw something which made him shudder.

'Come on, Anji, we're nearly there.' Dail and Anji were near the bottom of the pile. With a great effort, it was the girl who put the last weapon (which looked like a rocket launcher) on the ground.

'Found it.'

'Nice work. Now help me get it out. There should be a handle at your end, same as mine. I'll give the thumbs up to Yana and she can pop the hood. We'll swap the exhausted cells for this one. Leave me to do that.'

'No problem.'

'Right, on three...two...one...'

Anji put all her might into wrenching the cell from its recharge housing and was surprised to discover it weighed little more than a plate.

'There we are. Right, I'll come your way and we'll put it in the hood.'

They replaced the fuel cells with minimum effort and began to put their armoury back in the boot. Then Anji saw what Rader had seen a second earlier.

'Dail.'

'What?'

Anji looked on in horror. 'There's something in the grass!'

Dail's right hand reached for the handgun inside his coat pocket and aimed it directly where Anji was pointing.

'Keep loading.'

Anji began to breathe heavily. Frozen by fear, she couldn't move.

'Now, dammit!'

Tears forming in her eyes, she leapt into action.

The car doors clicked open and Yana and Rader, rebreathers in their mouths, jumped to the side of their comrade, machine guns in hand. A dull thudding, like the sound of hooves in a silent desert, echoed all around.

'I'll help load up, you've got this,' Yana said after seeing Anji struggling with some of the heavier weaponry.

'It's muts, I know it is!' screamed Rader.

'Just keep your eyes on it!' Yana shouted.

Anji began to weep. She hated herself for that.

Through the tears she doubled her efforts, longing to be back in the relative safety of the car.

The rumbling was getting closer. The grass was waving wilder and Anji's heart was beating faster.

'Target 20 seconds away. Get a move on!' Rader began to shake. He'd never seen a wild mut before. If his fears were about to come true, they'd be the last thing he ever saw.

Suddenly, the grass parted.

'FIRE!' screamed Dail.

Anji screamed. Yana threw herself to the floor and started shooting along with her friends.

An army of muts stampeded towards them, running headlong into the barrage of laser fire. Now that Anji could see them clearer, she saw their hideous deformities.

They were human in nightmare form, with their faces contorted at the front with limp, open mouths dripping unspeakable fluid from within. Their eyes were swollen and thick with blackness.

And they were fast. Very fast.

Anji threw herself to the ground and rolled under the hover car. She gazed on in terror.

The rebels' firepower made light work of the first few rows of muts but they were outnumbered. More of them poured out onto the road, their faces yellow and grey, putrefied flesh dangling from their emaciated bodies.

Anji watched on as her new friends struggled to keep them at bay. Bodies began to fall to the floor, the muts emitting a horrific death scream as they fell, their high pitched screech reminding Anji of the kind of zombies she'd seen in *The Walking Dead*.

'Fall back,' Dail ordered. They began to edge back to the car. They had only limited ammunition in their hand guns. Yana allowed herself a second glance at the boot. It was still open and she could see an impulse immobiliser lying there on the floor.

'Anji.'

The girl screamed through the horrific noise from her hiding place.

'I..I can't move.'

'You've got to hit the button on the immobilizer. It's right there, on the floor. We can't hold them back. Do it!'

Anji, her hands over her ears as the screeching of the muts became too much, took a deep breath and rolled out of her hiding place. As she did, the muts took control. They brushed aside the rebels with ease, pushing them to the floor, ready to kill.

'Muts...feed...muts...feed,' one of them chanted. Rader struggled to move but was pinned to the floor. The talking mut loomed over him.

Yana threw a punch at her captors but to no avail. Three muts circled her helpless form. One threw a punch back, making contact with her chin and causing the rebreather to fall out of her mouth. Mercilessly, the mut trampled on it.

Suddenly, a massive energy surge blasted the horde of muts. It swept through them and knocked them all to the ground. The explosion blew some of them back into the field and scattered them like matchsticks.

The rebels yelled in agony as the wave hit them too, knocking them all unconscious.

Then there was silence.

Anji started to breathe normally.

Unaffected by the blast, she quickly returned the immobilizer to the boot, ran over to her friends and checked their pulses. They were okay. She began to drag them to the hover car, first Yana, then the two guys.

She then managed to put the final few pieces of weaponry in the boot, closed it, raced into the car and slammed her door shut.

Her face smeared with snot and tears, she took the rebreather out of her mouth and hyperventilated.

As soon as she got her breathing under control, she tried to start the car, having put the unconscious Rader in her place in the back. Amazingly, the principles of the vehicle were pretty much the same as the ones on Earth.

She had never driven herself, but she'd seen enough people do it to pick up the idea.

There was no gear stick, but there were foot pedals. As she released the button labelled "handbrake", she put her foot down, initially on the brake and then on the accelerator, as they were the only two options available. As the car tore away from the scene, she could hear the engine running through the gears.

She wiped her face with her sleeve and dared to look in the wing mirror. The muts lay dead in the road. There were so many of them just lying there. She sniffed and returned her eyes to the road.

She hoped that she'd never see anything like that again.

XVI

'So, what do we do now?'

Jake was back in the land of the living and helping himself to the glass of water originally poured for Random. His purple skinned friend paced up and down the cell, hands behind his back, mouth pursed in concentration.

'How many people are in this mine, Delilah?'

'No idea,' Delilah lay on her bunk, picking tiny bits of dirt out of her nails.

'Helpful. Benaya?'

Benaya signed that she didn't know but it must be in the hundreds.

'Thank you. How many people would you say are transferred here every day?'

'Why do you ask?' asked Jake.

'Because if there are new prisoners like us then they still have the fight left in them to break out. Their spirit is still intact, unlike our friend here.'

'Who says it's broken? I've always been this cynical,' Delilah declared.

'If we can convince those among us to revolt and turn on the keepers, then we stand a decent chance of getting back to the surface.'

'And what about this Soul Destroyer thing?' asked Jake. 'I mean, if it's as powerful as you two say it is then can't it just kill us if we try to escape?'

'It's immobile, Jake.'

'Y'what?'

'Immobile. It can't move.'

'So?'

Random sighed. 'Gadzup it, why was I lumbered with the slow one?'

'Hey! I'm trying to follow you. I've woken up in a cell miles below the surface of an alien planet of which I used to be the richest man just 24 hours after leaving my home, which was blown up by a man from sand after a boy from space crash landed in a spaceship right in front of me!'

'Fine,' said Random, 'I'll put it down to culture shock.'

Benaya gestured to Random that she was aware of a security level inside the mine where the robots are housed and regenerated.

'Benaya I could kiss you!' beamed Random.

Her face dropped. *Try that and I'll break your thumbs*, was her response.

'If we can get there, we can turn the keepers off, all at once!'

'IF we can get up there. Plus how do we know that's where we can shut them down? Has anyone ever been there and lived to come back to confirm it?'

'Nope,' huffed Delilah.

'Right, well it's clear what I have to do then. I have to get myself arrested and take a look.'

'You'll die!' said Jake.

'No I won't. I'm indestructible,' beamed Random.

'What do you think you are? Some kind of god?'

'Definitely not, Delilah. But I'm less likely to be harmed than any of you. It would be deadly if anyone else tried to. But trust me, I'm made of harder stuff.'

Delilah laughed. 'I've seen it all before you know. The bravado, the heroics. No one ever comes back alive.'

Random smiled. 'This time...I will.'

'Right, what's the plan then?' Jake sprang from his bunk and stood beside his friend.

'We wait for the first shift. Then, on my mark, we'll start a fight with one another, break free from the chain gang and run amok.'

'Good plan!' said Jake before turning to Delilah. 'Just don't hit me in the face...or hard...in fact, don't hit me at all.'

'I can't make any promises,' Delilah replied.

'Then I'll be taken to the security level and I'll scout what's up there. If I can, I'll shut the keepers off there and then.'

'And us?'

We'll be sent to the Soul Destroyer, signed Benaya.

'Exactly. I'll make sure I'm back in time to stop you from getting killed. If the keepers shut down then you'll be free to go anyway.'

'This is all very impressive, but I doubt we'll be successful. You won't be able to get back up the shaft. The Government will be alerted and we will be slaughtered before we step out of the lift.'

Random paused.

'Hmm. Good point.'

He paced the room again.

Benaya pulled on her sister's arm.

'No, it's suicide.'

Benaya implored her to speak.

'Go on, Delilah, we're all ears.'

Delilah sighed. 'A few years ago, some people did manage to escape. There is a tunnel in the main chamber, but it runs dangerously close to the Soul Destroyer. Since then, it's been heavily guarded.'

'That's it!' Random yelped and jumped in the air. 'Then it's simple. We just need to shut the keepers down.'

'But if we do that the authorities will still find out just as soon as you slip the switch. They know of the tunnel now, its suicide!'

'No.' Random darted to the door, suddenly reminded that some prying ears may be listening in to their conversation. 'Not if we can adapt the keepers to protect us!'

'If only we had Skateboard with us,' sighed Jake.

'Who says we don't? We can contact him through the security level unhindered on a scrambled frequency. He can help us remotely!'

'If they haven't captured him yet,' reminded Jake.

'Skateboard's a wily thing. He won't let that happen.' Random turned to Delilah and Benaya. 'Are you with us?'

Benaya nodded enthusiastically.

Delilah stood unmoved.

'Too many ifs and buts for me.'

Random placed his hands on her shoulders.

'We can do this, Delilah. We can do this.'

Delilah looked at her fellow inmates and sighed.

'Well, one way or another, we'll end up dead in here. Better to live fighting than to die doing nothing.'

'Nicely put,' said Random.

'As soon as we're on shift we'll swing into action. We'll see that this Soul Destroyer and all those up in the Grand Chamber face justice.

We're not leading a rebellion. We're starting a revolution.'

Samuelson watched as the body bag was wheeled out of his office. Within moments, Consula appeared, flanked by two guards who stood aside as Zatterson was wheeled away.

She looked on remorseless, a stern look upon her cold features.

'You'd better have a good explanation for this, Samuelson,' she shouted.

'I tell you, it was his lifestyle that did that to him. His heart must have just given out.'

'And you must think I was born yesterday.'

Consula thundered at her Chancellor. She made for the drinks cabinet in Samuelson's office.

'A coroner's report will declare foul play.'

'We can cover that up,' said Samuelson, snatching the decanter out of his superior's hands. 'It had to be done. It was me or him.'

'I don't know who I'd prefer right now, Chancellor.'

'Well, if there's one way to get ahead in politics it's to dispose of the competition.' Samuelson sat down behind his desk.

'Did I tell you to sit down!' yelled Consula.

Samuelson sat unmoved.

'This is my office, I can do what I like.'

'Including murder members of the Cabinet, is that right?'

'If it's necessary for the continued success of Genocia, then yes.'

'Samuelson, I warn you...'

Consula trailed off. Her guards moved forward, their frames tall and muscular.

'You won't go unpunished for this.'

Samuelson flinched in his chair. He knew what his malevolent superior had in mind. He'd killed a member of Parliament. He had to be taught a lesson.

'Tell me about these youngsters you and Zatterson discovered.'

Samuelson was shocked. She'd been monitoring his plans all along.

'That is top secret information!' he screamed. 'It was a strictly need-to-know project.'

'Come, Samuelson. You're planning a mini empire, soon to develop into a coup for my position. By obtaining the money these aliens had, you could use it for your own means. Probably to overthrow my authority on Genocia.'

'It was not a coup. You are much mistaken, Consula,' sniffed Samuelson.

'Well, we'll soon find out,' said Consula.

She snapped her fingers and the two heavy guards advanced on
Samuelson. The Chancellor suddenly looked scared. He hadn't
been beaten since his school days. Now he had to be prepared for
the beating of a lifetime.

'Find out what you can. If you can't get everything out of him,
bring him to the detention centre for further interrogation.'
Consula turned to leave the office.

'Supreme Leader you have it all wrong. Believe me!'

A fist smacked into Samuelson's pointy chin, lifting him out of
his chair and sending him reeling into a book shelf. Consula did
not look back. She shut the office door and left her heavies to do
their job in peace. She was met by more of her personal guards
outside.

'Find out more about this Captain Random. Check every
surveillance tape and log book. When you've located him and the
money, transfer them to me. Understand?'

The guards nodded.

'Take me to my office, we've got work to do. If Samuelson
doesn't give us the information we want and fails to co-operate,
then we'll feed him to the Soul Destroyer.'

Consula smiled as she was escorted away.

XVII

The hover car continued on its long, lonely journey. It had been
well over an hour since Anji had set off the impulse immobilizer.
Her rebel friends had yet to regain consciousness.

Nevertheless, she had continued the plotted course to Terran's
hideout and was now very close to finding the one person who
could help her find her friends.

She looked down at the map on the dashboard display. She was roughly three miles from her destination. The poisonous blue sky had been left behind and the air now seemed thick with the horrible grey fog she'd been used to while driving through the wastelands. What a planet! Unbreathable air, zombies, a Government killing people to power their city and wealth. She dreamed of getting away on the Venus II, safe with Random, Jake and Skateboard. It had barely been a day since she'd last seen them but it felt like an eternity. She sighed to herself and checked her face in the mirror, wiping the tear stains from her cheeks. She had to be strong for her friends. She was strong for them. It didn't matter if she cried.

'Come on Anj, you've got this. Nearly there,' she encouraged herself.

Before long, the hover car turned into what looked like an abandoned settlement. It reminded Anji of a town from an old western film. The ground was dusty and ash coloured. The primitive buildings were made of wood and looked like they hadn't been maintained for decades.

Anji brought the car to a halt and took in her surroundings. She pondered for a moment whether to leave the relative safety of the car to try and find Terran on foot. Then she remembered the muts, those horrific zombies who'd attacked her. She looked down at Yana's side and noticed her hand gun. Anji took it for herself, hoping she'd never have to use it, and got out of the vehicle.

She took a look around and consulted the map again. Terran's hideout was in the fourth house on the east side of the settlement. She summoned all her courage and walked into the fog.

A few minutes later, she wished she'd never left the safety of the hover car. Anji peered through the fog but to no avail. She was lost.

Suddenly, she jumped as she heard footsteps up ahead. She drew her gun and pointed it in the direction of the noise.

'Who's there?'

She jumped again as more footsteps came from behind her. She started to breathe heavily.

'Don't come any further. I'm armed!'

But the footsteps continued to approach. She realised they were coming from all around her now. She stayed put, waving the gun.

'Look, if you're trying to scare me...you're doing a bloody good job!'

The footsteps were almost on top of her now. She began to panic. Would she really have to kill? She couldn't do it.

A scream pierced the cold air. The footsteps belonged to muts and they were on top of Anji ready to kill.

Suddenly, a shock of blue shot through the muts. They screamed as they fell to the ground, dead. Anji dropped down and curled in a ball.

'Miss, it's good to see you.'

Anji unfurled and looked at her rescuer. She smiled with relief as she clapped eyes on a friend she'd thought she'd never see again.

*

The prisoners had been rudely awoken by a shrieking alarm that rang throughout the mine. Random and Jake jumped out of their bunks, shocked and shaken. Delilah and Benaya had grown more used to the sound in their time enslaved deep underground.

'Five-minute warning. We must get to the central mine shaft immediately. If we don't, we will be punished,' Delilah yawned and picked up

a shovel next to her bunk. Benaya followed her out of the room. Random looked at Jake.

'You ready for this, Jake?'

'Ready as I'll ever be, Random.'

'Good, if we get separated, we'll meet at the security level. If I'm able to switch the keepers off then it might just be the safest place to be in this mine.'

The pair followed Delilah and Benaya out into the tunnel where all four proceeded to put on the radiation suits which hung on the wall there. They then walked to the nearest shuttle car port and were taken by escort to the central main shaft. It was the same shaft the boys had seen on their descent into the mine.

The group disembarked and saw hundreds of fellow prisoners, their suits grimed by dirt, slouching along, worn down by endless manual labour.

Random, Jake, Delilah and Benaya fell in with the others, standing in lines facing a plinth on which a line of keepers stood. One robot stood a few feet in front of the others and began to speak.

'I am B7405. I am your shift leader for today. We have located minute traces of ESOL19 in the south shaft. That is where we will concentrate our efforts. Any disobedience will be met with force. Now, pick up your tools and head to the shuttle bay. Dismissed.'

'How close to the security level is the south shaft?' asked Random.

'Almost on top of it,' said Delilah.

'Our lucky day,' whispered Jake.

'Move!' A keeper prodded Jake sharply in the ribs and pushed him and the others towards a shuttle car.

The trip to the south shaft didn't last long. They were extremely zippy, Random thought to himself. He made a mental note of their speed in case their plan didn't come to fruition.

Upon arrival, the foursome, accompanied by nearly one hundred prisoners, were put to work on the deepest tunnel in the south shaft. They were clamped together into a line with chains around their necks and feet, a keeper separating them all, monitoring their every move. They tunneled along a narrow path, below which was a sharp drop into nothingness. A laser drill was thrust in their hands and they were put to work, blasting away at the black rock, clouds of soot raining down on them.

Jake turned to his robot.

'What does ESOL19 look like anyway?'

'You'll find out if you come across it,' it stated unhelpfully.

Jake groaned and continued to laser away at the rock. He soon grew tired.

'Random, I'm knackered!'

Random's sensitive hearing ensured he could hear his friend over the drilling.

'It's the radiation from the ESOL19. It's draining your energy. Must mean we are right on top of some.'

He was right. Before long, the laser blasted the rock and a brilliant ray of light tore through the dull blackness.

The robot spoke into the communicator on its wrist.

'H979 to B7405. ESOL19 located in N17 South shaft.'

'NOW!' screamed Random.

He lifted his laser and shot it straight at his robot guard. The keeper had little time to retaliate before it fell into the abyss below.

Random used his lightning quick reflexes to shoot his laser directly at the other keepers in his vicinity. Every single shot burrowed into their chest units. They had no time to retaliate. With a chorus of electronic groans, a dozen or so of the metal overlords clanked to the floor, dead.

The prisoners stood aghast.

Random levelled the laser at their chains and blasted them free.

'Well don't just stand there. You're free! Take your tools and use them as weapons, come on!'

'VIVA LA REVOLUTION!' screamed Jake. To his surprise, the prisoners repeated his rallying cry.

'Well, that felt good.'

'Come on,' ordered Delilah.

They followed Random to the shuttle bay, the purple boy opening fire on the keepers as he saw them, again too quick for any return fire.

'I thought you said we were going to start a fight?' said Delilah.

'Yes, but when I saw the ESOL19 I thought we'd catch the robots off guard,' Random justified.

'And it worked,' said Jake.

'Exactly. Right. Stick with me and you'll stay safe.'

'Hold on, where did you learn to shoot like that?' Delilah was suitably impressed.

'He's an alien,' said Jake.

'What? From a military planet?'

'Kind of,' said Random as he familiarised himself with the controls of a shuttle car. 'Right, all aboard. We've got to get to the security level.'

The group got in and Random put the car into drive. The shuttle car flashed away at high speed.

The freed prisoners they left behind were dog fighting with the
keepers. Those who were strong enough were shooting the laser
tools at their guards who were starting to converge on the south
shaft. The keepers were firing back and both sides were taking
some casualties, but it was the enslaved that were on top of their
captors. The revolution had begun!

*

'Skateboard!'

Anji could barely hide her delight. She threw herself at the AI
robot and hugged his metal frame with all her might.

'How did you get here?'

'I'll explain in a bit, miss. But first, let's get you out of danger.'

'Wait, hang on a minute. There's three of my friends
unconscious in the car. We have to help them.'

Skateboard whirred towards the vehicle. Anji, wary of more
muts lurking about to attack her, stayed close to her metal friend.

He scanned the life forms on board.

'They've taken a fairly nasty shock from an impulse weapon.
They should regain consciousness soon. Can you get inside the
vehicle, miss, and follow me to the laboratory?'

'Laboratory?' asked Anji.

'Yes, I'll escort you out front. Come, we must get inside before
more of those mutants attack.'

Anji did as she was asked. Skateboard escorted the car to a
nearby shed. The door opened automatically and, when the hover
car was safely
inside, the floor gave way and the whole garage seemed to
disappear below ground.

Anji sat in the car, enjoying the ride. Now she was with
Skateboard, she felt safe and reassured.

A groan came from the direction of Dail's sleeping body.

'Skateboard, they're coming round!' said Anji excitedly.

The sunken garage ceased its descent and Anji got out of the car
to check out the surroundings.

They appeared to be in an underground bunker.

'This is great!'

Yana also began to stir in the back of the car.

'How did you find this place?' asked Anji.

'I'll tell you in a while, miss. First of all, there's someone you have to meet.'

A secret door opened. There stood an old man with white wisps of hair sprouting in different directions on his head.

'Anji, this is Terran,' confirmed Skateboard.

The old man smiled and held out his hand.

'Hello Anji. I believe you have been looking for me.'

The shuttle car tore through the tunnels like a bat out of hell. The searing heat of laser fire shot past its occupants.

'Keep down!' Random shouted.

Jake, Delilah and Benaya had taken up positions behind the seats, returning fire at every available opportunity. They were unsure if their attack was successful, however, as Random was driving the shuttle car at such a rate that everything was just a blur.

The group continued to shoot. Random checked the scope next to his steering wheel.

'We're nearly at the security level. We'll have to be ready for more of this when we get there.'

'Bring them on!' roared Delilah. The escape and subsequent fighting had given her back her old spirit. No longer was she broken from what had seemed like an eternity in the darkness. Now there was a chance to win. Especially with a super-being like Random by her side.

Suddenly, a bolt of laser fire struck the shuttle car, knocking it up in the air. The foursome yelled in panic before Random got it back under control. He wrestled with the controls and managed to calm his friends..for a moment at least.

Another barrage of shots flew towards the shuttle car and its crew. A brilliant explosion of light and heat shot up in front of Jake and Benaya. Without warning, the car started to split. The vehicle yawned as metal began to twist and break. Random looked on helplessly as the shuttle car shattered in two.

'No!' he yelled but there was nothing he could do.

The section containing Benaya and Jake started to disappear into the darkness. Despite the laser fire still focused on them, Random began to slow the shuttle down and put it in reverse.

'What are you doing?' said Delilah. Now that their speed had decreased, she could see her targets and was taking the robots out with relative ease.

'We have to go back for them,' yelled Random.

'No, we must keep going.'

'They'll die if we don't!'

'We'll all die if we don't keep going. If we get to the security level before the keepers reach them, we can save them. Come on, Random, you know it makes sense.'

'But, your sister!'

'She'll thank us for it if we're successful. Please, Random. We have to keep going.'

Delilah was right but Random felt nothing but guilt. He'd got his friends into this awful mess. He should never have taken them with him when he left Earth. Now Jake was in mortal danger. He frowned and speeded the shuttle car up again, leaving his friend alone with a stranger in peril. Reluctantly, they went on.

*

'Hey! Come back!' Jake was powerless to do anything. He watched and gulped hard as the other half of the shuttle raced off without him. He felt a touch on his arm. It was Benaya urging him to keep shooting. The keepers, along with wall-mounted defense weapons, were still shooting at them. As their speed decreased, the barrage of lasers was getting closer and closer.

Benaya looked desperately at the tunnel. She noticed they were coming up to a lay-by and spotted a crevice they could use for cover. She clasped her hand around the collar of Jake's radiation suit.

'Hey! What are you doing?'

Without warning, Benaya jumped off the shuttle, dragging Jake screaming with her just as the lasers shot into their dismembered craft. As the shuttle blew up behind them, the duo ducked into the crevice.

There, they drew their guns, ready to attack the advancing keepers.

XVIII

Consula brooded from behind her big desk. She had always suspected Samuelson of being a traitor.

Why not?

In the pecking order on Genocia, the Chancellor of the Exchequer was the next in line for the head of Government.

But why now? Had he discovered the truth about the Soul Destroyer? The real reason as to why so many more workers were being sent to the mines? That is what she was about to find out.

She returned to her paperwork and awaited news. Before long, her intercom fizzed into life.

'Ma'am, we've got him here for you,' said the guard.

Consula placed a long finger on the intercom. 'Bring him in. But do watch the carpet,' she snapped.

The doors swung open and two heavy guards approached, dragging a bloody and beaten figure towards her. The prisoner hung like a sack of spuds between them. There was a grunt as he was hurled to the floor before Consula's desk.

'Thank you. You may leave us.'

The guards bowed and retreated from the room. As soon as the door closed, Consula got up and approached the broken man.

'I must commend you, Samuelson. They tell me that you put up a brave fight. I'm also relieved that you were not privy to the information I have been purposefully keeping from you. But, there's this boy. This alien and his friends. I was intrigued to discover their unlikely story. Now I have a fairly good idea as to what you were planning to do with their money. Being a man of financial integrity, I'd have expected nothing else of the finest Chancellor to serve under me. It has been procured. Don't worry about it, it's in a safe place. But there are more pressing matters in the affairs of state. Such as this boy.'

Samuelson stared at the floor, barely strong enough to hold himself upright. He just sat there, slumped against the desk, legs crossed, trying not to show his superior any hint of weakness.

The thin, boney frame of the ruler of Genocia towered over him. She knelt down and whispered softly.

'Tell me, Samuelson. Who is he?'

Samuelson stayed silent.

Consula chuckled.

'My my. Maybe my boys were too hard on you. Have they crushed your voice box? Tell me.'

'What good will it do?' croaked Samuelson, his voice dry and weak.

'The man speaks!' mocked Consula. 'It would help me to know more about him.'

'Why would I want to help you?' spat Samuelson.

'It could go a long way towards sparing your life,' bribed Consula.

'I've got nothing left to live for. You know it. My position is gone, you've stripped my dignity away. Kill me, send me to the Soul Destroyer and get it over with quick.'

'Well, aren't we feeling sorry for ourselves?' laughed Consula.

'For all I know, he may be dead by now. Eaten alive by that machine you've been using to slaughter so many of our people.'

'That cannot be confirmed or denied, Samuelson.'

'You're insane, Consula!' screamed Samuelson. He looked up, making eye contact with his former ally, his face covered with dry crimson blood and broken skin.

'Some of the old fight returning, eh, colleague?'

'I warned you about the mines. You claimed nothing could be solved without more labour and more keepers.'

'And I was right, supplementing that workforce with tourists who broke the law and the wasters who scavenged around the outside of the Grand Chamber. What do we care for them? Self-preservation, that's what my Government is built upon and you know it. We need more power!'

'And in doing so we have committed the biggest genocide this galaxy has ever seen,' Samuelson cried.

'We haven't been caught yet. We never will be. With the Soul Destroyer nearing full capacity, it'll ensure that no one will trouble us again. We won't need anything from these disgusting tourists. We will be totally self-sufficient. Nothing will escape the awesome might of Genocia then. We will send a message to our neighbours and it will be one of total destruction.'

Samuelson's jaw dropped.

'That's inter-planetary murder!'

'To keep us alive. To keep us safe.'

The ex-Chancellor shook his head. 'Safe? From what? We haven't been attacked. This isn't a planet of conflict.'

'Look outside these walls, Samuelson. Have you seen it? The stinking, festering pollution of our world? We will be dead in ten years if we didn't take action. The Soul Destroyer will ensure that we stay protected.'

'How?'

Consula kicked Samuelson's chin brutally, sending him sprawling to the floor.

'Enough questions. Tell me more about this boy.'

*

'How did you find this place?'

Anji sat on a stool surrounded by a myriad of jugs, files and liquids which looked like potions bubbling under crude Bunsen burners.

'I set the bunker up almost as soon as I escaped the mines,' Terran said as he busied himself with his experiments.

'The bunker was derelict. No one had lived in this part of Genocia for decades. I set up shop here, discovered a food replicator which after repairs could keep me sustained and set about my work.'

'And you've hidden down here for how long?'

'It's been three years since I was detained.'

'For what?'

Terran stopped his experiments, made for the food replicator and keyed in a few numbers.

'Back in the day, I was a scientist, just here on my holidays from Delta-12. Just minding my own

business at first. Then I discovered a mineral known only to this planet. ESOL19. It has benefits beyond our imagination.

It can sustain plant life, thus providing more oxygen and clean air, thus providing protective compounds for the environment. I then discovered its fantastic replenishing properties for electricity and renewable energy. Split down even further, it can even replicate food!'

The replicator buzzed, lit up and produced two steaming cups from nowhere.

'Cocoa?'

Anji nodded. 'I wouldn't say no to that.'

Terran handed her a cup. She blew on the brown liquid and took a sip.

'Wow, this is delicious,' she said, taking another glorious swig. After her ordeal over the last couple of days, she didn't know if it was the taste of the drink or the feeling of finally being safe, but she felt renewed with every sip.

'This old thing works off one kilo of ESOL19. Keeps it powered for up to 20 years.'

'That's amazing. So that's why the Government want it all to themselves.'

'No. They want it because it's so scarce.' Terran sat down on his stall. 'Also, they had begun to bring everything inside the Grand Chamber. The mineral is now so rare there's barely any left.'

'So that's why they are sending more and more people to the mines.'

'Yes, in an almost futile search for the mineral, and to power the Soul Destroyer,' said Terran solemnly.

A door slid open to Anji's right and Skateboard wheeled into the room.

'Yana and the others are almost fully recovered, miss. It shouldn't be much longer now.'

Anji smiled and hugged her robot friend again. 'I'm so happy I found you, Skateboard. But how did you get out of the Venus II?'

'I used the cloaking system on myself, downloaded the appropriate files and converted the capabilities to my hard drive. As soon as I was invisible, I opened a sealed hatch and escaped silently past the guards.'

'So where is the Venus II now?' asked Anji.

'It's still held in the detention area. I'm monitoring its current situation and it looks like the soldiers have given up on breaking in.'

'Y'know, if anything happened to that ship...' Anji stopped herself. She couldn't think of anything worse than being stuck on such a terrible planet.

'I followed your heat signature. But because I was able to hack your resistance group's computer, I knew where you were planning to go, so I thought I'd go on ahead and find Terran first; pre-warn him, as it were, as to our business and get him onside.'

'Wait. Hold on. You hacked our computer?'

The voice was Yana's, who'd been listening in the doorway.

'Modesty notwithstanding, I'm a genius,' said Skateboard.

'He's not lying there,' said Anji.

'Ah, good. You're up. Here, I'll get you some cocoa,' said Terran.

Yana massaged her neck and moaned. 'I don't suppose you have anything stronger?'

'So, if you can map heat signatures, then what's happened to Random and Jake?' Anji dared to ask. 'Are they alive?'

'Very much so,' said Skateboard. 'But they need our help. They are trapped in the mines.'

'This is where you come in, Terran. Can you help us?' asked Anji.

Terran's face fell.

'I can,' he replied, 'But I fear that more innocent lives could be lost if you go down there.'

'They won't. Not if we find Random,' said Anji.

'What do you propose to do?'

'Shut off the Soul Destroyer,' replied Yana.

Terran looked shocked. He turned to Skateboard.

'You didn't tell me that!'

'I wasn't aware of that part of the plan, sir,' he assured Terran. 'Why must we shut it off?'

'Because it's evil! It's taking the lives of hundreds of Genocians,' said Yana.

'And anyone else who looks upon it,' added Anji.

Terran leant on his work station.

'I don't think there is a way to stop it.'

'Have you seen it? Do you know what it is?' asked Anji.

Terran nodded.

'Yes. I've seen it. When we broke out of the mines, the tunnel opening was metres away from the beastly thing. I sometimes lie awake at night, hearing the screams of the innocent who were fed to it. I had a choice to make at that moment. Save my sorry skin or try to help those who waited to face it.'

'There was nothing you could have done, Terran,' said Anji.

'Maybe. I remember as we found the entrance, just as the robots caught up with us and started firing mercilessly, I saw inside the cave. A shining light exploded out of the cave mouth every time a life was claimed but when the light grew dim...there was just these eyes...these vast hollow eyes. I looked into them and saw...nothing. No remorse, no pity. Nothing but...evil.'

'We have to get down there as soon as possible. Otherwise, Random and Jake could be next.'

Terran relented.

'Okay. I can tell you where the tunnel opening is. But it'll be heavily guarded, so you'll have to be prepared for the robot guards.'

'Don't worry,' said Yana as she reached for her hand gun. 'We've brought the goods.'

'I'll give you respirators too. You don't want to turn into one of those muts who attacked you. Too much poisonous air will rot your brain.'

'That's very kind,' said Anji, shuddering at the thought of the vicious horde that had attacked them.

'How far away is the tunnel entrance?' asked Yana.

'It's on the west side of the Grand Chamber. Roughly 50 miles from our current location.' Terran produced a map from beneath his work bench. 'The tunnel is seven miles long. It will take you a long time to get down there.'

'Not if we develop some form of jet pack. One that can descend as well as ascend. Shouldn't take any time at all with my expertise,' said Skateboard proudly.

'Well, I wouldn't put anything past our genius!' said Yana. 'But you're forgetting the big picture, you lot. What about Consula and the Government?'

'We should get Random back first then deal with the Grand Chamber,' said Anji.

'We must deal with both,' said Skateboard. 'When I read the encrypted files on the Soul Destroyer, I learned that it is connected with the ruler of the planet.'

'Consula? How?' asked Anji.

'I'm not sure. From all available data, a psychic link is my best guess. But my theory is that we stop one and we'll end up stopping the other.'

'Yana, what about the rebels you contacted before we left the hideout? Are they in?'

'I'll have to check. I've been out cold for the last…hey, how long was I out?'

'Not long,' replied Anji. 'We can go on ahead and they can meet us at the rendezvous.'

'Won't it be guarded from the surface as soon as we infiltrate the mine?'

'Yes, that's a point,' Anji thought. 'But they won't be expecting an ambush now, will they?'

Yana frowned in thought.

'I suppose not.'

'Great! Anything else?' Anji was relishing her seeming new role as team leader.

'It'll be dangerous. We'll have to shut down the robots as soon as we get in there,' said Yana.

'Skateboard? Can you do that remotely?'

'Negative, miss, I shall have to plug myself into the controls. The robots on the surface I can but the ones below, I am afraid, I cannot.'

A light bulb went off in both Yana and Anji's brains.

'Say that again?'

'I said the robots on the surface I can control but the ones below, I am afraid, I cannot.'

'Skateboard, that's it! You can shut down Genocia's defenses!'

'Not all. I still can't rescue the Venus II and not all guards and soldiers are robots.'

'No, but how many of them are?'

Skateboard's diodes whirred. 'Precisely 71.8%'

'Well, it's better than nothing!' cried Yana. 'Right, you do what you've got to do here. I'll
wake the boys up and we'll make for the tunnel. We can discuss the rest of the plan on the way!'

Terran had watched the plan unfold. He could sense the optimism in the air.

'If there is anything I can do to help, you know where I am. They won't be able to find me here if they track the signal.'

Anji hugged the old man.

'You've done so much.'

Terran smiled. 'I wish you the best of luck. If a silly old scientist like me can do it then so can you.'

'Thank you, Terran.'

Anji followed Yana through the doorway to tell Dail and Rader the good news.

Skateboard stayed by Terran's side.

'You are aware that, if we fail, then there is no stopping Consula's men from coming for you?'

'I know. I didn't want to spoil anything.'

'You will be safe if you come with us.'

'No. No you've got your battles to face. I have mine. Such as finding a way to replicate ESOL19. If I can crack this experiment and you can stop Consula and the Soul Destroyer, then this will be the best day that Genocia has seen in many, many moons. Maybe then I can get home.'

Skateboard's back slid open and a hydraulic claw reached out to Terran. The old man took a firm grasp of it and shook it like it was a hand.

'May you be successful.'

Skateboard's circuits whirred. 'You too.'

XIX

'Top left!'

Delilah shot another round of laser fire from her drill.

'Bottom right!'

Another shot of energy blasted into the chest unit of another keeper.

'Three o'clock!'

'What?' screamed Delilah.

Random twisted behind his pilot's seat, snatched the drill off his passenger and fired at a keeper hitherto unseen by the woman.

'That one.' said Random as he handed the drill back.

'We're almost there,' he hollered. The volley of firepower was indescribable. The laser fire rained sideways from an army of robots that were dotted around the tunnel. Most of the wall-mounted weaponry was gone, thanks to Delilah's prowess with the drill, but they were only a mile away from the security level and Random dreaded what kind of a welcome party they'd be greeted by.

The shuttle was badly damaged by now, scorched by the searing heat of the attack. Small fires were erupting in inconvenient places,

including on one half of the control panel Random was working from. Regardless, Random

somehow managed to keep it going.

Thanks to Delilah's shooting skills and Random's razor sharp reflexes, the shuttle was about to make it to their intended destination.

'As soon as we round this corner, prepare to jump and find cover, okay?' said Random.

Delilah nodded. Her heart was beating faster than it ever had done. Fear and adrenaline swam hand-in-hand around her veins. She had never felt more alive.

Random's eyes narrowed in concentration. With one final swing of the steering wheel, he rounded into the cave mouth. As soon as his eyes saw what was waiting for them, they widened in horror.

An army of keepers stood in a line at the lip of the shuttle bay, their arms outstretched with the barrels of built-in guns protruding from gleaming cavities in their limbs.

'Jump, Delilah!'

The duo leaped off the shuttle high into the air. The shuttle car tore through the lip of the cave, smacking headlong at high speed into the keepers, causing a massive explosion to rip through the cave mouth. Random grabbed Delilah as she fell to the floor and, using his own body as protection, pushed her hard into the cave face.

A fireball tore past them, the sheer heat of it melting some of Random's radiation suit. The roar of the explosion deafened them as they clung desperately on to one another. Within seconds, the whole ordeal was over. The sound of the explosion echoed down the tunnel. Scorched and battered, Random and Delilah slumped to the floor exhausted.

As Random gathered his senses, he looked up from the floor over at the cave mouth. The shuttle car had smashed into a good number of the robots waiting to slaughter them. The entire shuttle bay had been devastated. But he could see that some of the keepers had been merely damaged and were starting to recover.

He glanced up, furiously trying to spot the security level through the smoke and smog but with no luck. He could see nothing but blackness.

Suddenly, a red LED light cut through the smoke and aimed itself at him. Then another. And another. Random took a couple of deep breaths and reached for his drill. It was smashed beyond repair. He cursed it, throwing it away to one side. His eyes adjusted to the gloom and he discovered that those were not lights that were coming for him. It was the keepers.

The leader of the pack loomed over Random's fallen body.

'You're coming with us.'

*

Unaware of their friend's capture, Jake and Benaya were having trouble of their own. Backed into a cavern, the duo were bravely fighting off the advancing menace of the robots.

Piles of dead metal lay smoking, flames licking from the open wounds of the slain keepers. But Jake was noticing that his weapon was starting to falter. The stream of laser that erupted from the barrel was growing transparent and shorter.

'I don't think this drill's going to last much longer,' he said but the mute girl was unmoved.

She let off a volley of shots and took out a dozen of the closest keepers. As soon as their metallic screams ebbed away into the blackness, she grabbed Jake's hand and pulled him out of the cavern and they ran as fast as they could.

Several explosions of laser blasted around them and, for all Jake's screams, any onlooker would have thought that Benaya was unfazed. Determined to escape their predicament, she would carry Jake if she had to. Why had she been lumbered with this useless boy anyway? Why couldn't she have been marooned with the impossible purple one. Grunting as she ran, she was practically dragging Jake behind her like a child would drag a teddy bear.

'Mind the suit!' he yelled but Benaya wasn't listening.

The laser fire started to sound further and further away. At last, the couple found a reprieve. Benaya stopped in her tracks and threw Jake to the ground.

'Thanks,' said Jake sarcastically.

Benaya looked at Jake scornfully and put her finger to her lips. They could hear a noise of metal on rock. The keepers were starting to catch up.

Jake scrambled to his feet. 'Oh god. Not more!'

Benaya gritted her teeth. Seeing the red laser lights that announced their advance, she flashed her drill up at the roof of the tunnel and blasted it along a line. A rock fall crashed at her feet, knocking Jake to the floor once more. He pressed his hands against his ears but his protective hood did nothing to keep out the sound of the tumbling rocks. Before long, Benaya ceased firing and peered through the murky fog at a wall of rubble that had completely sealed off the tunnel.

'Nice one,' exclaimed Jake. 'But what about the people who are still stuck in there?'

Benaya signed that they would have to pray that Random shut the keepers down, but Jake didn't understand a word.

'Look, I'm sorry but I don't get sign language. Is there some other way we can communicate?'

Benaya had completely lost her patience. She made a gesture with her hand.

'Well, okay, I understood that,' said Jake. He laughed. Benaya's stern expression melted away and she smiled at the ground.

Come on, she mouthed.

'Yes, I got that bit. We'd better find the others.'

Benaya broke into a jog and disappeared in the black.

'Oh no, please, don't make me run!' Jake sighed. He took a deep breath and made off after her. They still had a few miles to reach the lip of the cave mouth and, hopefully, their friends.

XX

'Come in all units. Come in all units.' Rader was awake and full of life and vigour. Yana had made sure of that. His face still stung a little from her backhanded swipes as she implored him to wake. Dail had had an equally rigorous alarm call, and both were suffering from a dull headache. Still, at least they had escaped with their lives. The gang had left the relative safety of Terran's hideout and driven to the edge of the abandoned town. Here they would spark the revolution.

The speaker system emitted a loud static, interrupted only by Yana's worried statement.

'They can't hear us out here, can they?'

'Give it a chance, Yana,' said Anji.

The party stood intently around the shuttle car, waiting for any acknowledgement from the rebels.

'We are a long way out. There is a chance that the signal isn't reaching,' said Dail. 'I'll try to boost it.'

He fiddled with some buttons on the dashboard. Suddenly, a voice cracked through the speakers.

'GEN5 to GEN3, are you receiving me?'

Rader turned to his friends, his face aglow with happiness.

'GEN5, this is GEN3, reading you loud and clear.'

Another voice came through the airwaves.

'GEN6 to GEN3, we are receiving your transmission.'

'GEN2 to GEN3, we're with you, over.'

The group was ecstatic. All the various groups that had escaped Consula's clutches were coming through the little car speaker. Soon all twelve rebel factions were in touch with the group. Anji hugged Yana with delight.

'Whoa, hang on, kid. They haven't heard what we've got to say yet,' she warned.

'GEN3 to all units. We have located the secret entrance to the mine. With help from alien life forms and artificial intelligence, we are planning to descend into the mine once the planet's defense systems have been de-activated and, with our allies, we shall eliminate the Soul Destroyer. But we need your help to guard the tunnel entrance and make sure that our mission is a success.'

'GEN1 to GEN3,' the radio interrupted. 'What do you mean "disable the planet's defences"?'

'One of the alien party is a robot. It is currently working on breaking through the encryption codes,' confirmed Rader. 'They have friends

inside the mine who intelligence confirms are currently leading a coup. As soon as we get down

there we will need help from above ground to fight off the army, otherwise the plans will be futile. We cannot do it without you, over.'

The radio became static once more.

'Do you think they'll help?' asked Anji.

'It's hard to say. Even if we get a few of the rebel groups on our side, then we stand a fighting chance. But we'll have to act quick when we are down there to kill the Soul Destroyer.'

Anji nodded.

'GEN3. This is GEN8. I'm afraid we need a little more assurance that this plan of yours is valid.'

'GEN3 to GEN8, what do you mean?'

'GEN3, we are confident that our forces can withstand a small army. But what you are attempting will put the whole planet on high alert. Even with the defence system shut down there is the possibility of massive resistance.'

'Understood. Stand by.' Rader turned to Anji.

'Any chance we can get your robot pal to convince them?'

Anji nodded and turned to the laboratory. Skateboard had almost completed the construction of four jet packs - seemingly adapted from old vacuum cleaners, thought Anji.

'Skateboard. We...'

'I heard, miss,' he said without looking up. 'I can transfer the plan to the conference call now. Tell them to stand by for my message.'

Anji ran back to the shuttle car and relayed the information to
Rader, who in turn passed it on to the call. In a few seconds, a
beep was heard eleven times over.

It was now their turn to wait while the rebel teams made up
their minds.

'How long until we can shut down the defence system?' asked
Dail.

'I'm cross-referencing a network of encrypted and nano-
encrypted interfaces at a rate of fifteen BHz per second. But as I
am also constructing my third jet pack and having this
conversation, it's going to take a little longer. So far I have been
quite successful, but it's going to take another three minutes
before the final encryption is broken.'

'Good. I think our friends need a little demonstration.'

Three minutes passed. Still the radio was silent and still they
waited.

'Rader, pass the communicator to me, I have a plan,' said Dail.

Rader looked reluctant but handed it over to his colleague.

'All units, all units. Speak to your tech members and please ask
them to use the fireball mainframe to check on the status of the
Government's defense network.'

'Roger,' came the reply.

'Skateboard?' said Anji.

'And...now!' Skateboard gave the command.

*

All around Genocia, in the streets of the citadel, in the grand
Chamber, in the market places and in the high security buildings
like the central bank, everything shut down.

In the army and air force barracks, roughly 71% of the workforce
simply went to sleep. In the airport, where the Venus II was being
kept like confiscated goods, the workforce ceased, including
those in Immigration who had given Random and his friends such
a hard time when they landed.

It was as though most of the planet had fallen asleep.

The blackout had not gone unnoticed. Especially by Consula herself. As the power went off, she got up from behind her desk and looked out of the large window overlooking the whole of the Grand Chamber. From here, she could see all of what she called the "civilised world" of Genocia. It was black, dark as night. She could hear sounds of chaos down below. The screams of her subjects, not knowing what to do.

'Ma'am,' her personal security chief announced himself. 'It appears there has been a severe worldwide power cut.'

'It's not a power cut, General. Someone's got into the mainframe.'

She powered past him and made for the door.

'Get my car ready. Despatch all available units to the mine where that purple boy was sent. I want all possible shaft openings guarded at all costs.'

'Y-yes, ma'am.'

'And try to get the power operational again,' she gathered some things. 'Fetch me Samuelson too. We'll feed him to the Soul Destroyer while we're at it. He is of no further use to me.'

'Ma'am,' the General clicked his heels and left.

Consula was left alone in the doorway. She felt an eerie presence enter the room. Far from unnerved, she closed her eyes and titled her head back.

'Not long now, master. You will have the final sacrifice. Then, we can begin...'

*

The radio fizzled with delight. Chirps of excitement glided over the airwaves. 'I don't believe it...GEN3, the power has gone down, I repeat, the power has gone down!'

'It's only a power cut, granted a massive one, but it's enough,' said Skateboard. 'Only 29% of the planet remains active.'

'All units, are you with us? Has this done enough to convince you?'

'Roger that, GEN3. Please send us your co-ordinates and we will estimate a rendezvous time. All units, I advise you to do the same.'

As Rader read the tunnel entrance's whereabouts, Yana turned
to Skateboard.

'We'd better get moving. They can still track the root of the
power cut.'

'The packs are ready, miss. We can go now.'

Yana picked up her pack.

'Dail, Anji, pick them up. We've got to move out. Rader, are we
good?'

'Roger that. Over and out,' said Rader, concluding the
conference call. 'All units are in. It will take them a maximum of
two hours to get to the entrance.'

Dail's computer beeped. 'Yana. Consula is also on her way to
the mine. We've got to get there now.'

'How long is it to the entrance?'

Yana looked at the co-ordinates Terran gave them.

'Three miles, how long will it take us to get down to the
Destroyer?'

'Seven minutes,' confirmed Skateboard.

'And how long until Consula reaches the mine?'

'Seven minutes.'

'Jesus!' cried Anji.

'Quick, everyone in!' said Yana.

Anji and Dail finished loading the boot up with the jet packs and
jumped into the back of the car. Skateboard hurled himself onto
their laps. Rader started the engine and, before anyone could shut
their doors, tore off from the deserted town and shot like a bullet
towards the tunnel entrance.

It would be tight and it would be dangerous but Anji was
reassured in one thing. They were going to save her friends.

XXI

Random awoke with a start. He winced, feeling a sharp pain
behind his ear. He wanted to massage it better but his hands were
manacled down.

He looked around him and realised he was tied down to what
looked like a slab in the middle of what appeared to be a cell.

'Would the words "I come in peace" have been too much of a fib
for you?' he joked.

He tried the restraints. Although they were tight enough to keep a normal being restrained, he was confident he could snap the bonds like paper. However, considering there was an army of robots all primed and ready for any retaliation, escape was not an option right now.

Random suddenly remembered Delilah.

'Where's my friend?'

'Over here.' Random could not see her for the wall of metal soldiers surrounding him.

'Are you okay?'

'Fine. Except I think they want to torture us.'

'What makes you say that?' Random turned to the Chief keeper. 'You're not going to do that to us now, are you? We're all for co-operation and giving our plans away, aren't we Delilah?'

'Are we?' she said, still obscured from sight.

'Well, of course, we don't want to be violently mutilated now, do we?'

'Mutilation is not a method we use,' said the Chief keeper. 'It is a primitive way of extracting information from our prisoners.'

'There, you see, Delilah. No torture,' said Random cheerfully.

'We use something much more clinical in extracting data from the minds of the enslaved.'

'Such as?' asked Random.

'You had to ask,' groaned Delilah.

'The mind probe will scan your brain patterns for the information we require.'

Random's face fell. 'Oh...that's going to hurt, isn't it?'

'By the end of the process, you will barely remember your own name. It will drain all knowledge for a period of time and we will keep going until we discover what we need. You may recover but, for someone who has caused as much damage as yourselves, we will be setting the mind probe to its maximum capacity.'

The room fell silent.

'So, it'll sting a bit then?' said Random.

'Your friend is about to find out,' the malice dripped from the Chief's tones. Random's face fell. He could hear Delilah start to pull at her bonds, grunting in panic.

'Now come on, my head's much bigger than my mates. Not to mention my mouth. Why not drain my mind first?'

A keeper approached the Chief with what looked like a headset. Random could just make out spikes sitting dangerously on the inside of it, threatening to puncture the skull of whichever poor soul was forced to wear it. On this occasion, Delilah was about to be the victim. No wonder some people never recovered from it.

'I think your friend will do just nicely.' The Chief maneuvered over to the slab to which Delilah was fastened.

'Random, I'm not going to lie. I'm...'

'Come on, Chief...I'll do you a bargain. You don't need to do this. We'll talk. I'll talk. Just let her go. She's done nothing wrong.'

'EVERYONE'S done something to break our law to be down here.'

'Leave her alone!'

Random clenched his fists. He would have to work quickly if he was to burst into action. Delilah shut her eyes tightly and felt the cold touch of fear running through her body.

'Fine! You asked for it!'

A purple flash broke around the room as Random snapped his cuffs and began systematically disarming the robots one-by-one with savage blows to their chest units, head pieces and arms.

Random used his speed to punch, kick and head butt them all to submission. The Chief stood aghast.

His optical relay circuit couldn't keep up with Random's sheer speed.

Within seconds, all robots in the room were decimated – except the Chief. Delilah looked over her shoulder and saw the piles of wreckage. Random stood, panting for breath, over the pile of scrap metal.

'The helmet...or you are next,' he warned.

The Chief hesitated for a second and then made for his gun.

Random moved like lightning, snapping the arm holding the gun and used the disembodied limb to knock the Chief's head clean off his unfeeling body.

With a crash, the head fell to the ground, sparking and shifting. The body followed suit and the mind probe helmet slipped to the floor and smashed to pieces.

Delilah sighed with relief.

'Quick, get me out of this thing!'

Random winced. He looked down at his shoulder. He was bleeding. Somehow in all the confusion a keeper must have opened fire, or debris had caught him unawares. Either way, he was glad that it was just a flesh wound and not in a more serious place. He released Delilah from her bonds.

'You're hurt.'

'You're perceptive.' Random hated stupid comments. Unless it was Jake making them, in which case he had grown used to them.

'Here, let me have a look at it.'

'There's no time, Delilah. We've got to find the control room.' Random held his hand over his injured shoulder. Purple blood oozed onto the palm of his hand. He looked down at his person and noticed that neither of them was wearing their radiation suits anymore.

'We'd better act quick. The radiation levels might not be as high in this sector but we can't be too careful.'

Delilah looked at the scrap metal that scattered the room.

'Do you think we'll find many more of them?'

'Bound to be.'

Random looked out of the cell door. There appeared to be a corridor leading off the right.

'Delilah, maybe it's for the best that you leave this to me.'

'What?'

'Listen to me. We are in the detention block of the deadliest mine on this planet. We've already killed many keepers. They are probably all linked to a hive mind, they'll know what we've done. I can use my speed to get past them, but if I lead you into more danger and get you hurt then...'

'Random,' said Delilah. 'Don't you think leaving me in a room with a bunch of slaughtered guards will arouse suspicion too?'

'More will already be coming. We'll have to hide you somewhere.'

'Random, shut up and come on,' Delilah grabbed Random's good arm and led him into the corridor. They walked about fifty yards before encountering a security camera on the wall.

'Fifty yards and only now a security camera?' Random wondered. 'That's the arrogance of the people in charge of this place, I guess.'

'What do we do?' whispered Delilah.

'No weapons? No idea where we are going? We run! Hop on!'
Random bent down, beckoning Delilah to jump on his back.

She didn't argue. This man was some sort of a god. Even if he was a foot smaller than her, even she knew better than to disagree with a super-being.

'Hold on.'

Just as she fastened her arms around Random's neck, the boy hurtled as fast as his legs would carry him.

Ignoring the pain in his shoulder, he used his super speed to inspect the whole detention block.

They ran up the stairs, down the stairs, into rooms, out of them again, all at an incredible rate. If he had stopped for just a nano second, he'd have heard Delilah screaming in his ear.

Suddenly, they came to an abrupt stop.

'Here it is,' said Random delightedly. Delilah wasn't listening. As soon as she jumped off his back, she could do nothing but be sick, loudly, in the corner of whatever room they'd stopped in.

Wiping her mouth, she looked up. They had made it.

'The main control room of the security level,' said Random.

'Oh, and look, a welcome party.'

'Shoot and destroy!' came the command.

The security level was vast and open, not allowing for much room to hide.

Random picked up Delilah and ran her out of the control room door.

They stood either side.

'Too many,' said Delilah. 'Got any good ideas?'

'We need a bomb,' said Random.

'Oh yes, hang on, let me get on out of my bag.' Delilah rolled her eyes.

'Delilah! What happened to our drills?'

'No idea, Random. Probably destroyed.'

'What if we fired them at maximum capacity?'

Delilah's eyes widened.

'It could blow up a building!' said Random.

He raced off. 'I'll be back in a bit. Stay put.'

'Random, wait!'

The boy had already disappeared.

Delilah could feel the heat of the lasers. They were getting closer.

Trapped. She was stuck. Unable to move, not fast enough to evade the security cameras. There was no way out. What if Random didn't come back? She shuddered at the thought. He had to. He just had to!

Suddenly, she saw a blur hurtling toward her. The blur came to a halt. It was Random, looking very battered and worn out, with a drill in his hand.

The robots were firing at him. Laser fire bounced into the wall behind him.

'Random!' shouted Delilah.

The boy wasn't listening. Fiddling with the drill, he pulled open the casing and turned a dial within the mechanism.

'Down!' he screamed.

As Delilah dropped to the floor, Random threw the drill into the control room, pressing the trigger as he did.

The drill exploded, causing a bigger eruption of fire, blowing up all of the keepers and setting off an explosion that spewed out into the corridor Random was standing in.

The blaze threw him into the wall and he crumpled next to Delilah, who held her hands
over her ears and curled into a ball to protect herself from the blast. Random shook himself and groggily made for the doorway.

The only noise he could hear was fire. The control room had been completely destroyed.

In a breathy state of exhaustion, he turned to Delilah and beamed.

'That's it. The keepers are down.'

XXII

'And then...we found...Random...in...a...forest
...back on Earth. He...crashed...the...Venus II...
into a...lake.'
'Doesn't this kid ever shut up?' thought Benaya.

She was several paces ahead of her friend, whose lifetime of chocolate and fast food had done nothing for his fitness.

'Can we stop soon? I've got...a...stitch!'

He had to stop, clutching his chest, his radiation suit sticking to his sweaty skin like cling film. He was beat. Benaya disappeared from sight. She continued her descent into the tunnel and left Jake in the gloom. She noticed a warm glowing light up ahead. They were nearly there. She reduced her run to a slow jog and moved up against the tunnel wall for cover. Slowly, she moved into the cave mouth, fully expecting an army of keepers waiting for her.

'Hey, thanks for leaving me back there!' Jake's cry echoed towards her. She scrunched up her face and made a 'ssshhh' sign with her finger. Jake spotted this and slowly made his way to her side.

'Sorry,' he whispered.

With his faulty drill gun by his side, he lurched over to the cave wall. It sounded quiet.

'Too quiet,' he whispered.

Slowly, they stepped out into the shuttle bay, in full view of whatever might be waiting for them.

Surprisingly, there were no keepers. It was pretty clear that there had been one hell of an explosion in the area but the only robots in sight either stood charred and immobile or strewn along the ground, burning and shattered. Benaya looked past them and saw a gathering of prisoners looking bemused and scared. A man came towards them with his hands up, still chained to a keeper he was dragging along the rocky ground.

Jake and Benaya took their radiation helmets off and approached the man.

'Did you do this?' he asked.

'Yup,' said Jake smugly.

Benaya shot him a look.

'I mean...err...well, some of it. What happened?'

'There was a big bang followed by a second one. Some of us were working at the time and then...the keepers just stopped.'

Benaya beamed.

It worked, she signed to Jake.

'It worked. They did it!' said Jake grinning. 'The keepers have been shut down!'

Quite a crowd had surrounded the two heroes. They cheered, roaring in a chorus of victory. Tears started streaming down the man's cheeks.

He cupped Jake's face with his filthy hands and hugged him
tightly. Jake could hardly breathe but he did nothing but smile.
The man then hugged Benaya and then gratefully bowed to them
both. The prisoners all hugged one another, their cheers echoing
back throughout the caverns as the news continued to filter
through. They were free. And yet they were still trapped.

Random and Delilah staggered out onto the security level's
balcony. They saw below a crowd of people celebrating as though
they had won the Cup Final. Only this was far more important.
Their captors had been vanquished.

Delilah helped the injured Random to the hand rail to watch the
joyous scene.

'You've done it, Random. These people haven't seen hope in
years. Some of them were ready to die. Others were ready to give
up on life and finish the job themselves before the Soul Destroyer
did it for them. Tears of sorrow were drowning them but now
they cry tears of joy.'

Random noticed that Delilah was also shedding a tear or two.

'I can see that you're finally hoping again,' he smiled.

'Random!' cried out a familiar voice, some distance away.

'No, no, that way, that way!' it continued.

Random squinted.

'Jake?'

It was indeed Jake and Benaya, crowd surfing!

'Random you are a bloody genius!' he screamed.

'Benaya, are you okay?' asked Delilah.

Her sister made a gesture with her sign language.

'I know. I'll make it up to you.'

Benaya signed back. *You already have.*

Delilah smiled.

'Come on, let's get down there with them.'

'No,' said Random. 'I'm not finished yet.'

'Random, are you injured? Quick, let us down. We'll help you,'
Jake shouted up to the balcony.

'No time,' said Random. 'And I'm fine. You need to do
something for me.'

'What?'

'Get as many of the prisoners out of the mines as you can. Take the shuttle cars if there's enough power in them and get back to the main shaft. Pass on the word to all prisoners. Tell them to meet you there. You need to get these people out of here, okay?'

'Why, what are you going to do?'

'It's about time I met this Soul Destroyer. Shut down this mine for good.'

'But that could be suicide!' said Jake.

'I'll be fine. I'll meet you back up on the surface, okay?'

'No!'

'Jake!'

Jake sighed. His happiness melted away.

'Fine.'

'See if you can find Anji. She must be worried sick.'

Jake floated above the heads of the prisoners but his enthusiasm had all but gone.

'You'd better not get killed.'

'Oh, I'll try not to,' Random laughed. 'You'd better get down there too, Delilah.'

'No way. I'm staying put. You're in no fit state to take on this thing on your own. God or no god!'

Random sighed. It was no use fighting. He should be saving his energy.

'Benaya, I'll meet you on the surface. Stay with Jake.'

Do I have to? signed Benaya.

'Yes!'

She shrugged.

'Okay, you lot, we need to release every single prisoner and get everyone to the main shaft. Have you got that?' Jake shouted, rallying the crowd.

'Yes!' they shouted back.

'We're going to get you all out of here. Women and children first. Right, which way to the main shaft?'

The crowd carried the pair in the right direction.

'Oh, alright then. This is easy.' Jake allowed himself to be carried off by the tide.

He looked back and caught sight of Random over the crowd. The Rodasian waved and smiled. Jake waved back but deep down he knew he was far safer than his friend was going to be.

'See you soon,' he said meekly as he disappeared from view.
Random's face turned to one of pure concentration.
'Right, let's end this once and for all.'

*

'There it is!' said Anji, pointing.

The shuttle car's engines screeched to a halt. It had crossed the fields and now it perched on the road side. Anji fixed her rebreather, hopped out of the car and ran towards what looked like a massive sink hole. It was roughly three metres in diameter, enough to fit the gang down all at once.

'Get the packs on, quickly,' ordered Yana. She pulled open the boot and distributed the jet packs.

Suddenly, Skateboard's scanner started to twitch. 'Miss, I'm afraid I have some bad news.'

'What now?' asked Anji.

'There appears to be a small enemy fleet approaching at speed.'
Dail reached for his electronoculars.

'He's right! Dead ahead, five miles.'

'How long do you estimate it will take them to get here?'
Skateboard's diodes whirred.

'Roughly twenty minutes.'

Yana swore. 'We've got another thirty before back-up arrives.'
Her mood turned sombre.

'You go. I'll stay here.'

Anji was shocked. 'You'll die!'

'I'll do my best to hold them off. Go now!'

Rader stood beside his leader.

'I'm staying too.'

'Rader, this is suicide!' Dail protested.

'We'll do what we can to give you time. Go on, move!'

Skateboard knew it had to be done. 'Miss, we have to get down there.'

Anji started to well up. She hugged Yana and Rader. Dail saluted his comrades.

'For Genocia,' he said.

His friends saluted back.

'Ditto,' said Yana.

Dail sniffed and turned away.

'Right, are we ready? Just hold on to your packs, they're set to auto-pilot. I'll guide you through the tunnel. We won't stop until we find Master Random. Ready?'

Anji and Dail nodded. 'Ready.'

With a blast of energy, the improvised jet packs flew up into the air. Anji and Dail screamed as their bodies tore upwards into the sky before plummeting down again at high speed into the abyss.

'Good luck,' said Skateboard. He fired up his boosters and followed his friends down the hole and into the bottomless gloom.

Yana sighed and looked at her friend. They could feel a faint vibration in the air.

'Till the end?' asked Rader.

Yana nodded and loaded her gun, ready for battle.

*

To Mrs. Mamford, it was like the whole world had stopped.

It had taken a few moments for the sound of silence to disturb her from her paperwork. It was deafening. For years, she had worked to the sound of blood curdling screams, the sound of keepers beating disobedient sacrifices into line and the guttural roar of the Soul Destroyer shaking dust from the cave every few seconds.

But now, there were no screams, no roars of doom.

Nothing.

Suspicious, she glanced up from her work.

The sacrifices, who just moments earlier had been protesting their innocence and bothering her with pleas of mercy, stood silent in shock.

Unnerved, Mrs. Mamford replaced her pen lid, straightened her glasses and got up from behind the confines of her desk.

'What's going on here?'

Her question went unanswered.

'I said, what's going on here? Why have you all stopped?'

'They've...shut down,' said a stunned prisoner, clearing her throat.

Mrs. Mamford looked around. Every single robot guard had frozen in its place. One had paused just seconds before landing a savage blow on a cowering old woman who was now being helped to her feet by a fellow prisoner, both just as shocked as the dozens queuing to meet their maker.

'Stay exactly where you are!'

The secretary made for her desk. The tormented began to surround her. She felt hastily for an emergency button concealed under her worktop, alerting the security level to trouble. She pressed it hard. Nothing. She pressed it again. Still nothing.

'Keep back, all of you!'

A burly prisoner pushed his way to her desk.

'Where's your army now?'

Mrs. Mamford started to feel a trickle of terror down her spine. She jabbed at the button again, grunting, pleading with it.

'Come on! Come on! No, keep back. The keepers will be on their way any minute.'

'You're wrong,' said the burly man. 'Look around you. There's no-one here to help you now.'

A squeal of panic escaped Mrs. Mamford's quivering lips as the prisoner hurled her desk across the cave.

A few of the prisoners ambushed the trembling secretary and restrained her arms. She tried to kick her way to freedom but her legs were also pinned down. Before long, she was carried high up in the air by the angry mob, all trying to hurl fists and fury at the woman who, until moments earlier, had taken such delight in slaughtering them all.

She struggled to wriggle free but the resistance was too strong.

'Have you ever met the Soul Destroyer?' asked the burly prisoner.

Mrs. Mamford turned white, her hair sticking to her cold sweaty face.

'No...you wouldn't.'

The burly prisoner grinned.

'Take a look around you. Most of these people don't deserve to be down here.' He leant into

Mrs. Mamford, meeting her eye-to-eye, his breath rotten with the stench of decay. 'Petty crimes. Stealing food to feed their starving families. That sort of thing.'

His smile was malicious, black and evil. It was an evil Mrs. Mamford recognised.

'Not me though...'

The prisoner picked Mrs. Mamford up off the mob like she was a ragdoll.

She screamed, punching him hard wherever she could. It was pain he was immune to. He had felt it all too often before. With his final act, he'd be atoning for the thousands of lives Mrs. Mamford had signed to the same fate. By doing so, he hoped he'd wash his own conscience clean from sins too.

Slowly, they made their way past the cheering crowd. Mamford was crying tears of real terror. She hadn't felt this helpless ever in her life.

'Have you ever met the boss?' said the burly man.

'Please! I'm begging you! You don't have to do this! Please!'

'Yes, I do.'

They reached the mouth of the cave that housed the Soul Destroyer. Although the other prisoners were now free, none had moved. On the whole, they didn't agree with an eye for an eye. Well, maybe some of the more hardened

criminals did and, after the years they had been made to toil, perhaps some of their minds had grown as dark as caves where they had been incarcerated. But until this vile woman had been dealt with, were they really safe?

There was a good space separating the crowd from the Soul Destroyer's lair.

There were no protests from the would-have-been sacrifices, just a wave of shouting filling the hollow.

The burly prisoner held the squirming woman aloft.

'For the dead!' he screamed.

All watched as the man threw the screaming Mrs. Mamford into the cave. An explosion of light followed, and the evil lady was no more.

Her executioner, having been caught in the line of fire, fell to the floor, a smile on his lips. His job done, he could rest in peace, redeemed.

Mrs. Mamford, on the other hand, was taking a journey to a very dark place indeed.

The crowd ceased baying for blood and began to panic. The creature was growling, hungry to be fed more. They began to flee out of the cave of death, just as a secret opening a few feet away was about to be revealed for the first time in many years.

XXIII

Anji bit her lip hard. The descent was ridiculously dangerous but secretly, deep down she was loving it. The adrenaline flooded her body. It was like being on a rollercoaster, only this time she knew that the journey was truly fraught with danger. Skateboard remote controlled the jet packs past any jagged rocks or the walls of the shaft but it was starting to get narrower.

'I'll have to send you all through one by one,' he said but his update was futile. All Anji and Dail could hear was the rushing vacuum of air as they hurtled towards the end of the tunnel.

Anji looked up. She could see nothing in the pitch black. She thought she would have seen the tunnel opening soon enough. They'd been flying down for nearly seven minutes now.

'Err, Skateboard? Did Terran say anything about this tunnel being blocked up at all?'

Skateboard said nothing, although he heard her over the vacuum roar. Terran hadn't said anything about the tunnel being open.

'Um,' he muttered but up ahead he heard a loud thud and an even louder OUCH from Anji.

A glimmer of light pierced through the tunnel.

A second OUCH was heard, this time from Dail as Skateboard gracefully sailed through the hole and landed with ease inside the mine.

He glanced over at his two companions, who were lying in a heap, covered in dirt, their jet packs nothing but shrapnel strewn across the dirty floor.

'A bumpy landing,' stated Skateboard.

Anji and Dail lay groaning.

Skateboard scanned them.

'Nothing but a little bruising. You'll both be fine. Luckily, there was only a few inches of dirt to break through. This mine's dirt must consist of a much lighter mineral compound.'

Anji spat the mud out of her mouth.

'All of that tech inside your diodes and you can't detect a bloody wall!' she groaned.

'Still, no broken bones,' Skateboard cheeped.

Anji helped Dail to his feet. They took off their rebreathers and what was left of their jet packs and took a look around.

The cave was desolate.

'Where is everyone?' asked Dail.

'There's been a coup,' said a familiar voice.

Anji glanced up. At the other end of the cave was a face that she felt she hadn't seen in years.

Slowly, Random, aided by Delilah, walked towards the party.

'Did you miss me?'

Anji squealed with joy. She raced towards Random and jumped onto him, her momentum almost knocking him to the ground. He groaned.

'You're hurt!' Anji observed.

'Well spotted,' said Random. Delilah eased him to the floor.

'These your friends?' she asked.

Random nodded, cupping his shoulder injury. 'Skateboard, Anji...other guy, meet Delilah.'

'This is Dail, he is part of a rebel alliance here on Genocia.'

'We've got a whole army on our tail right now. We'd better work quickly and save pleasantries for later,' said Dail. He reached inside his combat jacket and produced a small first aid kit. 'We'd better get your friend cleaned up,' he told Anji.

'If I may, sir.' Skateboard's claw swiped the kit from Dail's grasp and made for Random's wounds. He scanned his biomolecular pattern and proceeded to treat his master.

'What happened down here?' said Anji.

'He caused a riot,' said Delilah. 'The whole security level has been destroyed thanks to him.'

'Please, you make it sound like it's a bad thing.' Random winced. 'Anj, the mine was controlled by robots enslaving the prisoners. We may have shut them down.'

'It looks like you did more than that.'

'Yes, and I don't want to be here when it comes to paying the bill.'

'Where's Jake? Is he okay?'

'He's fine. He's helping everyone up through the main shaft.'
Anji heard a noise from the tunnel. It sounded like laser fire.
'Yana and Rader!' Dail rushed up to the hole.
'Where are you going? Our jet packs are broken. You're stuck
down here,' said Anji.
Dail looked bitterly at his pack.
'I should have stayed up there.'
'I'm sure they've got a handle on the situation,' said Random
optimistically.

*

The reality was far, far different from Random's prediction.
Yana and Rader, having taken cover behind the shuttle car, fired
impotently on the advancing armada. The closer they got, the less
their chances of survival.
'Where the hell is our back-up?' Yana shouted over the sound of
rapid laser fire.
'Still minutes away,' replied Rader.
'We've got to stall them.'
Rader's eyes widened.
'Yana, the impulse bomb!'
'What about it?'
'We can use it on the armada!'
'That's suicide.'
'Have you got any better options? Get in the car, quick!'
Yana didn't stick around to argue. She made for the driver's seat
as Rader dodged through the fire and grabbed the impulse bomb.
He struggled with it into the passenger side of the car and, before
he had a chance to shut his door, Yana slammed on the
accelerator.
This was madness. She swerved past laser bolt after laser bolt,
artillery fire getting closer to its target the closer they got to the
battleships.

*

Consula gazed from her observation chair in the main battle
cruiser. She had spotted the shuttle car advancing on them.

'You and you, with me.' She ordered her bodyguards to accompany her to a small door. 'Bring the traitor.' The guards picked up Samuelson, who struggled helplessly and dragged him over to Consula's side. The door slid open and they disappeared inside. Hidden within, a small jet fighter lay waiting for her. Strapping herself into the command pod, she flicked a switch. The jet took off vertically and made for the tunnel opening, unbeknown to the army and completely obscured from Yana and Rader's view.

A shot from the battleship bored into the side of the shuttle car. Yana struggled to keep it on track.

'Rader, do it now!'

Rader flipped a button on the impulse bomb and, leaning out of the window, hurled it in the direction of the main battleship. With no hesitation, Yana performed an impressive handbrake turn and the car swung around.

'Ten seconds,' warned Rader.

Yana dropped into a lower gear and kept her foot fully down on the pedal.

The artillery bombardment drew ever closer.

'Six...five...four...'

Another bolt of energy tore through the bonnet of the car, knocking the car off course. Yana instantly threw it back into a straight line.

'Two...one!'

The impulse bomb detonated right underneath the main battleship, blowing a shockwave through it. The massive craft began to lose control, smashing into the other craft on either side and spinning towards the ground below. Rader and Yana checked behind them. A fireball shredded the toxic air as the battleship crashed into the dirt, igniting its companion ships and causing an explosion so large it looked like a nuclear detonation mushrooming up into the sky.

'Keep driving.' Yana had not outrun the impulse wave just yet. The shuttle car's bonnet started to smoke.

Rader couldn't take his eyes off the destruction they had caused. He smiled to himself.

'TAKE THAT!' he laughed. He turned around. The car bonnet was engulfed in flames.

'We've outrun the wave but I can't stop the car,' cried Yana. 'Jump!'

The pair launched themselves out of the vehicle and hit the dirt hard, the friction causing more pain and injury as they rolled over and over.

Mercifully, they finally came to a stop, their clothes torn and their flesh pink and red from burns. The car spun out of control and blew itself to pieces while the armada, depleted yet still advancing, drove on through the fire of the fallen battleship.

Yana and Rader lay unconscious, broken and beaten. Meanwhile, Consula's escape jet was at the tunnel mouth. They had failed.

*

Jake looked about him. Hundreds and hundreds of people had gathered around the main shaft. Cautiously, he called for the lift.

Benaya tapped on his shoulder.

'I know Benaya, I know. You lot ready?'

The refugees stood prepared, all armed with drills. Even some children stood ready for whatever greeted them.

The light indicating the lift's progress showed it was nearing the ground floor.

Jake readied his weapon.

The lift doors opened.

Jake raised the drill to eye level. It was Ki, accompanied by three gun-wielding soldiers.

'Put your weapons down and raise your hands, NOW!' he shouted.

'I should have known it was you.'

Jake stared at their visitor.

'Ki. Lower your weapons.'

'Jake, these people...they're criminals!'

'I don't know what that word means on this planet but where I come from it doesn't mean young children and the elderly being sent to their deaths.'

Ki dropped her gun and raised her hands.

'It's just the way it's always been on this planet.'

'You people have been committing murder. Cold blooded murder! It should be you down here, not us!' Jake raged.

'As a scientist, surely you have enough morality left to realize you're butchering thousands. Use your brains, woman, for Christ's sake!'

Ki began to weep.

'It's for the greater good.'

'Oh yeah? What is "the greater good", eh? What can be worth all of the lives lost?'

'I don't know,' she cried.

'You're just gutless sheep, aren't you? All of you lot. Jumping to attention at any order barked in your direction. You don't care for the consequences of what you are doing. What you can't see on the surface doesn't hurt, does it? Well take a look, Ki. Look at all these people. Tell me you can see evil here.'

Ki wiped away her tears and looked. Prisoners as far as the eye could see. All she could see was fear.

'I'm..sorry.'

Jake lowered his weapon. 'Tell your lot up top to stand down. We're getting these people out. Move!'

A soldier radioed in. With the planet's security defenses down, there was no way they had the numbers to contain so many prisoners.

Jake looked at Ki. She could barely return the look.

'Get these people out of here.'

Ki did what she was told. Benaya stood in awe of Jake. She never knew there was such a serious side to Jake's character. It even surprised him.

Slowly, Ki and the soldiers started to wave the first few dozen prisoners onto the lift. The evacuation of the mine had begun.

*

'Don't go in there.' Random stopped Dail before he could turn inside the cave. A maniacal growl belched from within. 'Nobody look at that cave!' Random pushed his friends well away from it.

'Skateboard, what do you know?'

'It's cybernetic, sir. Half machine, half organic,' he started a scan. 'I've never seen anything like it before.'

'What species is it?' asked Delilah. Good question, thought Random.

'It's known as the Yarvesh.'

'Never heard of it,' said Dail.

'No, that's impossible,' muttered Skateboard.

'What is?' Random crouched next to his metal friend.

'According to my data banks, the Yarvesh should be long extinct.'

'Like the dodo,' remarked Anji unhelpfully.

'It feeds on the life energy of other life forms.'

'Like a vampire,' said Anji.

'More of a space leech, miss. But yes, same principle. It can extract living matter by draining

the mind of its victims, simply by looking at them. As soon as their eyes meet, the victim is drained of its life within seconds.'

'The eyes are the gateway to the soul, hence the name,' said Random.

'Soul Destroyer,' Delilah realised. 'How do we kill it then? We can't walk in there blind.'

'Maybe you can't, but Skateboard can,' suggested Random.

'Unfortunately, not, sir. My organic matter is far too minimal. The machine the Yarvesh is attached to is purely helping to filter the life force it drains and thusly is not compatible with my circuits.'

'I can do it,' said Random.

Anji gasped. 'Don't be ridiculous, Random!'

'Skateboard, is there a way I can connect with the Yarvesh? Try and find out its weakness?'

'You can, but it could cost you your life.'

'I'm willing to take that risk. How do we do it?'

'You're crazy!' protested Delilah.

'Random, surely...can't we just, I don't know, blow up this mine?'

'Too risky. The Yarvesh might survive the explosion. We can't guarantee that someone won't find it down here. Another Consula, perhaps? Someone who can manipulate it for evil.'

'Sir, the Yarvesh race were said to have travelled the galaxy draining all planets of their resources. Whole races are now extinct thanks to the Yarvesh. This may be the last of its kind but don't be mistaken. It's as pure evil as you can imagine.'

Anji scoffed. 'And you want to mind meld with it, Mr. Spock?'

Random smiled reassuringly.

'I don't have a choice. Skateboard, shall we?'

'Ready when you are, sir.'

'Whatever happens in there, I don't want any of you following us in. Under no circumstances, have you got that?'

Anji nodded reluctantly.

Random shot his friends a look of hope and made for the cave with Skateboard.

'You'll have to hold me back,' Anji said to Delilah and Dail.

XXIV

Skateboard approached the creature first. Scanning for threats, his calculations were off the chart. The Yarvesh filled the room, a fat, greasy vessel of evil, its slimy skin rippling in acknowledgement that it had company. Edging along the wall with his eyes closed, Random approached cautiously.

'Don't go any further, sir. That's close enough for now.'

Random sniffed, his other senses working overtime to compensate for his lack of sight. The air reeked with the rotten smell of meat, coupled with a sweet, sticky scent.

'Ugh, is that the beast?'

'Yes, sir, and the bodies of its latest victims.' Skateboard circumnavigated the corpses of the fallen, including Mrs. Mamford and her executioner. 'I think this one must have worked down here. She isn't wearing the same clothing as the other prisoners.'

'Maybe someone thought she needed a taste of her own medicine. I don't condone it, Skateboard, but I can understand it. Now, where's the computer bank?'

'Turn 30 degrees left and move forward five paces.' Skateboard connected with the mainframe. Scanning the equipment, he discovered that the Yarvesh was connected up directly from its brain. Considering the monster looked more like a gigantic, glutinous hedgehog without its spines, he found it difficult to tell which end was which.

The creature growled again.

'It's making enough noise to start a rock fall. Can it talk?'

'Negative. The Yarvesh do not possess a digestive system and have no need for oxygen. They are totally dependent on brain waves and the life force of their victims.'

'So, it's indigestion, then?'

'Precisely. Judging from its current state, it's been overfed for quite a while now.'

'Why?'

'That's what you're about to find out, sir.' Skateboard's claw fashioned two cables into sticky pads. 'Put these on your forehead.' Random felt for the pads and stuck them over each temple. 'Like this?'

'Perfect. Now I must stress, sir, that what you are about to do is incredibly dangerous. My advice would be to...'

'Thanks very much, Skateboard but I know what I have to do. I need to know if there is a way of reasoning with this thing. Find out why it's been killing.'

'Judging by the equipment down here, sir, my best guess so far is that it may not be doing this alone. I'll try and find out some more on how and who could withstand such a dangerous being while you are out.'

'Check,' said Random, 'Oh and Skateboard, don't pull me out of the connection unless it's absolutely necessary. Clear?'

Skateboard whirred. 'Clear.'

Random smiled. 'Wish me luck.'

Skateboard completed the circuit. A wash of energy shot up the cables into Random's skull, shocking him into unconsciousness. The monster growled. Random slumped to the ground. His mind was at the mercy of the Yarvesh now.

*

'Stay down, pig!'

Rader felt the butt of a rifle smack across his neck. He had just regained consciousness and now he was about to succumb to the sweet embrace of nothingness again. Anything to escape the horrific pain he was feeling across his body.

Yana was in a similar state. She lay face down, her hands forced upon the back of her head, the barrel of one of the soldiers' guns thrust into her back.

The armada had been badly damaged but some of the ships had survived the impulse bomb that Rader had detonated and now they had found the culprits.

'Commander, the landing party is ready to infiltrate the tunnel. It looks like Leader Consula has already gone down.'

The soldier standing over Rader reached for his communicator watch.

'Roger that, Sergeant. Guard the entrance. Stand-by to infiltrate at Leader Consula's requests.'

The communicator fell silent again and the Commander returned to his two prisoners.

'Okay, you rebels have had your fun. The penalty for terrorism is death. Instant. Any last words?'

The air filled with the sound of jet engines. Yana smiled.

'No. Have you?'

A bombardment of laser fire shot into the armada, blowing up fighters and sending the soldiers scuttling for cover. The commander followed suit, barking orders at his troops. Yana got to her feet, picking Rader up as she struggled to get out of the way. As they retreated, more ships and vehicles flew headlong into danger.

Meeting the Genocian army head on, fighting fire with fire, it was the rebels. They had made it. The battle for Genocia had begun.

*

Random was overwhelmed by the darkness, his mind awash with the atrocities the Yarvesh race had committed over millennia. Once, they had been the most feared race in the cosmos. Hundreds of worlds had been bled dry, nothing left but the rocky husk of what used to be. Millions upon millions laid waste, unable to hold them back. They were virtually indestructible. Until, one day, after countless years of destruction, they finally met their match. By the time the majority of the Eastern cluster of Magnas 12 had been conquered, the final planet that stood in the Yarvesh's way was a white, crystal planet called Syno. The Synoians were a peaceful race - until provoked. The Yarvesh were no match for their advanced power and they were annihilated, broken down in numbers by the unbelievable force the Synoians possessed. It was a battle between light and dark that the former won with ease. It was a massacre. The Yarvesh were all but wiped out.

Some were executed. Only one was imprisoned. The one that Random was connected to right now.

It had fought with valour for its people. But then, with the Yarvesh on the brink of extinction, it was made an example of. Tortured and finally

imprisoned deep within the bowels of an uninhabited planet, unable to feed off the

produce the planet had to offer, it was left to rot and to die a slow, agonising death.

Except that this Yarvesh was exceptional. Upon imprisonment in the very outer core of the planet, he lay dormant, living off the remnants of those he had killed. There was enough life force within his body that he could wait for centuries. He would have the last laugh. The Synoians had failed in wiping his race out. In entombing him within a new planet, all he had to do was wait until he was discovered, and then he could feast again.

The years passed like a bad dream. Unwilling to use up his reserves, the last Yarvesh in existence put himself into a deep hibernation, awaking only briefly to check for life. But, after many lifetimes, he gave up. No life was coming to the planet.

Until, one day, an excavation deep in the bowels of the planet unearthed the monster. Sensing the presence of life forms and the blood coursing through their veins, he sprang into life. All those who gazed upon him were slaughtered within seconds. All except one, a woman, who the Yarvesh could see had potential within her soul.

Random regained consciousness suddenly, his head swimming, the dark thoughts slowly ebbing away as he returned to the light. He sat up, eyes wide open, away from the monster. To his shock, he was looking at another.

'Did you see anything of interest, Captain Random?'

Random caught his breath. 'Consula, I presume.'

Consula stood over his body. 'You presume correctly. You know, you've caused me a great deal of distress since you arrived on Genocia. Time for me to pay you back.'

*

'That's the last of them,' Ki confirmed.

Benaya nodded in agreement and along with Jake, they embarked on the lift as the last people to head up to the surface. Before he pressed the doors, Jake peered out into the empty mine. He couldn't hear a pin drop or see any signs of life.

'They'll be right behind us, won't they?' asked Jake.

Benaya smiled, her eyes full of hope.

'We'd better get a move on. There's nearly 8,000 prisoners up there who will need our help,' said Ki.

The guilt of what had been going on down in the mine had eaten away at her over time.

Deep down, she was grateful that Jake and Random had done what they had done. The killing was at an end.

The lift doors slammed shut and the trio made their ascent back up to the surface.

'Chief Ki. Chief Ki, come in please,' cracked Ki's communicator.

'Go ahead, Jed.'

'We have a situation, ma'am. There is a battle taking place near the south base of the mine. It's quite a way away but it's getting closer. We also have a problem with crushing. We have too many prisoners to contain them here safely. Suggest we bring them back down for their own safety.'

Ki looked over at Jake.

'Ha! Tell him if he and his twenty troops wanna try and shift 8,000 prisoners armed with laser drills, he can go ahead and be my guest. I wish him luck.'

'Did you get that?' asked Ki.

There was a pause on the other end.

'Yes, we did.'

Benaya signed at Ki and Jake and gestured at a row of warehouses nearby she had spotted on a map of the area on the lift wall.

'That's an excellent idea!' chirped Ki. 'Jed, can you escort the prisoners into the warehouses outside the mine?'

'With difficulty, ma'am. It's a dogfight out here.'

'At least they will be under cover. We will be with you in a moment. Ki out.'

Jake looked perplexed.

'Does everybody know sign language but me?'

'Better get learning, kid,' winked Ki.

Commander Jed led the first few dozen prisoners out through the main doors of the mine. They struggled, having been starved of sunlight and proper nourishment for years toiling in the darkness. The majority of the party being moved were women and children of varying ages and all of them were too weak to run. Jed beckoned them to follow him to one of the warehouses and yelled at them to pick up the pace. They could clearly see the battle raging between the rebels and the Genocian army miles away. The ground shook and the air smelt of fire. The danger was getting nearer. The ground troops continued to evacuate the mine and alleviate the pressure on the limited space above the surface.

Finally, Jake, Benaya and Ki emerged from the lift and raced for the gates to escape the mine for good. They could hear the destruction getting closer.

'God! I hope Anj hasn't got caught up in all of that,' said Jake quietly.

He shook his head. He should have stayed down there with Random. Now that they were separated, Jake felt truly alone.

'Head for the warehouse on the right,' said Ki, pointing. They ran towards the doors and leaped inside.

'Jed, what's going on?'

'Rebel factions from outside the Grand Chamber have ambushed Leader Consula's armada. It wasn't just the Chamber that lost power, it was the whole planet. Whatever your friend here did, he's brought the planet to its knees.' He shot an angry look in Jake's direction.

'Don't look at me!' cried Jake.

'Well, who did then?'

Jake searched his mind. 'Skateboard,' he muttered. 'What a ledge!'

XXV

'Where are my friends?'

'Don't worry about them. They are right where you left them. My guards are seeing to it that they don't miss your death.'

'Bit harsh considering you've only just met me.'

Consula thought nothing of Random's flippant manner. Random looked over at a third person in the room. He squinted, his vision still a little blurry from his link-up with the Yarvesh.

'I see Samuelson got off lightly then. What did he do to tick you off? Fail to tell you I was an alien? Not pay you back after borrowing money? He is, or I can guess WAS Chancellor, after all. It's always money and greed with that lot.'

'Everyone is an alien outside the walls of the Grand Chamber, Captain. Why do you think so many different species worked in these mines?'

Random scoffed. 'I've heard of drastic measures when it comes to immigration but that takes the biscuit. A dislike for the unlike?'

'It was necessary for them to work towards our ultimate goal.'

'Go on then. What is this ultimate goal when it's at home?'

Consula was now rather surprised by her foe's attitude.

'No one has ever spoken to me so flippantly and lived long after.'

'Well, you said it just then, missy. I'm dead in a bit anyway, so why not? What's Samuelson doing here?'

'You will be the last victims of the Soul Destroyer before the complete takeover.'

Samuelson looked maliciously at his former leader; his fists clenched.

'I'd rather take my own life than give it to you,' he spat.

'The Soul Destroyer is near full capacity. First, I'll feed your precious friends to it, Captain. You'll be able to hear their screams while their very life force is stripped from their flesh and bones.'

'Before you do, I've seen inside the mind of the Yarvesh. I know what you've been up to here. You've been using it to power your city since your precious ESOL19 ran out, haven't you?'

Consula laughed. 'We never ran out of ESOL19.'

Samuelson's eyes narrowed. 'What?!'

'It was a story fabricated by yours truly to improve the mine's workforce. It's all about life force, Samuelson. It always has been. The more people we could get down here to feed the Soul Destroyer, the quicker I could obtain full power.'

'Yeah, about that,' said Random. 'Why you?'

Consula looked upon the Yarvesh. Although Random and Samuelson kept it out of their line of sight, they could tell she was defying the creature's death blast. Samuelson was shocked she hadn't been obliterated, Random less so.

'So, the Yarvesh made a connection with you and has been controlling you ever since you met it?'

'I was a junior minister. I was here to unveil the new mining project we had developed. When the Soul Destroyer attacked us, I was the only one who survived. He saw something in me that could help him escape his tomb. And I saw something in him that could help me rise to the top.'

'Here we go. Yet another nut job consumed by power and greed. No wonder you both went into politics,' Random jeered.

A piercing light shot from the Yarvesh, sending Random sprawling to the floor, yelling in pain.

Anji heard the screams and made for the cave opening. But before she could get there, a muscular arm scooped her up and put her kicking and punching back in her place.

The guard stood over the group, who were powerless to help their friend.

She gritted her teeth, trying to erase Random's cries of agony from her mind.

*

Samuelson felt compelled to help the Yarvesh's victim, but he was powerless to do anything. To Random's relief, the light disappeared along with the pain that wracked his body.

'A life force the size of yours, Captain, will help us to complete the ultimate takeover. The Yarvesh will be able to free himself from his shackles and through me rule Genocia.'

'Consula, listen to me,' Random groaned. 'The Yarvesh will consume you. He will use your body. You'll be dead. I know. I've seen inside his mind. He's poisoned you since the day he spared your life.'

'You're so wrong. He'll give me eternal life. Centuries of ruling Genocia unchallenged, undying. Immortality awaits. Guards,' she called out, 'bring the captain's friends in here.'

'Anji! Delilah! Don't open your eyes! Whatever you do, keep your eyes shut!' yelled Random. Another blast of light shot from the Yarvesh, forcing him to the ground in agony.

*

The rebel ships continued their dogfight in the sky. As Yana and Rader watched from the ground, protected by a craft that had made contact with them when the fighting began, they witnessed Consula's depleted fleet slowly succumb to the rebel attacks. It didn't take much time for the rebels to force the upper hand. As the armada lay scattered and burning among the waste fields, homemade white flags began to poke out of the ruined vessels, once so mighty and now surrendering. For the first and only time under Consula's totalitarian rule, the rebels had won.

Yana looked up from the slab in the medical bay, her wounds being tended to by fellow rebels. She heard the cheers from the crew of the ship first and then saw her comrades warmly embrace one another.

'We've done it,' groaned Rader, who was also being treated. 'We've brought down the Government!'

Yana shared in the celebration, but knew that the fight was not over.

'Not yet,' she winced.

*

'No!' screamed Anji.

The guards produced two electric batons, which crackled as they swiped them menacingly.

'The Leader has spoken,' said one of the guards.

'She's not my leader,' spat Anji. 'Now Skateboard!'

The AI sprang in front of his friends.

The guards chuckled.

'Your toy's not going to save you.'

They raised their batons, ready to strike.

'Incorrect,' said Skateboard. Within an instant, a tiny stun gun sprang from within his casing and shot the guards to the ground. Each guard collapsed like an avalanche, nearly crushing Anji and her friends as they fell.

'Good job, Skateboard,' cried Dail.

'Quick, grab their batons,' said Delilah. They disarmed the sleeping guards and made for the cave mouth.

BANG!

The gang was thrown back against the wall. There seemed to be some form of shield around the cave.

Consula grinned. The Yarvesh was protecting her. Of course he was.

'Anj, get back to the surface!'

'We're not leaving you, Random.'

'You must. I have to finish this alone. Please, just go.'

Anji started to sob. 'You'd better be right behind me!'

'I'll catch up,' gasped Random. 'Skateboard, take them back through the tunnel.'

'Right, sir. Everyone stand on my back and hold on tight.'

Reluctantly they did as they were told.

'To what?' asked Dail.

'Good question,' thought Skateboard. Firing up his wheels, he shot back up the tunnel entrance. Anji held onto Delilah's arm but her face was forlorn. Their rescue mission had been futile. Jake was nowhere to be seen and Random was trapped. But if anyone could save the day, it was Random. She knew that. But would he be able to stop the Yarvesh? Anji looked upwards to the roof of the tunnel, the distant light of the surface getting nearer.

Of course he could.

*

'Right, let's do this. You and me, Consula. Forget your pet slug and the Yarvesh. No, I'm not sorry, Samuelson,' Random looked over at the wall of computers which fed back to the creature. 'Let's see, we have a filter system hooked up to the monster. A two-way connection for your little hook-up with lover boy over there, I know.'

He sprang up from the floor and vaulted towards the dictator.

'I challenge you to a little game. Call it cat and mouse. Actually, no. Scrap that. That's a rubbish

name. Hide and seek. I hide, you seek.'

Random leaped for the wires connected to the Yarvesh and he jammed them back onto his temples. He yelped as the current surged through his body again.

'What are you doing?'

'You need to connect with the Yarvesh before completing the takeover. Argh! You can't do that while I'm connected.'

'Stop it now or I'll tear you out of the machine,' snarled Consula, dropping her former poise.

Random's body jerked as the electricity coursed through his nervous system. He tried to resist the full connection with the Yarvesh for fear of becoming consumed. But, if he could just hold off the signal, then Consula couldn't make contact.

'You touch me and you'll die. There's enough voltage running through my body to turn you to dust.'

'Random, I warn you!'

Random screamed in anguish. 'Come and find me!'

He couldn't take the punishing current any longer. He collapsed, his consciousness once more within the beast.

'He can't do this to us. Not now!'

'Looks like you've been outsmarted, Consula,' smiled Samuelson.

'I'll wipe that smile right off your smug face!' she screamed. 'He thinks he can disrupt the signal as the Yarvesh can only consume one being at a time. He is wrong. The Yarvesh is stronger than he's ever been. Now that he has Random devoured, he doesn't need the final connection. All he needs is a host.'

Consula turned her back to Samuelson and faced her creature, opened her arms and let the Yarvesh take her.

Samuelson recoiled in horror as Consula's essence was engulfed by the Yarvesh, his own life force replacing hers as he consumed it. A second piercing light sped towards her. She screamed a howl of death as Random started to convulse on the floor. He was losing the battle.

*

The gang flew out of the tunnel. They disembarked from Skateboard's back and gazed in awe at the devastation all around them. As far as the eye could see, the rebel fleet had destroyed Consula's army. The entire armada was either captured or obliterated, scattered around the fiery cauldron of the battlefield.

Some soldiers were being rounded up and arrested by the rebels, others were being treated.

Dail whooped in delight. 'They did it! They did it!' he hugged the girls and punched the air.

'Dail.'

A familiar voice came from the nearest ship. It was Yana. She was battered and bruised but elated to see her old friend again. Dail scooped her up in his arms, making Yana yell in pain.

'Easy!'

'What happened? Is Rader okay?'

'Yeah, we're both fine. Just a little…tender. Anji, where is your friend? Did he stop the Soul Destroyer?'

Anji couldn't speak.

'I'm afraid Captain Random is still in the mine with Consula and Chancellor Samuelson.' Skateboard scanned the area.

'But Jake is alive and well and currently situated at the mine shaft.'

'My sister must still be with him too,' exclaimed Delilah.

'We've got to go, guys,' said Anji.

'We'll give you a lift,' said Yana. 'Get on board.'

The gang ran up the small ladder into the craft. Anji was overjoyed to know that Jake was fine, but she had abandoned Random.

'Skateboard, how's he doing?'

Skateboard used his scanners to monitor his master's situation, The life signs were diminishing.

'He's doing just fine,' he lied.

*

The murky, dank bleakness of the Yarvesh's mind swamped Random. He could feel the pain of millions of lost souls swimming about his essence. He tried to blot them out but just couldn't. The torment was too much to bear. He was deeper within the mind of the beast this time.

He had to be to have any chance of stopping Consula's conversion. He had to make sure she was trapped within the host, with the host still present too. But then what was he going to do? He began to panic, fearing he had suffered the same fate as all those who had perished at the hands of the Yarvesh. He started to worry about Anji and Jake and whether they would ever get back home.

They'd only come along with him for adventure, an escape into a new world. He'd brought them to this one. How could he have been so careless, so thoughtless?

The negativity drowned his thoughts. Then he began to notice that the other souls trapped inside the creature felt the same. The same thoughts and feelings echoed.

Missed loved ones, whole civilizations decimated by the relentless might of a truly horrific race. Random found the strength within his soul to keep fighting. It was what he had been created to do, after all. Fight the good fight.

There was nothing he could do for the souls of the dead trapped with him inside the monster. Some of them had been there for centuries. He could feel it. But he could put an end to the terrible Yarvesh and give their souls peace. A rage stirred within his spirit. He had to do it. For them.

Suddenly, the light rushed towards Random and he awoke startled, gasping for air on the floor of the cave.

'Random! We've got to stop her.'

Samuelson was busying himself at the machinery that Consula was connected to.

'Wha…what?'

'The Yarvesh rejected your soul. Consula bypassed your trap and he somehow managed to kick you out. Now don't just lie there. Help me.'

Random looked up at Consula. She was consumed by energy, her entire body sparkling with the light pouring from the Yarvesh. A wind blew through the cave, making it difficult for Random to scramble to his feet.

'You've lost, Random," Consula boomed with a voice not her own.

'Centuries I have waited. And now…I'm free.'

Random and Samuelson recoiled in horror as the Yarvesh consumed Consula's body, stripping her of her being.

She had been used, just as Random thought.

It was a long game, but the Yarvesh had won it.

XXVI

The energy continued to flow between Consula and her master, her body levitating like a possessed demon, her flesh grey and putrid.

Random continued to search the machine for answers. 'They must be stopped somehow!'

'Well get on with it, man. It's nearly finished!'

Random set to work. The wind tore through the cave and bolts of lightning shot from the Yarvesh.

'Samuelson, you'd better get out of here,' implored Random.

'No.'

'Samuelson, listen to me, listen for once in your life! I am trying to throw the system into hard reverse. It'll send a loopback reaction that'll blow the creature sky high. The barrier is down now, you can escape. So get to it, now! If you're here when the loopback completes, you'll be killed by the explosion!'

'I'm staying.'

Samuelson gazed intently at Random. He knew the game was up. Whatever happened next, if he did survive the Yarvesh, he'd be tried for murder, turned into a pariah for all that the Government had been up to for the past two decades.

'My life is over anyway. Go...now!'

Random was helpless to persuade him.

'It's suicide!'

'For you, yes. For me...let's just say it's the right thing to do.'

'How do I know you'll do it?'

'You can bank on it.'

Random tipped his head solemnly. The look of steely determination in Samuelson's eyes convinced him.

'Goodbye, Samuelson.'

'Forget about that. Just go!'

Random nodded. He pulled himself away from the cave and ran to the tunnel entrance that Anji and Skateboard had found. Clutching his wounded shoulder, he took a deep breath, a step back and sped up the tunnel. His momentum carried him up the almost vertical shaft away from danger.

*

Samuelson made sure that Random had left the cave and turned back to Consula. She was staring intently at him. He caught her eye and his life force began to pull towards hers. The Yarvesh began to slowly feast on his soul, taking its time to prolong the agony.

'Bow before me, Samuelson.'

He found the strength to laugh.

'Never again.'

A bolt of lightning shot from her fingertip. The Yarvesh had given her inhuman powers. The bolt smashed into Samuelson's chest, sending him flying against the computer banks.

Stricken yet alive, he staggered to his feet and felt for the connector switch that would complete the loopback.

'KNEEL, YOU WORM!'

He laughed.

'This worm has turned! I've always wanted to do this, Consula!'

'No!'

The voice of the Yarvesh boomed from Consula's mouth.

There was nothing it could do.

Samuelson, his body shattered by the lightning bolt, flicked the switch and died with a smile on his face.

*

A massive explosion tore through the mine. The cave itself was engulfed in flames as the Yarvesh's screams of agony bled into the roar of the fireball. A chain reaction of explosions began to tear through the entire mine.

Random heard the cave blow up behind him and raced the fireball to the surface, concentrating on escape.

Up ahead was daylight. The heat of the flames licked the back of his neck. Finally, he flew out of the tunnel exit and threw himself aside as the fireball spat out after him. He lay on the ground, beaten and bruised but alive. The roar of the fire subsided but he heard the chain reaction deep underground as it stretched into the distance.

He hoped that his friends and all the other prisoners had made it in time.

He took a moment to gulp in the air. It tasted toxic. He then became aware of the rebel ships that had surrounded the area. Someone was approaching him.

'Captain Random, sir?' said the Commander.

Random saluted meekly.

'That's me.'

*

The rebel ship sailed gracefully over the destroyed mine. It looked like firewood to Random from a great height but, as they landed nearby, he began to gain a sense of the enormity of what they had done. Thousands of people below were cheering, applauding the ship as it came in to land. He smiled. They had done it.

As the ship's landing haunches settled on the ground, Random noticed some familiar faces running through the crowds towards him.

He disembarked and threw his arms out to Anji and Jake, who engulfed their friend in a warm embrace.

'I knew you'd make it! See, I told you, Anj!' cheered Jake.

Anji kissed Random on the cheek. 'I never doubted.'

Random withdrew and smiled. 'Bet you did a bit.'

She smirked. 'Well yeah, a bit. What happened?'

'The Yarvesh has been destroyed. Consula with it.'

'You destroyed it?' said Yana. She, along with Rader, Dail, Delilah and Benaya, were now also standing with the trio.

'Well, technically, Samuelson did. He must have hated Consula more than we knew. He knew he didn't have a future. What better way to redeem himself than to set the planet free?'

The group hugged one another as the crowd continued to swell around them, everyone wanting to embrace them, to thank them for saving their lives.

'Where's Skateboard?' asked Random.

'Right here, sir.' The AI robot burrowed its way through the crowd and rubbed up against Random's shin. 'It's good to have you back with us, sir.'

Random grinned. He turned to the Commander.

'Commander, what about the rest of the Government?'

'We are taking care of that, sir. We are rounding up the members of the Genocian Parliament now for questioning. Sergeant?'

A member of the commander's taskforce saluted.

'Sir.'

'Take your men to the Grand Chamber and place Genocia under martial law. Send a message to all known outposts and rebel points declaring Consula defeated.'

'Yes sir,' said the sergeant delightedly.

'Well, Random, we've done it,' said Jake. 'The revolution won. We brought down the Government.'

Random slapped his friend on the back and took a moment, as did the whole group, to acknowledge the crowd. He stepped up onto a high step, ready to deliver a victory speech to the waiting crowd. It wasn't in his nature, but he felt it was the right thing to do. Just as he opened his mouth, Yana stood up.

'This is our planet, again!' she shouted. 'Make it a better one than it was. Make sure that nothing like this ever happens again. Make Genocia a planet to feel proud of. Carry the scars of what has happened here and use them to forgive...but never forget!'

The crowd cheered again, a thunderous roar of approval and jubilation.

Random looked a little miff and turned back to his friends.

'Oh, I was going to say that.' He got down and put his arms around Jake and Anji's shoulders.

'Oh well, maybe next time we liberate a planet, eh?'

Yana was carried off high on the shoulders of Rader and Dail.

The war was won.

The terror was gone.

Genocia was free!

Before long the intergalactic police arrived to restore some order. Many of the prisoners were kept in the vicinity of the warehouse for the time being.

Random, Jake, Anji and Skateboard were escorted back to the hangar where the Venus II had been confiscated by Yana and the others,

Having borrowed one of the rebel fleet's cruisers, they had no problems getting through customs this time.

'There it is!' exclaimed Jake.

'I feel like we haven't seen her in years!' said Anji.

'Good to see she hasn't been damaged,' Random remarked. They walked towards the gleaming ship, barely scratched by the battering ram still lying near the loading ramp. 'Anyone fancy a cup of tea before we go?'

'You can't leave now,' said Rader. 'You should be recognised for what you have done!'

'Oh can we?' said Jake gleefully. 'I've always wanted a medal!'

'Your people have regained control of the planet now. Parliament has been dissolved. As long as you tell them the truth then no harm can be done.'

'But we've barely had time to thank you for what you've done, or reward you,' said Delilah.

'No need to thank us,' said Jake, putting on a brave face. He'd get his medal one day. 'All in a day's work for us.'

Anji chuckled. 'We'd never boast about it.' She hugged Yana. 'Plus, it's me who owes you thanks. Without you guys I'd never have found this lot again.'

'Yeah,' said Jake to Delilah and Benaya, 'and without you two, we'd never have busted everyone out of the mine.'

'It was a team effort. You have your planet back and we have our ship back. That's reward enough,' said Random.

'Hey! What about our millions?' Jake had suddenly remembered the money which had got them into the mess in the first place.

'Keep it, you lot. Put it towards the rebuilding of your world,' Random smiled.

Jake looked crestfallen.

'Yeah, have it on us,' beamed Anji.

Jake looked dumbfounded.

'Fine! Just don't spend it all at once,' he snapped.

The gang laughed.

'Don't be strangers. Come and drop in anytime,' said Delilah.

'Who knows? We might be ruling the planet by then,' joked Dail.

'I'm sure they'll give you all something cool to do. You have a whole planet to rebuild. Best get a move on, eh? Just remember why we had to do what we did. Make sure that this planet isn't corrupted by greed and tyranny again. It's seen enough tragedy for one lifetime.'

The group nodded. They all shook hands and embraced. Jake even managed to sign goodbye to Benaya and thanked her for looking after him in the mines. She gave him a kiss on the cheek to show her gratitude. He blushed uncontrollably.

Waving goodbye, they made their way up the gangway and into the belly of the Venus II.

Random and Skateboard wasted no time in making their way to the cockpit.

'Come on, gang. We don't want to be around when the authorities catch up with us. Imagine the paperwork.'

Anji and Jake raced to the cockpit and waved at their friends.

'Releasing electric locking system now,' Skateboard reported. The Venus II was released from its shackles as its rockets fired. Yana and the gang moved away from the ship and waved as it sailed out of the hangar.

They kept waving until the ship had disappeared from view.

The Venus II flew valiantly over the Grand Chamber of Genocia and out into space.

*

Anji plopped herself down on the mid-section sofa and exhaled heavily.

'We made it,' she said, sprawling. 'I can't tell you how happy I am to be back.'

Jake sat beside her. 'I mean, we could have given them a little bit of the money. But all of it?'

Anji thumped him in the arm.

'Random.'

The captain made his way down the steps into the mid-section.

'I'm so sorry.'

'For what?'

'I should never have got you involved in all of that.'

Anji budged up so her purple friend could have a space next to her.

'You weren't to know what was going on down there...unless you did?'

'No. Of course not. It's just...there was a moment, when I was inside the mind of that horrible creature and all I could think about was not keeping you two safe. You've seen how dangerous this could be for us all, travelling with Skateboard and me. Give me the word and we'll turn back to Earth now.'

'Mate, you're being too hard on yourself,' said Jake, putting an arm on his friend's shoulder. 'And hey, we made it out alive.'

'It would be nice if we didn't have to face anything like that again though,' said Anji.

'Agreed,' said Random. 'Maybe a holiday planet would be just what we need next time. Right, we'd better be getting on then.'

Jake and Anji looked at each other curiously.

'Get on with what?'

Random pointed at the fruits of their shopping spree strewn across the floor.

'With the reason why we went to Genocia in the first place. Come on, we've got decorating to do.'

Jake and Anji groaned.

'Skateboard, set the Venus II to autopilot and help me put these curtains up,' said Random.

The Venus II and her crew sailed among the stars, off to find more adventures. Just as soon as the housework was done...

XXVII

The task ahead for the future of Genocia was long and arduous. The whole planet's government and international security were all but wiped out in a day, stripped of their powers. The rebels, however, were fair rulers. They arrested and tried the Genocian Parliament for its acts of barbarity against their own people and visitors to the world. Those who were found guilty of conspiracy were imprisoned, not killed. Genocia had seen enough killing to last a lifetime. Before long, elections were held again and the entire planet was opened up to visitors.

The keepers on the surface were reprogrammed and given fairer instructions than their previous.

The fire raged in the mine for two days. When the flames had died down and it was safe, Yana led a team to inspect the cave. They found nothing except the remains of three bodies, one of which was not humanoid, turned to ash.

No-one else was present anywhere in the mine when the explosion happened. Just moments after the inspection was completed, work commenced on filling in the mine and its secret tunnel.

The biggest shame ever to have been brought onto Genocia was gone, but never forgotten.

In the years that followed, it became a shrine to those who had fallen. The anniversary of the explosion and Consula's demise was celebrated, much like VE Day and remembered, very much like Remembrance Day on Earth.

The peoples of the planet began to rebuild their lives. With the help of scientists, the oxygen levels outside the Grand Chamber and the tourism complex were purified. Houses were built and, in some cases, rebuilt. People found jobs. There was an air of peace that fell over Genocia. It was going to take time but the peoples of the planet would get over the horrors of how things used to be.

Those who had been sent to the mine, and other places that had been posing as penal systems, had their cases reviewed.

Very few of the thousands who had been subjected to hard labour, with the threat of being killed by the Yarvesh, were actually deemed criminals and they were acquitted accordingly and some were awarded jobs in their chosen fields, something that was also promised as a way of compensation by the new, democratically elected rulers of Genocia.

The Grand Chamber was opened to the whole planet, no longer a fortress for all that was bad and evil.

The intergalactic police were called to help with the removal of those members of Parliament found guilty of their crimes and to help with the monitoring of prisoners. After a few years, the planet was thriving again.

Terran, before returning to his own world, continued with his work and succeeded in his experiments on replication. He managed to use the reserves of ESOL19 to duplicate stocks, ensuring livestock and power continued to keep Genocia going.

Not long after, a discovery was made under the vaults in the Grand Chamber where four tons of the mineral had been stockpiled. The Genocian people investigated and it transpired that Consula had hidden the mineral in her bid to exploit its rarity as a way of sending more and more of her people to the Yarvesh to feed her monstrous plan.

The Genocians were ashamed of their recent past and were keen to use it to point them towards a more peaceful and prosperous existence. With the help of a purple boy from another world, they were free once more. Generations of children were taught all about the deeds of Random and his friends on that day. There was even a statue in the centre of the Grand Chamber!

Books were written, plays were acted out before adoring audiences. They were looked upon like the heroes they were. Every story told about Captain Random and those who helped him liberate Genocia always had the same ending.

"...and they are still out there - helping people in need - fighting the good fight - doing the right thing..."

But that was all to come. There was still much to do to make Genocia safe again.

EPILOGUE

Some time had passed since the liberation of Genocia, but there was still much hard work to be done.

Delilah and Benaya, who had slipped away and gone underground not long after the Venus II left, had decided to get involved in the effort to rejuvenate the planet by establishing their own taskforce. It was a small team – just the two of them. For the right price, they could be engaged to find missing persons (of which there were a fair few after the mines had been closed and destroyed) or even hunting down and bringing to justice Consula's sympathisers and members of her Parliament who had slipped the net.

This latest job was arguably their most dangerous to date. Summoned by a mysterious benefactor, who had paid them in advance, the sisters had been tasked with journeying well outside the confines of the Grand Chamber and out past the waste lands. The air was still toxic, although this was being worked on, but a small gang of muts had been detected to the south of an abandoned settlement and needed bringing in.

The mutated remnants of a darker time were being taken back to the Grand Chamber to be

treated. True, they would never be what they were before, but it would be wrong to kill them for being different. After all, it was the poisonous atmosphere that had created them in the first place. But muts who had been brought in by the army were slowly starting to lose their hostile ways and were being rehabilitated into society.

'What I don't get, Benaya, is why we have been asked to do this when the forces have been at it for ages.'

Benaya shrugged, squinting through her face mask and breathing steadily into her rebreather.

The pair continued to move through the smog with nothing to guide their way but torches mounted onto their laser rifles. They were set to stun, of course. They were not killers.

Delilah stopped in her tracks. Her location system began to emit a beeping sound.

Then another.

And another.

They raised their weapons, prepared for a scrap.

'Get behind me, Benaya. This isn't going to be easy.'

The muts were starting to surround them.

'On my mark. Wait until they are close enough.'

The sisters stood back-to-back, ready, waiting.

The muts tore through the mist, just metres away. Delilah and Benaya opened fire, turning in

a circle using their weapons with deadly accuracy.

Within moments, two dozen muts lay unconscious on the ground.

Delilah smiled.

'Nice shooting, sis.'

She put her weapon down and reached for her communicator.

'Longboat, this is Red Fox, we have completed our mission. You are free to pick us up now.'

A familiar voice fizzed back over the intercom.

'Good job, Delilah.'

Benaya looked pleasantly surprised at her sister, who smiled back.

'Yana! You sly old thing.'

'Good to hear from you again, you two.'

'But...why couldn't you just do the job yourself?'

'What good would our recruitment drive be without testing out potential employees first?'

Delilah tutted. 'Yana, we're freelancers. We don't want to work for the new Government. We are just fine where we are.'

'Trust me on this one and stand by,' Yana replied. 'We will pick you and the muts up in a few minutes.'

'So, you've been monitoring us all along? You could have given us a lift,' said Delilah.

'Will make it up to you, I promise. A good day's work for you girls. 36 muts collected.'

Delilah's face dropped.

'36?'

Benaya stared in shock. The tracking system had been quietly beeping to itself for the last few seconds.

Without warning, more muts tore through the toxic cloud and knocked Delilah to the ground, sending her rifle clean out of her hand and the communicator far from her reach. Whatever Yana was shouting was inaudible over the screams and the shots being fired by Benaya.

The bounty hunter managed to take out a few of the muts but she too was overpowered. The duo was surrounded and held down.

Struggle as they might, they were powerless to escape.

As the muts raised their crude instruments of death over their prisoners, a terrible roar of engines ripped over their heads, scaring them away.

The muts left Delilah and Benaya and scattered back into the fog. Whatever had just saved them came in to land very close.

Benaya picked herself up and helped her sister to her feet.

It was a ship that had saved them. But who?

The sisters gingerly made their way towards it.

The ship was sleek but its features were obstructed by the dust and dirt it had landed in.

A ramp started to lower and a figure began to descend.

As they peered through the fog, they cried out with surprise when they saw who it was.

'Skateboard!'

'Miss Delilah. Miss Benaya, I need you to come with me.'

'How did you know where to find us?'

'There isn't time now. Please, we need your help!'

Delilah's smile turned into a frown of concern.

'What's the matter? What's happened?'

Benaya signed. *Where are Random and the other two?*

'They are in danger. Terrible, terrible danger. And they need your help.'

'But how?'

'We really do not have time to talk now. I can explain on the way.'

Another ship roared past.

'That's Yana. She can help too.'

'I am counting on it, miss. We need all the help we can muster.'

Benaya and Delilah shot a concerned glance between themselves.

'Listen to me, the fate of our friends may well rest in our hands. We need to get back to them as soon as possible. There is no time to waste. Will you come?'

CAPTAIN RANDOM
AND THE
RAINBOW CHASERS
HAYDEN GRIBBLE

CAPTAIN RANDOM

AND THE RAINBOW

CHASERS

HAYDEN GRIBBLE

I

All that Lon ever wanted was to be remembered. To achieve all he could in life.

Nothing was unobtainable, if he really wanted it.

Notoriety and success went hand-in-hand in his business and he liked it that way.

As the catacombs of Druis spiraled further and further into the darkness, he licked his lips as his latest prize was drawing him nearer.

He hadn't been the brightest at school, and yet he aced every examination he was subjected to by the harsh, totalitarian lecturers at Moftola University. He wasn't the quickest on the track either, not by a long shot, but he took part in arduous marathons and through sheer persistence and drive, he always finished first.

His mansion on the sunny side of Milas XII, a pleasure asteroid that circled a dwarf star in one of the most exclusive and desired settlements in the outer cosmos, mainly for its beautiful views of the cosmic ballet between the nebulas and the stars, but also because it was tax free.

A nobody would ever afford such a luxurious place to call his home.

Lon was far from a nobody.

He was prolific in his field of intergalactic archaeology. It had been his chosen subject back on his home planet. Maftola had a reputation in the Senas quadrant for breeding explorers and Lon was determined to be the best of the bunch.

Alfred Wolenhein, the man who found the lost treasure of Algonia? Lon wanted to make him a mere footnote in his planet's history.

Catalonia Trenaman, the first woman to uncover the hidden secrets of Rinan Berksop's latter day etching on the inner mountains of figabilons of Lagonias Valor? He wanted leapfrog her achievements.

Tred Walterquintan, the quantum-time award winning emotion wanderer who posed as hippy on the planet Earth and found the secret recordings of Jimi Hendrix that were so magnificent that if any being played them they would end up ripping planets in half for 400 million miles around, stored them in a container that became so hot they liquidated then finally decomposed into a gas compound that escaped his home and were found drifting in space in a state of detune that meant all that it would do to the listener now was give them a psychedelic trip so magnificent they would have to sleep for nine days just to shake the bad vibes out of their system...well...he was working on beating that guy.

And if he found what he was close to now..he would.

The Zedron Flux.

A helix of pure energy, binding the forces of Druis together in a way that could sustain the planet for what had been estimated by experts for a dozen millennia.

If he found it, it could save the universe.

Fossil fuels would be a thing of the past. Worlds like the Earth would no longer have to resort to polluting its atmosphere with the filth and grime it mined from within the bowels of its planet.

Even solar energy would be a thing of the past.

The Zedron Flux was the ultimate goal.

If Lon found it, the cosmos would be saved.

And he could retire a hero. A name never forgotten by the generations who would live in the safe knowledge that their species could live forever in perpetuity.

Money is a reward worth pursuing.

Immortality is all the sweeter.

Lon was now so close; he could taste it on the tip of his tongue.

'Nearly there, boss.'

Etherton removed his glasses, mopped his brow and returned them to his face.

'What makes you so sure?' said another voice.

Auger had been irritated by her counterpart's spasms of optimism. 'You've been saying since we got in this place.'

'Well, forgive me, dear lady, if my enthusiasm is somewhat, premature, but I firmly believe that the heart of the catacombs is right this way.'

'Would you two put a sock in it? We'll find it when we find it,' whispered Lon.

'Sorry, Lon,' said Etherton sheepishly.

He shot a look to Auger, who was doing her best to not be ticked off by either of her companions. It was common for Lon to get anxious on occasion, especially when he is honing in on a promise of a brilliant discovery.

But on this trip, he had seemed a little…tense. Almost as though there was more riding on them obtaining the Zedron Flux than their usual treasure hunts, and for good reason too. Normally, Lon had a twinkle in his eye when he told them off for their usual bickering.

Auger frowned. She didn't see the usual smirk either.

The twinkle had been extinguished for the time being.

Lon wiped the sweat from his brow.

'Damn it,' he cursed, 'is it me or is it starting to get really hot down here?'

Etherton nodded.

'It certainly feels like it.'

'That must mean that we are close!' cried Auger.

Her bespeckled counterpart removed his glasses once again and blinked hard. 'I thought eyebrows were supposed to stop sweat from going in your eyes?' he groaned. 'Mine must be broken.'

'Don't be silly, old friend,' Lon reassured. 'Auger's right. Just a little further.'

They passed a pillar that bore what looked like an old cave drawing. Etherton resisted temptation to down tools for a moment and study the curious etchings. Out of the three, it was he who regularly spotted those little details, the out of the ordinary, things which acted as clues as to what they were looking for. But since the group leader was preoccupied with his aim and seemed to be a bit on the nervous side, he thought he'd mention it on their return trip out of the catacombs instead, which was a shame, because he'd never get a chance to go back. But if they had of stopped and followed the markings, they'd have learnt a great deal about what the Zedron Flux and how it came to be deep in the bowels of the planet Druis in the first place.

In the ancient times, when the galaxy was ruled by almighty beings, omnipotent gods who after a couple of millennia, got bored of the wonders of the cosmos and surprisingly thought themselves out of existence because there was nothing else to do now that the beings that made up the population of their creation were running amok and untamable.

But before they did, they stored elements of their being in strategic places across the stars. All of them had perished over time, or so it was thought, except this one. The Flux was the glue that kept the energy of the universe bound together, and if it were to be harnessed correctly, it could save certain parts of the cosmos that needed its power the most.

And for Lon, and his two counterparts, it would mean galaxy-wide fame and adoration.

Not to mention wealth.

The light was pulsating a brilliant green, bright and eluring to the explorers, drawing them closer and closer. Finally, the team rounded the final, wall and witnessed the magnificence of the Zedron Flux.

The Flux beared a resemblance to the double helix, a compound of molecules which forms the very DNA of all living things in the history of creation, only this one was roughly two feet in height, almost a foot wide, and around it swarmed a glow of the most beautiful emerald either Lon, Auger or Etherton had ever seen.

Lon practically salivated at its sheer majesty.
'Behold, my friends, the element that keeps the entire cosmos alive, for centuries thought lost, a legend throughout the ages, before us now. Never forget this moment. We are the first people in all history to have gazed at its wonder.

Etherton, make sure you're getting plenty of pictures.'

The small man just stood there, mouth gaping open, unable to take his eyes off the Flux.

'Etherton?' Auger tore herself away and nudged her counterpart.

He instantly reacted, fumbled within his satchel and dug out a rusted, yet modern looking device, flipped a switch on the side and held it as it unfurled into the form of a rather old-fashioned camera.

'Won't the flash harm it?'

'Not at all, Etherton. The Flux is pure energy, remember? If it can provide the life force for all life forms who have ever lived, I'm sure it can withstand a flash from your camera bulb!'

'How do we take it, Lon?' asked Auger.

'Finally, a sensible question,' Lon searched inside his rucksack. He pulled out a long spherical tube and upon further rummaging, a set of thick gloves. 'When I was studying the awesome power of the Flux, I thought it would be best to come prepared.'

'Yes, but will the tube withstand its power?' said Etherton.

'Ah, ever the cynic, Etherton,' sneered Lon.

He turned to meet his friends in the eyes.

'There's only one way to find out.'

The intrepid explorer began to pull the gloves on.

'Good thing he brought those ones with him, all I could offer him are my gardening gloves!' muttered Etherton to Auger.

The team were standing a full ten feet away from the Flux but with extreme trepidation, Lon began to edge closer, taking one step at a time. He opened the tube, a hiss emitting from the void inside. As the neared the Flux, they were struck by the lack of sound coming from it.

'Lon, why is it so silent? I expected the Flux to be brisling with energy, weren't you?'

'Auger, please, not now. We'll discuss why and how's later,' Lon spat. His pupils were green from the glow of the Flux, as it span, levitating from the ground, like a ballerina in midair.

Lon thought he could hear angels sing in his mind. This was it. This was the moment he became a legend.

With one final step he was awash with green light, almost at one with the Flux. He held his arms outstretched like a toddler walking towards its mother. He took a deep breath, ignored the sweat cascading down his nose. Blinking back tears of joy, he lurched forward and held the Flux within his grasp.

Only he didn't.

He reached for the Flux again.

His fingers disappeared through the green light and failed to make contact with anything.

'What's going on?' asked Auger.

Lon tried desperately again and again and then another time but to no avail.

'The Flux...it's not here!'

'What are you talking about Lon?' said Etherton.

'It's a hologram!' he replied.

'It can't be! What's creating the heat then?'

'That would be me, I'm afraid.'

A fourth voice entered the fray. It sounded muffled, like it was coming through a communications device.

'I do hope you can hear me; we are quite far away from your current location.'

Lon's eyes narrowed with murderous intent.

'Strakonis! You'll pay for this!'

The voice at the other end of the device crackled with laughter.

'I doubt it, my old friend. Even as we speak, we are light years away from Druis. You were just too late on this occasion. Still, can't win them all. Isn't that what you used to tell me?'

Lon's fists clenched tight.

'I refuse to be beaten by you.'

'That's the trouble with you, Lon. You never know when to give up. Fine, well, if you can find us, which I certainly doubt, we'll talk it over then. Hey, maybe I'll even let you hold the Flux, so you can have a little moment of glory at least? Until next time, my friend.'

The communicator fizzed out of life.

Etherton looked at Auger with a terrified look in his eye. He knew how much this meant to all of them, but to Lon? This was supposed to be his crowning glory, his final job. And knowing his boss the way he did, he knew that Lon would not take this defeat well.

Lon never lost. Ever.

The explorer fell onto his haunches and howled.

'He is never getting away with this. I will not rest until Strakonis lays ruined, penniless in a hole in the ground!'

'Steady on, Lon,' Auger nervously interjected.

He got up and pushed his face right up to Augers.

'Nobody tells me what to do. Not today, not anyday. Do you understand!?'

She nodded hastily.

Slimeball, she thought to herself. It was about time you were knocked down a peg or two.

'Er, I hate to be the bearer of more bad news but I think I've discovered that heating issue down here.'

Lon turned back to Etherton who was studying a crack in the ceiling above where the hologram of the Flux had been cunningly placed by Strakonis. The heat was ebbing through the crack, which was widening second by second.

A tremor began to quake the explorers off their balance.

'It looks like Strakonis ripped the Flux from its housing and has disrupted the housing of these catacombs. Our presence has disrupted it further...so in short...RUN!!!'

Without a moment to lose, the trio tore themselves away from the fake Flux and ran as fast as their legs would carry them back up the windy catacombs. The heat became unbearable but they dare not look back.

Within a couple of minutes of running lat out, they burst back onto the surface of the planet and threw themselves to the ground as a fireball belched through the hidden door from which they came.

The tremors began to shake the planet even further and soon the whole planet floor within their vicinity began to fall in on itself. Lon and the othes kept their heads down as the area shook more and more violently until after a minute or so, the earthquake subsided.

Peering through his arms, Lon took a look at the devastation. As the dust began to settle, Auger and Etherton helped each other to their feet. Coughing and spluttering, they joined Lon, who was overlooking a lip of what now looked like a mountain.

In the distance emergency sirens were wailing and getting closer.

The catacombs had been completely destroyed. Where they once lay was now a precipice going down hundreds of feet.

Centuries of history, wiped out in an instant.

Etherton took off his hat, as if to mourn its passing.

The sirens were nearly on top of the explorers now.

'Strakonis will pay for what he has done. Just you wait and see,' said Lon through gritted teeth.

'Police! Hands on your heads and get down on the ground now!'

The explorers turned to see three squad cars from the Druis security service trapping them against the lip. Armed, chrome skinned officers pointed large dangerous looking implements in their direction.

They raised their hands in surrender.

'And in the meantime,' said Etherton, 'looks like we are paying the bill for this!'

II

Random was in trouble. As usual.

In recent times, he had managed to lead a relatively quiet existence, which he had worried would become a rare pastime for him.

Not long after being born in a giant tube on a war torn planet he was supposed to be the saviour of, he had found a talking robot in the shape of a skateboard and having stolen a spaceship from a man made of sand, crash landed on a little blue and green world in another solar system and had to pose as an orphan in a children's home at the insistence of two teenagers on a school trip who just so happened to be in the right place in the right time when he nose-dived the ship into the planet.

Soon after, he was attacked by the same man made of sand he had stolen the ship from, who had taken over his robot friend and pursued him to the home, which he proceeded to destroy in a fireball.

Not only that, with the help of his new friends and his freed talking Skateboard, they then decided that one violent act of criminal damage wasn't enough for one day, they then ended up blowing up the local school and killing the sandman in the process then fleeing before they had the chance to be reprimanded for both!

But at least he has company on his travels. Not only was his talking skateboard back at his side, but the two orphans who found his crashed ship in the woods were also along for the ride, although he had some concerns that in having allowed them to come along with him in his travels throughout the cosmos, that he may be exposing them to more dangers that the universe had in store.

He was right.

Their very next adventure was even tougher to recover from than their first.

Random along with one of his new friends, a boy called Jake, were incarcerated in the mines of a planet called Genocia, waiting to be fed to a demon from the dark ages of the galaxy friendly named the Soul Destroyer, whilst the other, a girl called Anji, was lost on the surface of the planet with a band of freedom fighters looking to overthrow a government that seemed hell bent on killing its people for profit and power.

So, after experiencing the exciting, thrilling and yet downright dangerous and corrupt ways of the universe, Random was bracing himself for an eventful existence.

But since then, not much had happened.

It was a blessed relief for all concerned. Anji and Jake, after their experiences on Genocia, had taken a little more time to get used to their new life as space explorers.

More time to acclimatize had definitely been needed and thankfully, it's just what they got.

For a few months now the trio, accompanied by their robot skateboard had planet hopped from many of the far corners of the galaxy. They had spent a good while in the effervescing bubble spas of Maltidorn XI, backpacked around the ice honeycombs of Victoliah and even discovered a new planet unbeknownst to Skateboard that could sustain life without having a breathable atmosphere.

Along the way...not one abrasive tourist, not one megalomaniac threatening to kill them, no murderous beasts hell bent on ripping them to shreds in the dark cavernous depths of the worst living nightmare possible.

Until now.

It had all started with a letter...

'Anj, what's keeping you? The water's going to get cold again in half an hour.'

Jake hollered for his friend from the relaxing confines of his lilo. He had been lying in the middle of the pool for what seemed like forever, but he wasn't planning to move out of his idea of heaven any time soon. Not even to go to the toilet.

'I'll be there in a minute,' Anji replied as she struggled into her bathing suit. With one final effort, she opened the changing room doors and

walked out onto the glorious sunshine that the resort had to offer.

The previous day, the explorer's luxury ship, Venus II had discovered a moon in the Caloni system which featured a range of free holiday resorts. The resorts were built onto the side of a vast mountain and hung vertically in the air, as gracefully as you'd expect a holiday resort to look when its defying gravity on the side of a sheer drop into oblivion but the view was fantastic, whichever way the holidaymakers looked and that was enough to blanket the knowledge that if the gravity dampers were to malfunction, the entire complex would end up plummeting down the cliff face.

As Anji joined Jake in the pool and the pair began to mingle in the water with other holiday makers, Random sat perched on his sun bed, his chin resting on his hands.

His purple skin glistened in the sunshine. In front of him he could see his friends having the time of their lives. Behind them, the heat of the white dwarf going supernova seven million light years away burnt brighter in his mind than the one that shone on them currently.

He sighed.

He was bored. Very bored.

'Still thinking about the white dwarf, are you sir?'

'Yup.'

Random didn't turn to face the direction the voice had come from. If he had, he'd have seen his faithful friend, Skateboard, perched high up on the sun bed next to him, a can of oil held up by a claw and a straw rising up out of the black liquid and surreptitiously leaning into a cavern where you'd expect a mouth to be.

In better moods, Random would probably have laughed.

'I'm sure there will be another supernova sometime soon somewhere,' said Skateboard as he took another slurp of oil.

'That's pretty presumptuous, old friend.'

'Well, every cloud, as the humans say. You're restless, aren't you?'

'What gave it away?' said Random sarcastically.

'Well, pretty much everything, sir,' said Skateboard.

Random sighed again.

'I want adventure, Skateboard. I need adventure! This kind of thing is okay, every now and then, but come on! We left Rodas to explore the cosmos.'

'I suppose, an optimist would say that we are right now.'

'Well, some of us are.' Random's gaze turned to Anji and Jake. The former, along with two green headed aliens were having a whale of a time trying to overturn Jake's lilo.

The shaggy haired blonde was clinging on with all his might, begging them not to chuck him out into the water.

'They are new to this, sir.'

'So am I, Skateboard. Okay, yes, it's fine every once in a while, to take a holiday, of course it is, but we've had SIX recently! I didn't expect that.'

'Maybe you need to talk with them both. Express your frustration?'

Random turned to his robot and witnessed the crude oil rising from the can and zig-zagging its way up Skateboard's silly straw. He allowed himself a little smile.

'You're right. I'll have a word with them tonight. Hopefully we can move on in the morning.'

'That's a pleasant compromise, sir.'

'That's what I do.'

Skateboard put his can down on the side table, rolled on his back wheels onto his back and laid back on the lounger.

There was a question he knew he had to ask, but there was no way he wanted to ask it now. Against his better judgment, he decided that now he and his fellow Rodasian were alone, it was the best time.

'Are you still having those nightmares, sir?'

Random's eyes widened.

'Why do you ask?'

'You're welfare, sir.'

Random bowed his head.

'Yes.'

Skateboard's circuitry whirred a little.

'Still the same. "You're the only one who can save your people," "You alone can put a stop to the madness," y'know, usual thing.'

Back on their home planet of Rodas, the war devastated red/blue planet that for centuries had been divided by the warring factions the Crimson Empire and the Sapphire Regime continued to rage. Random was created by rebels from both sides to put a stop to the chaos and save his world from oblivion. But instead of stay and fight, he had fled and hid and his conscious knew it. Every night since his birth, the same two voices, who by now he had presumed were his parents, had plagued him, urging him home, towards his true calling and his destiny, and Random has resisted.

'Maybe it's time to go back,' Skateboard asked cautiously.

'No,' Random snapped. 'Not yet.'

'If you wanted to, I could have a look into your visions myself. Analyse them further, just to put your mind at ease?'

'It's a kind offer, my friend but one I'd rather not think about just now.'

He clicked his tongue and gave a heavy sigh.

'I'll see you back at the Venus.'

He got up from his lounger and walked away from the poolside.

Skateboard was right. He was always right. But to go back now would be suicide. He wasn't ready, not strong enough to face Kalor Maloso again. He needed more time and yet, the more he thought about Rodas, the more he knew he should be there, putting an end to the suffering.

He was a coward for not doing what he was born to do.

No, not a coward, how could he be? Technically he had saved two planets already, not to mention countless lives. So why not Rodas?

He shook the thoughts from his mind as hard as he could.

Random walked towards the docking bay that housed his wonderous ship, the Venus II and ignored the merry holidaymakers that he wandered past, practically oblivious to their existence.

What he needed was another adventure, another distraction.

Thankfully, for him, he got one.

As he rounded the corner, the glorious view of his ship, the Venus II, honed into view. It's smooth, silver outline and vast size made it the envy of the docking bay, nay the universe. It was truly a one of a kind.

Random raised a little smile as he saw his home. He'd seen it not a few hours earlier, but every time he gazed upon its magnificence, he was filled with a feeling of reassurance and safety.

'It's you, the purple one!'

Random rounded towards the voice.

A stick thin being, with a nozzle for a mouth and big, oval eyes that blinked out of sync, stood before him, quivering.

'I-I'm so s-sorry. I d-didn't expect y-you to b-be h-here.'

'Where am I supposed to be then?' said Random.

'Ap-pologies. I w-wanted to just leave t-this with your s-ship.'

The being held out its spider-like arms and showed Random what looked like a 3-D realisation of the letter 'P'.

'Who are you? And what's that?'

'A l-letter.'

'I can see that,' Random tutted. 'What do you want me to do with it?'

'R-return it.'

'To who? And why can't you do it?'

'B-because...the Osirans...t-they b-banished me. I s-stole a v-vital com-p-ponent from them. T-told them I d-did not t-take it. B-but I h-had to. My f-family were s-starving. The Os-sirans took no m-mercy. My b-business w-was g-going under.'

'So, you're only a criminal through desperation, not desire?' said Random.

'N-no. B-but the c-component…it is t-to powerful. I d-did not k-now w-what it w-was. I j-just n-needed the m-money.'

'Hold up a second. So, what you are saying is that you want me to take something that was stolen from a race and return it to them?'

The being looked sheepish.

'I-if you can. I-I have h-heard w-what you d-did on Gen-nocia.'

'How?'

'E-everyone has.'

Random looked surprised.

'I suppose news travels quickly in the cosmos.'

'Y-you are heroes.'

'Not us! We won't be signing autographs anytime soon. I don't carry a pen on me, for a start!'

'Y-your humour i-is lost on m-me. P-please. W-will you take it?'

Random huffed. He took the letter from the alien and examined it.

'What is it exactly?'

'I-it is a engine c-component. W-without it, the O-osirans are s-stranded in space.'

'That wasn't very nice of you now, was it?'

'L-like I said. I-I was d-desperate.'

Random glared at the being. It cowered a little further to the ground, the intensity of the his red/blue eyes all too much for the thief.

'Supposing I do give it back, who shall I say gave it back to me?'

'O-oh, t-there's n-no need to m-mention my n-name. They w-will know. I-it doesn't m-matter one b-bit who you g-got it from. When t-they g-get it back, you w-will b-be rewarded t-that's f-for sure!'

'I'll have to examine it before I say yes.'

'I-it's not harmful in any w-way, I p-promise.'

Random scoffed. 'Said the criminal whose trying desperately to get rid of it!'

The alien looked forlorn.

'Please...i-it isn't safe for m-me to h-have it. A-and now I k-
know I c-can't get anything f-for it, it n-needs to go b-back. I-if I
did it, t-they will k-kill m-me for w-what I d-did. I am already r-
running from them for my c-crime. T-they have a-agents
everywhere. It's n-not safe for me to have i-it and I can't sell it to
a-anyone because they k-know w-who it belongs to.'
  'So, the Osirans...not a friendly bunch then?'
  'Y-you'll find out...will y-you d-do it?'

*

'Seriously?' Jake said in disbelief.
  'Yep,' replied Random, his arms crossed in staunch defiance.
  Jake swung his legs over the side of the lilo and inadvertently
splashed Anji, who wore a worried expression.
  'So, you want us to leave what I think we can all agree on as
paradise to run a dangerous errand for a man who you only just
met that could result in certain death? Sign me up!'
  'Gotta hand it to you Anj, you're very good at laying out the lie
of the land!'
  Anji scowled at Jake.
  'I'm being serious. Random, this isn't a good idea.'
  'Look, what's certain death for that alien out there is a picnic for
us. We haven't taken the component ourselves. The Osirans will
know that. The fella who had it was known to them. We would be
greeted as heroes! Again! Yes, I know that might not necessarily
be a good thing in the long run, but look, it's a chance to meet a
new civilisation. It's an adventure! Come on, it's been ages since
we had one. We've got to go!'
  'Random, I know you are itching to get back out there. But the
Yarvesh...Consula...' Anji shuddered at the memory of both, and
the muts who nearly killed her in the polluted fields of Genocia,
'...I was so scared. I could have lost you all for good.'
  'I know,' said Random. He sat next to his friend and put a hand
upon her shoulder. 'I know how terrified you both were. And I
promise I will never put you in such danger again.'
  'Then promise us this,' Anji's eyes pleaded with her purple
friend. 'Don't put us in danger now.'

387

A whirring of mechanical instruments emitted from behind them as Skateboard rejoined his friends at the poolside. At the group's insistence, he had been instructed to run a diagnostic on the component, to double check it was not harmful to the travelers.

'I've completed my checks, sir, and I can conclude that it is nothing more than a fuel cell for an ancient spaceship. The component is similar to the hydro fuel cylinders that the Venus II uses to power herself. Conclusive evidence of danger is zero percent.'

'That settles it then, come on you two! Dry off and let's be on our way!'

Jake rolled his eyes back.

'But we don't even know where to find them!'

'Oh yes, we do. The Osirans have been stranded in the Magidon cluster for four decades in your Earth terms. We have their co-ordinates...please guys, look if it makes you feel any better, you can all sit this one out and I'll go alone. I need this.
I can't just sit relaxing all the time. There's a whole galaxy out there to explore..and to be fair I did warn you from the start that things may get a little dangerous. It's not like I have done any of it on purpose.'

Anji put her head in her hands. 'I don't know, Random. It just feels a little soon.'

'Fine. I'll go by myself then. Skateboard, chuck us the keys, I'll come and get you all when I am done.'

Jake scrunched his face up.

'Arrg...fine, mate, we'll come along.'

'No, don't worry, if that's really how you feel-'

'It's okay, I get where you are coming from. I'll just finish my drink and we'll come along.'

Anji flashed a look of annoyance at her shaggy friend.

'Jake, what are you doing? Reverse psychology won't work. He means it.'

'I think we'd better keep an eye on him Anj, after all, if he never comes back, we'll be stranded here. Besides, he's useless without us.'

Random chuckled. 'That I am.'

Anji took a look around her. The golden glow arced in the
atmosphere that twinkled with glorious majesty.

'I can think of worse places to be stuck.'

'We can't abandon him. He needs us. Who knows? This time, it
won't be as dangerous.'

Anji gave a frustrated cry and wheeled back to Random.

'Alright, Captain, you win. Let's get a wiggle on.'

III

So now, here he was, approaching with extreme trepidation the
throne room of the Osirans. The tunnel leading to his destination
had been long, dark and dusty, as though it hadn't been used for
centuries. Although his mind was clouded by the mystery of this
supreme race he was about to meet for the first time, he doubted
they had anyone to clean up around the place!

He remembered Skateboard's recon. On the way they had been
briefed on exactly who the Orisons were. Supreme gods, legends
of the cosmos, who back in the dark ages of the universe had
influenced the religious leanings of the ancient Egyptians. Anji
and Jake were astonished to learn that names and stories they had
learnt at school were actually true, or at least based on fact.

Despite their newly-found enthusiasm to accompany Random to
return the fuel cell, he declined their offer and told them to hang
back.. and keep the engine ticking over! As he walked out into the
grand hall and focused his eyes out of the gloom, he half wished
they were with him.

Circling him, gazing down from on high, was a multitude of
figures sitting still on what looked like sandstone thrones.
Random's jaw dropped.

Not only were there dozens of them – hundreds, perhaps – but
they towered above him like skyscrapers.

Ten of which seemed to, somehow, dominate the room more
than the others, sitting in a circle, almost like a gladiatorial
colosseum. Random soon realized he was standing in what looked
like a pit, coarse sand crunching under his feet. He looked
nervously around him. Any minute now a giant tiger could leap
out from the darkness and try to make him his lunch.

The vast auditorium was silent. An eerie air lingered around him.

He gulped.

Hard.

Remember what Skateboard said, he thought to himself, *speak clearly and with respect.*

'Oh mighty gods...'

Yes, that's a good start, keep going.

'...I am honoured to have stand before you today...'

Oh, I'm a natural at this!

'...and I come baring great news.'

Silence.

Okay, keep going Random.

'My friends and I have reason to believe that we have found something that belongs in your possession.'

Still nothing. Random frowned a little. Were these just statues he was talking to? Were they dead? Maybe there was something to do with the fuel cell having shut down?

'A-anyway,' he stuttered, 'I've brought back to you a fuel cylinder...of...erm...great power.'

A loud creak omitted from one of the giants. To Random's amazement, one of the "statues" began to stir into life.

It's body, like it's fellow Osirans, resembled that of a human form. Its head differed from the others and resembled that of a bird. If Random could tear his eyes away from it, as its giant beak and moon-like pupils began to peer down on him, all of them had differing heads.

'Come closer.'

Its voice boomed throughout the auditorium, a shockwave of vibration disturbing the sand beneath Random's feet. He winced as his ear drums reeled and did what he was asked.

'Show it to us.'

Random produced the fuel cylinder and held it aloft for the Osirans to see.

A huff, loud enough to start an earthquake on a neighouring planet, emitted from above him.

'Where did you get this?' asked the bird.

'Whom am I addressing?' he dared to ask.

'It is not for me to reveal who I am to someone who we cannot be sure is a foe...or a friend.'

Random decided to chance his wit.

'Well, it would make conversation easier.'

The bird leaned back in its throne.

'I am Horus, God of the Sky.'

Random bowed.

'Delighted to meet you, blimey, not every day that you meet a God.'

'Gods,' bellowed Horus, 'for we are many.'

Random looked around him and for the first time in quite a while, began to feel quite nervous.

'All of you?'

'We are many,' boomed another, this time with a longer beak that almost looked like a sword.

'Thoth, please, we are not to entertain this insect,' said Horus.

'Hey! That's a bit strong.'

'SILENCE!'

A third voice shrieked from on high. 'The Mother Goddess allows passage within these walls but we shall not tolerate insults towards a stranger.'

'Mother Goddess, we should not take this boy on his word. We must be cautious. After all, was it not an over trust of strangers that led to our crippled state?' said Isis.

'It would be wise to listen to my Mother,' said Horus. 'Would it not, Thoth? Are you or are you not the God of Wisdom?'

'Prey, Horus, do not speak to Thoth on the subject of wisdom. He is wise by title, not by nature. Do you not remember that it was Thoth who allowed us to be robbed of our power in the first place?'

'Hold your tongue, Horus, or I shall have it cut from your mouth!' Thoth shook with indignant rage and forced himself up from his throne. The dust and debris from centuries of dormancy began to fall towards Random.

'Err...did you want to be left alone? I can step outside if now's not a good time.' He thumbed towards the tunnel he came from and failed to notice that it was slowly closing.

'We said silence!' a lightning bolt shot from the raised finger of the Mother Goddess and hurtled towards Random. He rolled forward spectacularly, kicking up a dust cloud as he evaded the strike.

'Woah, woah, what was that for!'

'You have brought the lost fuel cell for our ship to move freely throughout the cosmos once again, but we will not grant you a free pass,' said Orisis.

'You're an accessory to theft and shall be punished.'

'What? I'm here to help you!'

'The Osirans do not require you any further.'

The Gods all arose from their thrones in unison and raised their arms. As Random turned on his heels, he saw the door was almost shut.

'You will not escape,' boomed Horus.

'Think again,' Random scowled. Picking up the fuel cell, he moved as fast as he could and squeezed under the descending door, skidding under its crushing weight as the sound of thunder stormed towards him. He had escaped in the nick of time and fumbled for the fuel cell.

'Ah, nuts!' he exclaimed as he realised that he had dropped the cylinder on the other side. He witnessed it separate from him completely as the trap door slammed shut.

Cursing his own theatric getaway without the possession that had got him into this mess, he made immediately down the tunnel, picking up as much pace as he could muster, tripping as he set off. Even for someone of his immense pace, Random wondered how long it would take him to escape, and indeed even if he were to make it out alive at all.

As he hurtled towards freedom, he was becoming aware that he was setting off all manner of traps as he ran. Poisonous darts whizzed past his head, threatening to put an end to his life one-by-one. He ducked and weaved, and felt a sharp sensation prick his senses into full alert mode when one of the offending weapons whizzed mere millimeters past the worst place to be stung by a dart. Gritting his teeth, he continued on...

Back in the landing bay where the Venus II was parked, Anji and Jake sat on the ships' ramp waiting patiently for their friend to return.

'What's taking him so long?' said Anji, nervously checking her watch.

'Relax. He'll be here in a sec,' Jake reassured.

A distant rumble of activity echoed towards the pair. Jake shot a look as if to say, "I told you so," to his friend.

'Anj, you worry too much. He's got it covered. See?'
A purple blur shot out into the hangar. Followed by a barrage of explosions.
'Oh, really?' Anji retorted.
'Skateboard!' hollered Jake up the ramp. He scrambled to his feet and followed Anji inside the bowels of the ship. Seconds later, an out of breath, and slightly battered Random joined them, taking out a kitchen cabinet in the mid-section which acted as an unintentional barrier to stop his incredible speed. A tremendous crash of rockery and metal made the occupants of the Venus II's cockpit jump. They looked back into the mid-section just in time to see Random picking himself up and storming towards them.
'I thought I told you to keep the engine ticking over!' he barked, broken bits of crockery hanging like sharp dandruff in his thick brown hair.
'Oh yeah...I stalled it,' said Jake sheepishly.

'You certainly pick your moments to shine, don't you?' he spat, kicking his friend out of the pilot's chair. 'Skateboard?'
'Already on it, sir.'
The AI fired up the motors and the Venus II groaned into life. Random grabbed a hold of the steering column and pulled it towards the ceiling. A volley of laser fire exploded all around the hangar, jolting the passengers forward as it thundered into the craft.
'Shields withholding,' Skateboard announced.
Another crash of fire threw Anji and Jake to the floor and Random and Skateboard from their chairs.
'Shields down,' groaned Random.

He thrust the steering wheel up, catapulting the others to the back
of the cockpit. With a roar of agonized Rodasian engineering, the
Venus tore out of the hangar and exploded through the blast
doors, which has remained shut, into the comforting blackness of
space. In all the suddenness of the attack, Skateboard had
neglected to think about opening the hangar doors. Even if he had
requested, considering the reception Random had received, he
sincerely doubted they would reciprocate with giving them an
easier route to freedom. Even so, he could have thought ahead,
anticipated the danger, he could have easily hacked the systems.

The cymatics had clearly shown him in his research on the trip to
the Osiran mothership that it could be easily done. The ship was
ancient, broken, immobilized. Hacking the security system, even
that of ancient gods, was as easy to him as it was for a tin opener
to make light work of a tin of soup.

But he hadn't, and now here they were, running for their lives
on a ship that was now damaged.

Anji gingerly got back up to her feet and clung on to the back of
Random's pilot chair.

'Anj, Jake, get back to the mid-section now and strap yourselves
in.'

She looked to her left. Jake was nowhere to be seen. Anji gasped
as she saw the slumped frame of her friend on the ground.

'Jake!'

'Get him out of here now!'

Anji wasn't going to argue with Random. She picked him up,
struggling under his weight, and dragged him away.

'Sir, the Osirans ship is starting to move.'

'They must have got that fuel cell up and running again pretty
quickly. Right, priorities. Skateboard, how bad is the damage?'

Skateboard's circuits whirred.

'We've lost shields. Port engine fire is being dealt with by the
internal sprinklers and we've almost lost the starboard thrusters
all together.'

'Can we outrun the Osirans?'

'For now, sir, yes. But we need to move quickly.'

'Can we go to lightspeed?'

'Negative, sir. If we go to light speed, we risk burning the thrusters out completely.'

'Suggestions?'

'We need to find a planet with a breathable atmosphere...'

A deadly array of sparks began to shoot out of the central dashboard.

'Do it!'

Skateboard searched the navigation system.

'Got one. 5 clicks away. Sector 9V4XB.'

Random punched the co-ordinates into the navigation system.

Anji finished clipping the unconscious Jake into his chair and strapped herself in. She slipped and slid in her place and tried desperately to tighten her bonds but no matter how hard she tried to stay secure, the velocity and buffeting of the broken Venus II was enough to make her sick. More explosions of sparks emitted around the ship, threatening to set the interior of the Venus on fire.

Flashes of fire and smoke surrounded the travellers as Random struggled to keep the Venus afloat. The cockpit began to fill with a cloud of smoke.

'Almost there, sir!' Skateboard screamed.

Random peered through the fog in the cockpit and saw a myriad of colours getting ever closer.

He shook his head, wondering whether the fumes he was breathing in was making him hallucinate. Great, that's all he needed during a crash landing!

'Nose up, sir, you've got to keep it up!'

Random's eyes began to feel heavy. His head began to whirl.

'Sir...'

Skateboard pleaded with him to keep focused but it was no use.

As Random slumped off his chair and onto the harsh metal floor, the Venus spun onto its top.

Skateboard heard Anji scream in the mid-section.

Random was down.

The Venus II was on a collision course with a planet...with no one at the wheel...

IV

Skateboard set to work immediately. He was already connected into the ship's steering matrix but it was going to take reactions of lightning quickness to stop the Venus II from plunging into a planet.

He activated the emergency procedure. A safety belt shot out of a gap in Random's chair and anchored his unconscious body firmly to it. He checked his external clock.

0.349 click until impact.

There was nothing else he could do except hope, pray to whatever God might be listening and crossed his diodes. Even the ones that were hard to reach.

The Venus had come in hot. Too hot. It smacked into the surface with a terrible force, so great that Anji blacked out almost immediately. The ship bounced with a terrible ferocity across the rocky plane. Sparks flew as the twin engine system on either side of the body of the Venus II turned into huge Catherine wheels of fire.

Inside the spaceship, Skateboard tried all he could to keep the nose up but the gravity of the planet was doing its best to keep the crash landing as uncomfortable as possible.

Explosions began to ripple like deathly ripples around the place. Skateboard, already terribly worried by their current predicament, now had fire and three unconscious friends to worry about. Luckily, the sprinkler and foam system kicked in and began to spurt all around him.

Struggled as he might, the ship just would not come to a halt. And then, something terrible happened.

A shriek of metal threw his audio systems into overdrive.

Suddenly Skateboard sensed a harsh breeze blowing in the cockpit.

He dared to look around.

The mid-section had gone.

In this distance he could just make out the rest of the Venus II as it receded further and further into the distance.

Then, just as he turned back around to face the cockpit view port, his prayers were answered.

396

The ship has come to a sudden halt.

It had smacked straight into another ship.

This threw the cockpit section of what was left of the Venus II onto its side and finally Skateboard's mission was complete.

And then, just as he thought the day couldn't get any worse, he caused himself a massive embarrassment.

He leaked oil all over the floor and passed out.

'What on Milas was that?!' came a voice from within the vessel that had halted the Venus' less than glamorous landing.

Three beings clambered out of an opening in the opposite side to the ship. They studied the half a spaceship that had collided with them in complete bemusement. One of them, the smaller one who resembled what Anji and Jake would know as a mole, rubbed his neck vigorously and looked at the nose cone that had embedded itself in the hull with astonishment and agony.

'What do you think happened?' he said.

The girl, with pale blue skin and a hair that seemed to look like an elephant's trunk lying in its side, threw a look dirtier at her companion than a ton of manure being dropped from a great height.

'Clearly they crashed you moron!'

Etherton looked back at her with indignation.

'Ever the wit, aren't you Auger?'

'Shut up, you two,' spat the third member. 'Look.'

He pointed with two of his seven fingers at the smashed window of the cockpit towards the prone body of what looked like a boy.

'Come on,' he gestured.

Lon ran to the other end of the nose cone, closely followed by Auger and Etherton.

'Wait, there's more of the craft over there!' Auger pointed into the middle distance at the rest of the wreckage.

'You two go and check for survivors, quick!'

They obeyed as Lon clambered inside the gutted remains of what until very recently was a mildly tidy cockpit.

He dodged the small fired that were still ablaze and stepped over the debris that lay strew over what was previously the wall but was now the floor of the craft. He bent down to fit through the door and immediately slipped in the oil that Skateboard had produced before shutting down. Lon's outstretched arms stopped him from hitting his head on the dashboard and he cursed before turning his attention to Random.

Lon winced. The kid looked like he was in a bad way. He checked him for any physical injuries and apart from a gashed arm, which had practically ripped the flesh from the bone, he would live unless he had terrible brain damage.

'Lon?' called a voice from outside the nose cone.

'What is it?' he replied.

Skateboard's circuits began to whirr back into life.

'We've found two more.'

'Get the stretchers out of the ship. I've found one here, doesn't look too clever. We'd better being them on board our ship quick.

Skateboard groaned in the way only an AI robot can, startling Lon.

'What are you? What happened?'

Skateboard tried to focus his optical lenses on the stranger who stood over his master's prone body.

Trying to find the words, but unable to while his system continued to boot up, he struggled to produce just 3 words.

'A bumpy landing.'

It was Anji who came around first. As she blinked back into consciousness, a piercing light streamed into her eyes, aggravating an already splitting headache. She emitted a deep, guttural groan and closed her eyes again.

'Oop, sounds like one of them's back with us,' said Etherton.

He took his feet off his desk and swung himself upright and over to his...patient...he supposed she was.

'Oh, my head!' moaned Anji, placing both her hands against her ears as though there were some terrible earth-shattering noise shredding through her head.

There was.

'Must be concussion or something similar. I don't know, sorry, you've been lumbered with the least medical of our party, I'm afraid. You should have seen the wreck we rescued you from. It's a miracle you aren't dead.'

Anji tried to get up, wincing through the agony.

'No, but your bedside manner clearly is,' she quipped. 'My head…please, do you have anything that will…'

'Oh, yes, hold on a second,' the mole like creature scurried around what Anji presumed was the medical bay. It was certainly bright enough to resemble one.

'Could you turn the light down too?'

'Hold on, I only have one pair of paws!'

Finally, he grabbed a sachet of liquid, tore the corner slightly and handed it to Anji.

'Take a few swigs of that, should sort you right out.'

She did as instructed and instantly her headache began to subside. Anji began to sit up straight and forced her eyes fully open, no longer shrouded by pain, she took in her surroundings.

'Is this a hospital?'

Etherton snorted. 'Hah! Far from it.'

'Then where am I then?'

Suddenly her eyes shot wide when she realised she was alone.

'Oh my god, Jake and Random!'

She tried to get to her feet but was gently pushed back onto the bed by the strange alien who had saved her from a potential death by headache.

'Please, little lady, you have to remain still. The drugs won't have fully worn off yet.'

The mention of drugs began to make Anji really panic.

'You've drugged me!? Get off me!'

'No, no not like that! Please miss, stop struggling!'

'What the hell do you think you are doing?'

Auger had entered the room and as usual was shaking her head in dismay at her travelling companion.

'You've never been very adept at talking to women, have you Etherton?' she snorted, pulling him away.

Auger could see the panic in Anji's eyes.

'You and your friends are safe, now please take it easy.'

'Where are they?' Anji demanded.

'They are right next door.'
'Can I see them?'
'Of course – just as soon as you have fully recovered.'
'Why? What happened?'
'You don't remember?' asked Etherton.
Anji searched her memory. Of course, she did. The Osirans. The ship was gunned down. They had crashed!
'I do, oh my...' she caught her breath. 'Are they alright?'
'They will be, now.'
Another voice had entered the room.
Anji surveyed the newcomer.
He stood a proud six feet tall, thick black wavy hair floating down his short forehead and over his left eye. His arms were muscular with his biceps popping out from underneath his sleeveless jacket and Anji noticed that he had seven fingers on each hand.. and there were three of them!
Whoever he was, he was definitely the best looking alien Anji had ever seen.
'Now? What happened to them?'
'Let's just say that you were in much better shape than them.'
Anji gasped.
'I'll let you see them just as long as the drugs have passed into your system.'
'What drugs?'
'Truma supplements. You and your friends have been through hell by the looks of it.'
Lon dragged a chair across the room to Anji's bed.
'Now, why don't you tell me what happened to you and your friend while we wait for them to wake up?'
Anji fell silent. She was unsure what to say. Should she mention the Osirans? Were these people good guys? Could she trust them?
'We had engine failure and just happened to crash land.'
'Emphasis on the crash and less on the land, I'd say,' butted Etherton.
'Etherton, hush,' said Auger.
'Well, how do you expect me to feel? Her ship took out my living quarters!'
'Took out? Oh no, we didn't crash into you, did we?'
'Crashed! You put a hole in our ship!'

Anji began to feel a little awkward.

'Didn't you see us coming?'

Auger laughed. 'We were parked!'

Anji blushed.

'Sorry.'

'Don't worry about them, we'll fix it. Are you sure it was engine failure? We've surveyed the wreckage and there were what looked like scorch marks on the hull.'

'Well, we were on fire...from what I remember...' Anji said, rubbing her head.

'I wasn't born yesterday; it was from laser fire. So come on, tell us, what really happened?'

'What's going on in here?'

Yet another new voice entered the medical bay.

Lon, Auger, Etherton and Anji turned around in unison and couldn't help but look deeply shocked at their visitor. Instantly they all shot their gaze away again.

'What's your friend's name again?' said Lon.

'Jake! What are you doing?' Anji sounded shocked.

'Why, what's the matter?' said Jake.

'Jake, is it? I take it he isn't very clever.'

'Hey! That's a bit personal, you haven't even met me properly yet!'

'That's my fault, sorry,' admitted Auger.

'Right, well take him back to the main medical bay and for god's sake put his surgical gown on the right way around this time!'

V

A few hours later, the crew of the Venus II were almost as good as new, having recovered from their injuries and along with the people who had rescued them, had congregated in a meeting area of their ship.

Random slurped the last of his revitalizing tonic and replaced the cup on the table they were sat around.

'Thanks for that, it really was a lifesaver.'

'You're not kidding. Always handy to keep around in our line of work.'

'What is it you do?' asked Jake, who was over his embarrassment from earlier and had also fully recovered from his injuries. When he was found by Auger and Etherton, his body was broken in so many places the pair had severely doubted he would make it back to their ship alive. Despite their lack of optimism, he had and after they had delicately managed to zip both he and the others into bio suits, designed to help regenerate damaged body tissue, and pumped him and his friends full of trauma supplements, he had made a full recovery in a matter of hours.

'We're archaeologists. We travel the cosmos looking for rare and sometimes mythical artifacts, find them and sell them,' said Auger.

'Sounds amazing! I've always wanted to be an archeologist,' said Jake.

'No, you haven't, you've always wanted to be a footballer,' Anji retorted.

'Well...' said Jake, slightly embarrassed, '...that's what I tell people to look cool.'

'Anyway, what are you doing here..and where is here anywhere?' asked Random, trying to steer the conversation back on course.

'Before we answer any more questions,' said Etherton, 'I think it's only fair you tell us who you are running from.'

'Oh, no-one at all. We got caught in the crossfire of a little space skirmish, that's all?'

Lon searched Random's face for any hint of a lie.

He found none.

Random was a very good liar.

'That's as well, because if anyone were to find out what we are doing here they'd probably end up firing on us too.'

'How come?' asked Anji.

'We are here to find the Zedron Flux.'

'Never heard of it,' said Jake.

'I'm very surprised at that. Where are you from?' Auger was astonished. Everybody in the universe had heard of the Zedron Flux.

'Well, let's just say we travel a lot and don't really belong anywhere,' said Anji. Jake shot her a look.

'That's a bit on the nose, Anj, everyone belongs somewhere,' he replied.

'That's what we like to think,' she said.

'The Zedron Flux is pure energy. Used correctly it can be the one thing that can save the universe from all its ills.'

'Sounds a bit grand. How comes it needs finding, something that strong.'

'It doesn't. It was stolen.'

'Stolen? From who?' asked Anji.

'From me,' said Lon bitterly.

'From us,' Auger corrected. Lon shot a dirty look at his counterpart.

'Who pays you, Auger?'

The explorer bit her lip.

'And the person...or people who took it from you are here on this planet?' asked Random.

'Yes, and hopefully so is the Flux,' said Lon.

Random clapped his hands and got to his feet. 'Well, we don't want to bother you any longer than we have, come along you two.'

Lon laughed. 'Where exactly? We haven't even told you where you are. Besides, you left us with a hole in our hull and we could use some extra pairs of hands.'

'We don't want any trouble,' said Random firmly.

'You won't get any. Don't worry, we'll look after you.'

'We don't need any looking after.'

'If you say so. But you've left us with heavy damage. It would only be fair if you repaid us in kind. So, what do you say? Wanna join us on a treasure hunt?'

'Yes please!' said Jake.

'We all know you do, Jake,' tutted Anji.

'As long as we stay safe,' said Random.

'I can't guarantee that, but we can do our best,' replied Lon.

'We'd better speak to Skateboard first, see how the Venus II is doing.'

'There's little point in that, from the mess your crate was in I doubt it will ever fly again,' chuckled Etherton.

At that moment Skateboard slid into view.

'Self-repair mode is currently at 38 percent. According to early diagnostic tests she'll fly again, sir,' he chirped.

'Good,' Random smirked cheekily in Etherton's direction.

'It'll take quite a while for the Venus II to pull itself all back together again, we could be here for days, weeks even,' Skateboard informed.

'It looks like you have no choice but to join us then,' said Lon.

'Yes...but it would be nice to know where we were exactly.'

Lon made for a side door and pressed the release mechanism. A blaze of colours bled into the ship.

'Welcome to Spectronia.'

The travellers gazed in sheer wonder at the mass of colourful beauty that surrounded them. They all cooed at the wonderous collection of rainbows that painted the clear blue sky. Rolling mountains surrounded them, each one coated in a wash of all the colours of the spectrum. Random's eyes glimmered as he gazed at the shimmering mountain tops, the snow a glistening snow drift of colourful glory.

'Are we in heaven?' cooed Anji.

'This is...I mean, wow!'

'Couldn't have put it better myself, Jake,' said Random.

'Every colour imaginable!' squeaked Anji.

'Yes. It's a pity there were no rainbows on Rodas,' mused Random as he spotted a purple colour matching that of his pigmentation all around him. 'There would never have been a war in the first place.'

'Your people went to war over colour? Seems a little senseless to me,' said Jake.

'Says a human,' Random replied.

'Fair point.'

Jake went back to concentrating on the beautiful view. He thought back to his days at primary school, when he and his fellow classmates would play with rainbow crayons. It was as though someone had gone to town on the whole planet with a lorry load of them.

The horizon seemed to glisten in the sunshine, which seemed to resemble the one back in Anji and Jake's solar system.

Random, without taking his eyes off the pretty mountains, tried to tear his attention away from the wonder and to the task in hand.

'How long have you been here?'

'About two days,' said Auger.

'Do you ever plan to leave?'

'As soon as we have the Flux,' said Lon, who began to rummage through his backpack.

'But surely people of your occupation can take huge pleasure being in a place as gorgeous as this!' said Anji.

'Oh yes, I agree!' said Etherton. 'After all, Spectronia is one of the nine wonders of the galaxy. Picturesque, peaceful, majestic in all of its splendour. The trouble is Lon is such a grump he refuses to take it all in!'

Lon glared at Etherton, enough to make him nervous.

'A-anyway, would you like some warmer clothes? Spectronia can get quite cold at night.'

'We should have some on board the Venus II, thanks,' said Random. 'Come on gang, let's tool up. How long before you wanted to get on the road, as it were?'

'What road?' said a bemused Auger.

'It's an Earth phrase, blimey, you two must have rubbed off on me more than I realised...see!' he grinned.

'What time shall we meet you back here?'

'You're crashed vessel isn't far away, just be as quick as you can,' said Lon.

The trio, led by Skateboard made the small journey on foot towards the shipwreck.

To the naked eye, the ship looked an absolute state, beyond repair. Shard of metal and debris lay a path guiding the travellers closer and closer.

The Venus II was still torn in two, but there appeared to be a blue energy glowing around the rim of the nose section, pulling it very slowly towards the rest of the craft. Jake noticed the sound of metal being hauled together and hydraulics somewhere from within the ship, working overtime. It sounded like a building site.

'Alright, Skateboard, full damage report please,' asked Random.

'Um...it's dead!'

'Far from it, Master Jake,' insisted Skateboard. 'The Venus II is equipped with a self-repair mechanism powered by microscopic organisms manufactured in the seda metal. In other words, unless it is completely unsalvageable, it'll always pull itself back together, although it has to be said that this was a close call.'

'We're a lucky bunch!' chirped Anji. 'Random, I'm not sure about those three. They seem...cold.'

'I know what you mean. Especially that Lon fella. I think we should try and keep our wits about us on this trip, just in case.'

'Well, we could always just stay with the Venus II?' said Jake.

'And miss this chance to explore one of the nine wonders of the galaxy?' exclaimed Random.

'Come on Jake, like Random said, as long as we stay on our toes there's nothing to worry about.'

'Also, you heard Skateboard back at their ship. It could take days for the Venus to repair herself.'

'Maybe even a week or two,' Skateboard confirmed.

'Exactly.'

'Also, the self-repair system would make the Venus II quite uninhabitable until it is finished.'

'But who will look after it? I mean, who knows what kind of monsters might be lurking around the next rainbow?'

'He's got a point, Random,' said Anji.

Random looked at Skateboard.

'During the main reconstructive phase of the rebuild the outer hull of the ship will be sending electrical pulses throughout. Meaning it would be impossible for anyone to get close to it...'

'...and keep their face in the process?' said Random.

'Eloquently put, sir,' said Skateboard.

'How long until this...phase, starts?' asked Anji.

'As soon as we are ready to leave. Remember I am connected to the ship. I can initialize any command or override remotely.'

'Just like a set of car keys, you can make sure the riff raff are locked out,' said Jake.

'Precisely.'

'Well then, we'd better not lose our keys then,' joked Random. 'Come on you lot, let's get packing.

VI

For such a sunny day as it was, Anji was expecting the heat to be baking them as they continued in the open top buggy. Yet somehow, the temperature on Spectronia was more than adequate for them. Not too hot, not too cold. In a word, it was perfect. Just what she thought the planet was too.

Deep down she had been more the skeptical about going on another adventure so soon after the crash. But whatever Lon and the others had given them had certainly worked. She didn't feel any after effects of the accident at all. Which was weird, because for someone who just a few hours previously had broken all of her limbs, suffered a major spinal shattering and to top that all off, a splitting headache.

Although their new friends had confirmed that she had got off better than the other two, she hadn't wanted to enquire what had happened to them. That kind of information could really put someone off their tea.

And now here they were, sitting in the back of a dune buggy holding on for dear life as the sun shone its warm rays down upon them.

It wasn't the coziest of rides, but it was a damn sight comfier than their crash landing!

Back at Lon's ship, Random had asked how they were planning to track down the Flux.

'With this,' Auger had answered, brandishing a device which looked like a cross between a fish fork and a TV remote. 'It's an energy giga counter. When the Flux is near, energy will spike. So far, we have determined that it is roughly 200 miles south west of our location.

'200 miles? In space terms that's, what? Ten minutes away, yeah, Skateboard?' said Jake.

'It does seem like a very short trip,' said Skateboard.

'On the contrary. We weren't joking when we said this was a long trip,' said Lon. 'We've been tracking it for the best part of seven months. Unfortunately, the person who is holding it to ransom has detected us on every occasion. Why? Because of this thing. He's able to detect our vessel from a distance. So, this time, we have to be cunning, take him by surprise and take what should be mine.'

'Ours,' corrected Etherton.

''I know what I mean,' spat Lon. 'Now come on, before he moves again.'

So now here they were, in the back of the buggy, no seatbelts, holding on for dear life as it negotiated its way up the sand dunes.

'Is there any way of this going a little...slower?' said Jake. The steep inclines and falling declines were making his teeth chatter and his cheeks wobble. He wasn't the only one. Looking over at Random, Jake could see nothing but a purple blur.

'Fraid' not. We are making good time.

'Any chance we can get on a smoother road? Those rainbow roads look nice!' shouted Anji over the loud buggy's engine.

Jake leant closer to Random.

'Not being funny, mate, but it's making me numb.'

'I don't think our driver wants to, sorry, I'm not the captain here.'

Jake huffed.

'According to the map, the route should level out soon,' Etherton said, emerging from underneath what looked like a large duvet.

'Told you you should have gone digital, Etherton,' joked Auger.

'Hey, when you're navigator, do what you want, but when I'm in charge-'

The buggy came to a sudden halt, hurling its incumbents forward. Anji nearly hit her head on the back of Auger's seat. She caught a glimpse of Lon's expression in the rear-view mirror. He did not look happy.

'Will you all, please, for one minute just keep your mouths closed?'

The car fell silent.

'Thank you,' Lon huffed.

Skateboard, who was lying across the laps of his companions as there was little space in the buggy for a seventh person, started to whir.

'Er...sorry to break the silence...'

'Not as much as I am,' Lon interrupted.

'But I am picking up life forms on the mid-range scanner.'

The crew of the dune buggy looked around, alert to danger.

'How many, Skateboard?' asked Random.

'Roughly 60..no 70..80..I'll get back to you on that figure, sir!'

'I'm swinging this buggy round,' Lon declared.

Random got out of the buggy and walked up the dune to get a better look. His eyes widened.

'Wait, we don't know if they are hostile,' said Anji.

'We're about to find out,' said Random ominously.

On the horizon was a stampede of beings, seemingly riding on the back of other creatures. They were still a little too far out for Random to see any more than this except that they appeared to have some form of weapons on them...and they looked sharp.

'Get in the car!' hollered Lon.

He ticked the engine over and grappled with the steering wheel, swinging the car one hundred and eighty degrees. Random jumped gracefully into the back of the buggy, panicked.

'Drive.'

The buggy tore away from the oncoming threat and kicked up a cloud of sand and dust in its wake. Random, Anji and Jake kept their heads turned towards the chaos. The creatures had already gained so much ground that they were closer to them than they were to escaping. Much closer. The beasts pursued them with relentless intent and Anji cried in terror when she was able to see them clearly through the dust cloud. They looked to her like black horses. Five legged horses, with one in the middle of the front two and all had what looked like hooves made of spears, just as pointy as the colourful jockeys who rode upon them.

A sharp object was hurled towards the buggy and Random used his super speed abilities to intercept it and pluck it out of the air.

'Do that again and I'll buy you a drink!' said Lon.

'I'm not old enough to drink!'' Random replied, instantly regretting his response and relegating it to least cool thing he has said during a chase.

'Incoming!' yelled Jake.

A spread of spears hit the back of the buggy and one imbedded itself in the seat where Random had been sitting.

'Leave this to me, Anj, Jake, keep down!'

'Their almost on top of us Lon, hurry!' cried Auger.

Splinters and shards of weaponry flew above them. Despite Random's best efforts a pile of debris was starting to collect in the foot wells beneath Jake and Anji's feet. Seeing their predicament as a chance to be heroic and impress their new friends, Jake picked up one of the broken spears and stood up from his seat, brandishing it and gritting his teeth in a "come and have a go if you think your hard enough pose".

Within seconds, it had been knocked out of his hand and with a whimper, he sat quietly down.

'Get down!' said Random, just as his concentration had been distracted for long enough for another sharp weapon to fly into the vehicle.

'We can't outrun them!' said Etherton.

'Yeah, I don't need a running commentary people!' shouted Lon angrily.

But his mole-like friend was not wrong. They were almost outrun. He was out of control of the situation. He hated it when this happened...and it wasn't often that he felt like this.

The buggy continued to lurch up and down the sand dunes at breakneck speed and yet it was all but surrounded now.

Whoever, whatever were following them began to try to climb on board the buggy, but Random, helped by Anji and Auger, tried with all his might to fling the uninvited guest off their vehicle, but it was becoming impossible.

'It's no use,' cried Random as he struggled with five of them.

Giving into the chase, Lon reluctantly began to slow the vehicle down.

The buggy came to sad, inevitable stop.

Amazingly, the natives began to climb down from the buggy. Jake dared to open his eyes and gaze through the cracks in his fingers. The hunting pack had circled them. There was no way out.

The beasts whinnied exactly in the way that horses don't as they reared, resisting the urge to trample the buggy and its helpless incumbents to death.

The explorers looked around them. There must have been a hundred of the creatures.

Instinctively, they all put their hands up.

'Okay, we don't want any trouble,' said Lon.

Silence.

'We come in peace,' said Random.

'You don't get to do the talking here,' spat Lon.

'Do you think this is a good time to argue?' replied Random.

A female voice came forth from the hoard.

'Who among you is the leader of your tribe?'

'I am,' said Random and Lon at the same time.

The circle parted a little. From the void, a warrior rode forward, wearing a crown that looked like a collection of pan pipes.

'How can this be? There can only be one who makes decisions for your tribe?'

'We're a committee,' said Random. 'Who may I ask is addressing us?'

'Very formal,' Anji muttered.

'You are trespassing along our territory Trespassing is punishable with incarceration.'

'I'm sorry we didn't know. We were following a trail and it led us through here. Believe me, we did not mean to intrude,' said Random.

'Who are you?' asked Anji.

'I am Solenia. Ruler of the Spectronians.'

'What are they saying?' asked Auger.

'Of course,' exclaimed Random. He turned to his friends. 'Remember the translation capabilities of the Venus II? It must be working, that's why we know what the Spectrons are saying!'

'And Lon and the others,' said Anji.

'Not a clue,' said Etherton, answering Auger's original question.

'Pleased to meet you Solenia,' replied Lon.

Random looked at the explorer curiously.

'You speak Spectronian?'

'You pick up all kinds of languages when you've been to as many places as I have,' said Lon.

'You are strangers here. We cannot allow peoples of this world to roam our plains without having approved of them first.'

Jake gazed at Solenia with teenage lust. She had long, flowing, golden locks and a body that he had only seen in movies. True, she also looked like she had bathed in a rainbow fountain, her skin just as vibrant as the rest of this amazing planet. Indeed, had it not been for the strange alien horses they appeared to be riding, Jake was certain he wouldn't have seen her at all...except for that glorious hair.

Anji looked over and noticed that Jake had a vacant look in his eye...far vaguer than that he usually possessed, and immediately thought it inappropriate to laugh.

'We mean you no harm,' Random assured her.

'Then why do you come here to Spectron.'

'Spectron. I thought this planet was called Spectronia?'

'That is what the non-we call it. Only true natives of Spectron call this great planet by her full name. Now I shall ask you again, why do you come here?'

'I can't tell you,' replied Lon.

Solenia and her warriors raised their spears.

'Woah, woah, woah, there's no need for that!' said Random.

'I've come a long way. I'm not giving away our intent,' Lon said in a hushed tone towards him.

'We do come in peace though, I assure you.'

Solenia's eyes narrowed.

'You come with us.'

'I'm afraid we cannot,' Lon argued.

'You come with us!' Solenia repeated forcefully.

Lon exhaled.

'Yeah, let's go with her,' Jake dribbled.

Anji shot another look of disapproval at him.

'Do what they say,' Random urged Lon.

Lon growled in anger and sat back in his chair.

The circle began to move forward, the beasts maintaining their formation around the captured explorers, like travellers surrounded by Indians in the Wild West.

'Random? What are we going to do?' asked Anji.

'I'm sure we'll work something out,' he smiled, placing a reassuring hand on her arm.

Anji's eyes were a pool of worry.

Random hid his by closing them.

VII

Random's arms were going dead. He looked up at them as they dangled from the wall. Try as he might to wiggle them back into life, the manacles were too tight around his wrists. He huffed and looked at his fellow captives.

Anji and Jake looked thoroughly fed up. Auger had spent the last two hours pulling at her restraints and was still convinced she could snap them from the wall. Etherton looked sad, scared for he and his counterpart's future. Lon just sat there; a steely expression of cold determination washed over his face.

'They are going to eat us, I'm sure of it!' cried Etherton.

'If they do then I hope I'm the starter. I don't think I could stomach seeing you lot being served up on a platter,' said Anji.

'How's Skateboard holding up?' asked Jake.

Anji looked to her left to check on their AI robot. He was in a hell of a state. The Spectronians had clamped him down in a contraption that resembled a vice and had placed a magnet on his back, incapacitating his circuitry so he was less likely to hatch an escape plan.

'DWATERFUNGERNUFF,' he waffled.

'Did anyone get that?' Jake asked hopefully.

'Yes, it means, "shut up everyone, I'm trying to think!"' snapped Lon.

Random scowled.

'You may be angry, Lon, but snapping at my friend won't get you out of here.'

'Oh yeah, what will then?'

'Telling them what they want to know would help.'

Lon spat on the floor. 'I'd rather die than give them any advantage over me.'

'What advantage?' asked Anji.

'The Flux of course! If we tell them what we are here for then it's highly conceivable that they will leave us to rot in here and go get it for themselves.'

'Well, what if they did? You could always break out and take it back then? In a way they'd be doing your dirty work,' Random pointed out.

'No one, no one, but me are getting their disgusting hands on the Flux!'

Anji looked over at Etherton.

'Has he always been like this?'

'Ever since we lost the Flux, yes.'

'Well, he must pay well.'

'What makes you say that?'

Anji raised her eyebrows.

'I can't see why you'd still be with him if he didn't.'

Lon glared at Anji. If looked could kill, she'd have been dead instantly.

'Anji,' Random tried to temper his friend. 'Antagonising each other isn't going to help things. I'm getting a bit fed up of hanging around myself but we have to think of the positives.'

'Such as?' asked Auger, finally taking a break from her efforts.

'Such as, if we can get the Spectronians on our side, reason with them, we might be able to get the Flux back quicker than we expected.'

'And how do you propose we do that?' said Lon.

'By talking and being civil.'

'Ha!' cried Lon.

'Well then, let me have a go. Maybe I can reason with her.'

'No.'

'Lon.'

'You're a child.'

'Random's much more than that,' said Anji. 'You think you are the only one whose keeping secrets? If we told you what we have done in the past you'd start to take us a little more seriously.'

Lon's fists unclenched.

'Go on them enlighten me.'

'Not until you tell us who's got the Flux currently,' said Random.

'No.'

'Why not?'

'Because it's nothing to do with you, that's why.'

'We are risking our lives here Lon, for goodness' sake, give us at least that!' Random was starting to lose patience with him.

'Strakonis,' said a voice.

Lon looked over in Auger's direction.

'Traitor!'

'Whose Strakonis?' asked Anji.

'Come on, everyone knows who Rogar Strakonis is,' said Etherton.

'Well, we don't,' said Jake.

Auger continued.

'Rogar Strakonis is known the galaxy over as one of the richest explorers in the twelve-belt system. For years he and Lon have fought, testing one another, racing against themselves to find the treasures of the cosmos.'

'In short then, he's a rival,' affirmed Random.

'More than that,' said Lon. 'Strakonis has used his wealth to buy real estate in the twelve-belt system.'

'What's that when it's at home? asked Jake.

'A ribbon of planets hanging in twelve rows in the stars. Strakonis has taken over half of that sector of space, built his empire of wealth on selling the land.'

'So, he's a sort of intergalactic landlord?' asked Anji.

'It's a little more complicated than that,' said Lon.

Before he could continue his story, the dungeon gates swung open. An impossibly tall warrior stood with weapon in hand in the doorway.

'You. Come.'

The warrior was pointing at Random.

'Oh, alright if you insist.'

The prison guard, key in hand, made for Random's manacles. Deep down, Random knew that he could snap them as easy as a child could a twig. That's one of the advantages of having super strength. Luckily, neither Anji or Jake had given that fact away. Judging by their moods, he guessed that they knew that he was buying time for something. But then what would he have learnt of the explorers he and his friends had aligned themselves with? But he had wanted to know what Lon was really up to. There was something fishy about the three of them, and now he was getting close to the real reason of Lon's secrecy. But then why didn't he want to tell them the full story in the first place? He'd have to find out.

But first, he had to make sure he could bargain for their freedom.

Solenia heard the knocking from the other end of the court room. She took her time making her way back to her throne, resplendent in gold and burgundy materials, flanked either side by guards and two handmaidens. Sitting down, she beckoned the two footmen at the door to allow her prisoner to enter. As the long doors creaked open, Random, accompanied by two spear wielding guards, made his way of the long rainbow coloured gangway to the throne.

'Lovely place you've got here,' he said. 'You should see where they have put us up!'

Solenia smiled.

'A cheeky one. Very brave too.'

'Well, I try my best,' he smiled. Random looked above him. A glorious diamond window hung high above them, the sun blazing through and washing the court room with its brilliant rays.

'Tell you what, after you threw us in that dungeon, I never thought I'd get to see the sun again.'

'It clearly is not yours judging by the colour of your skin.'

'Oh, no one should be judged by the colour of their skin,' he retorted.

'And yet many do. We've had visitors from other worlds here before. None so much like you. Each and every one of them have threatened to disrupt the peace that we fight so hard to retain on Spectronia.'

'Can't be a lot of peace if you are fighting,' said Random. He
nodded at the spears. 'I mean, these can't be just for decoration,
can they?'

'We are at liberty to protect ourselves. Show me a Queen who
does not protect her subjects and I'll show you a broken world.'

Random smiled at her with appreciation.

'I wanted you brought to me as I thought I may get answers
from you. You seem different to the others in your party.'

'I am. Myself and the two humans, we crash landed here and
were rescued by Lon and the others.'

'What caused this accident?'

Random thought hard and fast to hide the truth. If this truly
were a peaceful planet, how could he tell the ruler of it that they
were on the run from Egyptian gods, who if they were unlucky
could turn up at any moment and blow the planet up? In that split
second, he believed that the truth was not what Solenia needed to
hear right now.

'An engine malfunction in our ship. Our AI robot has managed
to fix the fault and within a few days we should be able to leave
again.'

'If you are allowed to leave my custody, that is.'

Random blinked.

'Yeah, good point.'

'What is your name?'

'Random.'

'Random. My people are great in number but we prefer to live a
life in the shadows. We do not ask for the attention of others, nor
do we seek the treasures that I am sure your companion Lon
desires. However, my main priority for all is the safety of my
subjects. I suspect that your friend has come in search of another
here on our world.'

'I believe so,' said Random.

'He has eluded our grasp. Answer me this truthfully, purple
one, is this stranger likely to be a threat to us here on Spectronia?'

'It's hard to say,' said Random honestly. 'I believe there is a rivalry between said person and Lon. Whether it's a violent one, I don't think so. But it's clear to me he has something that belongs in Lon's possession. If you could let us go, not only can I keep my eye on Lon, but I reckon we could make sure that this Strakonis fella also leaves this planet well alone.'

'Oh?' said Solenia. 'How so?'

'Well, if Lon takes back what he believes is his he certainly won't hang around Spectronia to lose it again.'

Solenia got up and stood in front of Random. He stood at the foot of a row of steps leading up to her. She towered over him, looking down but not lowering her head to meet his gaze.

'This...thing, he is in possession of. Is it a weapon?'

'In the wrong hands, it could be.'

She reeled.

'Then we must not let the prospect of conflict linger.'

Solenia sat calmly back on her throne.

'Random, I shall give you your freedom. On one condition.'

Random bowed. 'Thank you, your grace. What can I do in return?'

'There is more to you than meets the eye. I can sense it. A great power resides within you. If you can prove my senses true, then I am fully confident that you can guide Lon to finding what he has lost and in doing so, ensuring that this Strakonis is also detained and taken away from this planet. Are you up to this task?'

'Saving worlds and stopping the bad guys? It's almost a hobby of mine.'

'Then go. I shall see to it that your friends are also set free. My chief architect can help you find easier routes to any journey you may need to take.'

'That's great news, thank you your grace.'

Random bowed again and turned for the door.

'And Random?'

He stopped and faced Solenia.

'Go well.'

VIII

Before long, Anji, Jake, Lon, Auger and Etherton had been released from their prison and joined Random in the throne room. Not that they were very grateful for it, especially Anji.

'So why couldn't you do your usual kick ass routine and get us out of there?' she whispered in hush tones as the group waited for the Chief Architect to arrive with some information Solenia had promised Random would be of some help.

'Because I wanted to find out what that lot were up to,' he whispered back.

'But did you have to leave us chained up for so long?' butted in Jake.

'Alright, I'm sorry I couldn't get us out of there sooner. But we need to know what kind of people we are dealing with here. Something tells me they aren't your average archaeologists.'

'Yeah, they're space ones!' said Anji.

'No, there's something else. Don't you feel it?'

Random knelt down towards Skateboard, who was busying himself scanning the area.

'Skateboard, found out anything interesting?'

'Yes, sir. It appears the Spectronians live underground. This throne room is roughly four hundred metres under the planet's surface.'

'How?' said Lon, overhearing the conversation.

'We didn't go down even a flight of stairs!' said Etherton. 'I think your robot might be broken.'

'I can assure you my diodes are functioning perfectly,' Skateboard replied. 'The tunnels are submerged but oxygen is filtered down here by air vents in the sand.'

'I'm surprised they don't get clogged!' said Anji.

'How did we get under here if none of us noticed we were going underground?' asked Random.

'The tunnels act on a pivot. As weight is transferred, the corridors at the entrance tip, but gravity keeps those walking towards the other end upright, replicating a normal experience.'

'Sounds cool!' said Jake.

'So how do we get out?' asked Auger.

At that moment, the Chief Architect arrived in the throne room, armed with roles upon roles of parchment paper. His head was the shape of light bulb, only fifty times bigger, and like everyone else on this Spectronia, his skin was all the colours of the rainbow.

'So, so sorry to have kept you all,' he said in a flustered tone as he tried to clear space on a small table. 'Oh! Wow! Aliens!'

'What did he call me?' said Auger.

'I know right?' said Jake.

'No, genuinely, it's starting to grate not being able to understand anyone on this crazy planet.'

'I've never seen real life aliens before! I mean obviously there's other beings in this universe, but to actually be standing in the same room as them. Wait until I tell the kids!'

Random offered his hand.

'Random.'

'Yes, isn't it!' the Architect enthused. 'Possil's the name.'

'Anji's mine, this is Jake, Skateboard and Random.'

'Oh!' I do apologise.' He scuttled over to Lon.

'And you are?'

Lon stared at him unmoved.

Possil's smile ebbed away.

'Right. Anyway, our great ruler has informed me that you would like to see plans of the area?'

'A little more than that,' said Lon. 'We are looking for stolen goods and every second we waste with pleasantries the further it gets away.'

'Ignore him,' said Random quietly. 'Any help you can offer us is greatly appreciated.'

Possil regained his smile. He unfurled one of the huge parchments and used the others to keep either side from folding back in on themselves and beckoned the travellers to the table.

'This is the Western Seam of Spectronia.'

'That's more like it,' Lon's interest was well and truly peaked. 'This is where we need to go.'

Anji ran her eyes over the crude drawings.

'Looks a bit rocky to me.'

'It is, Miss. You'll have to go easy along the mountain sides. But as soon as you reach the pinnacle you can get on one of the roads and it should make for a better journey.'

'Skateboard, could you scan these images?'

'Certainly, sir.' A small blue light began to swipe over the map.

'But these maps look ancient; won't the landscape have changed since they were made?'

'Jake's got a point; do you have anything a little more up-to-date?' asked Random.

'These maps may have been commissioned by our founding Mothers and Fathers twenty centuries ago, but the landscape has not changed in that time,' said Possil.

'What? Not even through climate change?' asked Jake.

'Climate what?' enquired Possil.

'You're all babbling again,' snapped Lon. 'What is the quickest way to this bit here?' he pointed to a void beyond the mountain scape.

Possil's face fell.

'This is where you want to go?'

'Obviously,' said Lon.

'Well...the quickest way to the Dead Space is through the mountains is the Silent Path.'

Anji tutted. 'Why do all these places have to have such ominous names? Why can't it be called Fluffy Field or something like that?'

Jake laughed.

'The names aren't meant to intimidate, Miss, it's just that no-one goes to these places anymore.'

'Why not?' asked Random.

'Well, they are not quite forbidden as it were it's just...'

'People went there and never came back, did they?' said Random in a grave tone.

'Typical,' muttered Jake. He rolled his eyes at Anji.

'Never a dull minute,' she tutted back and then shot a sneaky smile at him.

'Well, I suppose we'd better just keep out wits about us,' said Random as he got up off his haunches. 'How safe can we expect to be?'

'Oh, you should be fine. Spectronia as you know by now if a peaceful planet.'

'We should split into two teams. One goes along the Silent Path, the other through the mountain side. That way we increase our chances of catching up with Strakonis before he moves on...if he moves on,' said Lon.

'You mean, this could be a trap?' asked Random.

'You never know with him,' said Lon. 'Random, if you and your crew are still willing to come, we can take both paths. Are you with us?'

Despite the danger and lack of awareness of Lon's overall plan, Random had no hesitation to throw his hat in the ring. Even Anji and Jake, despite their recent urge for a quieter life, were both thinking that this adventure could be fun. They had caught Random's infectious quest for excitement yet again.

'I'll explain the plan again to Auger and Etherton in a moment. Auger can take your friends Jake and Skateboard through the Silent Path. The rest of us will take the rocky mountainside,' said Lon.

'Oh great, I get the one with the creepy name,' said Jake sarcastically.

'How will we stay in contact?' asked Anji.

'Ah!' Random's spontaneous response made them all jump. He pointed at his two human friends. 'You two, have you got your mobile phones on you?'

Anji felt for the front pocket in her dungarees and produced her handheld device.

'Check!'

Jake riffled through his pockets, producing all manner of fluff and rubbish before digging out his.

'Double check!'

'We can modify them so we can stay in contact, Skateboard?' asked Random.

'On it, sir.'

'We've got all the equipment we need with us in the buggy. I'm presuming our stuff is no longer confiscated?'

'No, you are free beings now,' Possil reassured. 'And I am relieved for it. You're welcome to scan all the maps you like, just please leave the originals here. They have been in my family for generations.'

'You didn't choose your job then?' asked Jake.

'No, I was born into it.' Possil offered his hand to Random. Good luck to you all, and stay safe. Before you go, can I just ask one small favour?'

'What's that?' asked Random.

'Get I get a photo with you all for my kids?

XI

Without any delay, mainly at Lon's behest, the travellers were on their way again. The buggy continued across the sand dunes, continuing their original journey and after a couple of hours they had reached the foot of the mountainside.

'Right, this is where we leave you,' said Lon.

'Now take care, you three, that's an order,' said Random.

'Yes Dad!' joked Jake.

They picked up their things and jumped out of the buggy. Jake disembarked first, but caught his foot in the strap of his back pack and fell backwards out of the vehicle and into a crumpled heap.

'Don't worry, I'll look after him,' said Skateboard.

'He's going to need it!' said Random.

'Keep in constant contact,' asked Lon, 'And Auger, make sure that you stick to the plan. If you find Strakonis before we do, do what you can to contain him. Watch out for traps too.'

'No one said anything about traps!' said Jake, dusting himself down.

'He's an archaeologist in possession of one of the most prized artefacts in the universe. He knows we are coming...and he isn't going to make it easy for us to take it from him.'

'We will do what we can, not sure what help the boy will be but the robot will be useful,' said Auger.

'Oi! I might surprise you!' said Jake.

'Goodbye Lon, and good luck.' Auger held her middle three fingers in a salute. Lon and Etherton reciprocated.

'See ya later, alligators,' waved Jake.

Auger threw a digital mapping tablet in Jake's arms and produced a compass from her pocket.

'Come on, time isn't on our side.'

Random and Anji watched on as the figures of Auger and Jake, with Skateboard gliding gracefully next to them disappeared into silhouette and off in the far distance.

The sun was baking down on them now and Etherton, a creature who was more used to the shade and darkness looked pensive.

'We'd better get a move on too, Lon. Any more time in this heat and you may have to leave me behind.'

'There's worse things that can happen than that,' sneered Lon.

The buggy swiveled and Lon, using the map that Random had Skateboard produce from the original copy, looked for the opening to the mountainside road.

'He's not very nice to people, is he? You'd have thought he'd be a bit kinder to get people on side,' observed Anji.

'I know. I'm surprised they put up with it, if you ask me,' said Random. 'You struggle in mild heat then, Etherton?' he asked, turning his attention to the mole like creature.

'My race, like the Spectronians live underground. We aren't used to prolonged periods on the surface.'

'But Lomes are great scavengers, the best even,' said Lon, 'So it's handy to keep Etherton around.

'Where are you from anyway?'

'Oh, you wouldn't have heard of it,' said Anji.

'Try us,' replied Etherton.

'Well, Jake and I are from Earth.'

'Never heard of it myself. What about you, Random?'

'I'd rather not say.'

'Looks like I'm not the only one keeping secrets, eh, Random?' said Lon, scoffing.

Before Random could respond, the buggy was thrown into chaos. The passengers screamed and shouted as they were catapulted from the vehicle and thrown onto the harsh ground. Random fell first and caught Anji and they rolled together over and over, spinning and twirling until they hit the mountain wall. A nearby sound of crunching metal was audible to all of them as they eventually came to a stop.

Panting, Random shook his head, trying to throw his vision back into focus. As he lay flat on his back, aching and hurt, he concentrated his gaze on the sun until there was only one of them and not the seven or eight, he saw initially.

As soon as they all bled together, he struggled to his feet.

'Anj – are you okay?'

She grunted, face down in the dirt.

'I'll live, what happened?'

He held out his hand and helped her upright.

'Take it easy, sit on that rock over there and catch your breath,' he helped her onto the boulder and went over to the others.

Etherton and Lon had fallen not far from them, but looked like they had come off worse.

'Ah, my arm,' cried Etherton.

'Let me take a look.' Random had limited knowledge when it came to medical situations, but he had skim read first aid during his short stay on Earth.

It didn't look good. The bone was jutting out at an awkward angle. Random held Etherton's arm gently, the bristles of his hairy arms rubbing against his coarse hands.

'Lon?'

'Yeah, don't worry about me, I'm fine,' said Lon with more than a hint of sarcasm in his voice.

'Then come and help me!'

Lon scurried to his feet and made his way over to his companion.

'Looks like a nasty break. I'll head over to the buggy and get the aid box.'

'I'd better call Jake and Skateboard,' said Anji. She got her phone out of her pocket. The screen was smashed.

'Urgh!' she cried, throwing it away. 'Just my luck!'

'Keep it on you,' said Random. 'They can still contact us if they need to.'

'Yeah, right,' Anji moaned. Back home she couldn't keep off her phone. Until Random turned up, that was. Since then, she's been so busy saving worlds with her new friends, and the fact that there was no signal in space, using it couldn't have been further from her mind. But now it had been tinkered with by Skareboard, maybe she could have contacted friends at home if needed. But now it was broken, the glimmer of contact with home was gone. Until she could nick Jakes that was, although the chances of him not smashing it up too were remote as he was often far more careless than she was!

Plus, who would pay the phone tariff for a phone call to Earth from thousands of millions of miles away?

Lon got to his feet and made his way over to what now was little more than a ruined pile of twisted metal. Most of the supplies and equipment had been tipped out and lay strewn across the path. Lon surveyed the wreckage and sighed. Most of their stuff was either on fire or broken.

'We may have to improvise,' he said back to Random. Taking his jacket off, he fashioned it into a sling and knelt down beside the stricken Etherton. Carefully, he and Random took the broken limb and fed it through the sling as Etherton swore in a number of languages that Random has never heard before.

'There,' said Lon as he tied a knot in the back of the jacket.

'Anj, go and take a look in the wreckage, see if you can find the first aid kit,' said Random.

'Why, what are you going to do?'

'Find out what caused the accident.'

Random and Lon made their way back to the spot where the crash took place when suddenly they walked into something hard that whacked into their shins.

'What the-' said Lon as he rubbed his lower legs.

Random held his arms out in place. Hesitantly, he felt for the anomaly. Although the area looked as normal as a rainbow road at the foot of a rainbow coloured mountain could be, something felt weird. Using his hands to test their road block he discovered what had catapulted the buggy into the air.

'Lon,' he said. 'Your Strakonis friend has wicked mind. Look.'

He pulled Lon to the side. From their new perspective, there appeared to be a three-foot-tall road block standing in the middle of the road.

'Camouflage,' spat Lon. 'Strakonis is far from a friend. He wants us dead.'

Random nodded.

'We'd better tread more carefully.'

'Random.'

Anji walked towards them, carrying a battered little box with its lid dented outward, full of what looked like pills.

'They will help to numb the pain, confirmed Lon. 'Good. We can't stay here.'

'You can't be serious?' Random was flabbergasted by his lack of care for the wounded Etherton.

'If we stay here, we are leaving ourselves open to more attacks. Take what you can, we're going to have to continue the journey on foot.'

Random shot a look of pure frustration at Anji.

'We'd better do what he says, otherwise he may leave all three of us behind!'

'Well, let's hope that Jake and Skateboard are having a better time than us!' said Anji.

*

Jake was through with walking. Auger was much faster, and taller, than he was, and seemed to be taking giant strides ahead of the rest of them.

'Any chance we can go a little slower?' he huffed.

'No.'

He despaired.

'Skateboard, any chance I can get on your back and you can take us?'

'Negative for now, sir. The extra weight would compound my circuitry and I would have to dedicate more run time to my gravitational elements to maintain a steady pace.'

Although Skateboard knew this information was true, he hoped he hadn't made it too obvious that what he really thought was that Jake needed to improve his fitness.

'Well, we can take our time, I'm sure.'

'We can't,' said Auger. 'We must get to the Silent Path before night fall. The temperature of Spectronia decreases significantly in the evening.'

'I'd rather freeze than drown in my own sweat!' he cried.

Auger did not possess the longest of fuses when it came to her temper and Jake was trying it thoroughly. 'Is there anything you do except complain?'

'Lady, I'm a teenager. Trust me, if it was an Olympic sport I'd have the gold, silver AND bronze medals!'

'You say the weirdest things,' she muttered. 'What's a teenager?'

'You don't have teenagers where you come from?'

'Well, I wouldn't be asking you if we did, would I?'

Jake frowned. There was no need to bite at him all the time. He began to wonder whether they had been unfortunate enough to find the three grumpiest explorers in the cosmos. Then he remembered. They were on a mission to regain what they felt was rightfully theirs. Of course, they were going to be needly. He decided fighting back wasn't the best response...for now.

'Well...it's the age you are at when you go from being a boy or girl into a man or woman.'

'Ah,' she smiled. 'So that explains why you and your friends are so small.'

'Small? On a good day I'm five foot one!'

Auger turned and gave Jake a little smile.

'Does your species not go through the same?' Jake probed.

'No, no we are lumed.'

'Lumed?'

'A fascinating form of gestation,' Skateboard interrupted.

Jake nodded his head as if to acknowledge he was completely in the knowhow of what the word "gestation" meant.

'My people do not reproduce in the conventional way that others do in the universe.'

'How then?' said Jake. 'Do they hatch?'

'No,' replied Auger. She leant closer to the blonde adolescent.

'We're grown. The Kataowa are grown in lumes and batches of 12.'

'I bet it's hell remembering everyone's birthdays then!'

'Of course not. We are all born on the same day.'

'Oh,' said Jake. 'Alright Christmas then!'

'Again, you'll have to explain that one to me,' she said.

'Maybe some other time, that's awesome! So, you are born fully grown adults?'

'Yes,' she took a glance down at the map, trying to maintain their pace.

'Why twelve? Six boys and six girls?'

'We are neither.'

'What neither boys or girls?'

'No.'

'But you look like a woman?'

'I look how I look,' she said firmly.

'There is no need for gender identity on Kataowa, sir,' said Skateboard, 'they do not reproduce like humans, remember?'

'Humans?' Auger cried. 'So, you're from Earth then?'

Jake's jaw dropped. 'How do you know about Earth!?'

'We've been there.'

'What?!' Jake was flummoxed.

'How? When?'

'Centuries ago. Long before your time.'

Jake turned to Skateboard for confirmation that he wasn't going mad.

'Centuries? But you look so young!'

'We don't age. We can live for a long time.'

'It is true, sir, the Kataowa's average life span is just short of two thousand years.'

'So...how old are you now?'

'Don't ask a woman such questions,' she quipped

Jake smiled. Finally, she was starting to warm to him which was something of a blessed relief.

'I have so many questions right now.'

'Well, which ones the most pertinent?'

'Why did you go there?'

'We were looking for an artefact in a dusty plane. Unfortunately for us we had to make a hasty exit. You see, the thing we came for was on a monument and we had to be hasty in our escape.'

'What was it you took?'

'An element that we had detected as one of a kind in its field. I won't bore you with the details but your people had built it into a monument and we took it under the cover of darkness. Bit of a fiddly one so we didn't do a good job but I'm sure they fixed it after we had gone. Knowing how stupid they were, they probably thought their gods had done something to punish them or something.'

'Wow. What was it that you actually took?'

'The nose.'

Jake frowned.

'Sounds familiar. Oh well.'

Skateboard searched his memory databanks.

'I don't suppose you came across the Osirans when you were there, did you?'

Auger looked down at the robot.

'They are long gone.'

I wouldn't be too sure of that, he thought.

'Ssshh!' Jake hissed. The group stopped in their tracks.

'Can you hear that?'

Silence.

'No.'

Skateboard turned up his audio sensors.

'There's something coming from just over that ridge,' he confirmed.

Auger craned her neck to get a better look.

A huge dust cloud began to fold over the horizon.

'Run.'

'What is it?' asked Jake.

'A sand storm. Quick, now! Run, run! Get back to the mountain!'

Jake fell to the floor in horror. A burst of brilliant colour exploded into view, crashing over the ridge and looming over them, blocking out the sky.

He scrambled to his feet and shot towards the other two. Ignoring his own wheezy breath and terrible lack of fitness, he pelted as fast as his little legs would carry him. There was a tremendous roar from behind them and a spray of sand particles. Jake began to panic. He reminded himself of the Sandman who blew up their school when they first met Random and the devastation he caused. This was like a thousand sandmen put together!

Auger and Skateboard were too quick for him and were tearing away and out of view.

'Wait!' he screamed but doubted they could hear him.

A stitch formed in his side and tears began to collect in the corners of his eyes. Surely it wasn't going to end like this?

He stumbled forward, his body giving up on him.

Jake didn't have time to curse. He didn't even have time to close his eyes and wait for the inevitable.

With a great whoosh of power, Jake was scooped up off his back and the next thing he knew he was gliding through the air, leaving the sand storm far behind.

'Skateboard?'

'Hold on, sir.'

Skateboard zoomed away from danger and into a cavity in the mountainside that Auger had found. They hid behind a small boulder and ducked as the sand storm slammed with such force into the mountain shuddered.

Cautiously, Auger looked up over the boulder.

'We'll have to wait here until the storm subsides, great!' she threw a nearby rock into the ground.

Jake held his knees close to his body and tried to regain his breath.

'So much for gravitational dampeners, eh Skateboard, but thank you. I thought I was a goner there.'

'It's quite alright, sir, and now you know why I lied first time around,' he quipped.

X

Unaware of the other groups troubles as they were on the other side of the huge mountainside, Random continued to fiddle with Anji's phone. Although he was carrying the main bulk of back packs and equipment, his friend had also insisted on him having a look at her broken device.

'I'm telling you, Anj, even though I am from another world there's nothing I can really do for this,' he gave up after a few minutes of tinkering.

'I thought you'd say that, thanks anyway. How are you coping, Etherton?'

'I've no idea,' said the injured member of the party. I'm relieved that what Lon lacks in bedside manner he will make up for in leniency.'

He was holding nothing else but the digital compass as the other carried the weight.

'The pills should reset your arm fully in an hour or two,' reassured Lon.

'Oh good, I'm relieved that you said that. Only two hours of constant agony to endure.'

'Of course, I could always make it go away instantly.'

'Really, how?'

'Because if you keep up your moaning, I'll put you out of your misery yourself!'

Random threw his load down on the floor firmly.

'Lon, if you continue to bully you're travelling companions, you'll certainly see a less charitable side to me!'

Lon turned. Random was fuming, fists clenched.

'Oh please,' he said wearily. 'You think you can lead this exposition?'

'That's not what I am saying,' said Random. 'But we are volunteers on this expedition and if you keep this anti-social stance up, we are well within our rights to return to the city and leave you to complete it yourself.'

'I don't want to order you, Random...'

'...Good, because I wouldn't advise you to try.'

'Random, please, there really is no need for all this. When you've been with Lon for as long as I have, you learn to ignore his bad moods.'

'That's fine for you to say but we aren't putting up with it,' said Anji.

Lon gave a withering smile.

'Look, this isn't a day trip to the zoo, this is a race against time!'

'We've dealt with worse than this is the past, we'll get over this obstacle, if you stop abusing your workforce. Do we have a deal?'

Lon begrudgingly admired Random for his stance. It takes a lot of courage to stand up to a person like him. But he wasn't the type to apologise.

'Let's keep going,' he replied, before starting off up the path again.

Anji sighed.

'I suppose that's his way of saying sorry!'

'You shouldn't provoke him, Random,' Etherton took his glasses off with one hand and rubbed them against his jacket.

'It's good for him to be reminded that he can't bully his way to winning back this Flux thing,' said Random through gritted teeth.

'Why not? That's how he has got to where he is in life.'

'If it ain't broke, don't fix it, eh?' said Anji.

'Exactly. Lon's a born winner. The Zedron Flux is the first artifact that has ever got away from his grasp. It's also the most important to him. Just take him cautiously.'

'So, he isn't always like this?' asked Anji.

'Actually, sadly he is.'

'Hey, come up here!'

Lon's voice carried back down the path. The others gathered their things up and raced up to meet him.

Turning the corner, they all noticed why his beckon wasn't an angry one.

'Ah,' said Random.

The path came to a sudden stop. In front of them was nothing but a tower of rock, piled up hundreds of feet into the sky.

'Strakonis again, I presume?' Random said.

Lon nodded. 'According to this map the road should continue through here and continue on for twenty miles.'

'Twenty miles?' Anji and Etherton said in unison.

'Strakonis must have blasted a charge deliberately.'

'Or a rock fall happened by accident?'

'This is no accident,' Lon cursed loudly. 'He's always one step ahead, isn't he?'

'Unfortunately for now we have to play his game to keep up,' said Random, 'but we can turn the tide.'

'There's no can't about it. We will. Just makes me mad that I have to dance his merry tune until that eventuality. It's humiliating...but I'll make him pay. Just you see.'

He began to rummage through his back pack.

'Right, there's only one way through and that's over the top.'

'You can't be serious?' said Anji.

'I am never anything but,' said Lon.

'Yes, we noticed that,' muttered Random. 'Fine, let's do it then.'

'But that's going to take forever...and look how high it is! We'll never make it!' Etherton despaired at the thought of climbing.

'Lomes are ground beings. Can't I burrow underneath?'

'The rock density will be too great for the tools we have with us, sorry Etherton, on this occasion I can't see any other alternative but go over the top,' said Random.

'What, with my arm like this?'

'I can carry you.'

'Not with all those bags!'

'Wanna bet?'

'Not really!'

Anji put her hand on Etherton's good arm. 'You'll be fine, Etherton, you'll be in good hands.'

'Oh, so he's taken you piggy backing on a mountain climb before has he?'

'Well...no, but he is incredibly strong.'

'And fast,' Random's eyes were friendly and trustworthy to Etherton. He looked up again and gulped.

'I don't like it.'

'Neither do I but again we are left with no choice,' said Lon as he produced three sets of laser picks. 'That's lucky, there's only three pairs of these anyway. I've got some boot spikes in here too and some bungee cord. Random, you ready to prove just how strong you are?'

'Always,' Random smiled back at him.

'Anj – will you be alright doing this?'

She nodded but deep down her stomach had turned into a
butterfly park. On Earth she has climbed a high wall on trips out
with the children's home her and Jake lived in and she was fine
with that, but comparing this challenge to that was like using
chop sticks to cut down a tree. But a spark had lit inside her and a
fire was burgeoning for her to be adventurous again. She'd been
heavily affected by her experiences on Genocia, almost hiding
from the universe on all those cosmic holiday resorts. But the
spirit was awoken within her again.

'Let's do it. But Random?'

'Yes, Anj?'

If you let me fall to my death, I'll kill you.'

She grinned as he laughed.

'I'll hold you to that. Right, Etherton, if I tie you to my waste
you can ascend up below me along with the bags if you want?'

'Sure, more padding for the drop!' he replied.

'Good man, right let's get a shake on then.'

He looked up again. The scale of the climb was intimidating but
Random hoped that his bravado had done enough to shake off
any indication to the others that this was going to much harder,
and scarier than he was letting on.

XI

Jake awoke with a startle.

'Sir, sir, Miss Auger has left the cave.'

'She'll be killed!'

'No, I can assure you that the storm has passed. You slept
though most of it.'

'Well,' yawned Jake, 'When you've ran as much as I just did, it's
wise to have a nap to refuel for the next life-threatening dash.'

Wiping his eyes, he got up and shook this head before leaving
the cave with Skateboard in tow.

He peered out onto the calm landscape. It was as though
nothing had happened. There was no devastation, nothing. Just
peace and quiet.

Jake scanned the horizon.

'Hey, I thought you said that Auger was out here already?'

'She is...' Skateboard took a look around him. '...At least, she was.'

They both looked at each other.

'Can you scan her? See where she's got to?'

'Doing it now, sir,' said Skateboard. He set his tracking parameters a little wider than the distance Jake could see in front of him and surveyed the land.

Nothing.

He widened them further.

Still nothing.

He then switched them to horizontal, in his mind thinking there may be quick sand nearby, in which case, she was in terrible trouble indeed, and they were probably too late to help her.

Skateboard switched his sensors with a sense of dread and learned the terrible truth.

'Sir, I've found her.'

'Great!'

'Not quite, sir. She isn't alone.'

'More tribal warriors? Excellent.'

'No, not that either sir. There's another heartbeat. A Much, much bigger heartbeat.'

The ground beneath their feet began to shudder. Jake tried to keep his balance. A rumbling emitted from under the sand.

Suddenly, a huge creature that looked like a giant snake, exploded from under them, knocking both to the floor. It kept going, raising higher and higher towards the sky, its brown and red body massive in diameter and wider than a skyscraper.

'Oh my god!' exclaimed Jake.

'Quick get back to the cave!' screamed Skateboard but before they could move, the creature's vacant, worm like head reared down towards them. From nowhere, a slit opened and a disgusting salivating mouth began to drool down upon them. Jake cried in fear. Skateboard leaked his fuel but it was too late to do anything now.

With one fell swoop, the monster swooped down and ate both of them whole.

The monster's belly was warm and squidgy. There was nothing for Auger to grapple on to even attempt to climb out from within its humid stomach. The gloop and remnants of previous meals lay in horrific piles all around her. She tried again, cringing at the slime oozing down the stomach wall before grunting in defeat as she slipped onto the floor of the monster's gut.

She turned to her bag, searching for some dynamite. If she wasn't able to climb her way out, then she'd have to blow it out. The only other escape route was less desirable than death to her!

Auger huffed. No dynamite. Only a knife. Fat lot of good that'd do, she thought.

All of a sudden, she heard cries from high above her. Quiet at first, but they were getting louder and louder.

She rolled to one side, covering herself in more of the slime, taking evasive action as Jake and Skateboard crashed into the prison with her sending volumes of yucky gut juice high into the air and crashing back down upon them. Their bodies bounced up and down for a bit, sloshing the contents of the creature's belly cascading all around.

Jake tried to talk but all he could say was a multitude of noises that were incoherent to even Skateboard, who was doing his best to work out what he was exclaiming. He gave up and checked his diodes.

'Anything broken, sir?'

Jake continued to moan and grunt.

'Miss Auger, I'm so relieved to see you're okay.'

'Okay...OKAY!!?' she raged. 'Look at where we are!'

'Present situation withstanding at least we are all well,' said Skateboard, doing his best to look on the bright side.

Jake coughed and wiped his eyes again, although instead of sleep descending this time there was a foul-smelling yellow liquid that poured down his cheeks.

'I think I'm going to be sick,' he declared. 'Am I where I think we are or am I dead and this is my hell? Cos' either way. I think I'm going to need to change my pants!'

'Stop waffling, we need to figure a way out of here,' said Auger as she picked him up. 'Skateboard, can you get us out of here?'

'Indeed, I can, Miss. But first we shall have to make good of two things.'

'Like?'

'Yes, I can get you all out of here. But first we need to make sure that the creature's mouth is open. We might also be quicker if we can ride a tidal wave of stomach acid.'

'You mean you want to give this thing indigestion?!' cried Jake.

'Precisely. If we stay here too long, we may be digested. I summise that we are currently standing in the creature's lower intestine. Who knows how long it will be before we move on...'

'Well, I'm not hanging around waiting to find out!' said Auger. 'Let's do it!'

'How?' asked Jake.

'I don't know ask your metal friend; I've never been inside a monster before.'

'What are we surrounded by? Smell the air,' implored Skateboard.

They both did and instantly regretted it.

'Poo!' exclaimed Jake.

'Not yet,' corrected Skateboard. 'Does it smell nocsious?'

'I'd say!'

'Then that's the answer. Right, you two, jump up and down and keep going. I'll start a small fire...'

'We'll go up in smoke!' said Auger.

'No, we won't. As soon as a burst of gas propels us upward, I'll swoop us up and send us on our way. Trust me, you two.'

Jake and Auger gave each other an uncertain smile and did what they were told. Ungodly gurgles surrounded them.

They all hopped and jumped as hard as they could, the sounds becoming louder and louder.

It didn't take long before the sand worm was beginning to feel the effects of the mayhem erupting within its stomach. From deep within its bowels a rumbling sound began to bubble from underneath their jumping feet.

'Oh my god, I think it's working!' exclaimed Jake. 'Please let this work!'

'Here we go!' said Skateboard, in a tone that made Jake and Auger think he was enjoying himself!

A giant surge of gas blew up from within the monster's stomach and spun its unwilling incumbents around and around like socks in a tumble dryer. Jake and Auger screamed and clawed for something to slow them down as they whirled around and around, faster and faster.

Their bodies rose higher with every passing second.

Skateboard, measuring the power of the whirlwind waited for the right moment to spring to life. He allowed himself to be whisked around like the others in the smelly gas cloud, getting closer and closer to his friends.

'Grab hold of me,' he urged. Auger did as she was instructed.

He maneuvered himself closer to Jake and the boy grabbed hold of the other side of Skateboard's chase.

'Hold on!'

With a jolt of energy, Skateboard fired his retros. This act would have been fairly innocuous were it not for the flammable gas surrounding them but, on this occasion, it wasn't a very good idea to light a flame when you're inside the body of a dangerous alien creature.

With an amazing force that nearly ripped Jake's face from his skull, the trio were propelled like a bullet back up the monster's neck, clinging to dear life whilst feeling the flames licking at his shoes.

Their velocity carried them further towards their escape. Auger began to lose her grip. Skateboard felt her palm imprint began to slip so he produced two grapples from within his body and fastened them around his friend's waists.

'We're almost there!' Skateboard yelled as another gurgling roar began to rumble. The explosion had ebbed away and they could feel the worm begin to sway. Skateboard adjusted their flight trajectory accordingly and whooshed around a junction that was actually the monster's neck. Within moments, they smashed through a glunky mass of putrid matter and slammed hard into what felt like a sandy floor.

Skateboard adjusted his optical settings and released the grapples around Auger and Jake's waists. Panting, struggling to breathe, they lay chests heaving in a gloopy mess. The sand clung to their flesh like a second skin. Coughing up a horrific amount of slime, Jake rolled onto his front and gagged repeatedly.

'Do you want me to hold your hair back?' joked Auger.

Finally, Jake managed to stop retching and wiped his eyes clear, rubbing coarse grains of sand back into them.

'Let's...never...do that..again!'

X

Unaware of their friends little diversion through the digestive tract of an alien sand snake, Random and Anji were nothing but the epitome of concentration as they made their assent up the rock face.

They had made a quick start, setting off after Lon who was in a rush to get over as quickly as possible.

'Slow down, man, what are you hurrying for, have you got a date?' Random bantered.

'You know damn well why I am rushing.'

'Lon, we have to put safety first, slow down.'

'Safety first? You know how funny that sounds coming from a boy who is carrying our whole entourage?'

'Hey! I'm doing just fine without any help, thanks!' Anji corrected him. She was. Random was proud of her efforts. He knew her adventurous spirit would be reawaken by their quest. This was the friend he had made back no Earth, not the one who was almost too scared to come out of a spa swimming pool and seek out the wonders of the universe with him.

'How far have we got to go?' said Random.

'I don't know, but I wouldn't turn back now,' gulped Etherton. A stiff breeze enveloped them and it was getting worse the higher they climbed.

The creature had made a terrible mistake in looking over his shoulder at the ground below. It was a disconcertingly long way away now.

'As long as our magnentic show clips work we shall be fine,' Lon reassured him. 'I reckon we are at about half way.'

With considerable effort, Random pulled one of his pick axes out of the rock face and smashed it half a foot higher up and repeated the same motion again and again. He had insisted on climbing up last in the off chance that Anji may get into some difficulty. But then, what would he do if she were to fall? He couldn't fly, so grimly, Random had come to the conclusion that he would have to smother her and plummet with his friend in his arms and do his best to break her fall. He knew he was strong and had a metabolism that would make an olympic rower green with envy, but could he survive a fall from such a great height?

Random shook the thought from his head, hoping he would never have to find out.

He felt the strain of his cargo. Clinks and sounds of tortured guide ropes shredded his nerves with every passing foot up the mountain.

'Anj, are you okay?'

'Of course, I'm just doing what you said and not looking down.'

Anji gritted her teeth. Inside she was screaming in terror. One false move and she was dead. No matter how hard she tried to reassure herself, this was the most terrifying thing she had ever done.

She had tried to brush off the climb by comparing it to a high wire event she had taken part in on a school trip. She had struggled to equate walking along a wire bridge suspended ten metres above the ground with a full scale climb up the side of an alien mountain. No matter how much she had tried to convince herself she was back in that adventure fun land, the mirage didn't work.

A cold sweat hung around her face, gluing strands of her hair that had fallen out of her ponytail to her face. Aware that she was shaking, Anji threw the pick axe into the rock faster and faster, trying her best to keep up with Lon.

Slow and steady was the safer method, yes, but the quicker they got to the top, the faster this ordeal would be over.

Noticing that Anji had picked up the pace, Random scowled.

'Anji! Slow down.'

'I can't Random, I just can't! I've got to get to the top.'

She picked quicker and quicker, her body aching to feel safe again.

'Anj please! Calm...'

Suddenly one of Anji's pick axes failed to imbed itself in the rock and it bounced out of her hand. Losing her grip, she fumbled at thin air with her now free hand and she screamed as her gaze followed the axe down below. She froze, paralysed with fear. Anji could feel her heart beating in her head. Nothing but terror coursed through her blood. She could hear nothing but her short, sharp breaths of fear.

'Zart!' swore Random. He picked up his own pace. Etherton complained as he and the cargo bounced after him, causing more stress on the already tortured guide ropes.

Anji's head began to swim. Her body was frozen but her mind was on the verge of blacking out.

Lon looked back at the commotion below. There was nothing he could do. It would be perilous for him to back up. He had to keep going. If he stopped for too long, who knows, maybe he may freeze up too? Reluctantly, he furrowed on.

'Anj, hold on, I'm nearly there!'

Tears trickled out of the corners of her eyes.

She tried to speak but could not easily.

'I-I-I don't think I can...' she croaked.

'Just a few more seconds, please!'

She planted her forehead against the colourful rock face. It felt smooth, cold against her clammy skin.

A small twang emitted from one of the cargo bags Random was hauling. Etherton's face turned white as he noticed what was starting to happen.

'Random...the weight, we can't take it!' he pleaded.

At that moment, everything was thrown into chaos.

Panic and terror overwhelmed Anji and she lost consiousness and slipped off the axe backwards.

'No!' yelled Random as he swung upward. As he leapt up the rock face, the guide rope tore in two, sending the cargo and Etherton falling from safety. The mole-like man managed to hang on with his harness and catch one of two of the bags before they tumbled back down the cliff face, but the bounce from the displacement of weight unbalanced Random. Stretching every sinew in his arm, he just managed to prop Anji up. Her boots were still implanted in the rock, but now that her weight was facing downward, they wouldn't stop her fall for long.

'Lon!' he hollered, but the explorer was too far away to help. Surely, he had heard the commotion?

Random grunted as he tried to pull Anji away from the wall as Etherton continued to whimper below him. He dared not look down to see how he was getting on.

'Etherton, are you safe?'

'No!' cried Etherton. 'There's too much weight. We're going to fall!'

'We are not going to fall!' cried Random. He tried to search his mind. His grip on the pick axe was starting to get awfully sweaty.

'Is there anything in those bags we can expend?'

Etherton struggled to find an answer.

'Um...in theory the tool bag.'

'Then drop it.'

'But without it we won't be able to pick up the Flux! The containment field is in there.'

'Just do it! I can't hold onto you all forever!'

Etherton hesitated. Then he remembered their predicament. Rather a bag of heavy tools than his own sorry skin. Scrunching his eyes tight, he let go of the bag.

Random levered himself upward and scooped Anji up fully with his arm. He held her tight to his side.

'Right, let's get moving again before anything else falls off!'

Etherton poked him in the back.

'Just one thing, Random. How are we going to climb if you've only got one free hand?'

Random went blank.

'Ah.'

'Random!'

They looked up. The voice in the distance was Lon's.

'Grab hold of this!'

From afar, what looked like a thin metal ladder descended from the top of the cliff face. Random sighed with relief.

He watched as the ladder tumbled further and further towards them and then it stopped abruptly roughly ten feet away from them.

'Lon, it's too short, bring it closer!'

'I can't,' came the distant cry.

Random searched his thoughts for an idea. All of a sudden, one popped into his head. A very silly one.

'Etherton, you're going to have to hold on for dear life.'

'As if I'm not already!'

'I'm going to have to jump for it. Hold on to my leg.'

Etherton's jaw dropped.

'We'll never make it!'

'Yes, we will, trust me!'

'No!'

'Okay then, humour me.'

Etherton did what he was told and clasped his paws around Random's leg.

'One.'

'No.'

'Two.'

'No!!'

With a fantastic leap, Random propelled he, the unconscious Anji and a screaming Etherton upwards, away from the pick axes. If he had miscalculated his own spring, then they wouldn't be getting any higher any time soon!

The whole world seemed to fall silent around them. It was like they were moving in slow motion.

With an outstretched arm, Random gratefully clasped his grip round the bottom rung of the ladder and gave an almighty sigh.

'We did it! We did it!' cried Etherton. 'I always knew you would.'

Random gave his companion a withering look.

'We made it! Right, winch us up!'

'No can do, I'm afraid,' replied Lon. 'The ladder is fastened down. I'm afraid you'll have to climb up.'

Random clicked his tongue.

'Fine, be with you in a minute.'

He turned to Etherton and smiled.

'There, you can let go now, how's that arm holding up?'

'You know what? A perilous situation seems to wonders for blanking out pain!' he said as the ache began to return when he noticed that it was his broken arm that was hanging onto Random's leg.

'Not to worry, about another hundred metres and we will be safe. Let's get going. We need to get Anji to safety.'

'Yes, and us!' Etherton reminded him.

Slowly, they began their assent back up the rock face.

Random did well to maintain his balance on the climb. Throwing Anji over one shoulder to give him better stability on the ladder, he began to curse this whole experience.

Oh Anji, he thought to himself, *I hope you will forgive me or putting you through this...*

A world of familiar voices whirled around Anji's head. They bounced to and fro around the blackness inside her mind. Slowly, she started to open her eyes and quickly wish she hadn't. The piercing light of the Spectronian sun swarmed her. She let them roll back into her head and slumped back onto what felt like solid rock.

And then, she remembered.

She'd blacked out on the cliff face.

But how was she still alive? Surely, she should have fallen to her death? Unless the ground beneath them was made of some sort of quilted material, she should be by all rights dead.

'Anj!' cried a relieved Random. 'Are you okay?'

She kept her eyes shut.

'I take it this isn't heaven then?'

'What makes you say that?'

'You're here.'

Random smiled. 'Oh, Anji Gummadi is back alright!'

She tried to get up but her head was still swimming.

'Just sit there for a bit. You've had a nasty shock.'

'What happened?'

'I asked too much of you. Anji, I'm so sorry, I'll never put you through anything like that again.'

'Too bloody right you're not!' she jabbed his arm. 'Are we back on the ground?'

'No, we kept on going. Lon was able to bail us out of trouble. Anj, we're at the top of the cliff face and the others have discovered something which might help us get to Strakonis much quicker than we thought.'

'A short cut?' asked Anji.

'You bet,' said Lon, 'we've found a cave opening. Etherton is checking the route out now for bugs and traps. How's it going, Etherton?'

Etherton had placed himself on a small rock and was watching a tiny monitor with great intent.

'The probe has covered roughly four miles of tunnels and there's no sign of any obstruction so far. I estimate its got about another mile to go before it reaches the surface...ah! There it is!'

Lon rushed to his aide's side. He pressed his face into the monitor.

A brilliant green shone through the screen.

'The Flux! But it can't be.'

Random got up and joined them.

'So that's what's causing all of this danger.'

'Isn't it worth it?' said Lon, with a look that was close to love in his eyes.

'It's very beautiful, I have to confess,' Random confirmed. 'It's a bit close. I thought we had much more of a journey on our hands than just in the centre of a mountain?'

'We did...but look!' Etherton's finger pointed at a figure moving in the shadows.

Lon's eyes narrowed.

'Strakonis...'

'What's he doing there?' asked Etherton.

The trio watched on as the shadow busied himself in what looked like a narrow cavern. It appeared that he was fixing what looked like charges into the rock walls.

'Setting booby traps for us,' said Lon.

'He doesn't want us to get out of this alive by the looks of it,' said Random, 'those charges are thermo detonators. As soon as a living being comes into range, boom!'

'He'll do anything to keep the Flux from my grasp,' Lon made for his bags and rummaged hastily.

'Well, I say it's time that we fought fire with fire!'

He produced a small laser gun from his bag.

'Not on my watch,' said Random sincerely.

'Look Random, you've seen he means to kill us.'

'It doesn't mean he will. Besides, we know what he has planned for us now.'

'Lon...surely you wouldn't?' Etherton had known Lon for a long time. He'd known his ambition to outstretch his capability to hold it together before but never had he witnessed his old colleague so driven as to even think about killing a rival.

'That man has taken the most powerful energy source in the cosmos. Think of what the Flux can do in the wrong hands!'

Random was silent.

'I suggest we proceed with caution. Nothing more.'

Lon cussed as he pocketed his weapon.

'Okay, Random, we will play it your way...for now.'

'No killing, Lon!'

'I'm not a killer, Random!'

'Not yet...'

Lon walked right up to Random, pressing his face into his own. Random did not flinch.

'Who the hell do you think you are?'

'I'll tell you. I'm someone who has seen madness and evil walk hand in hand. Make sure you don't join the two and we'll continue to get on. But if this Strakonis fella tips you too close to the edge, you better bet that I'll be the one pulling you back before you do something stupid.'

Lon's face was a picture of pure frustration. Desperation even. Anji got to her feet and was speechless. She knew Random could handle him, but the longer they spent with Lon, the more dangerous he became.

'Cool it, you two,' said Etherton, trying to squeeze between them.

'We should have left you back in your ship...'

His words chilled Anji. If they hadn't of rescued them, they'd be dead for sure.

Random just stood there, staring, unblinking, unnerved.

Lon moved away, staring with deadly intent at Random until he pulled his rucksack up towards him and fastened himself defiantly.

'Etherton.'

Etherton gulped and wiped his forehead.

'Coming.'

Random stayed exactly where he was standing. As Lon and Etherton moved off towards the cavemouth, Anji approached her friend.

'We can't go back.'

'I know.'

'So why do you keep provoking him? You're making an enemy of Lon.'

'He's making an enemy of himself,' Random watched as they disappeared around the corner.

'Besides, we've seen his kind before. Corrupted by greed, a lust for power. Sound familiar?'

'All too much,' Anji shuddered. Their experiences of Genocia was going to be a memory that would live long with her.

'If this Flux thing is as powerful as they have been saying it is, then think of the untold devastation it can cause.'

'In the wrong hands...' said Anji. 'So that's why we couldn't leave them. That's why we had to come along.'

Random nodded.

'We have to make sure the Flux ends up in the right hands. The universe may be depending on us.'

'Bit of a grand statement that,' Anji sniggered.

'I'm serious.'

Her smile evaporated.

'I know. Come on then. Let's go save the universe.'

Random wanted to smile, he really did, but the implications of their mission were weighing heavy. Anji was worried. Random seemed troubled.

'You okay?'

'Yes,' he lied. 'Come on.'

Random made for the cave mouth fast with Anji in tow.

She couldn't help but wonder what was wrong with him. Sure, the Flux was a dangerous component, but they've dealt with less in the past than this. Hadn't they?

Random gritted his teeth. Not now. Please, not now.
The voices were back.

XI

It was getting late and dark. On an alien planet, even one as
beautiful as Spectronia, to be stuck in the desert at night time is
not the wisest of moves. Especially when you have spent a portion
of the day trapped inside the intestinal tract of an alien sand
monster.

Jake had felt like they had been riding through the desert for
hours. When he stated this as an observation, Skateboard did
nothing but confirm that they had indeed been going for a very
long time. He had also stated, much to the boy's dismay, that
having carried them both for such a long time that his energy cells
were starting to drain. He insisted they get off and walk beside
him while he scanned for shelter so he could reserve his battery.

'As if you run off a battery,' said Jake.

'Doesn't all life in the universe?' said Skateboard sneakily.
'Sorry, sir, but as you can tell I am rather tired. I spent such
sufficient time on board the Venus II that I can absorb the power
from the ship whenever I start to run low. But I've never been
outside for so long and I could do with switching off soon to
preserve my run time. I'll scan the local area for somewhere for us
to recharge.'

Jake looked up. The sky was a brilliant wash of mauve light
blending in with the dark. Stars began to twinkle like tiny pearls,
shining brighter than any star Jake has ever seen before.

'Wow,' he whispered. 'I can think of worse places to be stuck.
What do you think, Auger?'

Auger was very quiet. She had barely said a word since their
escape and it unnerved Jake. In their brief time together, he had
come to accept that she wasn't the most talkative of people. But
his travelling companion had been as silent as a shadow for too
long.

'What's eating you?' said Jake.

Auger gave him a cold look.

'Are you serious?'

'Sorry, poor choice of words,' he replied, reminding himself of their ordeal by catching a whiff of his clothes.

'We should keep going.'

'Surely you can't be serious?' said Skateboard.

'Auger, we've already been eaten today. Who knows what else could be out here!'

'If we don't keep going, we are giving Strakonis a chance to escape. We can't let that happen.'

'I understand your frustration, Miss Auger, but if we don't stop, we might not get there at all.'

Skateboard completed his scans.

'There's a small hut roughly 500 metres due west. We can set up camp there for the night.'

'But we've only gotten miles left to go! We'd be there in a few hours!'

'Woman, I'm pooped,' said Jake. 'I'm siding with Skateboard.'

'Then I am going on alone!'

'I'm afraid that would be unwise,' said Skateboard.

'Oh yeah, right, because you two are so powerful. The child and the toy.'

'Hey, I'm 13!' said an indignant Jake.

'I don't care I am not stopping!'

'Miss Auger, I beg you to think rationally for a moment. Strakonis could have guards, an army even, we don't know how well protected he is. Safety is greater in numbers.'

'Company slows me down. I would have been there already, probably with the Flux already within my grasp, if it wasn't for you two!'

'You can't blame us for the sand snake, surely? You were the one who got eaten first!' said Jake.

'Hold your tongue before I cut it out!' Auger produced a knife from her pocket.

'Woah, Auger come on, will you just calm down!'

A small taser shot out of Skateboard's body and was pointed firmly in the direction of the threatening Auger.

'Drop it.'

Auger smiled. 'Sorry, I'm so sorry.'

Slowly, she put the knife away and Jake's heart rate climbed down greatly.

'I…that's not me.'

'You sure about that?' asked Jake.

Auger looked ashamed. Defeated.

'It won't happen again.'

Skateboard slowly retracted the taser.

'Let's get to the hut.'

Brilliant, he thought to himself. That's a recharge out of the question.

Skateboard knew that now he would have to watch Auger like a hawk.

Before long, the group had made it to the hut. Luckily it was uninhabited, although it looked like someone had been there recently. The place was small but a complete mess. Sand seemed to coat every piece of furniture within, although there wasn't much. A small table and a single chair sat beside a long-abandoned fire and a blanket that resembled a welcome mat in its cleanliness.

'Could use a spring clean,' said Jake wearily.

'If we camp here for a few hours, I should have sufficient power to carry us the final leg of the journey and we will be there before we know it. Do we have a deal, Auger?'

Auger nodded silently.

'Right, let's get some kip then. I think I've got the sleeping bags on me. Shame I didn't pack a mattress though!'

It didn't take long for Jake to fall into a deep, dreamless sleep. Which was odd for him, because he dreamt an awful lot. His favourite was a recent one he had when he and his friends had been staying on the health farm planet of Zlatacosta Meganion. It involved him being crowned footballer of the year for the ninth year in a row and being rewarded with a knighthood from the Queen before being fed into a canon and shot into the side of the moon.

Although it had seemed very real and vivid, and at the end pretty weird and scary, he'd thoroughly enjoyed it…but it did put into question whether he was eating too much cheese before he went to bed.

Skateboard was doing his best to fight back fatigue but his charge was now on 1%. He'd have to switch off soon. But Auger, he couldn't trust her, not after the last episode.

He would never forgive himself if anything happened to any of his friends.

Without warning, Auger stirred and got up, snaked her sleeping bag down her body and walked over to Skateboard.

'Miss Auger. Are you having trouble sleeping?'

'Yes.'

'Is there anything I can do to help?'

'I'm sorry, Skateboard.'

Skateboard whirred. 'It's alright, Miss Auger, I understand the frustration you must be feeling.'

'No, I mean I'm really very sorry.'

Suddenly. Auger plunged her dagger deep into Skateboard's body, hitting his energy pack. A short scream from the AI robot bleated through the still night as blue lightning-like energy seeped out of the wound. She stabbed the blade deeper until nothing but a low sigh emitted from the stricken robot.

Auger withdrew her weapon.

The cabin fell silent again.

Skateboard was dead.

Jake stirred from within his sleeping bag.

Auger flipped backwards and stood up over him.

'Skateboard?'

Jake's face peaked out from within the bag's opening.

With one cruel, swift swipe of her boot, Auger booted Jake full on in the face and knocked him out cold. She proceeded to stuff him back into his sleeping bag and using the chord, fastened the unconscious boy inside like a cocoon.

Auger picked it up and swung Jake over her shoulder and picked up the lifeless Skateboard.

'Sweet dreams, you two.'

XII

'You must go home.'

'Why won't you face your destiny?'

'How will Rodas survive?'

'How will the people survive?'

'Evil must not conquer.'

The voices continued...relentlessly plaguing Random's mind.

'Random...Random...Random...'

'Random?'

The purple boy turned to face his friend. His face was illuminated by the florescent light on the walls, caking the pair in a spectrum of light where anywhere else in the world they would have been submerged in darkness. Even through the colours, Anji could tell that something was wrong with Random's face.

'What's up?'

'Nothing,' Random lied. His face was caked in tiny beads of sweat. 'Hot down here, isn't it?'

'Far from it!' said Anji. She took her friend's arm. 'You know you can tell me if anything is the matter, don't you?'

Random smiled. 'Of course.'

He hesitated.

'Anj – I'm-'

Suddenly, they heard an explosion further on in the cave.

'Lon!' said Anji.

'Quick!'

Random and Anji tore towards danger, something they seemed to have done a lot ever since they first met. Soon they came to a cloud of rainbow dust. Anji held her sleeve up over her mouth. Random just coughed his way through.

'Lon!' Random spluttered.

'Yes, we're fine,' came a voice.

As the dust settled, Anji spotted Etherton lying underneath a pile of rubble.

'Well, speak for yourself!' he remarked. Anji and Random helped pull him clear as Etherton complained about them tweaking his still healing arm.

'Anything broken...again?' asked Random.

'Only my pride this time. We walked straight into a thermo mine. Luckily it didn't get us.'

'Lon, where are you?'

'Right here,' said Lon. He was concealed past the rubble. 'Blasted scout probe didn't pick up the mines. Had it not have been for my quick reactions we'd have both been killed.'

'You could have warned me!' complained Etherton.

'You're alive, aren't you? Now if you are quite finished moaning, we need to keep going.'

'Hold it, what if the cave is now unstable?' Random pointed out.

'What if it isn't?'

'You want to risk it?'

'I am willing to risk anything for the Flux, even you.'

'Well, that's not very friendly,' scoffed Random. 'And if that's supposed to shut me up then I'm afraid you've got me all wrong.'

'No, it wasn't, but this will.'

Instantly, Lon sprayed some sort of gas from a tiny can concealed within his hand. Before he had a chance to respond, Random was hit full on in the face with the gas. His head began to swirl and before long, he found himself falling against the wall and slipping to the ground.

'Random!' Anji dropped Etherton to the floor and raced over to her friend. 'What have you done to him?'

'Knocked him out of course, what else do you think I've done. Etherton, grab her!'

Anji acted fast and evaded the mole like creature's grasp and launched herself at Lon. She pushed him to the floor and attacked him viciously.

Etherton watched nervously as they grappled but Lon's superior strength soon told as he picked her up and threw her against the wall, completely knocking the wind out of her sails.

'Tie her up, now!' he demanded, wiping blood from his lip. His face was scratched.

'With what?'

'With rope, you idiot! Do it or I'll add you to the pile!'

Etherton made for a bag and began to rummage around.

'Lon...this is wrong, what are you doing?'

'Taking back the power,' he hissed. He drew a gun and levelled it at Random and Anji's unconscious bodies.

'I have an idea for where we can put them...somewhere they will never be found...'

*

Jake awoke with a startle, not to mention an angry headache.

His jaw ached badly. He groaned softly and moved his hand to cradle it.

Only he couldn't.

He tried again. Still no luck.

His hands were bound behind his back.

Jake's surroundings were dark, ominous.

Soon, he realised where he was.

He was in his sleeping bag. The opening had been fastened above his head. But why was he tied up?

Then he remembered.

'Auger! Let me out! Come on, jokes over. Very funny. I'm used to pranks like this. Granted I've never been physically assaulted at the same time, that's a new one...'

Shut up, he told himself. Stop trying to be funny. This isn't the time.

'Skateboard?'

He listened for a response. None came.

He smelt the air. There was an earthy smell surrounding him. He tried to wiggle himself free, but he was barely able to move.

Where was he?

Jake tried to wrestle his hands out of his bonds but to no avail.

He did his best to ignore the pain in his jaw but it was hard to do such a thing when it persisted to throb uncontrollably.

Then, with a terrible moment of realisation, he thought he knew where he was.

He was in the ground.

Surely not?

'Please, god no!' he pleaded as he tried to kick himself free.

But it was true. He was lying a shallow grave.

'Auger! Auger! For god's sake let me out please!'

Soon he began to hyperventilate.

Through gritted teeth he tried to force his hands through the bonds, but it felt like they were plastic, incapable of breaking.

Jake tried to calm his breathing before he was sick.

He tried to think clearly, come up with an escape plan.

A vision of a mobile phone came into his head.

'My phone!'

Of course, he thought, he could call Anji for help.

Desperately, Jake tried to pull his jacket pocket over. He knew it was there, he could feel it pressing against his stomach.

Auger hadn't removed it. Stupid...whatever she was.

Thankfully, he managed to reach it. Knowing his pin number off by heart, he opened it up. The screen illuminated his makeshift coffin. He wished it hadn't. The light all but confirmed that he was indeed buried under the sand. Grains were starting to trickle in the more he wriggled and the more the opening stretched.

Welling up, Jake tried to remember where his

contacts were stored on his phone. It'd be easy to find Anji's number in his call history. She was the only person he ever phoned and the only person who ever wanted to get in contact with him.

Dangling high above a perilous drop, Anji awoke with a startle. Her surprise escalated to sheer terror when she realised that she had been suspended by a rope around her waist above a cavernous, bottomless pit. She tried to scream, then realised her vocal cords were too shriveled with fright to emit any sound.

The more she moved the more she spun around, hands tied in front of her under the rope around her midriff, she noticed, much to her relief, that she was not alone.

'Random! Random wake up!' she demanded but it was no use. The Rodasian was still unconscious. Whatever Lon had sprayed in his face must have been strong to keep him under longer than she had been. She felt a tiny bruise on the back of her head and hoped that she had given Lon more than that before he knocked her out cold!

Anji's desperate eyes scanned Random's features. He appeared to be gritting his teeth, as though he were applying a great deal of force to something. Also, his eyes were screwed shut so tightly that tiny tears were collecting on his eyelashes.

She tried to maneuver her hands upwards to check his pulse but then she remembered he was an alien. It could be sky high for all she could know and that would be normal. It wouldn't be amiss for him to have no pulse either!

Something was terribly wrong with Random, and that in some ways scared that Anji more than the drop.

She sighed and her head fell against her chest. Powerless, she just hung there, limp, helpless.

Silence in the mountain. Lon and Etherton were long gone. They had failed.

All of a sudden, a familiar ring tone echoed around the cavern. Anji's eyes lit up.

'Surely not!'

Anji fumbled her bonded hands into the front pocket of her dungarees.

The screen was still as broken as it had been, but somehow, miraculously, it was still receiving calls.

She pressed the fractured screen to accept the call and tapped again to put the caller on loudspeaker.

'Jake! You're sense of timing couldn't be any better!' she returned it to her pocket and pulled the zip a little so she didn't lose the phone to the abyss.

'Anj...'

Jake sounded upset. Anji didn't like it when he was crying. It was so out of character for him.

'What's the matter, where's Skateboard?'

'Auger...she's buried me...in the desert.'

'Buried you!?'

Jake sniffed. 'She's tied me up and thrown me in the ground.'

'How? Why? Where's Skateboard?'

'I don't know, he's not here. Anji, you've got to come and find me...the sand...it's getting inside my sleeping bag. I'm scared.'

Anji's eyes welled up. 'So am I. Lon's captured us. Something's up with Random too. He's knocked out next to me and we're dangling above a pit.'

Jake couldn't speak. He allowed the sobs to take him over before snorting them back inside.

'A right pair we make, eh?'

Anji laughed.

There was a moment's silence between them.

'How did we let ourselves get into this Anj?' asked Jake.

'Random did warn us.'

'I know it's not his fault but...I don't know, I'm so scared right now I can't think straight.'

Anji sniffed.

'Me too.'

'The thing is…it's quite exciting, most of the time, isn't it?'

'Yeah.'

'Not now though.' Jake took a look in the murky gloom. 'Anj, I'm going to die here, aren't I?'

'Don't say that!' she pleaded. 'You're alive, that's all that matters.'

'I'm not sure how much longer I'll be able to breathe…'

Tears began to roll silently down Anji's cheeks.

'Listen, remember that promise we made to each other back at the pond? Before Random crashed right in front of us?'

'Kind of hard to forget, a thing like that,' he scoffed.

'Remember what we said to each other. The promise we kept to ourselves?'

Jake smiled. 'Yeah. If we were both single come prom then we'd go together.'

'Well, I'm game if you still are?'

Jake sniffed loudly.

'I'm not sure I will make it.'

'Of course, you will! Just hang on in there and I'll hang in here…' she cringed at her poor choice of words.

'Shh, Anj.'

Jake craned his ear.

'What is it?'

'I must be going mad…I could have sworn I just heard footsteps.'

'Well scream then!' Anji urged.

Jake hollered for help as loud as his lungs would allow. Again and again, he yelled, shouting so loud that it was a miracle he didn't rip his vocal cords the volume of his cries.

'For gods sake help me!'

Anji prayed on the other end of the line that their prayers would be answered.

There was a long, long silence.

Anji began to worry. Had Auger come back to finish off the job?

Suddenly, the sound of a spade plunging into the sand pierced through the airwaves.

'Anj…I'm being rescued! I'm being rescued!'

'Good! Then get your arse to the mountain and get us out will you!'

'As long as the prom date stands, I'll be there faster than you can say, "Should I wear my hair up or down, Jake!"'

Anji laughed. 'Alright mister, just make sure you are safe and get here as soon as you can.'

At that moment, her phone went dead.

'Jake? Jake? Jake!?'

Her phone light was dead.

She waited for him to call back, but the screen stayed black.

She sighed. The call wasn't coming. Her phone must have run out of battery. Unless Auger really had...no, she couldn't think like that. He was going to be safe, he had to be.

She looked at the void below her dangling legs and wished she was too.

The digging became more and more frantic. Copious amounts of sand kept surging into the sleeping bag, making Jake panic. Would he drown before he managed to get out? Through his screams he thought he could hear a deep, masculine voice.

'Stop moving, you're making it worse. Nearly there.'

It wasn't a voice that Jake recognised. He wondered if the owner of the shack had returned. If so, how lucky was he! Another brush with death that he had survived.

He tallied in his mind the scorecard between him and certain doom up until now.

Jake Three
Death Nil

Another one for old Jakey boy!

Soon, the digging stopped and a pair of gloved hands delved deep into the bag, clutching Jake's face.

'Oi, get off!' he muffled through what tasted like dirty leather.

He was soon startled as he was picked up out of the ground with considerable ease. Jake slumped to the bottom of the bag and groaned as his backside made hard contact with the ground.

Suddenly, a large knife split through the bag and tore it apart. It must have been early morning by now as Jake squinted hard as the bright sunshine bore into his barely open eyes.

He whimpered as he felt the cold metal of the knife up against his wrists.

'Hold still.'

Jake obeyed.

Shortly, the stranger had finished sawing his bonds off. Jake clambered towards him, clutching his leg and wrapped his body around it.

'Thank you, oh my god thank you so much!'

The stranger towered above him, his features protected by a cloth mask that concealed his nose and mouth.

'You should try and find better places to sleep.'

Jake giggled and then remembered.

'My friends…they are in danger too. We've got to help them!'

'One thing at a time.'

Jake clambered to his feet gingerly. He caressed his bruised jaw and winced as he felt the hot, split flesh.

'Who are you and what are you doing there?' asked the stranger.

'I'm Jake. I came here with friends but we've been betrayed…oh my god, Skateboard where is he?'

'Betrayed? By who?'

Jake held his hand to his eyes, shielding the sunshine from his gaze.

'First of all, who should I thank for saving my life?'

The stranger unveiled his mask. Jake recoiled instantly. The man's face was badly scared.

'My name is Strakonis.'

XIII

Somewhere, deep within his own psyche, a battle was enraging between Random and his sanity. Since he had been knocked out, he had been present in a sort of purple void. It looked like some form of tunnel, linking him between his inner thoughts and his own mind. He shook the concept of being inside his own head from his thoughts and began to wonder if he was dead. Maybe this was the afterlife. That's a turn up, he thought! He then groaned audibly as he realised that being gassed was perhaps one of the lamest ways to go that he could think of. Why couldn't it be something heroic?

Seemingly unable to move, he noticed what looked like people up ahead.

'Hey! What am I doing here? Not that I'm sure where here is. I need to get back, my friend is in trouble.'

They did not respond.

Instantly, Random knew he was unconscious. He wasn't really in limbo. But it felt like he was drifting between planes, flitting between life and death. Suddenly, it daunted on him who the two figures were supposed to represent.

'You're...the voices in my head, aren't you?'

Nothing.

'So that must make you...'

A feeling of shock convulsed through Random's body.

'...no, it can't be!'

He was confused, more confused than he had ever been.

'But...I don't understand. I came out of that big tube thing. You two can't be my...'

The ghostly apparitions remained unmoved.

Random tried to get a better view of them. They looked like completely different species. One was impossibly tall and gangly, with a sapphire blue complexion to its skin tone, the other much smaller and obviously feminine with a crimson red pigmentation.

'I know you've always been with me. I know what you want me to do. But I can't. Not yet. I'm not ready yet.'

Their silence was deafening.

'For zarks sake! Why would you haunt my every waking moment and not speak a word now! What are you trying to prove? Come on! Speak!'

Random attempted to run towards the phantoms but he wasn't able to gain any ground on them.

He stood in the void in his mind, feeling overwhelmed with confliction.

Up ahead were two figures that he could barely make out, and if he attempted to move closer towards them, they didn't get any sharper in focus or any nearer in proximity.

'Why? Why are you haunting me?'

The two ghostly figures were unmoved and remained silent.

'Is it something you put in my head when I was created? Are you trying to warn me now? Why won't you answer!?'

Random was becoming more and more frustrated. Anger was bubbling within the fiber of his being.

'Look, if you've nothing to say then go on, zark off! Leave me alone. I will fight on my own terms, when I am ready, not before. I am not allowing the ghosts of Rodas to bully me into rushing back. I didn't ask to be your saviour. I'm not asking you now. I'm just asking you, if you are who I think you are, to leave me alone.'

The apparitions stayed totally silent.

'GO!'

With a crushing blow, Random smashed his fists to the ground and awoke from his dream with a startle and in doing so, shocked Anji into a scream.

'Oh my god, don't do that!' she cried.

Random could feel the sweat pouring down his face.

'Anj! You startled me! Hold on,' he became aware of his surroundings. 'Right, I take it Lon's got away then judging by our current predicament?'

'Not before he left us here! What's the matter, Random, please tell me?'

'Not now, Anj, can't you see we're dangling above a pit?' he said curtly. 'Anyway, I'll be fine, I think it's all sorted now. So, let's look at the facts. We are tied up above what to the naked eye looks like a bottomless pit and we're miles away from safety either side.'

'How did he get us up here?' Anji pondered.

'Never mind that for now, we need to think of a way of getting out.'

'Random, listen, it's not just us who are in trouble. Jake phoned me. Auger attacked him in his sleep and left him buried alive!'

'What!? Where was Skateboard? Were they okay?'

'He's lost Skateboard, but someone was rescuing him while he was talking to me.'

'Let's hope it isn't Auger then and that Skateboard is okay.'

'Who do you think it could be? Could it be the Spectronians?'

'No, not this far out I wouldn't think. Hold on.'

A look a worry passed over Random's face.

'You said that someone was rescuing him?'

'Yes.'

'Well, if what we've been told is true, then there's one person we certainly don't want him to be rescued by!'

*

'Stay away from me!'

Jake pointed accusingly in the stranger's direction.

'I know karate! Ish!'

'I mean you no harm.'

'Oh yeah, prove it!'

Strakonis held his palms out in front of him.

'I just rescued you from a shallow grave...'

'Good point.'

Strakonis pulled the boy up to his feet.

'Now the question is, what were you doing down there?'

Jake hesitated. He didn't want to give away who he was travelling with.

'How can I trust you?'

'Look if you're going to continue to be evasive then I'll be on my way...'

'That might be for the best...'

Strakonis lurched down. Jakew shuddered at his terrible facial scars.

'You're afraid of me, aren't you?'

'No,' lied Jake, 'Whatever gave you that impression?'

'Then why hide the truth.'

Because I don't want you to put me back in that hole, screamed Jake's inner voice.

'Look...I've heard of you, and what you do, and I don't want any trouble.'

Strakonis looked confused.

'Tell me...how bad must a man be to dig a live being out from the ground and save their life?'

'I don't know...thank you, by the way,' said jake sheepishly.

Strakonis was right though. Auger had betrayed him and Skateboard but this man, someone he had been told was evil and percievably untrustworthy wasn't the one who left him to die a horrible death.

'I just don't know who to trust,' he admitted.

'Come with me. We'll go back to the shack, patch up that jaw of yours and see if there are any clues as to the whereabouts of your friends. I take it from your reluctance to tell me the truth that you were not alone?'

'No, I was with a friend and someone I thought I could trust.'

'Come on,' said Strakonis.

Jake walked with the man he had been led to believe was an evil mastermind like a child following their parent. He was so confused. But Auger seemed okay, he thought, well, until she did what she did to him.

The burial site was mere metres away from the shack, so as Jake and Strakonis was soon entering the tiny building. When Jake saw the familiar outline of Skateboard lying inert in the middle of the dusty floor, he immediately ran to his side.

'Nice place you've got here,' joked Jake.

'It's not mine, I've never been here before,' confirmed Strakonis. 'Is that your friend over there?'

A lump of motionless metal lay before their feet. Jake threw himself towards it.

'Skateboard, buddy it's me,' he said, shaking his lifeless form.

Jake scanned him for life signs. Normally the little AI would have little lights flashing, or a blue energy flowing through his metal work like blood coursing through veins, but this time, there was nothing. Then as Jake's hand caught the jagged stab wound that gaped open on his back.

'No!' he exclaimed.

'Let me have a look at that.'

Strakonis kneeled down next to the disconsolate boy.

'Get away from him!' railed Jake.

'Look, he's a robot, let me take a look and we might be able to fix him.'

Reluctantly, Jake handed Skateboard, who was surprisingly light, over.

Strakonis inspected the wound and then took a closer look at Skateboard.

'It's pretty bad. His energy pack has been pierced. It will take a lot of work to get him up to speed again.'

'You mean he isn't dead?!' said Jake, allowing a glimmer of hope to enter his world.

'I don't think I can, but I'm sure the Spectronians can.'

'Well then we've got to get him to them now!'

'No, I'm sorry but I can't go with you.'

Jake frowned. 'What do you mean?'

'There's something very important I have to get back to.'

'More important! My friend is dead!'

'No, not dead. I'm sure there are technicians back at the Spectronia city who can help patch him back up again. But I cannot go with you. I need to make a promise and make my rendezvous. I'm already late as it is.'

'But my friends need help too!'

'More of you?'

'In the mountain, yeah.'

Strakonis shook his head. 'I cannot help, I'm sorry.'

'But you must!'

'Look!' Strakonis snapped. 'It's terrible what's happened to you, I know. And in other circumstances I would not hesitate to lend a hand but there is something in my possession that needs to stay out of people's hands and I can't guarantee that unless I go on now. So I'll help patch you up then be on my way. Now, where's my first aid kit.'

'By "people's hands" do you mean Lon?'

Strakonis stopped in his tracks.

'You were with him, weren't you?'

Jake nodded.

'He rescued us when our ship crash landed.'

'A likely story!'

'It's true. And then he invited us to join him. Not the nicest of blokes it has to be said.'

'Was it him who did this to you and your friend?'

Jake shook his head. 'No, that was Auger.'

Strakonis' eyes widened.

'So, he's companions are here too...and Lon had endangered your other friends' lives?'

Jake sighed. 'Please.'

'If Lon is not alone then it's imperative that I move as quickly as possible,' he rummaged in his first aid kit and took out a futuristic looking plaster. 'Right, stick this to your wound and allow it to do the rest.'

He got up and delved into his pockets and finally produced a small gadget that Jake presumed was a communicator.

Strakonis held it to his mouth.

'Eago, Eago, this is Strakonis. Found wounded non-native and machine in shack. I am sending you my co-ordinates now. Unable to stay...the mission has become a little more uncertain. Lon is in pursuit and it's not known if your traps have worked. Please come quickly, humanoid boy is distressed. Strakonis out.'

'Thank you,' said Jake.

'Sadly, it's the least I can do, If I don't get the Flux to our rendezvous point then the fate of the galaxy is in trouble.'

'Lon's pretty determined to get his hands on it.'

'He always is, no matter what we are searching for. Our paths cross more times than I care to remember. Now please, stay here. You'll be safe as soon as Eago gets here.'

Jake gave a weak smile to his rescuer.

'Good luck.'

'Thank you.'

'Oh, one more thing before you go.'

Strakonis stopped in the doorway.

'This Flux thing – do you have it with you?'

'Yes.'

Jake paused.

'Can I see it?'

'No. Goodbye. I hope you find your friends.'

And with that, Strakonis swooped out of the shack and left Jake to cradle his dead friend, waiting for the promise from a stranger.

                                        *

'Try again!'

With what felt like the umpteenth swing of her legs, Anji tried
once again to throw momentum to her right. She and Random
swung like a pendulum, toing and froing between the two cliff
edges, but always falling several metres short of safety.

'Random I can't keep doing this!' said Anji, afraid to admit that
with the height of the drop they were swinging above she was
liable to black out as she did climbing the mountain.

'Okay, okay, so we're too far away to jump on the ledge, fine.'

'Can't you just snap the ropes and jump over?' Anji suggested.

'I don't think I am close enough to do that...unless...'

'...Unless?'

'Maybe I can, yes! Anj, if I snap out of these bonds, permission
to climb down to your feet?'

'My what?'

'You know them, boney things with toes on the end?'

'Don't be silly, I just don't understand why you'd want to climb
down to my toes.'

'Simple. Use your momentum and a longer length span to flip
back onto the ledge.'

Anji sighed.

'So, it's back to swinging again then?'

'Well, it's better than hanging around, come on!'

Random concentrated his efforts in the ropes around his hands.
He began to force them apart, grinding his teeth as the bonds
began to strain and pull. Before long, they twanged open. Random
beamed as he felt his wrists.

'Got them!'

'Great!'

'Only...'

'Only what?'

'Well, I've just realised. If I snap out of the rope that's tying me
to you, you will be free too.'

'What's the problem with that?' asked an incredulous Anji.

'If we do that, you might fall.'

'Oh.' Anji searched inside her head for a solution.

'Okay, I've got it,' she exclaimed. 'Untie my hands if you can. We are both going to have to swing. Do you reckon we will have enough momentum?'

'If we don't, we'll soon know!' Random gulped.

As Random and Anji were tied back-to-back, he found it easy to find his friend's bonds and roughly went about freeing her.

'Ouch!'

'Sorry, rough ropes,' he said.

Before long, her hands were also free.

'Right, hold on to the rope above us and hold on tight!'

Anji did as she was told.

'And brace yourself Anj.'

Anji did the best she could to get a good grip.

'Random, my hands are really sweaty.'

'Then tell them not to be.'

She frowned. 'Not sure how, humans don't work like that.'

'Oh,' Random replied, 'well, just do the best you can. Hopefully this won't take long. Ready?'

'Nope,' she joked.

'Me too,' said Random. He gave her a nervous smile and went about his work.

He grunted as he tensed his arm muscles. Suddenly the rope burst open and Anji screamed as she felt her weight fall from beneath her and up to her arms. She looked down, panting heavily, as she saw Random had fallen to her ankles.

'Random!'

'Yes, I know sorry I'm a lot heavier than I anticipated. I'll eat salads when we get back.'

'Stop messing around and swing!'

The duo swung from opposite ends, cancelling out their momentum.

'Not that way, the other way! It's making my hands slip!' panicked Anji.

Random shifted his momentum to Anji's movement and before long, they were swinging with significant force.

Anji heard a tearing sound underneath her screams. She dared to look above her and noticed that the weight on the rope was causing it to split!

'Random!'

'Now!'

Instantly, Random hurtled through the air towards the ledge and pulled Anji after him like a child who was walking upside down holding on tight to a balloon. They flew towards the ledge and with impressive precision, Random threw the lopsided Anji onto the safety of the ledge. She fell on her front onto the dusty sand, the rainbow flicks of which stuck to her face. Random landed with all the grace of a moose dancing the fandango on ice.

He rolled to the floor, laid on his back and panted hard.

'See, told you It'd work,' he patted Anji on her back.

She rolled onto her back and tried to catch her breath also.

'I'm never doing heights again.'

Random laughed.

Anji allowed herself a chuckle too.

'Look, there's a hold in the roof of the cave.'

She pointed right above the rope that was descending from a pin point beacon of sunlight.

'That's how Lon must have dropped us down here. We could have climbed up if we'd have seen that.'

'No, thanks, my climbing days are over!' said Anji.

Random smiled.

'That's the trouble with you sometimes Anji, you are always looking down on things. You've got to look up to find a way forward sometimes. '

'Says you!' she scoffed.

Anji sat up and took a look around.

'Er...Random...'

'What?'

'You know those two ledges we saw when we were tied up?'

'Yeah?'

'We're on one without an opening!'

Random's face fell.

'Oh.'

'Yup!'

'So, we're still stuck, aren't we?'

'Looks like it.'

Random sighed. He fiddled around in his pocket and produced a bag.

'Mint?'

XV

'We shouldn't have done that, you know?'

Etherton's conscience was working overtime. Lon's was clearly broken presumed missing.

'Spare me the guilt trip, will you Etherton?'

The little creature sighed. In all the years he had been with Lon, on and off giving his availability and the mission he was required for, he'd never seen Lon this driven before. Oh sure, he was ruthless, but then it's a big bad universe. But he had never hurt anyone before.

'How far away are we?'

Etherton checked the digital map.

'We're making good time.'

'That's not what I asked.'

'About two and a half hours away.'

'We can make it in two if we pick up the pace.'

'But...Lon...what will we say when we meet up with Auger?'

'We'll just say that we lost them on the mountainside and couldn't recover their bodies.'

Etherton was unnerved.

'This isn't you, Lon...'

'Isn't it?' he said, turning to meet his aide head on. 'So, what am I then? Go on tell me!'

Etherton cowered. Lon's eyes were burning with madness.

'Well, I don't know, but not this.'

'I've never lost a prize before. Never. Not once in my life. Not at school. Not in life in general. I'm a born winner, Etherton and I will not lose this one.'

He turned away.

'Not this one.'

'Lon...' said Etherton softly. 'Strakonis isn't as dangerous as you keep making out. He's just a rival.'

'He's more than that to me...and he is to me! Now come on, you're slowing us down.'

'No.'

'What?'

The mole-like creature was standing his ground, possibly for the first time in his life, he was putting his foot down.

'I will not help you.'

A deep-seated rage began to boil within Lon.

'This is a poorly timed display of defiance, Etherton.'

'I know,' he said, 'but I can't go on. You're consumed by the Flux.'

'So would you be if you really cared.'

'But that's the trouble, Lon, you care too much! Who cares if Strakonis has it? He won't use it. No one will come to harm.'

'And you think if I had the Flux people would?'

Etherton hesitated.

'You're not yourself, Lon.'

'That's your answer?'

Etherton screwed his fist up by his side. He was shaking, sweating. Trying not to give away just how terrified he was right now.

'When we have worked together before, throughout all these years, we've acted out of personal interest, chased the glory, but this time...people have got hurt. It goes against what I stand for. So yes, in short, that is my answer. You're losing it Lon. You need help.'

Lon had heard enough. He reached for the knife on his belt.

'You're wrong...you do!'

*

Jake sat patiently in the shack, still clutching the lifeless Skateboard to his chest.

He looked for a clock on the wall and then quickly reminded himself that this wasn't Earth and that he was being silly. Something he majored in. First class honours in being silly in even the most desperate situations. He checked his phone. It had been half an hour since Strakonis had left and still no word from the Spectronians.

Sat silently in a strange desert, millions of miles from home, is not the best place to be when you've just been buried alive and aligned yourself with someone who is willing to kill you and your friend to get what they want.

He needed a distraction.

He decided to try Anji again. He'd called a few times and yet no answer. His stomach was knotted with worry. For them, for Skateboard, for him.

Thankfully this time, she picked up.

'Bit of an awkward time to call, Jake.'

Anj! You're okay then.'

'Well, that depends on what you mean by "okay". We are free, but trapped. So Random's resorting to throwing me to the other side of the cave to escape.

'Hi Jake!' Random chirped.

'Hey mate,' said Jake nervously. 'Is that safe?'

'We'll soon find out.'

'Before you do that, I need to tell you something.' Jake looked down at the stricken Skateboard and sighed heavily. 'Skateboard's dead.'

'What?!' said Random. 'What happened?'

'It was Auger. She did it. She attacked us. Strakonis thinks he can be fixed though, well he seemed optimistic-'

'Wait, hold on, Jake, you've met Strakonis!'

'Yeah! He dug me out of the ground. To tell you the truth, Random, I don't think he is quite the baddie that Lon has been making out.'

Random looked at the rope dangling from the cave roof.

'You think?'

'Well, early indications say we've been hoodwinked!' said Jake.

'Is he still there with you?' asked Random.

'No, he's gone to meet someone. He said he had the Flux with him. But he's knows people on this planet and they are coming out to help us...well, if they ever turn up!'

'Random,' said Anji. 'If Strakonis is the good guy then we've been helping out the bad guys!'

'It looks like it, doesn't it?' Random moaned.

'Maybe we shouldn't be as trusting in future.'

'Forget about that now, we've got to stop Lon!'

'Jake, maintain radio...er...frequencies and let us know when you have any updates. Do you think Skateboard can be repaired?'

'He seemed to think so, but the stab wound is pretty bad, even for a robot.'

'Stabbed!' cried Anji. 'When I get my hands on Auger!'

'We'll be cautious,' said Random. 'Okay Jake, keep us in the picture. We'll get out of here and set off in pursuit of Lon. If you can convince Strakonis' allies to help us that'd be great too. We'll still meet in the same place. Just go easy and hopefully we'll be able to revive Skateboard somewhere along the line, okay?'

'Gotcha..and Random, Anj? It's good to hear your voices again. The last few hours have felt like years!'

'We'll be back together soon Jake, just you wait,' said Random softly. 'Okay, Random out.'

Anji sighed. 'Speak later, Jake, and stay safe!'

'Will do!'

The line went dead.

Jake pocketed his phone again and went back to rocking back and forth, cradling Skateboard, waiting for his friend's salvation.

Meanwhile, Auger was struggling with her guilt. As she continued her lonesome trek across the desert towards her destination, she continued to grunt through the occasional whimper of emotion.

She had killed them. Both of them. The annoying child and his even more annoying robot. And for what? To get her own way? Hardly an honourable way to dispose of people who were obstacles in the grand plan.

She hated Lon. For making her become this. For allowing these strangers to come along with them. They should have said no. Allowed them time to recuperate and then leave. It was a bad idea and now her conscience was stained. Is this what she was now?

She sniffed and wiped the tears from her cheeks roughly, sand sticking to it like a permanent reminder, if she needed another, of what she had done.

She was also exhausted. That intruding robot had been right. She had needed the rest. But for her, she would have to carry this with her. The pain, the guilt.

Suddenly, her thoughts turned to Random and the girl. How would she break the news to them?

What would she say?

Lon wouldn't care. She knew that for a fact. Lon cared for nothing and no-one. Well, except the Flux. It had changed him. Consumed his mind. Poisoned every fiber of his being. Auger knew he had the capacity to be ruthless. She had seen it. But when it came to putting people other than himself in danger? This was a new level and with it, he had dragged her down too.

Was the Flux really worth all of this? Immeasurably power, wealth and fame beyond the galaxy? Notoriety? They would go down in history for discovering it.

Auger took a deep breath.

It would be worth it.

She would make it worth it.

XVI

A distant sound of galloping broke Jake from his malaise. He gently put Skateboard down on the floor and made his way over to the door of the shack. Peering out into the brilliant sunshine, he could just make out a clan of Spectronians galloping over the horizon.

'Here they come, Skateboard!' he cried jovially, before remembering his robotic friend was incapacitated and thus unable to respond.

As he watched, a group of four Spectronians soon pulled up outside the shack, dismounted and moored their tamed beats to a post.

The leader of the gang strode purposefully into the shack, straight past Jake and to the stricken Skateboard.

'Uh, hey!' said Jake, a little indignant that the cloaked man hadn't stopped to see how he was.

'Hello!' said a new voice.

Jake allowed the second helper into the shack. She pulled her face mask down, allowing Jake to see her full beautiful features and making the teenager go a little weak at the knees.

'Uh...hi,' he voice cracked a little. The girl was roughly his height, shoulder length multi-coloured hair that matched her gorgeous complexion and lovely big eyes that he could have swum in for a week.

'And you are?'

'I'm Jake...'

The girl hummed. 'Jake...I've never heard of that race. Do you have a name, Jake?'

Jake chuckled.

'No, that is my name.'

'It's a pleasure to meet you, No.'

The girl held her thumb and finger out like she was encouraging Jake to give her a call.

'But we've just met.'

'Precisely, this is how we greet strangers on Spectronia, No.'

Jake rolled his eyes.

'No, No, Jake is my name, not No!'

'Alright then, No, No, Jake, let's take a look at you, shall we?'

As two more helpers came into the shack and made over to Skateboard to assist the head of the group, Jake was encouraged to sit on a nearby stool by his new, weird friend.

She knelt in front of him and sat her bag down next to her. She felt for something inside it and produced a small device and proceeded to buzz it around his head.

'So, tell me, No, No Jake, what are you doing out here?'

'Is it possible to just call me Jake?'

'I'm sure it is,' she smiled at him, making Jake involuntarily smile back. He winced and held his jaw.

'Looks like you took a nasty blow there.'

The girl delved back into her bag and found a box of what looked like tablets.

'This'll heal the wound. Before I give these to you, you're not allergic to asmosaline, are you?'

'What's that when it's at home?'

'That sounds like a no.'

She handed two tiny tablets, round in shape and white in colour to Jake who put them in his mouth and swallowed them immediately.

'What are you doing?'

Gulping, Jake's eyes widened with alarm.

'You're not supposed to swallow them!'

'Then where do I put them?'

The girl gestured to his posterior. Jake nearly choked in alarm. The girl broke out into a wicked laugh.

'It's okay, I'm just joking with you. You'll be fine in a few minutes.'

The boy sighed and laughed simultaneously. What a cruel joke to play on a frightened vulnerable individual.

He was so in love with her he'd have spat them out and stuck them up there himself if it meant she married him that afternoon!

'Sit there for a second and let them do the trick and relax.'

She flashed him another gorgeous smile and got up to go and talk to the group leader, who had appeared to open Skateboard's damaged battery system and was delving into his metallic inerds like he was playing Operation.

'I didn't get your name?' said Jake.

'That's because I haven't told you yet,' she said. 'It's Row.'

'Row,' Jake swooned to himself. He was going to get the name tatooed in as many places as possible on his person when he got home. If he ever got home.

He wanted to ask what the others were doing to his friend but then thought better of it. He didn't want to be the reason why an operation to revive Skateboard didn't work. What if they slipped and severed a vocal cord? Would Skateboard ever forgive him if he woke up with a lisp!

After several minutes, in which Jake's jaw completely set and healed, he could bare the suspense no longer.

'Is he going to be okay?' he called over.

'The main operator jumped.

'Careful!' he exclaimed. 'I nearly severed a vocal cord there!'

Row walked back over to Jake.

'It's going to take a little longer than we expected. Why don't I take you back to base? We can wait for your friend there?'

'No, I want to stay with him.'

Row placed her hand on Jake's shoulder.

'He is safe now, don't worry, he is in good hands. Come on, you can ride with me.'

'Okay,' said Jake hesitantly. As Row led him out of the shack, he shot a look over to his broken friend.

'You can get through this, Skateboard. You can do it mate.'

As he left the shack, Row had already mounted her stallion.

'Ever ridden a Dosa before?'

'If that's what that thing is then I'm afraid not.'

'Hop on.'

Jake approached the beast gingerly and carefully put one leg over the other and slid into the saddle behind Row.

The Dosa whinnied a little.

'See, she likes you. Now put your hands around my middle and hold tight.'

Jake blushed. The last time he put his arm around a girl's midriff, Anji had slapped him. He'd never had a girl ask him to hold on to her before. Gently, he reached around her slender waist and locked his fingers together.

'Here we go!'

The Dosa rose in the air and galloped across the soft sand, bouncing Jake and Row up and down as they tore away at great speed away from the shack that Jake was hoping to never revisit in person or in memory. Instead, he gave into the momentum of the Dosa and let his head lope on Row's back and sighed to himself a little.

So, he thought, *this is what heaven feels like.*

XVII

Meanwhile, whilst their friend was busy falling in love for the first time, Random and Anji had finally escaped the boredom of the pit and managed to stumble upon a passageway. The only trouble for the duo was that it was half blocked by a rock fall, so they had spent the last twenty minutes doing their best to clear as much of the rocks as possible and they were now so close to getting through.

'Phew!' said Anji as she wiped her brow with the back of her sleeve. 'First thing I'm doing when I get back to the Venus II is taking a shower!'

'You may have to join the queue!' said Random, whose face was soaked in sweat.

With a final push, they had made it out the other side.

'Finally!' declared Anji. When the dust had settled, they looked out on a clear and, hopefully, unabated path out of the mountain. A glimmer of light appeared at the end of the tunnel and it flooded Anji's outlook.

'Come on! We've got to stop Lon!' said Random. He tore off ahead of Anji and out of view. A purple blur shot away from her, and then shot back up the path towards her.

Without warning, Random grabbed her by the hand and yanked her along with him.

*

Solenia sat upon her throne, chewing over what the strange blonde boy in front of her had been saying ever since he had burst into the throne room and accidentally knocked over a priceless vase that was balanced precariously on a plinth next to the main doors.

In doing so, Solenia felt that she was well within her rights to condemn him to an eternity of embarrassing punishments. But as soon as she had deciphered the garbling gibberish he seemed to be spouting about being buried alive, a robot getting stabbed and Auger and Lon being murderers, she knew she had to step in.

'Enough of this, we have not a moment to lose,' she said standing up and making her way down towards the frantic boy.

'You have been through much; I implore you to stay here and rest. We will deal with the rest.'

'Your majesty, I must come with you. My friends will need me.'

Solenia put her hand on his shoulder, and then wished she hadn't with the clumps of rainbow coloured earth and what must have been sweat dirtied her hands.

'As you wish...but we leave immediately. Guards.'

The two golden robed strongmen standing either side of their Queen stood to attention even stronger than they originally were and waited on Solenia's next order.

'Summon the Valkaryies. We have no time to lose!'

*

High above the glorious skies of Spectronia, a fleet of mysterious flying pyramids were sailing ominously towards the illuminating planet. Dozens upon dozens of ships continued on their descent in a formation that rather unimaginatively also resembled somewhat of a pyramid itself.

At the tip, apex as it were, was the command centre, the same edifice that Random had escaped not too long ago after failing to get on the good side of the gods who had sat dormant for so long before he had disturbed their slumber.

And now, they wanted revenge.

How was Random to know that Gods were also susceptible to being a little cranky after a long snooze?

'The traitor is moving within range,' said Isis.

'Shall we open the laser canons?' asked Thoth.

'What would be the point from here,' said Horus. 'The target is too far away. We must move in closer. Crush the planet if we must. The traitor must die.'

'Wait!' Ra arose from his throne, dust falling from his frame as it moved for the first time in eons. 'I sense a great power. An orb with enough energy to power a thousand suns, or burn a thousand skies.'

'Ra speaks the truth,' came another voice.

'Bennut, you sense the same power?' asked Isis.

'I can smell it like the most pungent of herbs, it courses through my blood like a river of fire.'

Ra smiled sinisterly. 'Doesn't it feel good, Bennut?'

'It does..if we destroy this planet before obtaining this amazing power, we could lose the one chance we have of reobtaining our true place as the rulers of the universe.'

'Come on,' tusked Osiris, 'You expect us to believe that? What of the traitor? And if we do obtain the...orb...as you describe it, what makes you think the Syonians won't try to face us again?'

'We could easily crush the insulance of those righteous fake idols once and for all if we had this power, trust me,' smiled Ra. 'Listen to me, brothers and sisters, my fellow deities, this is the chance to gain life beyond immortality. To have the power to give or take life as and when we see fit, this will be a momentous day for the Osirans. It is the day that we can take control of supremacy in every single corner of the cosmos. Not even the furthest, darkest embers of the universe will hide from our supremacy. Galaxies can be bent to our will with a mere thought. We must seize the power..and ascend above glory, past myth..all will know of the Osirans, and they will grovel in the dust at the mere thought of our presence.'

'Not without the consent of Amun-Ra,' barked the Mother Goddess.

'I am Amun-Ra!' barked Ra. He was right. Amun-Ra was an amalgamation of the god of war, the very deity trying to wager a galactic war on the rest of the cosmos before his peers, and Amun, an almighty god, who was unwilling to merge with Ra since the Osirans had been paralysed and left abandoned in space.

'Amun, show yourself.'

There was silence in the vast bowels on the ship.

'I will not consent to this,' came a tired voice.

Ra laughed. 'You dare to let the opportunity of supreme power through your fingertips?'

From the shadows, a face, human in design, peered through the darkness towards its impetuous rival.

'The universe reeks of megalomania. In the eons we have both lived and imprisoned in dormancy, countless others have sought to control all living matter.'

'But Amun, we are hundred in number!'

'Exactly. The quantity of egos in this room negates democracy. We can never agree on anything. You and I are the same creature and we can never see eye-to-eye.'

'Amun, you forget, you need me to break this feeble spell of soul searching. I can handle the call to power but I am asking you to join me in a call to arms..solidarity can lead to our supremacy. Trust me!'

Amun sighed hard.

'Trust..now why would anyone ever trust a god of war? Destruction, devastation, disease. These are all brought about by Kings such as yourself.'

'Well, you did once,' said Ra. His comment cut though Amun's heart.

'I did, and it was a mistake that we must learn from here. No god should be above their peers.'

'No god,' spat Ra. 'But I!'

'Stop him!' cried Isis, but it was too late. Ra's form began to merge with that of Amun's. A brilliant struggle of wills battled it out in a blaze of white fire that enveloped the pyramid ship. Within seconds, the space that had been occupied by the two gods was unoccupied and a larger, bigger being began to emerge from the brilliant light. The vast creature descended to the floor, huge in stature and resembling little of Amun and more the face of Ra, it glared down upon all the gods of the Osirians.

'Kneel before us...'it boomed its thunderous order.

'Kneel before me.'

XVIII

'Lon!'

Auger had never been so pleased to see someone in her entire life. She had picked out the familiar outline of her colleague and ally across the sands and ran to be with him again. It had seemed like forever ago since she left the boy and his talking board for dead – and forever is a long time for one person to be alone with their conscience.

Lon was silent in response. He proceeded to move towards her but in a manner that was as though Auger wasn't even there.

As they got closer, Auger registered that Etherton wasn't with him. Or Random. Or the girl.

'Where are the others?'

Lon continued on his approach, his face drawn and his eyes black with fatigue.

'You look terrible.'

'Noted,' he brushed off the remark as he powered on past her. She turned on her heels and caught up.

'Woah, woah, slow down a second there, aren't you going to ask me what's been going on.'

'No.'

'Lon.'

'Enough.'

Auger frowned.

'What's happened?'

'Nothing's happened.'

'Don't kid a kidder, Lon.'

Lon stopped.

'Who said anything about killing?'

'No, you misheard me, look, I had to get rid of the other two.'

'Good, that's the first sensible thing you have done since you got here.'

Lon picked up the pace again, leaving Auger slightly aghast.

'Excuse me!?'

'Auger, I have neither the time nor the patience to carry on with this conversation. I don't care what has happened to your little friends and I don't think that I ever will, do you understand?'

'Lon, what's got into you?'

'Again, with the questions...'

'Well, if you are going to treat me like a child then I demand to know why you've gone rotten all of a sudden?'

'All of a sudden? I've always been rotten, Auger. Right to my very core!' he cried. 'If you don't know that about me by now then I doubt we've ever got to know each other in the first place.'

Auger reeled as it dawned on her why her friend was acting like this. She wanted to act out like he was too. That could only mean one thing.

'You killed them.'

Lon's eyes dimmed. He resisted temptation to dignify Auger's claim with a response.

'Look at what the Flux has done to us!'

'We can think about our actions when it in our grasp, and we are off this zarking planet!'

'I don't think I can live with the guilt...'

'Then after you've helped me retain it, don't.'

Auger was appalled.

'How dare you!' Is that what you really think?'

'I think of nothing but the Flux. The ultimate prize!' he spat.

'It's consumed you! Changed you! The very thought of it has poisoned your mind.'

'You sound like Etherton,' he sighed. 'Your minds are too narrow for ambition. I'm relieving you of your services right now.'

'Lon, you need help!'

'I need the Flux!'

Auger's eyes met with Lon's. She saw the madness that now consumed him, the same madness that was the final image that Etherton had seen.

'Leave me.'

'But Strakonis...'

'...is no match for me. Not this time. Not now I know what I am capable of. Go home, Auger.'

Auger let him continue his journey. She was through with fighting with him.

After all these years, this was it. He was beyond redemption. He had killed Etherton and the two Earth kids. She had killed too, but at least she still had her guilt. Lon was without redemption.

He had to be stopped.

As Lon marched towards the canyon, which was quickly appearing on the horizon, he suddenly felt a hot bolt of agony erupt in his left arm. He cried out in pain and crunched down to his haunches. Inspecting his wound, he noticed what looked like a laser injury.

Through gritted teeth, he reached into his boot with his good hand and spun around sharply. Without remorse, without compassion, he fired several shots of gunfire back at his old friend, crying out with all the rage and fire that burned within him until Auger lay motionless in the dust in the distance.

He pitied her. So close to the prize, but just as weak and feeble as the others when push came to shove.

Lon glared down at the wound. The heat of the laser shot had cortisone the hole that now lay searing hot near his upper shoulder, so at least he didn't have to stop to tend to it. The determination that burned in his soul wouldn't allow him to do that anyway. Nothing was going to slow him down now.

Lon flicked a small switch on his gun to recharge it. The finish line was in sight and when he got there, he was ready to end this for good.

No one was going to take the Flux from him.

No one.

*

The canyon was quiet, still. No living being disturbed the silence that hung in the thick, stuffy air. As venues for a showdown between two ruthless, ambitious explorers battling for the most powerful element in the known universe. As Strakonis watched from high above at the very top of the canyon, his trap laid and set to obliterate Lon and his cronies as soon as they set foot in the quagmire.

As he replaced his binoculars and reached for his satchel, produced a flat bread snack and taking a sizeable bite, thought about the boy he had encountered in the shack. He said that he had other friends who needed his help, but Strakonis wasn't able to come to their aid. He'd wanted to. He hated the thought of people getting caught in the crossfire of his long running feud with Lon. Besides, he had the Flux to protect, to hide. And if he hadn't made the canyon in time, it would never make its rendezvous.

Suddenly, his thoughts were disturbed by what appeared to be a flash of purple light far below his vantage point. He reached for his binoculars and gazed down on what looked like a young boy and girl. They were humanoid in appearance, but it soon became clear to Strakonis that his complexion was what had given off the impressive purple hue. This wasn't part of Lon's team, nor did they look like natives. These were the friends that Jake had been talking about.

And then he realised the danger they had just walked into and ran towards a cave opening nearby...

'Looks like we beat Lon then.'

'Looks that way?' said Random, gasping for breath. 'Right, let's have a little look around. See if this Strakonis is anywhere to be seen-'

As he placed on foot forward, Anji recoiled in alarm.

'Random watch out!'

A barrage of laser fire exploded from a nearby rock, causing Random to throw himself to the side and with cat like reflexes pull Anji down with him and before she knew what was going on, she was on the ground with him.

'That was close!' said Random as the barrage subsided. As he got up, a rumbling sound filled the canyon. Anji, who remained face down on the floor swore it was getting louder.

Random looked down at his chest and noticed a hologrammatic bullseye imprinted on his t-shirt.

Panicked, he grabbed Anji once again and threw the pair of them against the cliff face just as two huge boulders cascaded over the top of the canyon and smashed in the very space they were standing in, sending debris and dust up in the air like a mushroom cloud.

As the chaos settled, Random and Anji put their hands up in surrender, not daring to move their feet anywhere else but from where they were firmly planted.

'Stop! We come in peace!' shouted Random. He turned to Anji. 'Ugh, don't tell anyone I said that!'

'Forgive me,' said a faraway voice.

'Only if you stop attacking us!' shouted Anji in reply. She looked all around for confirmation of where the voice was coming from.

'The failsafe is in operation now. You are free to move around the canyon...if you confirm to me who you are and what you are doing here?'

Random lowered his hands very slowly.

'I take it we are speaking to Strakonis?'

'You are,' replied the disembodied voice. 'And who may I say I am talking to?'

'My name is Random and this is Anji. You helped our friends Jake and Skateboard out earlier.

There was a moment of silence.

'Hello.'

All of a sudden Strakonis popped up from behind them, making Random and Anji jump like cartoon characters startled by a mouse in old 1960s cartoons.

'I apologise for the less than hospitable welcome.'

'It's alright, we understand why you've gone to such lengths to keep the Flux safe.'

Strakonis surveyed the two strangers. Anji was startled by his appearance.

'Don't be alarmed,' he reassured her. 'Although my appearance is less than palatable, I can assure you my offer of friendship is.'

He held his hand out to shake Random's own, with the
Rodasian returning in kind by pinching his thumb and pulling it
up and down.

Strakonis laughed. 'Yes, well, we all have our customs. Follow
me. There is much that I need to know.'

'He's on his way,' said Random grimly.

'But I didn't fancy his chances against that lot!' said Anji.

'You can never be sure with that man, come let us talk inside.'
With that Strakonis led the pair through a concealed opening in
the canyon wall and they passed through what to them looked
like solid rock.

'Holograms!' said Random admirably.

'Cloaking devices,' Strakonis corrected him.

'Whatever it is its impressive!' said Anji.

'In my line of work, you need it,' replied Strakonis.

The trio snaked up a metal gantry.

'So, I take it this isn't a feature of the canyon, no?' asked
Random.

'Certainly not,' smiled Strakonis. At the top of the gantry, he
pressed a button on the wall. A door slid open unveiling an
impressive control room to an aghast Random and Anji.

'Oh wow!' cried Anji.

The place was the stuff of science fiction dreams. A myriad of
switches, flashing lights and what looked like important
instruments adorned the walls and a flat table system that sloped
ever so slightly up to the ceiling, which was just as dark as the
cabin.

'It looks like a Christmas fair in here,' said Anji.

'I'm going to assume that that's a good thing,' said Strakonis.
'Sorry about the mess, when you are forever travelling you don't
really have the time to clean up after yourself. Please.'

A bony hand offered Random and Anji to sit down on a large
brown sofa. They accepted in kind but turned down their new
acquaintances offer of what looked like a very muddy pot of
coffee.

'So then,' said Strakonis as he lowered himself down in a
command chair that Anji thought looked like a gaming one she
had seen in a shop window one time, 'tell me everything.'

'Wait a minute,' said Random, 'it's all very well you being so nice to us after, you know, trying to blow us up and crush us with your traps, and while we understand why you've had to do that, it would be good to know that we are actually on the right side this time. Who's to say that you are not as mad with power as Lon?'

'Because even though I have the Flux I do not want it.'

'You don't want the most powerful element in the universe?' said Anji.

'No,' said Strakonis.

'Then why are you going to all of this bother?' said Random.

'It's a fair question so I will give you a fair but fairly obvious response. Because I am hiding it.'

'Why?' asked Anji.

'Because the very thought of obtaining the Flux is enough to turn any being in the cosmos mad. Take Lon for example. Sure, we are rivals, we go way back. We've battled throughout the galaxy for treasure, but the Flux is the one thing any explorer desires, but should never have. I don't want to be in possession of it at all. I'm just a courier.'

'Courier for who? And can they be trusted?'

Random wondered who Strakonis might be working for.

'I believe so. I know so. The Flux should be protected from any being who desires it. So, to give it to a people who do not want it, and will pretty much forget about it in the years to come, is more than safe.'

'But from what Lon has told us it can do so much good for the universe,' said Anji. 'Put an end to famine, energy supplies, that's what he said.'

'It's true...' said Strakonis, '...but what if the person who uses it for that power becomes corrupted, started using it to take over worlds, destroy lives? It's happened before, it can never happen again.'

Then Random thought, somewhat misguidedly, that this would be the best time to ask the question that was on both he and Anji's minds.

'May we see it?'

Strakonis huffed.

'No.'

'Strakonis, we are willing to accept what you are telling us, but without seeing what you are protecting, it's hard for us to believe it's really worth all of this.'

'That's no justification to show you.'

'I know, but I thought it was worth saying.'

Strakonis exhaled. 'Okay, but I must warn you, it does have an immense power, more than many living beings can comprehend.'

'Alright, we promise we won't touch,' said Anji smiling.

Strakonis got up and made for the control panel. He flipped a few switches and before long a slow, hydraulic tube descended from the ceiling, slowly filling the room in a heavenly emerald glow.

'Behold,' he said, 'the Zedron Flux.'

Anji had never seen anything as beautiful as the Flux in her entire life – and that included her short lived but intense crush on Dylan Scott in Year 7.

'My god.'

Random was unmoved.

'It sure is...glowy.'

'I am surprised, my friend.'

'Random, don't you think it's gorgeous?' Anji purred as she watched it swirl almost balletically in its casing.

'It is a sight to behold, but I can see what Strakonis is talking about.'

'You're not feeling a lure towards it? No lust for power? No yearning for it to put anything right?'

Random had wondered about it. Ever since Lon had described to them what the Flux was, he had been slightly tempted by its power. With the Flux, he would have the ability to end the war on Rodas once and for all. Obliterate Kalor Maloso, slaughter the Crimson Empire and purge the Sapphire Regime until they were nothing but dust. But he was not a God. There were other ways of making peace without taking any more lives. The Flux was not the answer and it never would be.

'It's just an intergalactic pawn,' said Random, moving away from it. 'A weapon to hold and say, "ner-ner-ner, I have it, can't touch me now". I mean, that's pretty sad really, isn't it?'

Strakonis flipped a switch and the Flux began to raise back into his housing and the light began to fade back to normal in the cabin.

'Well, now I know I can trust you,' said Strakonis.

'We can help you get the Flux to where it needs to go,' said Random. 'But I would feel a little easier if I knew who is it going to for safe keeping.'

Strakonis nodded.

'It's Solenia.'

XIX

Light.

Then darkness again.

Then another flicker of light.

Followed by another embrace of blackness.

This sequence of events seemed to come and go for Skateboard but for how long he could not work out. In fact, he couldn't do much. There was nothing for him to compute, he found that he was unable to run a diagnostic, think freely, move or even speak. He couldn't even remember what his name was. No memory of what had happened, who he was.

Tiny hints to these questions kept cropping up every time the light flickered into view, before being cruelly taken away from him again and sending him reeling back into the vast nothingness.

Every now and then the moments in the light felt longer and he was able to piece together little bits of this information. But it still felt quite vague.

He knew he was on an alien world, far from his own. He knew that he had arrived with others, but their faces were faint, unrecognisable.

Something had happened to him; he knew that much. Something awful.

And then, he remembered.

The woman with the knife.

She'd stabbed him.

Worse still.

She had killed him.

Skateboard's hydraulics began to whir inside him at an erratic rate.

He couldn't stop himself.

He was having a panic attack.

'Shhhh,' said a soothing voice. 'Kepp calm, your safe now.'

Skateboard continued to writhe on the work table.

'Jes, I think he is having a panic attack,' said the nice soft voice.

'A robot? Having a panic attack? Must just be a malfunction, Dara.'

'Honestly for an AI expert you really lack compassion. He's had a shock, you know robots can suffer shock, surely?'

'Well, yes of course I do Dara but I haven't switched him back on yet!'

Dara looked down at the panic-stricken robot.

'Then his battery pack must have finished repairing.'

Skateboard lay there, wriggling from side to side.

The soothing hushed tones that Dara shushed did little to calm him.

'Please, do stay calm, your safe now.'

With a croak, like his vocal cords hadn't been used in a long time, Skateboard emitted a dry noise from his speaker grill.

'Try not to talk just yet. You've had a big shock. Just stay there and relax.' Dara stood up and looked at Jes.

'You're fine with us my little friend. Your companion is safe and well.'

Companion? Which one? Had Jake made it out alive?

'J-J'

'Yes, Jake, that's the one. He is absolutely fine.'

Skateboard's motherboard breathed a sigh of relief. He began to settle back down, reassured that these people were not trying to finish off the job that Auger had started.

'You'd better inform this Jake that the robot is back with us.'

'He's gone with her Majesty to the canyon, I'm not sure how we can reach him from there.'

'Contact Medical Officer Row, she'll put him in the picture.'

Dara rolled her eyes. 'Sure, Row gets the good jobs.' Although Row was her superior, Dara had been quite jealous of her of late. In fact, it was Row who had trained with her in the same medical teachings that Dara had attended but only one of them had obtained promotion and with it, greater freedom to roam the up-above surface of Spectronia.

'Put your jealousy to one side for a moment Dara,' implored Jes. 'You'll see the surface soon; I am sure of it.'

'Yes,' said a third voice. 'You can come with me now and tell him the news yourself if you like?'

Jes and Dara turned back to the work station, where their patient was no longer lying down flat but standing up on his back two wheels.

'What do you think you are doing?!' Jes flapped. 'Stay down, you've hac a terrible shock.'

'My dear doctor, I know,' assured Skateboard. 'But I'm not about to let an attempt on my life get in the way of what is threatening those of my friends.'

Dara reached for an electric tranquiliser rod.

'No!' said Jes. 'Put that down.' He yanked the instrument from her grasp. 'These are expensive to run. Now I'm telling you, robot-'

'I would prefer if you would call me by my name; Skateboard.'

'Fine,' said Jes, 'Skateboard. I cannot allow you to leave this facility. Not in your condition.'

'But I have no condition. I have fully recovered thanks to you and your colleagues. I am more than grateful; I can assure you.'

'You can assure me even more by staying still and fully recuperating.'

'Jes,' said Dara holding another, less threatening instrument in her hand, 'he is telling the truth; all systems working perfectly.'

'Then what of the shock he was displaying moments ago?'

'I'm a robot – these things change just like the weather. The shock of waking up from death is fleeting for an AI like me. Especially when there are more pressing matters at hand. Now please, let me go. I can take your associate with me to keep an eye on me, just in case I have anymore..." wobbly" moments.'

Jes looked at Dara and could tell that she had nothing but extreme keenness to take the robot up on his offer.

'Fine. I hereby discharge you from this workshop but insist that you stay under direct supervision until your carer deems it necessary.'

'Thank you,' whirred Skateboard.

'No, thank you!' grinned Dara.

'We haven't a moment to lose,' Skateboard declared as he hopped off the work station and with a metal clang landed abruptly on the floor. 'Transferring to horizontal mode,' he said as he flopped onto his four wheels. 'Please step on my back, Miss.'

'What?'

'It's perfectly safe, I can assure you.'

Hesitantly, Dara picked up her medical bag, packed her scanner inside, zipped up the pocket and stepped onto Skateboard's back. She felt a grip bolt the soles of her shoes to the surface.

'Just tucking you in tight, Miss, wouldn't want to lose you enroute,' said Skateboard. 'Right, off we go.'

With that, Skateboard tore forward a couple of metres and slapped firmly into the ground.

'Oh,' he cried, in a tone of embarrassment. 'Just one thing before we go...can you attach my wheels back on please?'

*

Jake had had enough of the Dasa...whatever they were. He had just got to the age where he was no longer conscious of having a squeaky voice that broke every five seconds or that a pretty girl was around. Just before he left Earth, he felt like he was finally on par with the other boys around him. Sure, some of them had developed at a rate that saw them hairier than a gorilla, taller than a giraffe and deeper voiced than...some other zoo animal he couldn't think of right now, but out here in the hitherto undiscovered charters of space, he was unique. He was the blue print for humanity that other species could look from and say, "this is what the rest of the human race are like". And then, he wondered if this was actually a good thing or not. He wasn't the neatest, best looking or had the highest levels of personal hygiene that many others possessed back on his home world. But hey, who was going to find out any time soon unless they went there? So that took an awful lot of the pressure off him when it came to the way he thought he was looked upon as a person.

He had grown since he had left the Earth some months earlier. Hell, he'd even got some downy fluff on his chest now! Any time now he thought he would probably have to take up shaving! But after thirty minutes of bouncing up and down on a black alien horse that smelt worse than he did after two hours of football practice, his voice was rapidly regressing to its girly, squeaky version.

What was even more concerning was that and he couldn't feel anything in the trouser department anymore.

'How much further?' he squeaked to Solenia's guard. He was holding on to his tree trunk like waist, although he hands kept slipping a little from the large quantities of sweat, he was producing. Jake had been bitterly disappointed when he was told he couldn't ride with Row, or that was wasn't being given his own Dasa. But nothing prepared him for the crushing blow that was having to cling to a half-naked man for the journey. Solenia had only his safety at hand, and he had insisted upon going with them, if for nothing else, so he didn't miss a slice of the action. Last time out he had felt a little ignored when Random and Anji had faced the Yarvesh back on Genocia. Sure, he was the one who had freed the slaves and got them out of danger, with a little help from other of course, but it hurt a little that they hadn't been around to see him being heroic. And now here he was again, alone without his friends. Well, this time he wanted a slice of the pie. This time he wanted to show them he could be just as heroic as they were.

If for nothing else, just to show off.

And if it took a humiliating and less than cool journey that resulted in his spuds getting crushed by the beast he was riding, then he just wouldn't tell them that bit.

'We are not far away now,' cried the Guard.

'Good!'

'Just do me a favour will you, little girl.'

Jake tried to remember that this was an alien he was accompanying, one who could crush him with one swat of his giant, rainbow coloured hand, so let the mix up of gender slide.

'Sure...'

'Please stop digging your nails into my waist, it really hurts.'

Jake embarrassingly recoiled his fingertips from the Guard's flesh.

'That's better.'

Blushing, Jake fell silent and decided to speak again until they got there...

XX

Auger lay still where she had fallen. Unmoved. Quiet. All for the heavy cries of pain and sobbing.

494

There was no one around to help her, no one to hear her.

She was well and truly alone.

She tried to move her leg again. Apart from a sensation of searing agony, she felt nothing.

This was how it was going to end for her.

She would bleed out, alone on the most beautiful planet she had ever seen.

And how had she treated her time on this blesses world? Instead of finding the wonder of it all, she had been consumed with nothing else but the drive to reclaim the Flux. Not that they had ever had it. And it had led her to kill, something she had never thought she would ever do, no matter how desperate the situation.

She loathed herself.

This was the end that was right for the person she was now.

To die alone, without comfort or companionship was her punishment...and she deserved every last second of it.

She peered up for a moment, trying to make out Lon in the far distance. He was now but a dark spec on the horizon, no bigger than her thumb.

Someone had to stop him.

But what if there wasn't anyone? What if Lon would end up taking the Flux, becoming a mad ruler of the universe?

She couldn't let that happen.

No.

She wouldn't let that happen.

With great effort, Auger rolled herself on to her side. With a cry of agony, she hauled herself upright. She heaved when she looked down on what was left of her leg. Calming herself, she ignored her wounds, the pain, the blood and with a yell got up on to her feet...well, the working one.

Grunting heavily, she dragged her broken body towards Lon's outline. The sweat cascaded down her face but she ignored, focusing more on the pain and letting that drive her forward.

She would die today...but not before she had saved everyone else.

*

'So Solenia is on her way?'

Anji studied the orange illuminating map that adorned one of the walls in Strakonis' ship.

'If we are lucky, she will be here in a matter of minutes.'

'Good, let's hope Jake and Skateboard are with her,' said Random.

'But Solenia told us she knew nothing of the Flux,' Anji pointed out.

'That's because Lon was with you. I had pre-warned her of his intentions.'

'Then if that's the case, why let us all go in the first place?'

'Good question Anji,' said Random.

'Believe you me, I wish she hadn't, but my best guess is that because she was unaware of what his intentions would be...and technically, his team, i.e, you lot, were not deemed dangerous, she must have thought she'd chance it by letting you all go and beating Lon to the prize, as it were.'

'And seeing you safely off this planet?' asked Random.

'That was the intention, yes. But my ship crash landed. I am stranded here, for the time being at least. There was no guarantee that my ship would be ready in time before Lon got here. Plus, I can't keep running from him forever.'

'Is there a way that we can destroy the Flux?' said Random.

'I have pondered that every day since I discovered it...well...saved it from Lon's possession. Unfortunately, no. I wish there was a way but there isn't. Even if you were to throw it into a singularity, the Flux would only make the black hole stronger and consume all of the life in its wake.'

'Oh great, so it's indestructible then!' Anji threw her arms up in the air.

'You could say that.'

'So, what makes you think Solenia won't be consumed by it?' said Random.

'She is a ruler, The Spectronians are a peaceful race. This planet is left alone by the cosmos. It's remote, hard to find, and so will the Flux if it stays here.'

'Well, we all found it,' said Anji. Suddenly, a blip on the map distracted her attention.

'Hey guys, there's another blip.'

Strakonis and Random went over to join her.

'Lon,' said Strakonis, who without hesitation made for his gun.

'And another, fainter one behind him.'

'Could be Etherton...or Auger, come on Anji, we've got work to do.'

'Like what?'

'We've got to buy Strakonis time, stop Lon from entering the canyon.'

'How?'

'Any means necessary,' said Strakonis.

Random saw the panic in Anji's eyes.

'We are not killing him!'

'No, we are not,' reassured Random.

'Hopefully it may not come to that,' said Strakonis. 'But you must do what you can to stop him from getting in here. Let the traps do their job and if they fail, or he finds a way past them, that's when we need to strike, I'll inform Solenia through our communication channel.'

'Look, Random, there's another blob on the scanner...it's really fast!'

Random grinned. 'That's Skateboard.'

'How do you know?'

'Oh, I know alright! Strakonis, the Spectronians are still further away than Lon, can you tell them to speed up a bit?'

Strakonis threw his microphone down in frustration.

'There's too much interference, I'll have to drop the cloaking device to get through to them.'

'Right, you do that, Anj, let's go.'

All three of them went about their work. As Strakonis dropped the cloaking controls and followed Random and Anji out of the room, a large cluster of blobs began to descend on the scanner. More and more appeared, completely unnoticed.

Before long, it was going to be hard to ignore that they were there. Especially with what the unnoticed intruders had for the people below.

Lon had found a way inside the canyon. Squeezing between what should have been a blocked off area, he had instantly found a chink in Strakonis' armour. It looked as though something – or someone – had blasted between the rock face. Fragments of jagged debris lay strewn all about his feet. As he placed his hands on the sharp boulder, he failed to notice that the razor sharpness had made two lacerations in the palm of his hands, like paper cuts right across the flesh. But such was his want, his drive, his mind had told him to ignore it.

High above, Random, Anji and Strakonis took up their places and watched like spectators in a stadium as Lon entered the playing field.

'What do we do, drop rocks on his head?' asked Anji.

'Good idea!' chirped Random. 'Nothing that will squash him though.'

Strakonis readied his gun.

'I can end this here and now with one squeeze of the trigger.'

'No, you can't. I haven't known you long Strakonis but I can already tell that you are not a killer.'

Random was right. Strakonis hated him for it but also secretly thanked him for his perspective. He couldn't stoop to Lon's level – he'd never do that. No, he had to stop him by other means.

'Okay, you win, Random. I'll go back to the ship and set up guard there.'

'Are your traps reset?' asked Anji.

Strakonis said nothing.

'Well?'

Without a word, Strakonis legged it back to his ship.

'Anj, try and slow him down,' said Random as he pegged it after the explorer.

Anji turned away and looked back over into the canyon. Lon was coming up to the very spot where she and Random were nearly fried by the concealed laser gun.

Nothing happened.

She turned away, desperately searching for something to throw. Quickly, she ran her hand along the ground, picking up chunky nuggets of gravel and started to rain them down upon Lon. But even as the timid rock fall cascaded at him from the sky, Lon did not look up. In fact, Anji didn't even think that he had blinked, even looking down from afar.

She looked around for more rocks and decided it might be a good idea to move onto slightly bigger missiles. She began to throw fist sized rocks, but her aim was less impressive than the cluster she had chucked over the edge before and they all missed Lon.

The power crazed explorer had spotted Strakonis' ship. He started to run towards it, his legs carrying him ever closer towards the vessel that might, no, MUST contain the Flux.

'Random!' shouted Anji. 'Plan A didn't work. Move to Plan B!'

Random could hear the cries of his friend but he was too engaged in making it back to the ship before Lon. But Lon had an almighty advantage as the entrance he had found to the cave was much closer to the ship than either he or Strakonis were. Even with his super speed, they still didn't stand a chance in getting there first.

Strakonis lagged behind, fiddling with his weapon as Random tore on ahead. He had to get there first, he just had to.

Throwing himself down the gravel path, he tumbled as he reached the higher point of the nose cone of the space ship. And as he slipped close to the rocket section a bolt of laser fire imbedded itself into his stomach, sending the Rodasian falling well over the cliff edge and plummeting towards the ground.

Anji screamed in terror as she witnessed Random's lifeless form fall to the ground and with a sickening thud, he fell at the feet of a grinning Lon.

'No!' she hollered. 'You murderer!'

Lon looked up and fired his gun in her general direction. Anji ducked behind a boulder and felt the heat of the fire shoot past her head and blow a hole in the rock face behind her.

As Lon made for the gantry up to the control room, Strakonis threw himself at his rival and the pair grappled for supremacy. Lon's eyes were as black as his soul as he landed several blows upon Strakonis' person, the protector of the Flux being far from a physical match for his enemy.

Lon punched him again, splitting what was left of his scared lip. Gripping him tightly by his collar, Lon pulled Strakonis close.

'You thought you could stop me? ME! I was always going to defeat you, Strakonis. You couldn't run from me forever.'

Strakonis spat. 'You haven't won yet...I don't see the Flux anywhere.'

'You're going to tell me where it is and you will do it now.'

Strakonis stared defiantly.

'No.'

Lon landed another devastating blow to Strakonis' badly scared cheek, sending the beaten man hurtling to the floor. Lon instantly picked him up again but his collar, half choking him.

'You will show me where it is!'

Strakonis began to black out. Only the pain of Lon digging his fingers into the scar tissue on his face kept him awake.

'Or I will finish the job I started a long time ago...'

Strakonis' breath became heavy with anger. So, Lon was responsible for the acid attack on Ulsamaynor.

'You...'

'Come on, in we go,' Lon dragged the injured Strakonis inside the spaceship, leaving Random laying injured, a trickle of purple blood flowing from the back of his skull.

As Anji raced to his side, she could hear the approaching sound of hooves. She tried not to pay attention to them as she made for the lifeless body of her friend.

XXI

Jake was one of the first to see his friend lying in the dirt. Without hesitation, he dismounted his steed and fell in a crumbled heap on the floor before running to be by Random's side.

'Anj!' he cried.

'Jake! His fallen, Lon's inside with Strakonis!'

'We'll see to him,' said Solenia. 'Legion!'

A dozen or so guards readied their spears, which suddenly a blue energy ribbon around the spikes in unison, dismounted their Dosas and ran towards the ship. At exactly the same time, all of them were thrown with great force away from the ship and landed in an undignified heap.

'Lon must have activated a forcefield,' said Jake.

'Never mind about that Jake, help him!' cried Anji. She cradled her friend's head and noticed the blood on her hand.

'Oh my god.'

'Stand back,' said Solenia.

'No!' screamed Anji.

'Don't defy me, little girl.'

'You're not my Queen and you won't tell me what to do!'

'Guys, please, don't shout I've got a terrible headache,' murmured Random.

Anji breathed a sigh of relief and held her friend tightly to her in an embrace.

'Ouch, not so hard, Anj, I've got a tummy ache.'

Random pushed her away and inspected the wound to his stomach. 'Ah, that explains it.'

'What happened?' asked Jake.

Random, still dazed by his great fall, felt it were better if he mimed a complete guide to his fall, complete with sound effects and hand signals. If for nothing else, it would help him discover the words in his vocabulary that he had momentarily lost after hitting his head.

'...and now here I am. But let's not concentrate on that. Where is Lon?'

'Inside. He's got Strakonis,' said Anji.

'Ah. That's not good.'

The hubbub surrounding Random's improbable survival was shattered by a large, pointed shadow enveloping the canyon and a deep humming noise echoing all around. Suddenly, another shadow descended and then another. And another. Within moments there were many a flying pyramid hanging in the air. If it had not spelt as much danger as it did, Random and his friends would have been impressed.

Anji, Jake, Solenia and the Spectronians were aghast, unable to utter a sound.

'Ah,' Random finally said. 'Neither's that!'

The pyramids swirled in the sky, high above them.

'Who are they?'

'Osirans,' said Random.

Solenia recoiled.

'I thought that they were just legend.'

'Evidentially not,' said Random.

'What are they doing here?'

Anji and Jake gave each other a knowing look.

Random knew what he must do. He had to tell the truth – no matter the consequences.

'Your majesty, I don't think I have the heart to tell you, but they were chasing us across space.'

'So, you lied...' Solenia gritted her teeth, a quiet rage slowly building within her.

'Please, we can deal with this some other time, but first we need to rescue Strakonis and deal with the Osirans.'

He was right. And a liar. But Solenia knew they had to attack two problems now... and the fate of her people, her very planet, hung in a balance.

She had heard of the myths surrounding the Osirans as a child, back in the old times of the Spectronian people, when her Mother read her the stories at bedtime. She remembered how terrified they made her, sometimes to the point that she'd ask her to stop and read something with a nicer ending. She had comforted herself at that young age that these were just stories, and the baddies in those particular books did not exist.

And now here they were, very much a reality.

'This is your Emperor speaking.'

A deep voice emitted like a sonic boom from the lead pyramid.

'There is only one ruler of Spectronia,' Solenia screamed back.

'Solenia,' whispered Random. 'Keep them talking, stall them.'

'What are you going to do?' asked Anji.

'We are going to break into Strakonis' ship.' Random got himself up to his feet, with a little help from his friends who steadied him.

'Good luck...'

Solenia's warriors grew closer towards their Queen.

'Who am I addressing?'

'You have the privilege of speaking to Amun-Ra, Emperor of the Osirans. I care not for who you are.'

Solenia sighed indignantly. 'Well, you should. You are trespassing my world.'

'We are Gods. We can go anywhere we like without prosecution.'

'This is a peaceful planet, we have nothing to give you, so if you could just be on your way-'

'Oh, but there is something in your possession that we must have. Our scans detected it, far away from your world and we will not leave your world until we have it.'

Solenia looked nervously over to the trio of aliens who had brought this threat to her planet. The purple one was walking around the landing haunches of the ship with a large stick. How she wanted to wrench it from his hands and beat him with it.

'What if we refuse.'

There was a pregnant pause from the pyramid.

'You can protest, you can fight us, you can appeal to our better side but you will do nothing but prolong your agony and suffering...I will not give you further time and this will be the last time we ask you. We must have the element...and we will take the element. It is your choice whether you live to serve us...or die for having the sheer audacity for standing in our way.'

Solenia's guards shivered. The air turned cold. There was nothing they could do but fight. Somehow. Buy the liar's time.

Solenia looked over towards Random once again and glared. He had brought death to Spectronia.

XXII

With another vile blow Strakonis flew across the control room and slammed painfully into the scanner wall, puncturing a hole in the glass and splintering it to pieces. He fell down.

'Where is it!' I will turn this place to pieces if you do not tell me!' Lon landed another savage blow on Strakonis' body, this time cracking a couple of ribs with his steel capped boot. He began to cough violently, a coppery taste developing in his throat.

'Have it your way!'

Lon left him reeling on the floor and began to trash the place, pulling tables and chairs about, tearing things off the wall. The resistance the stricken man had offered was pitiful and Lon's attention turned back to his prize.

'Lon, Lon please, for zarks sake open up.'

A voice from outside came over the comms system.

'You don't fool me, Random,' spat Lon as Strakonis lay panting on the floor.

He screamed as yet another potential hiding place again threw up nothing. Desperately, he picked up a large shard of glass that lay on the floor next to the crumpled Strakonis. Towering over him, he pressed the sharp fragment against his jugular.

'This is your last chance…where…is…it!!'

'Lon…you can break every bone in my body, kill me in the worst way imaginable. For the peoples of the universe, to save trillions of lives, I will never…ever…tell you.'

With a fell swoop, Strakonis slashed a similar piece of glass at Lon's stomach, making the crazed explorer recoil in agony. As quickly as possible, Strakonis crawled to the button that turned on and off the forcefield.

'Random…quick!' he cried before losing consciousness and falling to the floor. But in doing so, the injured archaeologist had brushed his arm against the lever that hid the Flux. Lon was breathing heavily in pain but had noticed that the control room was slowly flooding with a similar green hue that he had seen on Druis.

Finally, Random, Anji and Jake were aboard the ship.

'Quickly!' said Random as they began to tear up the gantry to the control room. But before they had chance to make it even halfway, the ship began to move.

'We're taking off!' cried Anji.

'We must stop him…the ship might not be ready to take off yet!' said Random, steadying himself and continuing the climb.

'Meaning?' asked Jake.

'Boom!' cried Random.

The roar of the engines sounded wrong. 'See what I mean?' said Random. Finally, they made it to the top and tore into the control room but the green light was now flooding the ship.

They had failed.

There, standing victoriously, was Lon, with the Zedron Flux in his hands.

*

Amun-Ra had had enough of Solenia's silence. To kill after so long was a lust too strong to resist.

'As you wish,' he said, the words dripping with malice.

'Get down!' cried Solenia.

Suddenly, bolts of green energy fizzed towards the Spectronians, but they all did well to avoid the initial volley of fire, despite a handful or guards being thrown from their horses.

'Take cover!' screamed the Queen as the shots continued to relentlessly pound towards them, thumping into the ground and sending Spectronians and Dosas sprawling.

*

Not far away, the chaos had stopped Skateboard in his tracks. Dara stared in horror as the Pyramids hung in the sky, raining down death from above.

'The Osirans,' said Skateboard.

'Who?' asked Dara.

'The gods in the pyramids...they found us.'

'They are killing my people...what are we going to do.'

Skateboard scanned for lifelines. He couldn't find his friends, but the people of Spectronia were in clear danger.

'We must act quickly. Get ready to hop off when I give you the word. We must save them.'

Skateboard's wheel span as he propelled himself towards the death zone.

*

Lon stared in total fascination as the Flux twinkled majestically in its holding cell. He started to chuckle, softly at first before descending into a laugh that chilled Anji and Jake's bones.

'Lon,' said Random, who tried to edge towards him, 'Okay, you win. You have the Flux. It's yours. So, let's call this whole thing quits, yes? We don't want to take the Flux from you now. But I urge you, you have to use it well and do you know where you should start? Do you know the first thing that you should do now. Listen to me. Those people out there need your help. They are being murdered by Gods who dare challenge your claim to that thing. Will you allow that?'

Lon said nothing, totally hypnotised by the power he held in his hands.

'Will you?' Random asked again.

'No.'

Random smiled. 'Good.'

'No, I will not help them.'

Random's smile fell.

Strakonis continued to move, out of sight to his bitter rival, but seen by Random. If he could keep him talking...

'Why not?'

'What's the first thing a man should do when no one around helps him in the first place? He should help himself!'

'Lon, you can't escape. The ship is falling apart. Its engines aren't ready yet. There is no escape.'

'But there is!' he spat. 'As long as I have this! No one can tell me what to do. No one. These Gods you speak of...they are not Gods...I will make them bow before me.'

With a swift swipe, Strakonis split the skin across Lon's shins. He screamed in agony and dropped the Flux towards the floor. In the blink of an eye, before Anji or Jake could implore him to, Random had swooped downward and collected the Flux's cell before it shattered on the cold metal floor.

Suddenly a laser shot burst from the open gantry door, sending Lon sprawling against the wall.

Anji and Jake screamed and looked towards the door as they ducked for cover.

There, propped up against the frame, her pistol shaking in her hand, was Auger. Her face was broken with emotion as she fired the gun again, glowing another hole into Lon's chest. A small flame lit his clothes on the outside of the impact and the fallen explorer began to slide down to the floor.

Lon knew he was finished. Betrayed at the last by his oldest friend. He had found Auger on her home world and asked her to accompany him on his explorations throughout the cosmos. They had history that stretched back throughout years. The things that they had seen, the things that they had done. It all ended like this.

With his dying gaze, Lon looked towards the harsh glow of the Flux. He ignored all else inside the room. His rival, his executioner. The three strangers he had taken with him and had ultimately played their part in his end. All faded to black except that luscious, glorious emerald glow. It was the last thing he saw, the only thing that accompanied him to his end and it was his. It would always be his.

With one final effort, Lon smiled. And then he was gone.

Auger, whose tears were already streaming down her face, sobbed ever more aggressively as she too sunk to the floor. Jake kept his distance from her but Anji kicked the gun from her hand across the floor.

'I had to do it...I had to.'

'It's done now,' said Anji.

Random placed the Flux under his arm and turned the engines off before going over to Lon's lifeless body. He placed his fingers on his wrist. There was no pulse. Slowly, he closed the explorer's eyes and then went over to Strakonis.

'Jake, give me a hand.' The teenager went to aid of the stricken archeologist and placed him gently on a chair.

'I had to do it,' Auger repeated again.

'To make up for what you did to me?' said Jake coldly.

Auger nodded. 'To redeem myself...to save you all.'

'Well, I'm sorry but I am not in a forgiving mood,' he replied.

'I thought I was doing the right thing.'

'How sick must you be to think burying someone alive is right!?' screamed Jake, tears forming in the corners of his eyes.

'Jake!' Random pulled him back with his free hand. He looked his young friend in the eyes. Jake seemed to know what he was thinking. He had been treated harshly, left for dead, but they could deal with that later.

'I know what she did to you was bad but there are people out there who need our help, can you keep it together for just a little longer?'

Jake sniffed and nodded his head.

'Good man,' said Random patting him on the back. The Rodasian made for the woman lying wounded on the floor.

'You will have to pay for what you have done.'

'It's too late to kill me...I'm already dead.'

'I'm not a killer. Unlike you. Nor will I thank you for saving us just then. You will not get find redemption at our door. When this is over, we will hand you over to the nearest penal colony and see to it that you never find freedom again!'

'I don't think you heard me,' she smiled. Anji noticed that she had been clutching a deep laser wound in her stomach.

'I have made my amends...' she said, her voice getting weaker. She looked at Jake, relived that she had not taken his life, a gesture that chilled Jake to the bone.

Despite the deplorable things she had done, Anji was finding it hard to hold back the tears. As was Jake. Random watched as life ebbed away from Auger's features and she too lay dead.

Putting the Flux down, Random scooped up his two friends and held them tight to him. He let them cry on his shoulder, he could feel their tears through his t-shirt and he didn't want to let them go.

'I am so sorry you both had to see that,' he whispered.

Anji and Jake hugged him harder.

'I'm never putting you two through this again. Ever.'

Strakonis sighed hard to himself. Despite his injuries, he knew he would be okay in time. But he worried for the three youngsters in front of him. To see such atrocity at such a young age, what would that do to them now? He then looked over at his fallen enemy. Lon was dead. The Flux was safe, until he remembered it wasn't.

'I'm so sorry you three but the Pyramids...the Spectronians!'

Random broke away. 'You three stay here.'

Anji wiped her eyes with her sleeve. 'Where are you going?'

'I'm going to use the Flux against the Osirans.'

'You can't, you don't know what it will do!' said Jake.

'I'm not going to use it really, just as a bluff, I swear.'

'We can't stay here. Not with these two,' said Anji pointing to the corpses. 'I'm going out there to help the Spectronians.'

'It's safer in here!' cried Random.

'It's what we do, isn't it? We help where we can.' said Jake.

Random sighed. 'Okay, but stay as close to the rock edge as you can! Whatever happens don't wait for me. Find Skateboard and go back to the Venus II, you got that?'

They both nodded. 'Be careful,' said Anji.

'Not as careful as you two,' he shot them a reassuring grin as they both tore down the gantry out towards the chaos outside.

For the first time, Random could hear the laser fire outside and could not believe he had led them to danger again. All for what? To satisfy his needs? To distract him from the voices of those two...strangers? Next time, he'd let them stay on a holiday planet for as long as they wanted.

No.

Next time, he'd take them straight home. This wasn't a life for them. How selfish of him it was to think he could keep them with him.

'Random,' said Strakonis, struggling to his feet.

'Easy Strakonis.'

'No, I'm fine, I'll mend, Listen, I can use the ship's laser canons to fight off the pyramids. The nose section of this craft envelops onto the canyon edge. Go up there, it'll keep you out of the fire.'

'Okay, thanks.'

Random made for the door.

'And Random?'

The Rodasian turned back.

'Yes?'

'Whatever you do. Make sure it is a bluff.'

Random nodded.

He would.

If he wasn't left with any other option.

XIII

Row tried desperately to stop the flow of blood but it was no use. The Guard lay there, his eyes vacantly gazing skywards, unmoved. With a grunt of terrible resignation, she threw the stained swabs to the ground and looked around. There were many Spectronians who lay strewn across the canyon like a sea of fallen dominos. She witnessed yet another blown sky high by laser fire.

All this death.

All of this destruction.

She'd seen too much.

'Over here!' came a cry over her shoulder.

Another Guard was being tended to by a comrade, his legs bleeding a sea of rainbow colours.

Row dodged the fire and the shards of rock being blown up all over the place and skidded to the ground to be next to the stricken man.

'I can feel them,' he said reassuringly, 'But, the pain!'

Row turned to his friend. 'Get him behind that rock, now!'

With a struggle, the pair lifted the injured man upright and guided him to a large rock that was roughly ten metres away. As they got close, they dived for cover again as the shots from the Pyramids blew them off their feet.

Row set to work quickly, producing a roll of gause from her backpack. As she tended to her patient, the other Guard fired back with his electric lance, but the range was just too short.

'They should come out and face us like real warriors,' he muttered.

'They are not warriors; they are Gods.'

'Who are you?' said the Guard.

Skateboard and Dara had arrived and were ready to do their bit.

'We are friends.'

'For now, at least,' Dara said to herself whilst sending a glaring look at Row.

'Dara, Miss, er?'

'Row. I helped you and your friend back in the shack.'

'I'd wish to formally thank you but we simply do not have time. We have to get you all out of the canyon. Dara, show Row the way we got in.'

'Hold on, I'm supposed to stay with you.'

There simply isn't time Miss, now please. I've got to find my friends and put a stop to this before anyone else gets hurt. Now go. I'll cover you.'

Skateboard produced a little laser gun from his body work.

'Now!' he shouted as he fired off rounds that projected far past the Guard's lance and penetrated one of the Pyramid's hull.

'Can we swap?' asked the Guard.

'Go!'

'Right, I'll go pull them out, you girls get moving!' the Guard bravely disappeared back into battle as Dara and Row helped their patient out of the canyon.

'I'm Row by the way,' said Row.

Dara stared indignantly at her. After all these years of being together. Through medical school. She had never taken the chance to even acknowledge her existence?'

'Unbelievable!' said Dara back.

Anji and Jake ran as fast as their legs would carry. They found shelter under a small lip in the cliff face and surveyed the horror around them.

'We've got to get these people out of here,' said Anji.

'How? Where?'

'Anywhere but here Jake!'

Tiny blue shots of light shot skywards towards the Pyramids, causing several explosions far away in the underside of the crafts.

'I wonder what caused that?' said Jake.

With precise timing, Skateboard burst into view.

'Yes!' cried Jake. 'Skateboard, you legend!'

'Anji, Jake, no time to speak. Where is Random?'

'He's going to bargain with the Osirons,' said Anji.

'Good. Hop on board. We need to collect as many people as possible.'

The two teenagers did exactly as they were told.

'Pick up who you can,' the AI robot implored.

'Not much room, mate,' said Jake.

At which point, a second length of board shot out of Skateboard's back area.

'Don't tell Sir that I keep my back up board there,' he said sheepishly.

Anji and Jake didn't have time to make a smart-arsed response as they began to hold out their arms and help those stranded in the gun fire onto the board. After two Guards had been collected, Anji notified Skateboard that they had run out of room.

'Blast,' said Skateboard who then headed for the exit, passing Dara and Row in the process. Jake's head swiveled and at the same time a divot on the floor made Skateboard's passengers rock uneasily.

Jake looked down and wondered why he was hurtling through the air whilst everyone else was Still on Skateboard's back and getting further away.

Then he remembered how he'd forgotten to tie his laces again.

As he coughed, picking himself up, he looked upwards as a volley of laser fire headed his way.

'You can't kill me!' he cried, 'I haven't got any shoes on!'

A hand hot out and grabbed him by the arm, hauling him out of danger's way.

It was Row.

'H-hi!' he stammered.

'Jake! Where are your shoes?'

'Um...'

'Never mind! Get as many people out of here as you can!'

'Yes, that's what I was doing,' he insisted.

'Then keep at it!'

She ran off into the dust again.

Jake looked up and could just make out in the distance the outline of Random, his silhouette bathed in a green light, jumping from the nose cone to the canyon ridge.

'You give them hell, mate,' he said to no-one in particular as he ran back into danger, crying out in discomfort as the broken rock hurt the soles of his feet.

'This is sport!'

Amun-Ra gazed out of the ancient viewer and watched with glee as destruction continued to rain down on the Spectronians.

'Prepare the armageddon beam!'

The Gods did as they were told. The Armageddon beam was a link between all Pyramids that when their energies met, had the ability to split a planet in two with its power.

'We'll fragment this world and obtain the element when we pick it out of that woman's cold dead hands!' he gleed.

'Amun-Ra, look!' came a voice from the dark.

The war God's attention diverted towards the image of a small purple boy carrying what looked like the element they so wanted, standing alone on the cliff top.

'So... another challenger...'

'He has the element, sir!' came the voice again.

'Not for long... cease fire...for now. Create the energy link.'

Mercifully, the lasers stopped. Solenia, who was flat on her back, let the dust and the eerie calm wash over her before struggling to her feet. Jake and Row rushed to her side and tried to help her up but she was adamant she could help herself. Apart from a cut on her forehead, she looked fine.

All three of them stood and watched as the Pyramids began to hum.

And on the cliff top, all alone, facing them down was one boy. Random.

<h1 style="text-align:center">XXIV</h1>

'Who dare face us?'

The voice boomed out of the head Pyramid.

Random stood defiantly.

'Don't you remember me?'

There was a pause.

'You...'

'Yes, me,' he said lightheartedly. 'I didn't have supposed Gods down as being short on memory. Short on brains perhaps.'

'You dare mock the Osirans!'

'I do!' he shouted. 'Because you dare to take what isn't yours and destroy a people you barely know.'

The canyon fell silent. Anji and Skateboard rushed to be by Jake's side. They were all glued to what was happening high above.

'You have the element.'

'Oh this?' Random said, swigging the Flux to and fro in his hands. 'This old thing? Well, I suppose you could call it an element. If you don't know what it is in the first place.'

'It is the most powerful element in the known universe.'

'It's called the Zedron Flux, look it up in your history books. And yes, I suppose it is. In the right hands it could do a lot of good for the universe. The trouble is there aren't many good hands about.'

'That depends on what you define as good.'

'True,' he agreed. 'But I doubt that you lot qualify.'

'I... Amun-Ra, the Emperor of the Osirans, defy qualification. It is my destiny.'

'No, you see you are wrong. No-one has a god given right to this thing, not even a God such as yourself. It should not belong to any one person, especially one who thinks they deserve it.'

'Who are you to judge?'

'I'm not, but I'll tell you what I am. I'm the person who currently has it.'

'Not for long.'

'What are you going to do? Take it from me?'

'But of course. But before we do, we have a little gift for the peoples of this repulsive world.'

'That's a bit harsh calling this world repulsive, I mean look at it. I think it's rather beautiful.'

'That depends on what you define as beautiful...' said Amun-Ra. 'I see fire. The universe awash with flame. I see a new order. I see the...Flux...in my hands and I see the Osirans as untouchable Gods!'

'Sounds more like a nightmare to me,' said Random.

'It matters not, you will be living in it soon.'

A massive hole began to open in the underside of the pyramid.

'What's that?' asked Random.

'Your salvation,' leered Amun-Ra.

Random started to panic a little. He held the Flux above his head.

'You even think about blowing these people away and I'll use it.'

Amun-Ra stalled.

'You wouldn't dare...'

'Wouldn't I? I suppose that's what you've got to consider...'

'One swift twist of this cell and the Flux can be unleashed. I will be able to bend it to my will. It will be able to destroy you. So why run that risk, eh? Why not go now, and never come back?'

'Are you trying to bargain with me, puny insect?' Amun-Ra was impressed. 'You are indeed a brave one.'

Random winced.

'Why not go home, use this immense power to put a stop to the war?'

He grew very concerned.

The voices were back.

'Think of how you could use the Flux, Random, to bring peace to Rodas. Put an end to all the hurt...the suffering?'

The voices were overwhelming.

Over and over again these two sentences bounded around inside his skull.

'Please...' he said, redirecting his efforts back to the Osiran fleet. 'Do the sensible thing and leave.'

'In no time at all this world will be nothing. Pulped. Pulverized. Squashed like an ant hill under a heavy boot. You with it. Your life is of no consequence to us. In fact, we would take much joy in destroying you and the rest of the pitiful inhabitants of this world.'

'But these people have no other home, you'd be committing genocide!'

Anji, Jake and the others were trying to work out what Random was saying, but being such a distance away, it was to no avail. But Strakonis had the advantage of being that much closer and he was starting to worry about Random's position. As he finished tending to his wounds, he placed a concerned hand on his forehead.

'Don't do it, Random. For all that's good in the universe, don't!'

'These people are nothing! You don't know them. Why are you willing to risk your life to save their worthless existence?'

'Because their existence is not worthless!' said Random. His hand clasped the release mechanism on the cell.

'I am going to give you five seconds to power down your weapons or so help me...'

Random pleaded with the situation. If he used the Flux, he would be saving the millions, nay billions of inhabitants on Spectronia, but he'd be committing mass murder, no, genocide himself if he just twisted the cell. Could he really do that? Destroy an entire civilisation if it meant the salvation of another. Maybe it was his calling to be judge, jury and executioner. After all, he was destined to put an end to war on Rodas. Why couldn't he end it anywhere else?

'Prepare to fire the Armageddon beam!' Amun-Ra barked to his fellow Gods.

The hum of the beam grew stronger. The link was complete.

Shivering, sweating, Random looked down over the canyon ridge and saw swathes of people. Spectronians, looking up at him. Counting on him.

Then he saw Anji and Jake and his faithful Skateboard. How could he let them perish? He'd never allow anything to happen to them or the Spectronians.

No. He had to do it. And he would have to live with his decision.

As the voices reached a crescendo, Random looked up at the pyramid.

'You asked for it.'

'Fire now!' cried Anum-Ra.

Random opened the cell and the Flux exploded in his hands. The purple boy was swathed in a green energy. He cried out in pain and horror as the Flux seeped through every pore in his being, consuming him completely. As he continued to be overwhelmed by its power, he began to levitate high into the air.

Anji and Jake were horrified. Their faces awash with alarm. And Skateboard who had turned up his audio bandwidth and listened to the whole exchange without telling the others, was shocked by the events unfolding in front of him.

Meanwhile in his ship, Strakonis fell to the floor in shock.

He had told Random not to open the Flux.

Random hadn't listened.

Now all manner of hell was about to be unleashed on Spectronia.

XXV

Random let the Flux explore every fiber of his body. He felt it surge like a monsoon throughout him, but at no point was he afraid, nor was he out of control. He let the Flux suss him out, just as much as it let him look into what made it so powerful. Random couldn't find any malice within it. He also could not see any reason to be as consumed with greed for the power that it could bring him like it had Lon.

The Flux could sense no reason to distrust him either His intentions were true. If he wanted, he could be the true owner of it. But Random had no need for it, he felt, and still felt.

The Flux was safe.

But it sensed the conflict in Random's mind. There was something going on in there it did not understand. Was it enough for it to reject him as a host?

Random concentrated hard to block the same two voices that had plagued him since his birth out. He needed all of his will power to obliterate the Osirians. He was beyond doubt. He was ready.

Random's eyes were emerald green. He readied his hands towards the pyramid fleet. Like bolts of lightning, the Flus exploded towards Amun-Ra's pyramid. The God stood his ground. Accepting his fate, he thrust his arms wide open and allowed armageddon to blow him away.

Molecule by molecule, the pyramids were hit by the green wave that eradiated from Random's fingers, rocking in the sky like ships in a storm.

Anji, Jake, Skateboard, Solenia and the surviving Spectronians watch aghast as they witnessed the green wave wash over the Orison's ships and bit by bit, they began to melt away to nothingness. Molecule by molecule the pyramids were fading into nothingness. Before long, all of them had disappeared and the green wave swept back into Random's body.

The Osirans had been obliterated.

Random exhaled deeply. The Flux flowed out of his mouth,
sweeping back towards its cell and within moments, Random had
his feet firmly back on the ground and the Flux was safely back in
his housing.

He looked down gratefully at his friends far below and watched
as Anji and Jake got on Skateboard's back and they made towards
him.

Random smiled as he saw the Spectronians cheering and heard
them whooping and celebrating the end of terror.

The threat was over. Random had saved the day.

But as Solenia and Strakonis looked up at him from his vantage
point, they were far from happy.

Random had done it. Saved yet another civilisation from a doom
that this time he had inadvertently brought upon them himself.
He would have to take responsibility for those who had perished,
but as with his decision to wipe the Orisons out, he would have to
learn to live with that burden.

Burden.

That was a word he was becoming used to.

He stood up and drank in the sound of silence.

Then his eyes grew wide with happiness.

Silence.

The voices had stopped.

They were gone!

He gave out a little chuckle to himself and went to pick the Flux,
which was trapped in its holding cell again, calm as a white cloud
in a sunny sky, but his vision suddenly went a little out of focus.

As he heard Anji calling out his name, he suddenly felt his body
grow very weary. He slumped onto the floor and stayed there
until his friends joined him.

'Random mate, that was awesome!' said Jake, thumping his
friend's upper arm as he sat cross legged next to him.

'Random, you did it! But what happened to them?'

'The Osirans...no more...end to...'

'Random?'

Before Anji could get an answer, Random had slumped into
Jake's lap, leading the blonde-haired boy to feel quite
uncomfortable.

'Uh…Anj?'

Skateboard ran a medical scan on Random.

'He appears to be asleep. The Flux must have drained all of his energy from him. If you could put him on my back I would greatly oblige.

Solenia and Strakonis had taken one of the rainbow roads up to the vantage point and made it just as the two human teenagers were bundling Random onto their robot friend.

'How is he?' asked Solenia.

'Stable but unconscious,' replied Skateboard. 'He will be fine in no time.'

'And the Flux?'

Strakonis let out a wheezing groan as he got down to pick the Flux's cell up off the dirt.

'Entact and neutralized.'

'Good,' she said before turning her attention to the travelers. 'What your friend did we shall be forever grateful for. But I cannot ignore that he committed genocide here on my world.'

'He saved your people, didn't he?' said Anji defiantly.

'Take a look down there.'

Anji and Jake peered over the precipice and saw many Spectronians celebrating their salvation, but it was hard to ignore the dead bodies that littered the canyon like a battlefield.

'Many of my men will never see another sunrise. They paid the price for the danger that you all brought to Spectronia.'

'Your majesty-'

'Silence!' she barked.

The trio uttered not a word.

'We Spectronians pride ourselves on peace and non-interference. You have brought death to our door. Despite your good deeds, I hereby banish you all from Spectronia forthwith.

'But he saved your lives!' shouted Anji.

'You can tell him how thankful we all are when he comes around. But not here. Go to your ship, leave and never come back!'

Anji and Jake were stunned and ashamed.

'We shall do as you please, your Majesty,' said Skateboard. 'We can do nothing more than follow your orders and apologise for the harm we have brought you.'

Solenia stared them down.

'Come on, you two,' said Skateboard sadly. 'Back to the Venus II.'

'Can't we say goodbye?' asked Jake.

'No.' said Skateboard firmly.

With their heads bowed, Anji and Jake followed Skateboard back onto the rainbow road and slowly they disappeared from sight.

'Your Majesty,' said Strakonis, 'Not that it is for me to argue with your excellency but was that a little harsh?'

'You know the power of the Flux,' she replied. 'You saw it with your own eyes as well as I saw with mine. Thanks to their intervention a whole race has just been obliterated in the skies of my world. Their blood is now a stain on our history. For centuries to come my people will talk about the day that Gods fell to the might of one man, consumed by the most brilliant power in all the galaxy. And you expect me to hide it here?'

Strakonis bowed his head. She had a point. He had warned Random not to use it. Indeed, he was surprised at how well he had contained it inside him.

'But his actions led to the survival of your race. Without him you would all be extinct.'

'This is true, which is why I have let them go freely. You do understand that we cannot be the keepers of the Flux now, don't you Strakonis?'

The explorer nodded sadly. 'Yes, I understand.'

'Will you be able to find somewhere else to hide it as quickly as you can.'

'I will. Someday.' He patted the cell and the Flux gave out a little hum. 'Although no one is looking for it now, it will still be hunted. Someday.'

'Then I wish you luck in your quest,' Solenia did not wait for a response and made her way back to her Dosa, who with a click of her heels reared up and turned away.

'Farewell Strakonis. And good luck.'

Strakonis held up his hand as Solenia rode away and left him alone with the Flux.

And so, unabated this time, it was up to him to leave the Flux on
a remote, technologically stilted planet where no one would think
of looking.

He walked back to his ship, deep in thought. What was the
name of that planet he had thought of before Spectronia but
decided against due to lack of fuel reserves? That one in the solar
system with the primitive people who hadn't even got any further
than their own moon when it came to space travel?

Strakonis wracked his brains and decided that as soon as his
engines were back up and running, and that he has remembered
the name of this illusive world, that he would set a course and
hide the Flux there, somewhere.

Surely the people of that world wouldn't be as dangerous as his
now dead rival, Lon...

XXVI

It had taken the travellers a few hours to get back to the Venus II
and on their long trek home they had barely said a word to one
another.

It was weird to them not having Random to keep them company
on their return to the Venus II and although he was there in body,
he wasn't there in spirit. He was sleeping like a baby, flat out on
his front. Anji had manufactured a blanket out of his combat
jacket, covering his torso so she could see nothing else other than
a ball of hair protruding from underneath it.

She felt hot. Whether she was warm from the sun or from the
shame of being banished, she couldn't tell.

A part of her had sympathized with Solenia. She was Queen.
She had to protect her people and sadly, some of them had lost
their lives. But that hadn't been Random's fault. The Osirans
would have caught up with them eventually, if they had crash
landed on Spectronia or not. It was just unfortunate but she didn't
feel bad that Random had gone to the extremes that he had. He'd
saved a peaceful race. Wiped out an evil too. Surely what he did
wasn't all that bad?

She looked at his unmoving frame again, still except for signs of
normal breathing as the coat rose and fell with every snore.

'There she is!' Jake said gleefully.

The Venus II stood proudly before them.

When the gleaming seda metal and shiny hull of their vessel honed into view, all three of them had felt such a relief.

'It looks good as new!' exclaimed Jake.

'So it should be, given the calculations in the self-repair unit,' said Skateboard, who connected back with the ship as he was now in distance and had already turned the oxygen, gravity and landing lights on. With a hiss of hydraulics, the ramp that led up to the mid-section hissed as it landed softly in the colourful sand.

'It feels like ages since we've been away from you old thing, we've missed you!' said Anji.

'It can't hear you,' Jake tutted.

'I'll pass your kind words on, Miss,' said Skateboard.

They all made their way up the ramp and were pleasantly shocked to see the interior was in such good condition too. For a ship that was ripped apart, gutted even in its recent crash landing, the living area looked like someone had given it a spring clean!

'Amazing!' said Anji.

'We'd better wake up Random,' said Jake. 'I'd have thought he'd have woken up by now.'

'To be fair to him he did absorb the most powerful thing in the universe,' said Anji.

'I'm sure that all he needs is to recharge his batteries, something I am never forgetting to do again,' quipped Skateboard. 'Now, do me a favour will you please? Take him to his quarters so I can get us up in the air, will you?'

'Sure, anything to get away from this colourful mess of a planet!' said Jake.

'That's a bit rude, man,' said Anji.

'Well, they didn't even thank us, did they? And I never got to say goodbye to Row.'

'Whose Row?'

Jake went hot with embarrassment.

'Uh, no-one!'

Anji knelt down to pick Random up, who had been face down on Skateboard's back for the best part of a few hours now. She went to pick him up by his arm and then noticed something that was not right.

'Hold on.'

Jake's attention was diverted from daydreaming about the crush he was never going to see again down to his friends.

'Jake!'

Anji sounded panicked.

She rolled Random over.

The two of them recoiled in horror.

'Skateboard, what's happened to Random?'

Anji and Jake stood back, unable to process what had happened to their alien friend.

Gone was Random's unique purple complexion.

He had changed colour.

He was red and blue, split down the middle.

One half crimson.

The other half a sapphire blue!

ACKNOWLEDGEMENTS

A few big thank yous this time out. Firstly, to my wife Sophie, who during the writing of this book has levelled up from girlfriend to fiancée to wife and given me unwavering support. To the hip injury that kept me off work for three weeks and provided the spark to write the follow-up sooner than I expected. To the writing group at work who meet every Tuesday and for their encouragement and counsel which was more than inspirational. To Steve Heywood, who proofed the book and spotted that I had used the wrong spelling for 'Penal' that may have got this book banned from the Young Adult section if unnoticed! To Nicola Gent for being another pair of eyes. To illustrator extraordinaire Anthony Moorin, whose visions of Random's universe really bring the books to life. And lastly to you, the dear readers, who read the first one, gave it a chance and gave me the confidence to turn Captain Random into a series of books. His adventures are far from over, so do please keep reading and supporting him!

The adventures of Captain Random will continue
in *Volume Two*.

Also Available:

The Lurking

ISBN: 978-1999865955

Rob is a hopeless loser in the game of life. With work, his relationship with his long suffering girlfriend Claire, with everything in general. Tonight he will change for the better, make a fresh start by taking it to the next step and propose to her.

But fate has other intentions.

After an accident that leaves him stranded, Rob takes shelter in an abandoned aircraft hangar and soon discovers that he is not alone. There is something lurking in the darkness, taunting him, haunting his every movement.

Soon trapped in a living nightmare, Rob must learn the terrible truth of his tormentor and escape its clutches before it is too late...

Available from all good bookshops.

Captain Random and the Eater of Souls

ISBN: 978-1999865931

Following their explosive battle with the Sandman, and struggling to come to terms with life out in space, the crew of the Venus II decide to throw themselves into a spot of retail therapy on the friendly planet of Genocia.

But almost as soon as they arrive, they realise that this new world is not all that it seems. Outside the splendour and vast wealth of the Grand Chamber lies a neglected wasteland where terror lurks within the poisonous gloom whilst deep within the bowels of the planet lies a terrible secret.

At the very heart of it all is the ruthless leader Consula, whose designs for supremacy mean ultimate devastation to all of those who oppose her. But the greed and corruption of the government is nothing compared to what lurks in the shadows for Random and his friends. Separated and fighting for their lives, Random, Anji, Jake and Skateboard must work quickly to save the lives of the prisoners stuck in the mines deep below the surface, where death is very close by...

What is the Soul Destroyer? What part does it play in Consula's diabolical plan? Will Anji ever see her friends again? One thing is for sure. The Eater of Souls is hungry...

Available from all good bookshops.

Captain Random vs the Sandman

ISBN: 978-1999865924

Rodas. The scorned planet of Ursa-17. Ravaged by centuries of war between two factions, the villainous Sapphire Regime and the ruthless Crimson Empire. The reason behind the conflict of red and blue? The people of Rodas were unable to make the colour purple.
Until one day, when two rebels, one from either side, combine to create the ultimate warrior. A being who could put an end to the battle of ages and bring peace to the volatile planet of Rodas once and for all.

There is one tiny drawback. The warrior is a boy.

***** Fantastic book, enjoyed every part of it!
Highly recommend it for Dr Who/Red Dwarf/Rick and Morty fans.

***** Hayden Gribble's writing is witty and clever with an essence of Douglas Adams in there too. Would thoroughly recommend for anyone with an adventurous spirit.

***** I really enjoyed it. I can well imagine Kids getting swept along with the interstellar, action packed adventure and chuckling along with all the funny scenarios and characters and wanting to know just what happens.

Available from all good bookshops.

Child Out of Time: Growing Up With Doctor Who in the Wilderness Years

ISBN: 978-1999865900

For 26 years, DOCTOR WHO was a British institution, capturing the imaginations of generations of children. But then, in 1989, it was cancelled. The Doctor and his on-screen adventures were no more. There was no longer a hero, a champion for the outcasts who struggled to fit in. It was as though he had walked into his TARDIS and set his controls for dematerialisation, never to return: a whole generation lost to the powers of Science Fiction's greatest creation. It was in this Doctor-less world that I grew up. This is the story of how one little boy would try to find the Doctor in any way, shape or form and the obstacles he faced in doing so. This is the story of growing up without Doctor Who in the Wilderness Years...and how I lived through it.

***** An engaging and enjoyable insight into a fan discovering Doctor Who during the wilderness years

***** A very passionate account of one fans discovery of the greatest science fiction of all time.

**** Perfect for fans of the Doctor in any of his or her forms.

Available from all good book shops.

The Man In The Corner

ISBN: 978-1500549862

A mysterious assassin wants out of his life as a cold and ruthless killer but must face one last assignment before he flicks the escape switch. As he closes in on the biggest criminal mind in the country, he is reminded of what he left behind and how getting closer to the light at the end of the tunnel might also reunite him with a person from his long and distant past. Who is the Big Chief? Why must he be brought down and will it be the end, not just for himself and his superior, but also to the only link to the life he has lost.

***** An exciting book! Whilst focusing on the dark story of an unnamed man, you find yourself sucked into a city of criminals. The chapters contain their own stories which really draw you in and make you want to read more. Great read! The only negative is that it was over too fast.

***** Brilliant read. Did not want to put the book down.

*** This book is a great little read about the path to redemption; not too long, in fact in some places I found myself wishing it might go on a little longer. It's got a sort of style all its own.

Available from all good bookshops.

Hayden Gribble was born in Cambridge in June 1989. He has always loved writing and released his debut novel, The Man In The Corner, as an ebook in 2013 before it went paperback the following year.

This is the first omnibus in the Captain Random saga.

Away from writing, Hayden loves reading, walking, sports, music, film and TV.

He has also been a regular member of the Diddly Dum Podcast, a show about Doctor Who, since February 2015 and curates his own James Bond podcast, Podcasters Royale. Both can be found on iTunes.

He lives with his wife and son in Suffolk.